SKYLARK'S SONG

ALSO BY ROY HATTERSLEY

Nelson: A Biography
Goodbye to Yorkshire
Politics Apart
A Yorkshire Boyhood
Press Gang
Endpiece Revisited
Choose Freedom
The Maker's Mark
In That Quiet Earth

ROY HATTERSLEY

SKYLARK'S SONG

MACMILLAN
LONDON

First published in 1993 in the United Kingdom by
MACMILLAN LONDON LIMITED
a division of Pan Macmillan Publishers Limited
Cavaye Place London SW10 9PG
and Basingstoke

Associated companies in Auckland, Budapest, Dublin, Gaborone,
Harare, Hong Kong, Kampala, Kuala Lumpur, Lagos, Madras, Manzini,
Melbourne, Mexico City, Nairobi, New York, Singapore, Sydney,
Tokyo and Windhoek

ISBN 0-333-55608-9

A CIP catalogue for this book is available from
the British Library

Phototypeset by Intype, London
Printed and bound in Great Britain by
Mackays of Chatham PLC, Chatham, Kent

Because the road is rough and long
Shall we despise the skylark's song

CHAPTER ONE

IT WAS the coldest December that anyone in Langwith Junction could recall. The pond in Scarcliffe Park was frozen over for more than a month and the film of ice which spread across every bedroom window at night retreated but did not disappear during the day. The sky was a cloudless watery blue and although the sentimentally inclined talked of a white Christmas, the occasional flurry of sleet never turned to snow.

At 11 Langwith Road, the Brackenbury family looked forward to the season of goodwill with a mixture of hope and apprehension. Agnes, old at forty-nine and huddled in a wheelchair with her crumpled hands folded in her lap, longed to begin her week of peace and security with her sister at Worksop. But she dreaded the ten-mile journey and the agony she would feel in every arthritic joint as the car jolted over the pot-holed road.

Brack, her husband – who complained bitterly about being deserted at a time that families should spend together – had arranged to celebrate Christ's nativity with Jane Wood, the widow of a Mansfield bookmaker who promised to provide all the home comforts which he had for so long been denied. But at the end of their discussion about buying the turkey and inviting a few friends round on Boxing Day for a hand of cards, she had given him an ultimatum. After Christmas he had to choose between her and Agnes. His inclination was strongly in favour of deserting his crippled wife. But it was a difficult choice for an urban district councillor to make.

Enid, their only daughter, pretended that she was so excited at the prospect of a holiday that anticipation of the pleasure kept her awake at night. She had been brought up to treat her aunt Anne – and Aunt Lottie, Anne's companion – with blind affection. And at the age of twenty-five, she found it difficult to distinguish between what she felt and what she was expected to feel. She knew that the two women, Skinner and Harthill, High Class Ladies' Dress-makers and Tailors, would make her a dress for Christmas, and the genuine highlight of her holiday would be the moment when she put it on and looked at herself in the cheval glass which dominated the fitting room. The pleasure, though not to the credit of her character, was entirely justified. She was fashionably thin and conventionally beautiful, with the biggest and bluest eyes that anyone in the district had ever seen. Enid believed that she was superior to her neighbours in more than looks and deeply resented fate's requirement that she should live amongst families who did not recognize her superiority.

She talked to her mother as if the Christmas Eve pilgrimage to her grandparents' grave in Steetly churchyard and the Christmas dinner itself would be equally joyous events. To suggest otherwise would have been regarded as unthinkable. Enid, therefore, did not think about it. She prided herself on 'managing' – an activity which she defined in her own mind as a determination to live in comparative peace and relative prosperity from one day to the next. In order to manage, she flattered and threatened her father in turn, saved every possible penny by searching from shop to shop for the cheapest groceries and pretended to herself that she loved aspects of her life which she hated. Despite her capacity for self-deception, she approached Christmas in the knowledge that, before New Year, she had a difficult decision to make. Enid Brack-enbury was engaged to be married to one man and in love with another.

She was engaged to John O'Hara, a collier from the west of Ireland where young men were not the red-faced Paddies of Eng-lish folklore but tall and fair with high cheekbones, long jaws and unembarrassed pride in their appearance. There was no doubt that he loved Enid with an unthinking devotion. And there had been a time when she loved him, if not with a blind passion, at least as much as most young women in the Nottingham coalfield loved the men they were to marry. She loved him because he was hand-some, the best dancer at the Miners' Welfare, the best player in the tennis club and pursued with shameless ardour by all the local girls who did not pursue his equally handsome, but more exciting, younger brother. But there was another and more important reason for her affection. She had loved him a little because he loved her so much.

However, even that little love had not lasted. Enid had aspirations. These were neither practical nor precise, yet she felt a fierce determination to do something and become someone. She longed for real education and made claim to more than she really possessed. Education was one of the many essential attributes that Jack lacked and he showed no sign of understanding his loss. She read with a constant desire to read more, both to escape from the real world and to pass the hours spent keeping her mother company. Jack read nothing except the *Daily Herald* and the *Sporting Life*. Enid found it impossible to love for very long anyone who did not possess a ticket for the county council lending library.

For a year, although she did not love him, she never thought of ending their engagement. She had got into the habit of courtship, and marriage was what everyone expected to follow the long silent evenings with Jack and her mother in the Langwith Road living room. Jack was also the swift and certain escape route from her father. So the loveless engagement survived.

Then the new priest came to St Joseph's. Father Hattersley was a young man, who had been given a church of his own before he was thirty because Langwith, a parish almost without parishioners, deserved no one more senior. He was tall, with shoulders which had been broadened by seven summers of rowing on Lake Albano but, because of his reticent manner, he seemed physically frail. His hair was still parted almost in the middle in the old-fashioned clerical style. But he had abandoned brilliantine when he left the seminary and, although he was cropped as close as respectability allowed, a few auburn strands always fell across his forehead. The gold-rimmed *pince-nez*, clipped to the bridge of his nose, completed the picture of a man who needed someone to look after him and Enid decided, almost at their first meeting, that she had been chosen by fate to perform that task. She had no desire to change or improve him, only to protect him from a world that he was too innocent to combat on his own. When he talked about Rome and old churches, books and bicycle rides, she thought, for the first time, that she might have met a man who would change and improve her.

Enid thought that she loved him because he knew so much. But in truth she loved him because of his quiet voice, his nervous smile and his unaffected humility. She had been used to the colliers' rough courtesies and to the miners' contempt for men who earned a living without breaking sweat or flexing muscles. Then she met a man who was what she thought of as genteel and refined. Naïvely she believed him to be a gentleman when he was no more than a Catholic priest.

Enid loved him sometimes without hope and often with a rage which seemed strangely like anger. But she loved him in a way in which she knew she could never love another man. And, more important by far, from the first meeting she was consumed by a determination that he would love her as she wanted and believed she deserved to be loved. Father Hattersley became an obsession which was a reflection of her desperate needs.

It was several months before the priest even admitted to himself that he was in love with Enid Brackenbury. He had no idea what it was that made him love her but, since he was unschooled in such matters, he did not believe that a reason was necessary. Rex knew that Charles Stuart – saint and martyr – had told his confessor on the night before his execution that he had fallen in love with Henrietta-Maria at first sight. So he was not surprised by his sudden passion.

When he felt sure that his feelings were more than one of the brief infatuations to which young priests are prone, he confessed to his bishop and asked to be moved away from Langwith Junction. Temptation, Bishop Dunn had told him, was unavoidable because he was a man. Because he was a priest, temptation must be resisted. Redemption would not be achieved by running away, but by meeting sin head on. *Tu ne cede malis, sed contra audentior ito.* So he had gone back to his parish and found the temptation irresistible. In a moment of uncontrolled anguish he told Enid that he loved her, and the three words that took only seconds to pronounce had changed his life for ever.

In November, after weeks of furtive friendship, they had

agreed that if they still loved each other at the end of the year, Enid would leave Jack and Rex would leave the Church. They had both kept their promise that, until the irrevocable decision was made, there would be no more secret meetings or coded messages. She had counted off the days and now the time had come for him to follow her to Worksop and carry her off like Father Lochinvar. Enid was frightened by the reality of what she had enjoyed as a dream. But she was more afraid that he would not come and that she would be left to marry Jack and struggle to remember that she had once been truly in love.

Rex, alone for half the day in St Joseph's Presbytery, found it increasingly difficult to believe that the joys of the summer might delight him for the rest of his life. They had been simple pleasures. Hiring a rowing boat on the Trent at Beeston. Cycling side by side to Newstead Abbey and picnicking on the grass in the shade of Byron's house. Reading together, not the classics of which Enid spoke so often and with such authority but the popular novels of the day – Jeffrey Farnol's *The Amateur Gentleman*, Edgar Wallace's *The Fellowship of the Frog* and Ian Hay's *Knight on Wheels*. In *Knight on Wheels*, the heroine had methodically removed the hero's spectacles before she kissed him for the first time. Enid had read Hay's description of that incident aloud. The memory of the moment and of the minutes which followed made the thick glass in his *pince-nez* mist over.

Even after he had bought the battered old Austin Seven from Brack, they had never enjoyed more than modest pleasures. A day trip to Lincoln, where he had felt sick when they climbed to the top of the Cathedral tower. Tea in the garden of the Crown Hotel at Edwinstowe after a walk through Sherwood Forest. An evening excursion to Sheffield where, disguised in his brother's old tweed sports jacket, they had sat gratefully crushed together in the gods at the Lyceum Theatre. Nothing – desperate shortage of money, need to be back in Langwith Junction at exactly the prearranged time or even the constant fear of exposure – had cast the slightest shadow over their time together. For he was with her and that, his new idea of heaven, was all that mattered.

As he waited for Christmas, his only fear – a denial of all that he had been taught during the long years in Rome – was that the idea of perpetual bliss was too good to be true and that the prospect of a life in Paradise was not so much a hope as a dream.

Fear that he would receive no answer made him reluctant to send the message which he had promised. But he forced himself to compose a cryptic greeting which would seem no more than a priestly platitude to the casual reader and wrote it out on his Christmas card. 'In the certainty of a better life ahead and the joy which will follow Christmas.' Unwilling to risk the vagaries of the Christmas post, he paid a boy sixpence to deliver the card by hand. Then he waited for Enid to send him some sort of reply.

It came on Christmas Eve, added to a plain white pasteboard card which looked like an invitation to a wedding or a first communion bore the message 'Season's Greetings from Ernest Brackenbury – Coal Merchant, Haulier, Cars for Sale and Hire', written in elegant italics. The brief postscript was scribbled in the margin between the deckled gilt edge and the discreet representations of holly and mistletoe which surrounded the rubric. Rex read the scrawl with difficulty. 'Expect coal delivery as promised. Earlier the better.' He was incapacitated by a mixture of joy and anxiety.

Rex had no doubt that he wanted to leave the Church and marry Enid. But until that minute when he knew for certain that she expected him, he had not faced the consequences of what he intended to do. He knew that he had neither the courage nor the capacity to behave as he should behave – the explanation to the bishop, the weeks spent in retreat, the final confirmation that the vocation was lost and the sad, but loving, farewell as he left the priesthood but strengthened the bonds of faith which held him tight to the Church. Loving Enid should have made him brave, but he was afraid that he would run away as if he were guilty and ashamed when, in truth, he was more proud than he had ever been in his life.

He counted off the hours of Christmas – midnight mass in his own church, a wedding performed at the desperate request of a sailor whose pregnant fiancée insisted on being made an honest woman before his ship sailed, and Christmas evening spent with his father and family behind the ironmonger's shop in Not-

tingham. Both his sisters were there, perched on the arms of their
husbands' chairs. So was his brother Syd, a scholarship boy at
Ratcliffe College. Aunt Clare, a dashing spinster of sixty who had
been pursued by Rex's father, before he had settled for her homely
sister, had travelled with him from Langwith to Nottingham. She
had sat in the uncomfortable passenger seat of the battered motor
car without complaining about the wind blowing in through tears
in the canvas hood. The whole family treated the priest in their
midst with proper respect.

Soon they would have two priests to be proud of. George –
twenty-three and five years younger than Rex – was soon to be
ordained at the seminary in Valladolid. He was not a great corre-
spondent and he had sent a single letter to Nottingham which had
been addressed to the whole family. It had been read and reread
over and over again by the time that Rex arrived on the afternoon
of Christmas Day, but Rex was required to read it once more to
the whole admiring company.

It described, in a couple of terse sentences, the turbulent state
of Spanish politics. A whole paragraph was devoted to the deterio-
ration in seminary food and half a page to memories of the summer
holiday spent with Rex in Langwith Junction. Comments on the
impending ordination covered both sides of a whole sheet of lined
paper. They concerned the pageantry rather than the spiritual significance of the occasion. George was looking forward to the
drama of the ceremony.

'Your mother would have been proud.' Rex's father was not a
Catholic but he was a sentimentalist. 'In all her troubles, it was the
idea of having priests for sons that kept her going.'

Of course, thought Rex, if his mother was there in the kitchen
– cutting up the boiled ham and making the sandwiches – she
would grieve at the thought of his leaving the Church. But she was
where there is neither grief nor sorrow. In heaven, he told himself,
his mother would understand that love was all that mattered.

When the cake was eaten, the beer drunk, his father's repertoire of songs and stories exhausted, he pleaded the need to rise
early on the following day and crept away to bed. Standing under
the sloping roof of the attic he was less certain that his mother

would understand. He talked, inconsequentially, to Syd until two o'clock in the morning and, as soon as his brother had fallen asleep climbed silently out of bed and took a pad of cheap writing paper from his suitcase. He had meant to leave notes of apology and explanation for his father and family. But he could not bring himself to tell the harsh truth. Instead, crouching in the faint light which came through the dormer window, he asked for their help and understanding during difficult days to come. He did not describe the nature of the difficulties.

He tiptoed out of the house at six o'clock. On the warmest mornings, the old Austin Seven only spluttered into life after two or three unsuccessful attempts to turn the engine over. In the freezing dark, with a sheet of ice stretching across the windscreen, he did not even reach for the starting handle. He rubbed at the front of the windscreen with his bare hand and, when he had melted a peephole, climbed into the driving seat and released the handbrake. He was at the bottom of the hill, with all hope gone, when a great convulsion under the bonnet sent the car lurching forward towards his new life.

As soon as he stopped worrying about starting his car he began to worry about where the car would take him. He could not go back to Langwith Junction. His parishioners believed that, in order to spend Boxing Day with his parents, he was saying early mass at St Paul's in Nottingham. He could not stay with his family. They believed that he was saying mass in Langwith Junction. Nor could he drive very far. If the cracked dials on his battered dashboard were to be trusted, his petrol tank was almost empty and he could only afford a couple of cheap gallons at the Russian Oil Products garage on the Mansfield Road.

He drove first to Steetly – only partly because of Enid's obsession with that village. At Steetly he could sit undisturbed in the back of the Saxon chapel. He could change from his black priest's suit and stock into the sports jacket and striped tie which George had left in the presbytery after his summer holiday. Steetly was in striking distance of Worksop. He could strike as soon as the hour was reasonable for a respectable visit.

The church was locked. He shivered in the porch for almost an hour. Then he pulled on his unconvincing disguise and stamped round the churchyard – his breath condensing in the freezing air and his shoes crushing footprints on the grass made stiff with frost – in the hope of reviving his circulation.

In order to improve his spirits, he made a mental list of all the reasons why he loved Enid. He loved her because she was beautiful, but although that was the first thought which came into his head he pushed it to the back of his mind. It was not a sufficiently elevated explanation for the noble passion which he felt. He loved her because she was strong and brave and he loved her because sometimes she was not as strong and brave as she pretended and needed him to look after her. He loved her because she was clever, even though her cleverness built barriers of resentment and frustration between them. But, most of all, he loved her for no reason at all. That, he decided – for he was beginning to learn about love – was more important than all the other reasons put together.

A farmer, feeding chickens in his yard across the road, saw Rex and told him when he had put the flowers on his family grave, a cup of tea was waiting in his kitchen. As the priest walked across the frozen ruts in the farmyard, a cockerel pecked at the back of his legs. It was, his benefactor said, a direct descendant of the fighting cocks which once were matched at Shireoaks where three counties met. Rex knew. Enid told him that story a dozen times. He made the tea last for twenty minutes.

'Better be off,' said the farmer, speaking of himself but thinking of his guest.

There was nowhere for Rex to go except Worksop. So he arrived at Brook House, 75 Newcastle Avenue, at just after nine o'clock and walked boldly down the path that ran alongside the little stream. To his surprise, his hand did not tremble when he knocked on the door.

Inside a dog barked. It was, he knew, Mick, Enid's wire-haired terrier and grandson of the best rat catcher in Nottingham. As the bolts scraped and locks turned, he heard Mrs Brackenbury warning her daughter not to let the dog run into the road. There was a pause before the rusty hinges swung.

He had agonized for days about what he would say and had, at the last, decided to rely on the inspiration which the emotion of the moment would provide. At the sight of Enid, he was speechless.

'What are you doing here?'

He could not think of how to reply.

'I thought you'd come tomorrow.'

Before he could ask what a difference a day made or explain that he had nowhere else to go, she hissed at him through almost closed lips.

'I haven't told them yet. Come back after tea.'

The door slammed shut. Mick barked again and the bolts slid back into place.

ENID TOLD her mother that the caller was a gypsy and was congratulated for having shown the proper Christmas spirit by giving the beggar a threepenny bit.

At Worksop, where they believed that the old ways were always best, presents were distributed on Boxing Day so as to separate the sacred celebration from the profanity of material pleasure. The festivities got off to a bad start. Mick was more than usually aggressive towards Chum, Aunt Anne's elderly sheep-dog. Several interventions were necessary to prevent bodily harm. Agnes was in such pain that, had it not been the season of joy and good cheer, she would not have got out of bed. The warmed-up dinner was virtually inedible and Enid found it almost impossible to join in the chorus of voices raised in its praise. In a single nervous sentence she announced that she would not have a second helping of plum-pudding and that she 'wanted a little talk'.

Her hope was to address the whole assembled company and the reply was made on behalf of them all by Uncle Ern, Agnes's widower brother, an object of unconcealed family idolatry and a visitor who effortlessly assumed the role of host.

'There's a time and place for everything,' he said, choosing the most appropriate cliché from his extensive repertoire. 'Best get the presents over with.'

It was in that joyous spirit that the revellers moved out of the kitchen and into the fitting room which was, except for Christmas and confrontations, reserved for the most prestigious of customers. Agnes half sat, half lay on the *chaise longue* whilst Lottie perched on one of the gilt orchestra chairs. Enid stood by the window and looked out into the road until she noticed that Anne, who remained in the doorway in sight of the dogs, was silently signalling an instruction to concentrate on Uncle Ern, who coughed in preparation for the ritual distribution of his gifts.

For Lottie there was a huge and obviously expensive jar of crystallized fruit, which Agnes – who had, long ago, worked at Ashton's High Class Grocers and Provision Merchants – priced, *sotto voce*, at more than five shillings. Anne's box of mixed biscuits, although wrapped in sober paper and therefore less frivolous in appearance as well as content, was valued at half a crown more. Agnes herself received a tin of chocolates which had the circumference of a cart wheel. An envelope, stuck to the lid by the gum on its flap contained a five-pound note.

Agnes began to search the tin for a hard centre before the small package was handed to Enid. Inside the plain brown paper were two second-hand books – *White Fang* by Jack London and Walt Whitman's *Leaves of Grass*. The gifts visibly revived Enid's spirits. They were neither as expensive nor as spectacular as the other presents. They were, however, exactly what she wanted. Indeed she had bought them herself, at Uncle Ern's suggestion and handed them to Anne in exchange for the four and sixpence which they had cost. There was no more thought behind Ernest Skinner's other gifts. They had come to him as marks of respect and hopes of future business, tributes paid by various suppliers of goods and services to Hirsts of Retford where he was the incorruptible chief clerk.

Anne virtually ignored her present, but seized with obvious delight on the paper in which the Christmas boxes had been wrapped. She carefully smoothed out and folded each sheet into neat squares. Then she took the string and ribbon with which the parcels had been tied and wound each piece into a tidy skein. Watching her aunt adding to her hoard of useless clutter, a terrible truth was suddenly revealed to Enid – a truth so hideously obvious that she could barely believe that she had not understood it before.

The women who had brought her up did not behave like other women that she knew. Her father – with a mistress in Mansfield and an obsession with gambling – was the most normal of her family.

He had told her that the Skinner women were all peculiar, Agnes and Anne and their mother before them, and he had said that they all hated men and that, if she was not careful, she would grow to do the same. At the time, she had thought of her father's assault as his usual coarse abuse and the sordid justification for his constant adultery. Now she feared that what he said was true. She would be like them – unless she married the only man that she could ever love. Desperation made her brave.

'Shall we have our talk in here?'

The fitting room was far less comfortable than the kitchen, but Enid wanted to discuss her future amongst the elegance of her aunt's trade – the bulrushes in the tall vase, the pattern books on the low table and Chinese lacquer screen – rather than surrounded by the debris of Boxing Day dinner.

'We ought to take the dogs down Stubbing Meadows,' said Anne. 'They've not had a walk all day, poor things.'

'The dogs can wait.'

The expression of so shocking an opinion startled Enid's whole audience into apprehensive silence. Enid seized the moment.

'I'm going to get married.'

'Don't say that.' Lottie would not have been more distressed if Enid had announced that she was to volunteer for white slavery.

Ernest Skinner coughed, smoothed down his moustache with the back of his hand and looked at the ceiling immediately above the fireplace.

Enid's wedding was regularly discussed and regularly postponed and Anne always asked the same question.

'Who's going to look after your mother?'

'Jack's always been very nice to me,' Agnes said.

'Not him,' said Lottie with fine disregard for Enid's long engagement. 'Not that great Irish labourer.'

'No,' said Enid. 'Not him.'

There was another agonized silence before Uncle Ern decided that, as the head of the family, it was his right and duty to ask the obvious question.

'Who, then? Who's the lucky man?'

Ernest Skinner called every bridegroom 'the lucky man' no matter how unsuitable the match or potentially disastrous the union. But Anne stared at him to demonstrate her disgust at the idea of a successful marriage. She suspected him of recalling with affection the happy months he had spent with his young head-strong wife before she died in childbirth.

'I'm going to marry Rex.'

Enid knew that the name meant nothing to her aunts and uncles but she could not produce quite enough courage to use his full name and title.

'Is he a foreigner?' Lottie asked.

'He's the priest,' Agnes answered. 'And he's always been very nice to me.'

'You don't mean a *Catholic* priest?' There was no irony in Anne's incredulous question.

Enid answered in a continuous stream of self-justification.

'It's Father Hattersley from St Joseph's. We had a lovely time in the summer all of us together. Mam, his brothers and me. He was at the English College in Rome for seven years and he's the best-read man I've ever met. He's from Nottingham.'

Then she added as an afterthought, 'And I love him.'

'Does he love you?' Before she became ill and foolish, Agnes had been in love. Despite the agonies of her marriage to Brack, she still believed the message which was engraved on the locket that he had given her as an engagement present. A.V.O. 'That,' she proudly explained to the puzzled visitors, 'means love conquers all.'

'Hold on.' Ernest Skinner began to exercise his authority. He had assumed the manner which he adopted when a near illiterate farmer argued about a valuation of standing timber. 'I don't think you understand. Priests never get married. They take vows.'

'I know that. But he's left already. It was him at the door this morning, not a gypsy.'

'You see.' Anne put a comforting hand on Agnes's arm. 'He's started her telling lies already.'

'Even if he does leave,' Uncle Ern added, 'they'll persuade him to go back. Leopards don't change their spots. They'll find him and fetch him back.'

'And think,' Lottie implored, 'what will have happened by then.'

It was as if the assault on Enid had been carefully planned. For an hour, they begged and threatened in turn. Ernest Skinner was certain that, whatever the priest said now, he would never break Rome's bonds. Anne could not believe that any good could come of a relationship which was born in deception. Lottie warned of humiliations which could not be described. And Agnes, frightened by the constant suggestion of desertion, asked who was going to look after her.

At first Enid tried to convince them that she and Rex together would look after her mother for as long as she needed them and that his love was certain and unchangeable. But all her life she had been taught to believe what Worksop told her. Arguing with them was against her nature. Gradually their disbelief broke her confidence down and she was driven back to repeating the same, increasingly frantic promise over and over again.

'He loves me and he's coming for me this afternoon.'

DURING HIS years in Rome, Rex had made a list of all the great churches in the city and methodically visited them, one by one, ticking off the name on his inventory after each pilgrimage was done. He did not go to pray, though in a sense all his visits were acts of worship. He was infatuated by the splendour of the Church Beautiful: the great mosaic pictures which sparkled in the shafts of sunlight between the corinthian columns, the gold bosses in the high roofs, the tombs of saints and martyrs and – even more sumptuous – the memorials to the bishops who were the Church's founders. He knew nothing of architecture and little of Roman history. In the churches he enjoyed the profane pleasure which comes from the enjoyment of magnificence.

Back home in England, the fascination persisted, but it became historical. The coats of arms of Charles the Martyr, the effigies of Knights Templars, the stained glass celebrations of wool merchants and the battle honours of regiments which fought in the Low Counties and the Peninsula all fascinated him. With time on his hands on Boxing Day in Worksop, it was natural enough that he should drive from church to church. It was an entirely unrewarding experience.

St John's was locked. St Mary's, being Catholic, he only dared to examine from the outside. St Anne's contained nothing of interest except a pallid marble figure who turned out to be the wife of the benefactor, a Victorian brewer and county alderman. Some sort of service was going on in the Priory, so Rex stood in the gloom by the east door. The gatehouse, in which Cardinal Wolsey had spent a night during his last journey, was a ruin.

Rex decided to find warmth in the waiting room at the railway station. It was locked and the station deserted. He bought two penny bars of chocolate from the scarlet vending machine and went back to his car to think.

Sitting in the cold of that joyless afternoon, with all the Christian world in celebration around him, it was impossible for Rex not to feel neglected and deserted. If Enid really loved him, she would not have sent him away with a silly excuse about it being the wrong day. After an hour, when he felt as if the frost had got into his bones and the little groups of daytime revellers peered into the car as they wandered home from the public houses, he decided that Enid did not love him at all. Then, because the idea was so painful, he amended it to the hope and fear that – although she loved him – she was afraid to make the leap that their love required.

His first instinct was to return at once to Brook House and claim her. Then he thought that she might not want to be claimed. He could not bear the idea of rejection. Extinguishing even the hope of future happiness paralysed him with fear. Rex was, by nature, disposed to settle for what he was sure to get. He would not frighten Enid by his ardour or risk a rebuff by demanding her immediate commitment. He would talk to her about when the time should be and how the difficulties of their condition could be overcome.

As he knocked on the front door, Enid was sobbing through

her tears. 'I tell you, he will look after Mam. He wants to as much as me. I only want her to stay here for a couple of days. But he's coming to take me away tonight and I must go with him.'

Her determination had been strengthened by all the stories of the Church never letting go and always fighting back. If they did not go at once, they might not go at all.

Anne answered the door and grudgingly asked Rex in. She did not suggest that he took off his black gaberdine coat. So when Enid saw him, sitting on one of the gilt fitting room chairs with his collar still turned up against the December wind, he still looked like a priest.

Rex knew that he ought to say, 'I love you and I have come to take you away.' But he saw Uncle Ern standing in the doorway, so he said, 'I'm sorry that I've caused you all this trouble.'

Enid, so close to Rex that he could feel her hip bone against his, took his hand.

'Tell them what we're going to do.'

'That's what I've come to talk about.'

'So you mean it, then?' Lottie asked, still hoping that he was a philanderer who would leave Enid to decent spinsterhood.

Enid squeezed his hand.

'We just have to decide how and when,' Rex said.

The grip on his hand relaxed.

'She said that you wanted to take her away tonight.'

Rex mistook Anne's accusation for relief.

'No. We said we'd talk about it today.'

'What's there to talk about?' Enid asked, again on the verge of tears.

'We have to think about things.' Rex was determined to sound dependable.

'What things?' Enid asked.

'It's a big decision,' said Rex. 'We need to sit down and decide—'

'There's nothing to decide,' said Enid.

'There is,' Rex tried to sound patient and reassuring. 'We can't just—'

'There's nothing to decide.' She spoke with a disconcerting calm. 'I don't want to marry you.'

'But I thought . . .' Uncle Ern sounded puzzled but he added, almost under his breath, 'A woman's prerogative. A woman's prerogative.'

'So did I. But I was wrong.'

The announcement that she did not love him was intended to provoke a statement of his undying devotion to her. Rex was supposed to beg, plead and implore that she went away with him at once. But instead of a sudden explosion of passion all he offered to convince her of his devotion was an appeal to reason.

'Can't you and I talk about this? On our own. It's difficult discussing things in front of . . . in front of . . .'

A demon inside Enid persuaded her to advance when she knew that she should retreat.

'In front of my family? I've nothing to hide from them. Anyway, I've told you. There's nothing to discuss. You don't love me. And when I saw you sitting there, I knew that I don't love you.'

As she walked towards the door, Enid was completely calm and so dignified that she was slightly ridiculous.

'Would you like a cup of tea?' asked Lottie. She turned apologetically to Anne. 'After all, it is Boxing Day.'

'I think,' said Uncle Ern in a rare moment of understanding, 'that the young man will want to be on his way.'

Rex walked slowly back to his car and looked at the cheap, compressed-cardboard suitcase lying on the back seat. The remnants of three labels still stuck to its scratched side. On two of them the word 'Rome' was clearly visible. It was, Rex decided, a suitcase that could only belong to a priest.

When he saw the suitcase he wanted to go home to his family. And, at that moment, his family was not his father sleeping off his Boxing Day dinner, his brother George waiting for ordination in Valladolid or Syd worrying and wondering about his future at Ratcliffe College. His family was the Church and his home was the presbytery at Langwith Junction.

Rex took the starting handle from under the front seat and slotted it into the hole in the front bumper. Three times he tried to turn the engine over and three times he failed. Then, when at last the bonnet shook and trembled, the engine would not fire. He turned the handle time after time, rested inside the car, and turned it again. Nothing happened. A group of boisterous youths on their way to or from a party pushed the car for what seemed like half a mile. Still it would not start. He decided to walk. At least the Austin had been moved a respectable distance away from Brook House. It was still only five o'clock. He could be home well before midnight.

After he had walked for almost two hours – and still had eight miles left to go – he hid behind a hedge in a field outside Cuckney, put on his stock and clerical collar and became a priest again. Evening revellers, on their way to the pubs and clubs of Langwith Junction, recognized Rex. They fell abruptly silent and touched the peaks of their Sunday caps. His gratitude was tinged with envy. Back in the safety of the Church, he had begun to fear that he had returned not to a refuge but to a prison. The men he saw in the street were normal men who lived normal lives. He resented them enjoying the family pleasures which he might be for ever denied.

The key to the presbytery was where Rex had put it, under the brick outside the front door. But he was surprised to find his house exactly as he had left it. His letter to the bishop was still on the kitchen table with the cleaning woman's wages and a note telling her to post it and wait for the Vicar General to come out from Nottingham and tell her what to do.

Rex took the letters up to the bedroom and put them on top of his wardrobe where he had once kept all his other secrets. There was a whole night to pass before he could begin to rebuild his life. He shivered when he sat down on the side of his bed and after a moment's thought, pushed his feet under the blankets without taking off his socks. When he had checked and rechecked that the alarm clock was set for half past five, he said his prayers – as he had been taught – as the very last act of the day. Had he not cried himself to sleep, it would have been as if he had never been away.

CHAPTER TWO

FOR REX, the start of his first day back in the presbytery at Langwith Junction was easy enough. He woke, as he had woken on every morning since his ordination, just before the alarm clock rang. Then everything – from the quick shave in cold water to the last words of the mass – was done, as always, without much thought or any hesitation. Only a quartet of communicants, 'the faithful four' who attended each morning, knelt by the altar rail. After the service Rex came out of the vestry to offer a personal greeting to each of the regular worshippers, a habit which he developed in the belief that his little courtesy would encourage their return on the following day. He repeated the blessing and the greeting which he had used a thousand times before. They all offered the hope that he had enjoyed Christmas and he replied with exactly the same answer to each question.

'Very much, thank you. Quiet, you know . . . With my father. Quiet . . . I enjoyed it very much.'

As always he returned to the presbytery, not along the dusty corridor that connected vestry to kitchen, but through the front doors of both his church and house. Normally, he waved goodbye to his parishioners and hurried home with something approaching relief. On that morning, he dragged his feet like a child on its reluctant way to school. When the mass ended, he had begun to think again about his future and the thinking immobilized him.

On most days the routine which followed the service was as automatic as the mass itself – cigarette lit, kettle boiled, bacon fried and back page of *News Chronicle* read. The worrying about how he was to spend the day and which bills could wait for another week rarely began before nine o'clock. On that morning he did not possess enough interest or energy to turn the tap, light the gas or decide which of the various half loaves of old bread would make the least unpalatable toast.

19

All he could think about was Enid. He had told himself, as he walked home from Worksop, that he only wanted her because she could not be his and and that he was well rid of a woman who demanded his entire attention and expected his complete devotion. Back in the presbytery, he no more believed that he was better off without her than he believed in his vocation to be a Catholic priest. He wanted her and there was still the possibility that Paradise could be regained. The faint flicker of hope was more painful than the dull ache of despair. If there was still the chance of happiness, he had to decide how he could grasp it. And, that morning, he was not sure if he was capable of deciding anything at all.

He had taken his original decision to leave the Church during sleepless nights spent staring into the darkness above his bed and half listening to 2LO on the wireless which the parishioners of St Philip Neri had given him to celebrate promotion to a parish of his own. He had never prayed for guidance. It seemed impertinent to seek advice from a God whose existence he doubted and whose laws he was about to break. He was surprised as well as proud that, without any support or encouragement, he had dared to do so much. It was totally unreasonable of fate to expect him to prove himself again.

He sat and stared into space for almost an hour. The outcome of his anguish was an initiative that was comfortingly close to inactivity and therefore, as well as preserving what little dignity had survived the previous evening, reduced the risk of a second and fatal blow to his self-confidence. He would telephone Brack on the credible pretence of asking him to rescue the disabled motor car and see where the inconsequential conversation led.

To admit that the Austin Seven had broken down in Worksop was to risk raising Brack's suspicion that he had visited Enid. But Rex could think of no other excuse for his telephone call. Comforted by the certainty that neither Agnes nor her daughter would ever tell the story of his Boxing Day humiliation, he walked to the telephone kiosk in the station yard.

It took Brack so long to answer that Rex almost lost his nerve and put the receiver back. Then he heard a grunt.

'It won't start. Not even with pushing. It's in Worksop, just round the corner from St Mary's.'

'It never!' Brack sounded amused. 'Do you want me to bring it in?'

Rex hated Brack for talking about the car when he should have been talking about Enid.

'I don't think you'll be able to drive it. It may need a tow.'

'I'll manage. But if it needs a lot of work, don't expect to be driving it this side New Year. And it'll cost a bob or two. I don't know what you've been up to. It was all right when I sold it you.'

There was, Rex decided, nothing to be gained by contesting Brack's claim. He made one last desperate attempt to introduce the only subject that interested him.

'Well, all the best for the coming year. To all of you, Mrs Brackenbury, Enid . . .' He could not bring himself to mention Jack O'Hara, but he added '. . . and Enid' again in the hope that, having heard her name twice, Brack would feel obliged to say something about his daughter.

'And the same to you.'

There was such a terrible finality about the reply that, out of pure instinct, Rex said 'God bless you', the proper ending to all his conversations. He recovered his composure just in time and, shouting so that he could be heard even if the ear-piece was half way back to its hook on the wall, he threw himself a last life-line.

'Hope to see you soon.'

Rex feared that he would not survive the silence which followed but he was rescued by a torrent of false *bonhomie*.

Brack's relationship with Rex had passed through several phases. At first, he had been treated with open hostility. His predecessor, Father Froes, was a racing man and – since gambling in general and horses in particular fascinated Brack – the old priest had spent many happy afternoons at 11 Langwith Road, studying form books and smuggling furtive bets to bookmakers' runners. Rex could not name a single Derby winner. He was, therefore, held responsible for the early retirement and the subsequent end to a rewarding friendship.

When Rex started to perform little acts of kindness towards Mrs Brackenbury, her husband's attitude changed. Each courtesy to Agnes was a convenience to Brack, as it saved him from having to execute some trivial but uncongenial task. The discovery that

Rex had political opinions, as well as views on faith and dogma, added to the attraction of his visits. He became a sounding board for Brack's prejudices and, although he did not enjoy the sustained derision that his host called argument, he returned night after night to defend the Church against charges of condoning slavery in the Congo, imperilling the lives of working women by encouraging perpetual pregnancy and worshipping statues.

Brack's attitude changed again when a gambling crony suggested, as a joke made funnier by its improbability, that Enid was 'sweet on the priest'. Brack never repeated the libel to his daughter, whose high opinion he craved without ever craving it so much that he attempted to deserve it. And he was no more prepared to confront Rex openly than he was to warn Enid of the dangers to her reputation. So he opposed Rex's visits with stage whispers about 'being eaten out of house and home' and loud demands for the local newspaper whenever the priest was noticed reading it.

The antagonism lasted until he heard his daughter telling Jack O'Hara that she would never speak to Father Hattersley again. During the examination of the catechism, which was essential to the preparations for her marriage, the priest had committed the unforgivable offence of treating her as if she were a backward child. The story rehabilitated Rex in Brack's esteem.

True to form, the effusion of bogus joviality which thundered down the telephone ended with an outright lie.

'I was saying to our Enid, only the other day—'

The magic name having been spoken, Rex leapt in.

'How is Enid? Did she enjoy Christmas? I haven't seen her about for a bit.'

'I was only saying that it was about time you came round again for one of our little discussions. They'll be back in a day or two. Call round after the New Year.'

Brack was gone and Rex's hope of contentment died in the silence. As he walked home to the presbytery, he wondered how he was going to live until bedtime. Only two things were certain. He dared not return to Worksop and face the renewed prospect of doubt and disappointment. And he could not bear to go on thinking about what he should do. Somehow, he must put Enid out of his mind. It seemed unlikely that he would be distracted by Hilaire Belloc's *Reply to Mr H. G. Wells' History of the World*, but he opened the book at the turned-down page and tried to concentrate on the good news that the seals' lack of agility disproved the disreputable doctrine of natural selection. The robust assault on Darwin and Darwinism reminded him that he had spent the first part of the day worrying exclusively about the risk of losing Enid and had not thought at all about the certainty that he had lost his immortal soul.

Rex had barely got through a page when he heard the letter box rattle. There was, he knew, one chance in a hundred that he had received a letter from Enid. The overwhelming probability was that a couple of late-posted Christmas cards lay on his mat. But he nevertheless rushed out into the hall. The long, white envelope was a communication from Bishop's House, informing him of the papal encyclical that was published to mark the end of the year. It was entitled Casti Connubi.

> How great is the dignity of chaste wedlock . . . may be judged best from this. Christ Our Lord, Son of the Eternal Father . . . restored it to the original purity of its divine institution . . . Let it be repeated as immutable and inviolable fundamental doctrine that matrimony was not instituted or restored by man but by God.

He could not prevent himself from kneeling before the Sacred Heart in his living room and praying for forgiveness. With Enid he was a man. Without her he was in danger of becoming a priest again.

BISHOP DUNN stood, hands clasped behind his broad back, and stared disconsolately out of his study window. He was a prelate of such determined faith in human nature that he resented being forced to acknowledge the wickedness of the world. Yet his secretary, Father Ellis, a clever young man from the English College

in Rome, persisted in drawing his attention to the minor consequences of original sin. He could tell by the young priest's manner
that a minor indiscretion, committed in some remote part of the
diocese, was about to be elevated into a matter of major moral
concern.

'It's Father Hattersley, my lord . . .'

The bishop's huge pink face lit up with interest. Father
Hattersley was one of the bishop's many protégés, taken out of a
terraced house in Nottingham and sent, first to Ratcliffe College
and then to Rome.

'Father Hattersley stayed with his family in Alfreton Road on
Christmas night and I walked round to see him yesterday morning. He wasn't there.'

'What's so strange about that?'

'His father said that he'd gone back to Langwith Junction to
say mass.'

'And?'

'He hadn't. I said mass for him yesterday so that he could stay
with his family. He was expected to serve for the Vicar General
and he wasn't there.'

The bishop had picked Father Hattersley out of the Nottingham cathedral choir when he was a boy in glasses as thick as
beer bottle bottoms and had convinced him of his vocation. He
had been a Bishop's Scholar at Ratcliffe and the Bishop Dunn's
nominee at the English College in Rome. Only an honourable
explanation of his conduct was possible. It was agreed that Father
Ellis should find out what it was.

'Give him my love and my blessing. Tell him that I'm still
proud of him. Tell him that the salamander survived the fire as his
friends always knew that it would. It is not by running away from
evil that we overcome it.'

Father Ellis hurried towards the door. He had no wish to hear
yet again, the whole Legend of the Salamander. It only made him
wonder why Bishop Dunn based all his aphorisms on such bad
theology.

The bishop's secretary did not own a motor car so it was well into the afternoon before he arrived in Langwith Junction. The presbytery was dark and locked, but a dim light glowed through the church windows. He pushed the door open and stood in the half light waiting for his eyes to adjust to the gloom of the small, ugly nave. An elderly woman knelt on all fours beyond the altar rails, cleaning the carpet with a hand brush. Father Ellis, having briefly prayed for strength, approached her with the soft tread appropriate to a place of Catholic worship. He bent down and touched her on the shoulder.

'Lord bless us and save us, Rex. You could have frightened me half to death, creeping up to me like that.' She was looking at the thick black shoes and black trouser legs.

'It isn't Father Hattersley. I'm looking for him. We're old friends.'

The woman swayed back on her haunches and tried to recapture the lock of dank hair that had escaped from the bun at the back of her neck as she pushed herself to her feet.

'I'm sorry, Father. I thought—'

'Of course you did. Do you know where he is?'

'I've not seen him all day. Not since mass.'

'He said mass here, this morning?'

The woman looked at him in bewilderment.

'This is his parish now. Father Froes left over a year ago.'

'I know all about Father Froes. I thought that Father Hattersley was on holiday.'

'Yesterday. Yesterday, he was. A priest came from Nottingham yesterday. But he was back this morning.' She picked up the brush from the carpet. 'You'll have to excuse me, Father. If I don't finish this in half an hour, I'll be late home and my husband's tea won't be ready.'

'The presbytery seems to be locked.'

'The key's under the brick on the step. I'm sure he won't mind you waiting inside, you being a friend. I doubt if he'll be long. He'll be out on one of his walks. He goes for a walk nearly every afternoon, rain or shine. I'd make you a pot of tea only . . .'

Father Ellis sat in the one easy chair in the dismal living room and marvelled at the moral resources of a man who was able to live in such conditions without the comfort and companionship of other priests. The furniture was cheap and old, even by the standards of Catholic presbyteries. All that decorated the walls was a faded picture of the Pope, a garish representation of the Sacred Heart and, surprisingly in the place of honour over the mantelpiece, a calendar advertising the services of a local coal merchant. The books added to the impression of poverty. Because the presbytery did not boast a bookcase, they were piled on the floor like a heap of building bricks.

It was, Bill Ellis decided, unwise to draw the curtains along the fragile wire, even after he lit the gas. So he turned the back of his chair to the window and, hidden from passing pedestrians, waited. He waited for almost two hours. All that Rex saw, when he arrived home from the longest walk of all his years at Langwith Junction, was a light in his living room.

'It's me,' he shouted from half way along the gravel path. 'It's me. I didn't think you'd come. I really didn't.' The gibberish continued as he charged into the hall. 'Thank God. It's been killing me.'

It was then that the Bishop's Secretary seriously considered the possibility that the parish priest of St Joseph's, Langwith Junction, had gone mad. They had known each other for more than ten years. Bill Ellis had met Rex off the train at the Termini Station on the day that he arrived in Rome. He had watched him struggle through the doubts and depressions which every seminarian suffers and he knew – for Bishop Dunn was indiscreet as well as sentimental – that there had been some crisis during the summer, which had almost ended in Rex leaving the Church. He had assumed that it was the usual temporary loss of faith which was experienced by most young priests in lonely parishes.

'My God.' The sight of the Bishop's Secretary rising from his chair turned delight into despair.

'Nothing to worry about, Rex.' Bill Ellis was frightened. 'Don't be upset, it's only me.'

As Rex walked towards him, fear turned into pity. What the Bishop's Secretary saw was not a lunatic, but a sane man in torment who had to force himself to greet his visitor.

'I didn't expect to see you.'

The greeting was so banal that it broke the spell. Bill Ellis needed time to decide how he should deal with a trauma which he did not understand. He touched Rex – first on the arm, then on the shoulder and finally on the bare flesh of his hand.

'Have you got any whisky in the house? I could do with a drink.'

Rex disappeared without a word and he returned with an unopened bottle and one glass.

'You're lucky.' He spoke like a man in a dream. 'I was going to give the whisky away tomorrow.'

'I've never seen a man look so disappointed to see an old friend.' Father Ellis took a gulp from his glass and made another attempt at joviality. 'Who was it that you hoped was here? Who was it that you would have rather seen than me?'

There was another long silence. Bill Ellis decided that the conversation must be moved on.

'Look, Rex. I went round to see you at the shop yesterday. Your father said that you'd left before six to come here and say mass.'

'You thought that I might have run away. But as you see, I haven't.'

'Where were you on Boxing Day?'

'It doesn't matter.'

'Don't be so stupid. You're a priest. You've taken vows before God. You don't tell lies about saying the mass. You've—'

'I don't want to talk about it.'

'You'll have to talk about it to somebody.'

'Why will I?'

Rex reminded the Bishop's Secretary of the recalcitrant school children who had been such a trial to him during his brief service as an assistant parish priest. He found the reluctance to accept the certainty of retribution even more irksome than the refusal to admit error. He decided to change tack again.

'I'm here to help. One old friend to another. Just between you and me, are you in some sort of trouble?'

'No trouble that you can help with.'

Despair had liberated Rex. He spoke what he believed to be the simple truth without concern for the offence which it might cause.

'Of course I can,' said Bill Ellis. 'Let me try to smooth your path.'

'With God?'

It was important, Father Ellis told himself, to behave as an old friend as well as a priest. A rebuke would certainly have been in order. There could be no excuse for a flippancy which bordered on the blasphemous. He chose to treat Rex gently.

'Talking may help you to find grace.'

'I'm not looking for grace. I'm not even sure that I believe in it any more. I thought about it, night and day before Christmas. But now I'm not sure. What I'm looking for now is happiness. I don't look like finding it.'

Bill Ellis drew a deep breath before he replied.

'You're not making sense.'

'That's because I'm frightened and I don't know what to do.'

Bill Ellis was frightened too. Priests know only one way of driving out demons.

'The thing to do is pray.'

'I can't. That's the strangest thing of all. I tried to pray for forgiveness of my sins before this morning's mass. That's what I was taught to do. You don't forget something like that. I tried, but I couldn't do it.'

'Perhaps you felt that it wasn't a genuine repentance.'

'I don't repent. I came back here last night because I had nowhere else to go and I said mass out of habit. Sometimes I believe. Sometimes I don't. This minute, there's nothing. That's the truth of it and I'm not in a mood to dress it up.'

Bill Ellis poured himself a second glass of whisky with a shaking hand and sank back in his chair like a man who was already exhausted by his battle with the devil. Then he forced himself to ask, 'What are you going to tell the bishop?'

'You tell him for me, Bill. I wrote him a letter. If things had turned out differently, I would have posted it today. You've got your duty to do. You tell him and it will be off my chest.'

'I don't know what to tell him. I don't know what is going on.'

'That I'm leaving, that's all. I'm not sure why, but I'm leaving.

Priests have left the Church before and will do again. I probably shouldn't have gone to Rome in the first place.'

'I told him that you'd rot in this parish, but he wouldn't listen. Would you feel better in Nottingham?'

'It's too late for all that. I asked for a move last September and he wouldn't give me one. In his own terms he was absolutely right. It wouldn't have helped.'

'Look here. I don't suppose that there's much point in talking about your duty of obedience. But you do owe it to the old man. He's done a lot for you – and for your family. He'll take it hard, anyway. If you just sneak off . . .'

'I'm not sneaking off. I'm not ashamed of what I feel. Just confused.' Rex was no more prepared to discharge his debt of gratitude than he was to observe his vow of humility. 'And I'm not sure that I've got all that much to thank him for. If it was all a mistake, it was his mistake, not mine. I was a little boy when he took me over.'

'Rex, you've got to tell him yourself. It's the only decent thing. I'll take any message you want to send. I'll prepare the way. Then you come yourself. You owe it to him.'

Rex hesitated and Father Ellis stumbled on the magic words.

'I know that it will take courage to face him. But if you really are going this time . . .'

Enid had told Rex that meeting the bishop face to face was the only way to leave the Church and instead he had written a letter which, when the time came, had proved not to be worth the trouble he had taken to write it. She had told him to make a clean break and he had hung on to the trappings of his old life long after he had begun to lose the convictions which went with the clothes. 'If you don't have the courage to do it properly, you won't do it at all.' It was as if Bill Ellis was quoting her words in order to remind him of the price that he was already paying for his cowardice.

'I'm going, Bill. I'll tell him. I'm not sure why any longer, but I'm going. No need for you to talk to him first. I'll just do it.'

The bishop's secretary stood up, determined to start the journey before Rex lost his nerve.

'I knew you would, old chap.'

'I'm not going before eight.'

Bill Ellis did not argue. He knew that there was no hope of Rex changing his mind and leaving the presbytery until he was certain that the other visitor – the one for whom he longed – would not come. After a couple of attempts at desultory conversation, the two men sat in silence, one watching the clock and the other listening for the sound of footsteps on the gravel drive.

It was then that Father Ellis realized that, within the evening, a gulf had opened up between them which, despite all their years together, would separate them for the rest of their lives. Since Rex had returned from Rome, they had met almost every week, and they had always talked about their calling. They had not discussed the bodily assumption of the Virgin Mary, the infallibility of the Pope or even the latest papal encyclical. They had gossiped about the idiosyncracies of their colleagues, joked about the vagaries of the priestly life and the preferment prospects of their old friends from the English College. That night, he felt unable to speak about any of those things. His life was the Church. And whatever Rex wanted for himself and his future, it was not that. Father Hattersley was lost to the priesthood for ever. God willing, thought his old friend, we can save him from being damned as well.

'WELL, WELL, WELL, this is a nice surprise.'

By the time that Rex was ushered into the study it was not a surprise at all. For, as it befitted his calling, the Bishop's Secretary had asked Bishop Dunn if he was prepared to grant an audience to the parish priest of St Joseph's, Langwith Junction, before the unexpected guest was allowed to kneel and kiss the episcopal ring.

'Bill told me you were ill.'

'With the greatest of deference, my lord . . .' Father Ellis sounded hurt.

'Don't stand on your dignity, Bill. It doesn't matter. We all make mistakes, even you. See if Mrs Griffith is still in the kitchen and ask her if she'll make us a pot of tea, unless you'd like something stronger.'

'I think,' said the Bishop's Secretary, 'that it would be best if I left. Father Hattersley has something to tell you.'

'Father Hattersley! Father Hattersley indeed! How long have you two known each other, *Father* Ellis?' The bishop was still not wholly serious when he turned to Rex.

'Is it private or can Bill stay as long as he sits quietly in the corner and doesn't interrupt?'

'He knows all about it, my lord.'

At last the bishop accepted that the two priests had come on serious business. But he could not keep silent for the moment that Rex needed to compose himself. He stretched out his legs in front of the dying fire, folded his arms behind his head and showed every sign of looking forward to the discussion which was to follow. Rex did not have the composure to soften the blow.

'I'm leaving. Leaving the Church.'

There seemed nothing more to say and Rex waited to be engulfed in a tidal wave of regret and recrimination. His great fear was that the bishop would ask him not to change his mind but to postpone the ultimate decision until he had talked about it – talked to Bill Ellis, talked to the Vicar General, talked to the bishop himself. Because he could not bear the thought of another day's indecision, Rex prepared to reply with uncompromising honesty. In his mind, the weakness became a virtue. He was about to justify all Enid's faith in his courage and determination.

Bishop Dunn sat silent. He had drawn up his knees and he sat hunched and crumpled like a man in pain. Rex forced himself into offering some sort of comfort.

'It's all for the best. If the vocation was ever really there, it's gone.'

The bishop still did not speak and Rex, moved not by guilt but pity, filled the silence.

'You know I thought about it last September. I should have done it then. You were right not to let me move away from St Joseph's. That wouldn't have solved anything. I know that I've let you down.'

Rex could not stop talking. Irrelevant detail ran into bold statement of principle.

'I haven't told anybody yet – except Bill, that is – though my family know that I'm having doubts. But my mind's made up. I've paid the housekeeper's wages. I'll write to George in Spain.

Perhaps Syd knows. I more or less told him on Christmas Day. There's no going back so I don't mind if he talks about it at Ratcliffe. I'll send the letters as soon as I get back to Langwith Junction.'

'Stay here tonight.'

'I don't understand.'

'Stay here. It's simple enough. You don't want to be alone tonight. Not in that terrible house. Father Froes designed it himself, you know. That's why it's so cold.'

Bishop Dunn always made the same joke when the presbytery at Langwith Junction was mentioned. No matter how sad the mood or solemn the occasion, the habit was too strong to break. Rex did not laugh.

'I'm best out of your way, my lord.'

'No, you're not. I'm your pastoral as well as spiritual father. It's not just your soul that concerns me. It's your . . .' He flinched from saying 'mind,' and added '. . . your body as well. Have a good night's sleep. Bill, can you go out to Langwith again tomorrow? Nobody will know that anything is wrong.'

Rex's nerve, which had held out far longer than he would have anticipated, snapped. He was being tricked. If the bishop accepted that he had renounced his vows, there was no point in scheming to keep his apostasy secret for another day.

'It's no good. If I stay here for a month, I still won't change my mind.'

'I know that, Rex. If you say that you've made up your mind, I believe you. I just make two requests, two humble requests. That proves I've given up, doesn't it? Have you ever known a bishop be humble with a priest? I'm not treating you like a priest. Don't treat me like a bishop. We're old friends. And, as an old friend, I ask you only one thing. For the parish's sake, let's do it with as little scandal as possible. You must have friends there whose feelings—'

'Believe me, I don't want a scandal. I've tried to avoid it for months.'

'Good. Very good. I'm more grateful than I can say. So just one other favour. Stay here tonight. Have a lie in in bed tomorrow morning. You can't have had many of those.'

'It's no good. I've finished.'

'I didn't realize that you meant finished with the Church. I thought you meant finished with the priesthood.'

'I don't know whether I've lost my faith or not.'

'Is it that young lady, Miss Brackenfield?'

'Brackenbury. Yes, it is.'

It was still an effort not to add 'my lord' to the end of every reply but Rex concentrated hard on avoiding the old deference. He accepted the bishop's authority no longer. He was free to say what he believed.

'I am in love with her. Nothing can change that.'

'You told me about her last summer.'

The bishop's complacency was intolerable. There was no doubt what he intended. Enid was again to be treated as an example of the occasional aberrations which overcome young priests, not altogether dissimilar from boils, unhealthy interest in corporal punishment and wet dreams. The bishop thought of Enid as something for him to grow out of without scandal or damage to the righteous illusions which sustained the Catholic Women's League and the Society of St Vincent de Paul. The desire to shock Bishop Dunn into taking him seriously was irresistible.

'In September it was only in my mind.'

'And now?'

'Now I want her more than I want anything in the world. And I thought that she wanted me. We were serious about it, you know. We planned to go away together.'

'You thought . . . ?'

Rex was impervious to interruption.

'I don't know if she even really meant it, but I did. Still do. Until yesterday, I daren't jump unless she jumped first. So I talked about us jumping together. I'm ready now. Ready to risk anything. Ready to build my life on a chance.'

'I'm sorry you feel so wretched, Rex. I don't know what else to say. I'm supposed to understand these things. But it isn't easy. I wish I could help more.'

'You have helped. It's helped just having somebody to talk to. Do you know, I've never told anybody that I loved her before. I've

33

barely told her. Telling you – just saying the words – has made it all seem real. It all seems possible again. Something worth fighting for.'

'Talking to me has made you more determined. Is that what you mean? More determined to leave the Church?'

Bishop Dunn did his best to look distressed, until he was out of the study. But, on his way to bed, he put his head round the door of the living room and when he saw his secretary sitting at the table, reading the Bible, he grinned like a boy who was about to embark on an enterprise of which his parents disapproved.

'So far, so good, Bill. I've done very well. Even if I say so myself. It's only the woman. The vocation's still there. Get her out of his head and he'll be all right.'

ON THE MORNING of the Feast of the Holy Innocents, Rex sat in Bishop Dunn's study waiting impatiently to say goodbye. He did not look forward to the parting, for he had no doubt that the attempts to keep him in the Church – which he had expected since his arrival – would at last be made. And he was eager to be on his way back to Langwith Junction.

He began to explore Bishop's House for no better reason than that moving furtively from room to room was better than sitting in front of the bishop's desk and staring first at the clock on the mantelshelf and then at the clock on the wall. The kitchen was deserted, but two saucepans boiling on the gas stove suggested that the housekeeper was not far away. He closed the door so quickly that it shut with a bang.

'Were you looking for me?' The bishop's secretary stood behind him. 'I'm afraid that the bishop is held up. He's round at the convent. Some problem about new desks for the boys' school. Sister Maria Fidelis thinks we can afford them. The Administrator doesn't. His lordship's adjudicating. Not with very good grace, I fear.'

Rex could barely believe Bill Ellis's account of how Bishop Dunn was spending the time. He had taken it for granted that the morning would be devoted to wrestling over his future. Yet, instead of fighting to save a soul from the devil and a life for the Church, the Bishop of Nottingham was arguing with nuns about the cost of furniture.

There was no question, Rex decided, of his waiting for the bishop's return. No matter how desperate the entreaties, he would say firmly, but politely, that the time had come for him to be on his way. He was sorry to hurt the old man, but he had taken a new vow – the vow of frankness.

'He wants you to know that you'll always be welcome – welcome to stay here in the house. Actually, he thinks that's what you should do whilst you're getting things sorted out; a job and so on. He would have liked to have told you himself. You know what Maria Fidelis is like if she's kept waiting. Anyway, you were looking for me. On your way, are you?'

'I wanted to make a telephone call.'

'Of course, come into my cubby hole. And don't forget what his lordship said. It goes for me too. We've known each other too long for . . .'

Rex was not sure if he should shake his old friend's hand, or embrace him in a final show of affection. Before he could make up his mind, the secretary turned on his heel.

'I'll leave you to make your call in private. Remember, we want to see you. We'll be thinking of you and praying for you. God bless you.'

Father Ellis crossed himself. Rex caught his breath. It was the one moment during the whole conversation when Father Ellis had behaved like a Catholic priest. If the sudden reversion to the habits of Rome had been planned as a final reminder of the life that was being left behind, it had exactly its intended effect. Rex's hand trembled as he lifted the telephone from the desk.

Jack O'Hara answered. Rex almost hung up without speaking, but remembering that it was the beginning of a brave new life, he asked for Brack without identifying himself. Jack recognized his voice.

'Are you all right, Father? The Father who took mass this morning said that you weren't well.'

'I'm fine. Anybody there I can speak to?'

Jack was not offended by the implication.

'Enid and Mrs Brackenbury are back some time today. That's definite. Brack's gone out to get your car. I'm holding the fort. It's afternoons this week.'

'Tell him that I'll be round to pick it up at about three.'

The train arrived at Langwith Junction at half past one and since everything in his new life had to be planned decisively and executed with firm precision, Rex spent almost an hour walking in the Top Wood before he returned to the presbytery. When he had changed once more into George's old clothes, he sat on the stairs waiting for zero hour. At exactly five minutes to three, he walked out into the cold, clear afternoon.

'Lord above!' Brack sounded shocked. 'You must be froze solid. Come inside before you get your death. Where's your coat?'

'I don't have one. At least not one that's suitable.'

Rex began to tremble. Dressed as a priest he would have felt all the authority of the station and expected to receive the respect which was due to his calling. Without the protection of the cloth he felt all the fears of a man who dreams that he is naked in public.

Brack began to search through a pile of papers which were held down on the kitchen table by a rusty horseshoe.

'You'll need a new starter motor. It'll cost at least a quid for parts. That's rock bottom. Not much in it for me. Pay me when you can. But not bit by bit. I lose count.'

'What time do you expect them?'

'Bloody hell! I don't know. I only know they're coming at all because they sent the girl a telegram about airing the beds. More money chucked away – money we can't afford.'

'If the car's working, I could go and get them!'

'Pass 'em half way, more like. Anyway, do you feel like driving? Jack said that you were off work ill.'

The moment that Rex had been waiting for had arrived, the moment when he proved that courage and conviction had changed his life. On Boxing Day he had failed because he had dissembled and procrastinated. On the Feast of the Holy Innocents, despite his fear, he would succeed by answering every question with the certainty which came from being proud of his intentions.

'Mr Brackenbury, I'm dressed like this because I'm not a priest any more. I've left the Church.'

He spoke slowly, for he was determined neither to stutter nor stumble over his words. Brack nodded gravely, like a man to whom a long suspected truth has been confirmed.

'I'm not surprised. Educated chap like you. I never did understand how you could believe all that mumbo-jumbo. Tell the truth. You never did believe all that about statues coming to life and bleeding real blood, did you?'

'It's not that. It's Enid.'

They were not the words in which he had intended to proclaim his love. But he had borne witness. He was ready for anything.

'Enid? You don't mean . . . ?'

'I mean I love her.'

'Don't be so bloody daft.'

Afterwards, when he relived the extraordinary moment, Brack always told himself that his responses had been carefully constructed to humiliate Rex. In truth, he said the first thing that came into his head. He had occasionally suspected that the priest harboured impure thoughts about his daughter. But he had always treated the supposed infatuation as a silly joke. The discovery that Father Hattersley's feelings had grown from secret vice into normal love shocked him deeply. He was, by instinct, censorious of all scandals other than those which were necessary to his personal gratification. The idea that his own flesh and blood had encouraged the advances of a Catholic priest was so repulsive to him that he dared not risk Rex saying anything that justified the presumption of Enid's love.

'I'll tell you this. She's never done anything to encourage you. I know that, you great soft sod. I ought to give you a bloody good hiding. Nobody would blame me. Just bugger off before Jack O'Hara gets here or he'll have the skin off your back.'

'It's true, Mr Brackenbury, and you must believe it—'

'Must! Who says I must? Who's going to make me? Not you.'

'We were going to go away together.'

Brack thrust at the one chink in Rex's armour.

'Were? If you were, why didn't you? She's going to marry Jack

O'Hara, you daft bastard. She wears his bloody ring. Aren't you teaching her to be a Catholic?'

'She was going to marry me. She might still.'

'That'll be news to him and, what's more, it'll be news to her. He's getting a pit cottage and he's moving in. She said that they'd get married after Easter.'

'When did she say that?'

As she had never said it, Brack needed to make the reply convincing.

'The day before she went to Worksop. That's when she told me.'

'I need her to tell me herself.'

'Then wait, you lying sod, till she gets here and ask her. Wait outside in that little motor car. I'm not having you sit in my house, pretending . . . pretending things.'

As Rex shuffled towards the door with as much dignity as tight jacket and short trousers allowed, Brack felt sudden and uncharacteristic remorse. He was not a bad fellow, the priest. Knew a lot. Clever talker. Always a pleasure to argue with. And, on the afternoon's evidence, not backward at coming forward. He liked a man who stood up for himself. Brack had not believed that the priest had it in him. In a moment of rare compassion he called after Rex with what he imagined was a message of comfort.

'Our Enid wouldn't be the one for you, even if . . . even if you weren't a clergyman. She needs someone she can put on, somebody she can look down on. You couldn't stand her airs and graces.'

'I love her, Mr Brackenbury.'

'Bloody hell.'

Brack was not used to public demonstrations of love. Love was what young men felt for young women but were embarrassed to admit it. He had once been in love and, as a result, had been encumbered for thirty years by a sad and crippled wife. The thought of what he might have made of himself had he married a woman of spirit – perhaps even a woman with a little money of her own – was too painful to consider. As Rex stumbled out, Brack consoled himself by listing his own achievements. He was a councillor, he was a coal merchant and garage owner, he had snatched Mrs Wood from under the nose of a pork butcher who had offered to marry her and he was the best card player in the coalfield. Nobody need feel sorry for him. He had managed very well without love.

CHAPTER THREE

As TIME passed, reckless elation gradually turned into accus-
tomed anxiety and Rex began to walk nervously up and down the
road. He had gone through all the fantasies of despair when, in the
half light of early evening, headlights bobbed at the distant end of
bumpy Langwith Road. He was still fifty yards from the gate
when the car turned into the yard. The engine was still running
when Mick leapt out and ran, howling, round the back of the
house. Rex waited to hear Enid call the dog back. But no sound
came from inside the car. He held back while he marshalled his
reserves of courage. After several minutes, the driver climbed out
and, very carefully, opened the back door.

'Don't touch her. Just wait there till I've moved her legs.'
Enid's tone changed. 'Sit still for a second, Mam. If we get your
legs out first, it will be easier.'

Enid was not looking her best. Her coat was fastened on the
wrong buttons and her hair was so dishevelled that it looked as if it
had not been combed all day. But Rex noticed nothing about the
details of her appearance. The sight of Enid – Enid in general, Enid
in any shape, condition or form – filled him with more emotion
than he could manage. He was at once exhilarated by hopes of their
life together and incapacitated by fear that he had lost the chance of
happiness.

Rex watched in fascinated silence as Enid walked round the car
and, opening the back door, reached into the passenger seat.

'Don't worry about that, Mam. We'll clean you up as soon as
we get you inside. I'm going to push you along the seat and you'll
be half out before we have to lift you.'

Enid, having pushed her mother as far as she would go, skipped round to the other side of the car and began to pull. Rex
watched in awe. At that moment, Enid seemed like all the female
saints and ministering angels of whom he had ever heard. He also

watched in anguish. For the heroic confrontation which he had planned was no longer possible.

If Rex had seen two unknown women in such distress, he would have gone to their aid at once. But it was Enid – the woman he loved and had almost lost – who was struggling to heave her mother out of the car. He could not walk boldly towards her and, ignoring the cripple on the back seat, announce that because they were in love, nothing else mattered and they must spend the rest of their lives together. Nor could he bear to approach her as priest and friend and offer his help without telling her that nothing in the world mattered except them being together for the rest of their lives. So he watched in guilty fascination as Enid pulled her mother out into the yard.

He waited until Agnes was half carried, half dragged across the patch of muddy ground which separated car and house. Then decency required him to wait another few minutes, whilst Enid did all that was necessary to make her mother clean and comfortable. He stood for more than half an hour in the dark road. Gradually his confidence came back, and as it returned he came to the firm conclusion that waiting until the travellers were re-established in their home, was less an act of bewildered cowardice, than a tactical triumph.

Instead of approaching the house with a sickening void in his stomach, as he had anticipated, he walked towards his destiny with such assurance that, even when Brack opened the door before he knocked, he did not allow surprise to disturb the appearance of calm confidence. It was a moment for dignity.

'I would like to see Enid.'

He thought of adding 'please' simply for reasons of courtesy. But Brack was the sort of man who would interpret good manners as a sign of weakness. He was stating a fact, not pleading for a favour.

'You've chosen a bloody awful time.'

Enid's voice from inside the house supported Brack's judgement.

'We don't want anyone in here, Dad, whoever it is.'

'What's happened to Mrs Brackenbury?'

'She looks as if she's had a bloody fit.' He spoke over his shoulder to Rex who was following him towards the gate. 'Brought up her dinner all over her coat. Shivering and shaking. She had some sort of upset at Worksop. Her ladyship up to her old tricks, I wouldn't wonder. She'd never happy except when there's a row on.'

The doctor's car turned into the yard before Rex could speak up in Enid's defence and Brack hurried towards the road to show the respect and deference which a coal merchant and motor car dealer owes to a professional man.

It was almost an hour before the doctor left and Rex – shivering in his draughty car – was still wondering if the visit had lasted so long because of the invalid's health or her desire for extended conversation, when Brack came out of the house. He was, Rex felt sure, on his way to Cobbler Jack's for his nightly game of cards. His departure gave no clue about his wife's condition. He would have gone to Cobbler Jack's at nine o'clock if she had died at half past eight.

Rex, for whom waiting had become a sort of pilgrimage, sat in his cold motor car and stared at the first-floor windows. When the gas was lit in the bedroom, he would know that Mrs Brackenbury had been hauled upstairs and that Enid would soon be alone in the kitchen staring at a book in the half daze which came from imagining that she was one of the characters. He concentrated so hard on identifying the moment when he could, at last, correct the errors of the previous days that he did not hear the front door open.

It was Mick, choking on his collar, that made Rex look down. The dog was, as always, straining on its leash and Enid was, as usual, making no real effort to restrain him. She was pulled out into the yard, with her arm stretched out in front of her. Instead of protesting, she was congratulating Mick on the patience with which he had waited for his evening walk.

'Enid, it's me.' Rex did not mean to startle her, but he leapt out of the dark so suddenly that she flinched, cowered and then turned away. 'It's only me.'

Mick growled. Enid stood absolutely still.

'It's only me, Rex.'

'I know it is. What do you want?'

'I've come to explain. I left the Church like I promised. Look!'
He spread his arms wide to reveal his tweed jacket to best advantage and, frightened by the shadow that he cast, dropped them
down to his sides again with a little gasp.

'It's too late. I told you that on Boxing Day.'

'I didn't think that you wanted to go.'

'That's a lie. You're only saying that because you want to get
out of it and want to put the blame on me.'

She knew that it was untrue. But the demon inside her would
not allow a reconciliation.

'I love you. Nothing else matters.'

'It matters to me. You made me feel a fool. Anyway. I can't
talk now. Mick's not had his walk.'

'This is more important than the dog.'

Rex, one pace behind, followed her out into the road. She
addressed him without turning around.

'You keep telling me what's important. Things matter to me
that don't matter to you. Mick matters. He's always there when I
need him.'

'I love you. I've told your father. Ask him. I want it all
straightforward and definite.'

'I wouldn't ask him. I wouldn't dream—'

'Then, let's forget about the past and talk about what happens
now.'

He tried to catch her hand, but she pulled away before he could
touch her.

'I can't forget about it. I'd been through all that. You can't
imagine what it was like. Then you said that you didn't want to
take me away. I shall never understand how you could just leave
me there, for Anne and Lottie to laugh at.'

'Did they laugh?'

Since the answer was inconvenient, Enid ignored the question.

'I understand it all now. You never meant it. You never meant
to go away with me. I know that now. All you want is what you

can't have. If I told you now that I'd come away with you, you'd find a new excuse.'

'Did you tell your aunts?'

Rex persisted with the question because of the hope that the answer might bring. If Enid had told her aunts she had really meant to marry him. And if she had meant it three days ago, she must mean it still.

'Of course I did. You spoilt Christmas. It was because of you that Mam got ill. It was worry that did it.'

'Your mother was worrying about me taking you away? She seemed all right when I saw her.'

'It's no good you trying to catch me out. I know you're cleverer than me. That's why you didn't come, isn't it?'

'Don't be ridiculous.'

'How dare you call me ridiculous? If I'm ridiculous, it's because I've been waiting for you.'

Enid stopped and Rex prepared himself for her onslaught. Then he noticed that the dog was defecating under the hedge by the side of the road.

'Good boy. There's a good boy. Look at that. Almost bursting, but he waited until he got to his own bit of grass. He knew he had to wait because his missus was busy. I can always trust him.'

Rex, although not proud in the presence of the incomparable Enid, resented his loyalty being compared unfavourably with the devotion of a dog which had displayed its fidelity by not fouling the footpath.

Exasperation trapped him into asking the wrong question. She was still possessed by the need for self-destruction.

'What does it matter? We can get it all sorted out now.'

'It's too late.'

Enid hoped that it would never be too late for Rex and she knew that it would never be too late for her. But she could not bring herself to say that she loved him and wanted to live with him more than anything else in the world. She had risen to heights of emotion from which descent was, at that moment, impossible. She believed she could punish him a little more and reprieve him later.

She jerked on Mick's lead. The dog, its head having been

forcibly turned towards home, led the procession back to the coal yard.

'I didn't have to ask about your mother, I knew. I saw you bring her home.'

'You did what?'

'I saw you bring her home. I was sitting in the car waiting for you.'

'And you just sat there and let us struggle . . . let me drag her in, pulling at her and hurting my shoulder. I don't believe it.'

The irony was lost on Rex. 'I thought it was the best thing to do.'

'That does it.'

'Does what?'

'I can't talk to you now. Mam can't be left on her own.'

'You've left her on her own for the last ten minutes whilst you walked this damned dog. I just can't understand you.'

Rex's mild aggression was intolerable to her. She escalated her denunciation to the stratosphere of passion which from time to time was her only way of sublimating feeling that, in other young women, were gratified by more carnal confrontations. Satisfaction was dependent on total victory, Enid said what she judged necessary to secure a moment's triumph. Neither the truth nor the consequences were important. All that mattered was the defeat of the moment's adversary.

'Just get it in your head. It's all over. Whatever happens now I'm going to marry Jack O'Hara.'

REX HAD misjudged Brack. He had not hurried off to Cobbler Jack's, the squalid room above the boot and shoe shop where he normally ended each night by cheating young miners at brag and poker in a desperate effort to recoup some of the losses which he had suffered with local bookmakers during the day. Instead he went to the Manvers Arms, the nearest approximation to a respectable public house that Langwith Junction boasted.

He sat alone in the snug with a glass of brandy in front of him. Brack was a gambler, an occupation which he thought inconsistent with drinking, so he had never acquired a taste for beer or spirits. But he believed that, in the later evenings, gentlemen drank brandy. So he ordered a glass of Cognac and left it standing untouched on the table. He stared across the room with the expressionless patience of a poker player.

It was twenty minutes before Jack O'Hara arrived. A pace behind him was his brother Eamon – a little younger, a little shorter, just as handsome, but perceptibly less upright in stature and character. Eamon had arrived from Ireland just before Christmas (for what was planned as a brief holiday) and had shown no sign of wishing to return. Before they had sat down, Eamon hissed over Brack's brandy.

'He's having doubts. Bloody cold feet. That's what he's got. What are we going to do?'

Jack looked guilty but did not speak.

Instead of replying, Brack rose silently from his chair and walked across to the bar. He knew that the brothers drank pints of stout. He slowly carried the two pint glasses back to the table. As he intended, Eamon began to show the strain of waiting for a reply.

'Did you hear me?' Eamon asked, accusingly. 'He's got the jitters. And I can't do it on my own.'

'Well,' said Brack, 'my coal-shovelling days are over. And one of you can't do it. Not in two hours.' He turned to Jack O'Hara. 'How much did you take home last week?'

'Twenty-five and six, bottom line. I did three days.'

'And you're turning down five pounds for two hours' work? You're off your bloody head.'

'I didn't say I wouldn't.'

At that moment, a small man in a Crombie coat and bowler hat – the sort of man who was at home in the snug of the Manvers Arms – pushed open the glazed glass door and looked furtively around the room.

'We're over here,' Brack cried. 'And the lads are drinking pints of stout.'

The small man put a florin on the bar and then tiptoed towards Brack's table. Eamon whispered to Jack that the adventure was more important than the money and that they were in for the most exciting night of their lives.

'This,' Brack shouted, 'is Timothy Kennedy, the company's agent. Tim and I cut coal together once at Shirebrook. I lost m'job when there was a strike over using forks instead of shovels. Mr Kennedy didn't.'

The agent winced more because of Brack's loud identification than because of the reference to his strike-breaking past. Brack continued with his introduction.

'In the end he became a nark. If he heard a shovel scrape he'd be round the corner of the stall like a greyhound, would Mr Kennedy. Many a man was sacked for shovelling, thanks to Mr Kennedy.'

The owner's agent licked his lips nervously.

'What shifts are you lads working?'

'Jack's on two till ten,' Brack said. 'I'm not daft. But we've got a problem. He's got cold feet.'

Jack O'Hara was about to defend himself when Timothy Kennedy burst into justification of the plan to steal a waggon-load of coal from the colliery sidings and split the profit in equal proportions, to the O'Hara brothers for doing the work, Kennedy for planning the time and place and Brack for having the idea.

He explained, with eloquent integrity, that there was no question of asking the young man to black-leg. Quite the reverse. The trucks, which had been standing so long in the Langwith sidings, were now intended for Scotland and Northumberland where the miners were on strike against the owners' refusal to implement the Coal Mines Act and cut the working day to seven and a half hours. By stealing a waggon-load of Langwith coal, they would be cutting supplies to the tyrannical Scottish colliery companies and helping their brothers in the northern coalfields. Kennedy emphasized that Brack, being a good Labour man, would not have even contemplated action which might undermine the cause.

'Solidarity,' said Kennedy. 'That's the thing. Solidarity.'

'Bugger that,' said Brack. 'These lads couldn't care a damn about that sort of talk. They're Irish. They just need the money. Before the company started to move their waggons, there was no chance. Now there is.'

'Are you with us, Jack?' Eamon asked. 'Five pounds. Think of it.'

'They're Best Brights,' said the agent, hoping that the reluctant thief would be impressed by the quality of the coal.

'It's breaking the law.' Jack spoke for the first time.

'We won't get caught,' Brack reassured him. 'Mr Kennedy will see to that.'

'You won't, anyway.' Eamon did not smile. 'You'll be at home in bed.'

'I won't if this yellow bugger's too nesh to do it. Old as I am, I'll be there with you.'

The discovery that it was Best Brights that had stood in the sidings for over a year had rejuvenated Brack. Even after Kennedy had taken his extra cut, he would make the best part of fifteen pounds on the night. Without giving Jack a chance to change his mind, he stalked out of the snug to change into his working clothes.

Eamon O'Hara stayed to finish his drink and Jack, ashamed at his respectability, slunk off into the night. As he walked towards his bus and home he saw Father Hattersley wandering, like a man in a daze, towards his presbytery.

'Goodnight, Father.'

'I'm fine,' said Rex, without being asked how he was. 'But did you know that Mrs Brackenbury is unwell?'

Rex expected Jack to turn and dash up Langwith Road to Number 11. But, instead, he fell in step behind his priest.

When they arrived at the presbytery door, Jack O'Hara began to shuffle his feet like a man who had something important to say but was nervous about saying it.

'Father, I need to have a word. But it's a bit difficult.'

Rex had no doubt that Brack had already begun to tell his story.

'Best get it off your chest. Just say it any way you like.'

He knew that he sounded like a priest encouraging a parishioner to confess. He hoped that the familiar form of words would both give Jack confidence to get the unpleasant job over quickly and remind him that he had an obligation to show proper respect for the cloth.

'I know that Enid's a handful. But I'll tell her to behave. Will you start the instruction again? My mother would turn in her grave if we didn't have a proper wedding.'

IT TOOK longer to load up the car than Rex had anticipated. On Christmas Day he had bundled up a pile of clothes, buried his few precious possessions between the creased folds of his second best suit and crushed the essentials of his new life into his old compressed-cardboard suitcase. On the eve of his second departure he did not mind if he left the presbytery looking as if he was going for ever.

Simple prudence demanded that he took with him as much of his portable property as he could carry away. His crystal-set and a coffee table (made for him by the boys of St Philip Neri elementary school) were tied into the passenger seat. Behind him, books spilled down on to the damp car floor and saucepans rattled against basins underneath a shroud of patched sheets, torn pillowcases and threadbare towels. He thought of wedging his leatherette armchair into the open dicky-seat but, lacking confidence in his practical skills, decided that it was better to leave it in the presbytery than on the road between Shirebrook and Nottingham. The imitation Jacobean dining table and the four almost matching chairs he decided to leave as a bequest to his successor.

He could not decide what to do with the painted plaster Buddha which he kept, like a guilty secret, in his bedroom. Enid had bought it for him during what he believed had been the happiest day of his life. Even by the modest standards of his joyous summer, it had been nothing special. He had driven Enid to Leicester and they had spent the morning doing no more than walking around the town looking for a café in which they could afford to buy lunch. They had eaten quickly and badly and then wandered on, doing nothing which was exciting in the eyes of the world but feeling excited because they were in each other's company.

Beyond the prison and the de Montfort Hall they had come to a second-hand bicycle shop and Enid had told him, in her imperious way, that he must buy a bicycle. He had talked about the Raleigh Cycle Works in Nottingham and she had – to his immense embarrassment – sat astride a rusty old boneshaker and pedalled ten yards down the road. When the proprietor came out and offered to sell them a tandem for ten shillings, Enid had dared him to ride it with her. After the argument about who should sit on the front and who should sit out the back, which Enid won, they attempted to pedal off in unison. But suddenly, and at the same moment, they began to laugh – uncontrollably and for no sensible reason.

They had laughed all afternoon – at everything and at nothing. And when they had walked past a junk shop Enid had pointed to the pot-bellied Buddha in the window and begun to giggle. When Rex told her that it reminded him of Bishop Dunn, they had both been near to hysteria. Enid had searched for and found the secret ten shilling note which she kept in the lining of her handbag and insisted on buying the two and sixpenny idol. They called it 'The Bishop'!

As he packed his few possessions he could not decide whether he wanted to keep the Buddha for ever or never see it again. In the end, he decided that, whatever happened he would never put Enid out of his mind. So he wrapped it in a dirty shirt and wedged it under the passenger seat where he knew it would be safe.

By the time that he was ready to drive away, it was after midnight. Waking his father in the small hours of the morning would add more drama to a life which was already too dramatic. He lay fully dressed on the bare mattress of his stripped bed and shivered through six hours of fitful sleep.

He drove slowly into Nottingham, determined not to arrive at Alfreton Road before his father was out of bed. At the end of the passage which led to the back yard the gate was swinging on its creaking hinges. The noise of rust grinding against rust reminded him of childhood afternoons spent playing in the passage and made him feel simultaneously sad and at home. The back door was locked. A faint smell of bacon confirmed that, inside, the morning had already begun. He felt guilty that he was about to disturb such an agreeable start to his father's day.

'All right. I'm coming.'

His father's voice, just audible through the door, was not

intended to reassure his visitor. He was complaining about the interruption to his daily routine. After years of failure, Herbert Hattersley's life had come to rest in an ironmonger's shop. Rex could visualize his father, breathless and bent double, as he pulled back the bottom bolt.

Herbert Hattersley was a big man who had changed with age from raw-boned into stout. But his hair was as black and shiny – and as carefully parted just to the left of centre – as it had been during the years of glory when his baritone solos had been in demand at clubs and smoking concerts all over the city. There was a hint of white at the corners of his carefully trimmed moustache. But when he opened the door, that hated proof of his mortality was hidden by lather. The sleeves of his thick vest were pushed up almost to his elbows and his braces hung down in loops against his knees. The razor, which he held with surprising delicacy, had been sharpened so often that the cutting edge had been worn into a deep curve and most of the maker's mark had been ground away. Herbert was a time-served cutler who had come down in the world. He looked relieved by the discovery that the intruder was only his son.

'Syd saw the priest who came round on Boxing Day. He told a cock and bull story that a kid wouldn't have believed. I thought you'd gone off with that woman.'

'She wouldn't go off with me.'

Herbert, not knowing what to say, reached for the kettle and poured more hot water into the enamel bowl on the kitchen table.

'If you give me a sec to finish this . . .' He rubbed his brush furiously against his stick of shaving soap. '. . . I'll make you some breakfast. You must have left Langwith at the crack.'

Rex filled the kettle.

'I hoped that I might come here for a bit.'

'Of course you can. It's your home.'

It was a home in which Rex had never lived. He had left the house where he was born when he was sent to Ratcliffe at barely sixteen. And then, less than two years later, he had gone to Rome expecting never to live in a real house again. When he returned to

Nottingham for his mother's funeral, he had not known the way to the ironmonger's shop in Alfreton Road.

'I'll get some sort of a job, clerking or something, as soon as I can.'

Herbert nodded as if he had only half heard. A year before, there had been talk of his marrying a lady from Lenton. But although he had longed for the comfort and companionship he could not bring himself to make what he believed would be a break with his past. He was trying unsuccessfully to turn himself into the Jolly Miller of the song he used to sing. Herbert was essentially a gregarious man.

'Money's not too tight at the moment. You can spend a week or two looking, if you have to. Best get something that suits you. It would be a shame to waste all that education.'

'I'm all right for a bit. I'll sell the car. It's worth twenty pounds at least. I paid nearly forty for it.'

'Forty quid . . .' Herbert whistled softly.

'I had special reasons, Dad.'

Herbert reached his shirt from the hook on the back of the kitchen door.

'Kettle's boiling. Will you mash?'

Everything his father said and did was consciously welcoming, but it only made Rex feel more unwelcome.

'You don't mind, Dad? You don't mind me being in the back bedroom for a bit?'

'I was just thinking about your mother. Thinking how she'd feel. I just remembered what your aunt Clare said on the day that you were what's-its-named.'

'Ordained.'

Clare's words were embedded too deeply in his memory for him to have any doubt about what his father meant, but he was surprised that his father wanted to remember. For it was on that day that Clare had told him that his mother, up in her hard-working heaven, would at last feel that her life had been worth-while and that all the hardship and suffering had been endured for a purpose.

'It wasn't true. It wasn't the only good thing in her life. There was you. She doted on you.'

'And what did she get in return? Nothing. She didn't even get properly looked after when she was ill. I didn't mean to neglect her . . .' Herbert sat down. 'You know that. I didn't know how bad she was.'

It was true. After Clare Martin had turned him down, he had fallen gladly into her sister's comfortable embrace and, throughout his marriage, he had treated her with affectionate gratitude. He had failed to look after her not because he was brutal or callous, but because preoccupation with his appearance and his reputation had prevented him from noticing what she needed.

Huge tears filled his bloodshot eyes and overflowed down his purple-veined cheeks. He wiped his jaw with the back of his hand just in time to prevent the rivulets of remorse dripping from his pink jowls on to the front of his clean shirt.

Herbert Hattersley was an emotional man whose frequent tears were almost always genuine. In singing circles he was famous for weeping during the performance of his repertoire of sad songs. He cried to the end of 'I Hear You Calling Me' but, when he sang 'Trumpeter, What Are You Sounding Now?' the sob in his voice disappeared when Gabriel sounded reveille. He was incapable of remaining melancholy for more than a few minutes.

Reassured, Herbert returned to the practical business of the morning. He hung his ironmonger's apron round his neck and reached behind him for the strings which were to be tied across his formidable belly.

'I'm opening in twenty minutes. If you want a hand with your things, we'd better start straight away.'

'Give's a chance, Dad! Let me finish my tea. I've only just got here.' Rex could think of only one reason for urgency. 'I don't have to drag it all through the shop. There's nothing that can't be carried through the yard.'

His father was unusually determined.

'Let's get started straight away. Then you can shift the car. I'd rather have it gone by the time we open.'

It was then that Rex understood that his father was ashamed of what he had done. It was not, according to Herbert Hattersley's canon of respectability, decent to leave the Church – even a Church which he had always disliked and often feared.

Abandoning the cloth sounded almost as disreputable as being defrocked. Perhaps his son would be defrocked as punishment for breaking whatever vows he had either broken or was about to break. For years he had boasted about his son – his son at Ratcliffe College, his son in Rome and his son the priest. His drinking cronies – Methodists to a man and all equipped with medals from the Band of Hope – spoke of Rex with a mixture of awe and incredulity. Herbert did not want to explain that the steady progress towards a bishopric had been interrupted by an aberration which he had assumed to be a woman even before Syd had told him that part of the story. His son had come down in the world and he did not want to admit it. When he became part owner of the shop he had hoped that coming down in the world was behind him for ever. He was neither a brave nor a subtle man, but he had tried hard to hide his feeling of bitter disappointment. His attempt to counterfeit contentment failed.

JACK AND Enid did not celebrate New Year's Eve. Mrs Brackenbury was judged too ill to be left and shortly before midnight Enid announced that she was too tired even to welcome the new year into her own living room. Jack walked down to the Miners' Welfare in the hope of finding his brother sober enough to shake his hand. He kissed Enid a tender goodnight before he left. Because he was not allowed to spend the night at 11 Langwith Road he would start New Year's Day with the long walk back to his lodgings in Alfreton.

The excuse for always sending Jack home was at least plausible: 11 Langwith Road was not equipped to accommodate visitors. Three of the four bedrooms were permanently occupied by Brack, Agnes and Enid and the fourth, which was furnished with no more than a bed, was only used when a visit of mercy from Anne or Lottie was not completed before the last train left for Worksop. Downstairs there was only the kitchen, the living room, a dark, damp scullery and a ramshackle bathroom which Brack had agreed to add to the ground floor during a month of prosperity and a moment of goodwill. Casual callers had to sit cheek-by-jowl with the invalid in the wheelchair. Brief visits, and the diversions which they provided for Mrs Brackenbury, were encouraged and welcomed. But nobody stayed the night.

Yet, in the early hours of New Year's Day, Brack burst into the kitchen and, with no concern for his sleeping wife, shouted upstairs to his daughter.

'Get up and put some sheets on the spare bed!'

Enid, still half asleep, tried to calculate if refusal or acquiescence would, in the long run, cause least trouble. She had still not made up her mind when he shouted again.

'What the bloody hell are you doing? Eamon O'Hara's had an accident. For Christ's sake get a move on.'

The view from the landing confirmed what Brack had claimed. Eamon O'Hara leant unsteadily on the banisters. His face and hands were black with coal and dust and a trickle of blood was smeared across his brow. His pit clothes were no more grimy than pit clothes are expected to be, but the back of his shirt was torn open to expose his clean white shoulders and a huge purple bruise which ran across his spine.

'I'll give him a bit of a wash in the sink,' Brack said. 'Then I'll bring him up. Half a ton of coal fell on him.'

It was, Enid thought at the time, a peculiar way to describe a pit accident. But everything about the night was strange – not least her father's appearance. At the end of the night which she assumed he had spent in Cobbler Jack's, he was dressed in the overalls which he usually wore to service the lorry. His hair was matted and a handkerchief bound up his left hand.

'Stop gawping and get the bloody bed done.'

'If he's broken something shouldn't he go to Mansfield?'

'Mind your own business and get that bed ready. Then come down here. Mr Kennedy will be round in a minute.'

Enid was immensely comforted by the news that the colliery agent was on his way. The presence of a man of such professional standing would add much needed respectability to the night's events. She started to make tea. It was important to be downstairs when the agent and her father discussed Eamon's injury.

'You still don't think we need to send for a doctor?' Kennedy asked nervously.

'I'm still bloody sure that we can't risk it,' said Brack. 'That night watchman will have told the police by now. The soft sod stays here till he's better.'

'It was his own bloody fault,' said the agent, 'climbing up on to the top of all that coal.'

Brack could still barely believe what had happened. At first everything had gone exactly as he had planned. The coal truck had been shunted into a near deserted siding. The lorry had been driven, almost silently, alongside the track. The side of the waggon had been let down and something like half the coal had been shovelled out of the colliery company's possession. Then, without warning or reason, Eamon O'Hara had run, whooping, up the pyramid of coal that remained to be stolen. Inevitably, it had collapsed under him and he had disappeared under an avalanche of Best Brights.

'He's bloody lucky to be alive. He's cracked in the head.' The agent was sweating.

'The important thing now is to make sure that he's not done for all of us. That's why he's staying here, broken ribs or not. And I've got to get that coal to Sheffield before people start looking for it.'

He looked at Enid, who gave every impression of concentrating on tidying the table.

'Take that bottle of whisky into the yard and smash it. He's a real wild one, that. If he doesn't kill himself one way, he'll kill himself another.'

FATHER WILLIAM Ellis pushed open the shop door and paused with surprise when the bell above his head rang to announce his arrival. He was not used to the mundane events of ordinary life. Herbert Hattersley, counting the morning's takings in the till behind the counter, did not need to ask how he could be of help.

'You'll have come to see Father Hattersley.' In the presence of a priest who was not his son, he was showed the respect which he thought was due to the clergy in general. He lifted the flap in the counter. 'He's in the back. Come through.'

Bill Ellis did not accept the invitation. Instead he waited between a pile of zinc buckets and the display case which exhibited the products of Joseph Rodgers and Company 'King of Knife-makers and Knifemakers to Kings'.

'You'd better ask him if he wants to see me. He may not.'

'Of course, I do.' Rex was standing in the doorway which led from shop to kitchen.

Father Ellis squeezed past Herbert Hattersley who was half filling the gap in the counter, and followed Rex into the kitchen. He closed the door behind him as a sign that he would take charge of the conversation which was to follow. He was not sure that the composure, which Rex continued to radiate, was real or counterfeit. So he lowered himself into the most comfortable chair, and tried to lighten the atmosphere with what he believed to be small talk.

'Wish I had time to read the papers.' The bishop's secretary picked up the *Daily Mail* and pretended to study the football reports on the back page.

'I wish I hadn't. It's more than a week since I had any work to do. Dad won't let me help. Doesn't trust me to weigh out nails and thinks that delivering orders is beneath my dignity.'

Bill Ellis decided to risk serious conversation.

'One of the things I want to ask you about is money. Are you managing all right? The bishop wants to know. You probably left with twopence in your pocket.'

'I've got a bit and I'm going to sell that old car.'

'That won't last for ever. There's a fund at the cathedral. The bishop wanted to know —'

'The Distressed Priests' Fund?' To Bill Ellis's relief, Rex was laughing. 'Well that counts me out. I'm neither distressed nor a priest. I don't qualify.'

'If you need any help, you just have to let us know. You don't need to call round or even telephone. A postcard will do the trick.'

'No tricks needed. But many thanks. In the circs . . .'

'In the circs.' Bill Ellis wondered how many times he had

heard Rex Hattersley say that. It was one of the qualifying clauses that Rex used to diminish any opinion which seemed in the slightest degree superlative. He had first noticed them during their first summer together overlooking Lake Albano. The food at Palazzola, the summer retreat of the English College, was intolerable to everyone but Rex, who found it excellent, 'in the circs'. Whilst other seminarians had blossomed or wilted in the August heat, Rex had found it 'so-so'. He had evaluated the rival pleasures of rowing and swimming as 'fifty-fifty' and invariably distributed blame and praise on the principle of 'six of one and half a dozen of the other'.

The bishop's secretary believed that his judgement had been vindicated. Only a brainstorm could have made a man, whose past life was dedicated to moderation, suddenly behave with total disregard for the conventions that had shaped his life.

'The other thing is St Joseph's. We haven't told them much up to now. But next Sunday the Vicar General's going there to say mass. He'll have to tell them something. The question is what.'

'I thought,' said Rex, all moderation exhausted, 'that you'd tell them the truth. I don't see what else is to be done.'

'At the moment they think you're sick. That's what the bishop thought best and you agreed to keep things as quiet as possible.'

'But they've seen me drive away with my car stuffed with junk. I've actually told one chap that there's nothing wrong with me. Have I had a relapse?'

'It depends on what you're suffering from.'

'You tell me. You and the bishop invented it.'

'We told them what we suspected. I suppose we gave them to believe that you'd already seen a doctor. But we honestly believed – still believe – the diagnosis.'

There was only one possible interpretation of what Bill Ellis was saying, but Rex found it so difficult to believe that he was more incredulous than angry.

'You don't mean that you've told them I've gone off my head.'

'A nervous breakdown. It is not the same thing. We've told the parish, and we believe, that you did not behave rationally. That, my dear Rex, is a matter of fact. When a man suddenly turns against his whole past – denies all that he's ever believed in or stood for – something has gone wrong inside his head. You really ought to see a doctor. That's another thing I promised to talk to you about.'

Rex knew that it was a moment for righteous anger, for fury at the presumption of the bishop and the arrogance of the bishop's secretary. But all he could feel was a grudging admiration for the way in which the Church had acted to protect its reputation and preserve the façade of priestly virtue.

The diagnosis clearly owed more to theology than to medicine. If he was mad, the Church had not been defiled by a renegade priest. A madman was not to be blamed for his madness and a lunatic had no sins to confess. He had not deserted Rome, but simply taken leave of his senses. If he cut his throat in despair, he would still be buried in consecrated ground for, instead of being accused of the ultimate blasphemy, he would be certified insane. Rex wondered if he had once been taught the proper description of his invented condition – the equivalent, or was it the opposite, of 'baptism of desire'. The diagnosis of lunacy allowed Rome to claim that he would have remained a priest, had he been free to make a conscious decision. He became curious about the process by which such an elegant solution had been devised and developed.

'What brought my illness on, Bill?'

'I am so relieved that you accept what happened. That's the first step to recovery.' The bishop's secretary showed no sign of understanding the irony. 'You'll see a doctor? Of course, I'll arrange it.'

'What brought it on?'

'St Joseph's, Langwith Junction. That terrible presbytery and the constant worry about money. You should never have been sent there in the first place. Frick Wilson called it a "punishment station".'

At the mention of an old friend's name, Rex became momentarily animated.

'How is old Frick? I expected him to come and see me. He looked after me when I was really ill. Looked after me in Rome.'

'I'm surprised he hasn't written,' Bill Ellis said. 'It was Frick who suggested that you had a holiday. He thought you'd like to go back to Palazzola. But we told him that you'd prefer to go and see your brother in Valladolid. It goes without saying that we'll buy the ticket.'

'Distressed Priests' Fund?'

'We're trying to help, Rex.'

Rex knew that self-respect required him to respond with more than a gentle irony which Bill Ellis would not appreciate. He thought of how Enid – still all that was brave and strong as well as beautiful and desirable – would have expected him to drown the suggestions of insanity in an avalanche of outrage. George, smiling his superior, secret smile, would have told him to dismiss the whole idea as too ridiculous to warrant discussion. Only respect for the cloth would have prevented Syd from telling him to frog-march Bill Ellis through the shop and out into the road.

'Will you think it over?'

The conversation being completed to Bill Ellis's satisfaction, he opened the door which led into the shop and expressed the hope that Herbert Hattersley had not felt excluded from his own kitchen. Herbert insisted, with equal emphasis but less conviction, that he in no way felt offended.

'Nice of him to call,' said Herbert. 'Everything considered. A real gentleman too. Was he a big friend of yours in Rome?'

'Half and half,' said Rex, pulling on his priest's black gaberdine.

CHAPTER FOUR

EAMON O'HARA was quiet and obedient for almost a fortnight. The man from the St John's Ambulance brigade who was bribed to make a secret diagnosis felt reasonably confident that the ribs were cracked rather than broken, but there was hardly an inch on his body which had not been bruised by the avalanche of coal. So he lay in bed and felt sorry for himself whilst he waited for Enid to bring him food and Brack to ask anxious questions about when he would feel fit to leave.

Jack visited him for a few minutes each day and then descended into the living room to sit, patiently adoring, with Enid. After ten days, although his back was still too sore for him to contemplate returning to the pit, he was profoundly bored. He had money to spend for Brack had sold the stolen coal without difficulty. The pound notes under his pillow only added to his frustration. Enid, bringing his breakfast, provided an opportunity for amusement.

It began with innocent horseplay. Eamon pretended that the teapot handle was too hot for him to hold and that he was in imminent danger of scalding himself by dropping it on the bed. Then he complained with mock disgust about the amount of bacon in his sandwich. When he pulled the two pieces of bread apart to substantiate his claim of neglect, Enid leant over to examine the evidence. He pinched her bottom.

'How dare you?' she asked him with real passion. 'I'm engaged to be married to your own brother.'

'I don't believe it,' said Eamon. 'Leastways, I don't believe you want to be.'

Enid, afraid that he had heard rumours about Rex, told him that she had no idea what he was talking about. She was half way to the door when he began to explain.

'You've got some life in you. Our Jack's like a man of fifty. He was born elderly. You get precious little fun out of him. And not much else.' He leant out of bed and grasped her hand. 'If you've any sense at all, you'll take on his little brother instead. He'd know how to get on with you – good looker like you.'

She shook herself free and tossed her head in what she believed was a gesture of contempt.

'I meant no harm,' Eamon called after her. 'Just a bit of fun.'

He had no doubt that Enid had enjoyed the compliments. Thinking about how he could exploit her susceptibilities helped him pass the time during his recuperation.

IT WAS more then ten years since Rex had been to Ratcliffe and although he had always thought of it as timeless as Rome he was still surprised to find Pugin's grey gothic façade and stunted towers looking exactly the same as they did on the day when he had left. The great expanse of grass which separated the college from the Fosse Way still made the buildings look like two-dimensional scenery for a Victoria melodrama. As Rex walked up the long drive, the figure standing at the front door suddenly became recognizable as Syd.

Syd possessed all the confidence that comes from being seventeen and successful. He had followed Rex to Ratcliffe, but he had not followed in his footsteps. He was gregarious and good at games. Although not as clever as his brother, he was clever enough. He was short, square and as dark as his father but – brilliantine being forbidden in school – his hair, instead of being arranged in neat waves, was a halo of ragged curls above his round face.

Syd was, in all matters of consequence, triumphantly typical of the glorious world in which he lived. Rex had been plucked out of a Nottingham terraced house and dropped into a public school without preparation or warning and had expected boarding school to be like Greyfriars in the *Magnet* and St Jim's in *the Gem*. Syd had taken it for granted that he would follow his brothers to Ratcliffe. Life had turned out as he expected.

Syd shook his brother's hand and patted him on the shoulder in a gesture which was as near to an embrace as either of them would have thought respectable. Once Rex was disentangled he stepped, instinctively, towards the front door and the porter's office. Syd stopped him. It was only then that Rex noticed the bottle of lemonade and the buff envelope that Syd was carrying.

'Let's walk down to the boat shed. We can talk in peace down there.'

Rex had never seen his brother look so miserable. He could not believe that Syd, who had never lain claim to a calling, was distressed by the news from Langwith.

'It is all right you know, me being here. I wrote and asked the President the day I wrote to you. He said he'd like me to come and put your mind at rest. Explain things to you. Strangely enough, he seemed to think you might be worried about how I was getting on.'

'He never mentioned it to me. Father Atkinson came down from Derby on the day after I got your letter and told me not to worry. Said he knew you better than anybody and you'd pull through. Then Father Ellis. He talked as if you'd gone crazy, but I could tell he didn't believe it. But the President hasn't said a word.'

They sat on the steps of the boat house and looked at the river on which Rex, being too short-sighted for ball games, had rowed on Saturday and Wednesday afternoons. Not knowing quite what to say next, they skimmed flat stones along the surface of the water. Syd's bounced. Rex's sank.

'Father Atkinson was very nice. Told me not to be put off. I couldn't tell him that I'd never had a calling. He thinks I'm next in line.' Syd imitated, not Hugh Atkinson, but his image of priests in general. 'Sure, it's a glorious thing to have three brothers in the Church.'

'He's not Irish, you ass. He's a real English gentleman.'

'And there won't be three brothers in the Church, not Hattersley brothers, anyway,' Syd said. 'One at best. I suppose George will get ordained.'

'Do you mind?' Rex asked. 'Have I made life very difficult for you?'

'Course not.' He pushed the marble down the neck of the lemonade bottle. 'Do you want some?'

'You first.' After Syd had gulped, Rex took the bottle but did not drink. 'Honest, now. Are they making life difficult for you? People being unpleasant?'

'The brothers are fine. They never mention it. You'd think that they didn't know. It's the other men.'

'I've not gone off my head, whatever Bill Ellis says.'

'They don't say that. They make jokes about you being silly in a normal sort of way. You know. G. K. Chesterton walking in his garden with a wastepaper basket on his head, so the neighbours can't see him. That sort of silly.'

'Has it come to that? Do they laugh at Chesterton now?'

'They laugh at everything. We all do. Anything that's silly.'

Rex had never before considered the possibility that his behaviour was foolish. He had thought that it might be wicked and hoped that it was heroic. On cross-examination, he would have admitted incompetence and perhaps even lack of moral courage. In his more romantic moments he told himself that he had loved not wisely but too well and that the world was well lost. At times of despondency he wondered why fate had been so unkind and if he was being punished for trusting fate in the first place rather than relying on divine guidance. But silly was a new description of his behaviour and one which he found very difficult to bear.

'I'm sorry.' Rex always apologized when uncertain what to say.

'They'll get over it. So will I.'

It was clearly time for a change of subject. Rex reached down from the steps and picked up a handful of pebbles. He threw them into the river without attempting to make them skim across the water.

'What's in the envelope?'

'Have a look for yourself.'

Rex took out Syd's New Year report and read every mark and comment without looking up. Then, since they were alone, he hugged his brother.

'Why, that's marvellous from start to finish. Nothing worse than B.'

'Nothing worse than B Plus. Have you read what the President wrote?'

'Course I have.'

Syd leapt on his brother and held his free arm in a half-Nelson.

'Well, read it again. Read it out loud.'

'Only if you let go, you little brute.'

'Swear.'

'I swear, but let go. You don't know your own strength.'

'I don't trust you.'

'That's isn't very funny.'

'I didn't mean that, for God's sake.' The grip on Rex's wrist gradually relaxed. 'I'm sorry.'

'Shut up and listen. "Sydney's most successful term to date. This year he has not allowed his love for the games at which he excels to stand in the way of his academic work. Excellent examination results of which he will be rightly proud. I have recommended him for the Bishop's (Lower VIth) prize." Dad will be like a dog with two tails.'

'Will you take it home to him?'

'He can wait another couple of weeks. You want to show him this yourself.'

'I'm not going home this term. Perhaps not even for the holidays. I hoped you'd come down after on Easter Sunday.'

'Why aren't you going home? Aren't you getting on with Dad?'

'*She'll* be there.'

'Mrs Nicholls? I'd forgotten all about her.'

'Well, Dad hasn't.'

'I've not seen hide or hair of her whilst I've been there.'

'He's trying to break it off. But he won't manage it. She'll be back by Easter. I can't think why she wasn't there at Christmas.'

'It can't be that bad.'

'Worse. Anyway I've got it all arranged here. I'll stay with the Indians. Moving from classics to science, I could do with the extra swot. And the nets will be up by then.'

'Is that the real reason? Tell me. Are you staying here because of the chance to play cricket?'

'Don't be daft.'

'I'm too old to change, Syd. I'm daft for good.'

Syd put his arm round his brother's shoulder. 'You mustn't let it get you down.'

It was meant as comfort and encouragement but Rex, still worrying about the idea of being silly, was only made more depressed. Syd would take life by the scruff of the neck and force it to go in the direction which he chose. He was seventeen and fully qualified to offer comfort and advice to a brother more than ten years his senior.

'Anyway, I think you did the right thing. Mind you,' Syd grinned, 'you'd expect me to. I'm your little brother.'

Rex forgave Syd everything. The simple statement of the obvious had instantly revived all the old emotions.

'Don't you worry. I'll be all right. I only wish I'd known about you not wanting to go home and about Mrs Nicholls coming. Perhaps I'm standing in Dad's way.'

'He'll get things sorted out.'

'So shall I,' said Rex.

'What sort of things?'

After a moment's thought, he decided not to answer. He had no idea how he could sort anything out and he did not want to sound silly.

MONSIGNOR PAYNE, parish priest of St Paul's and Vicar General of the Diocese of Nottingham, struggled to put the idea of Rex Hattersley out of his mind. He feared that if his thoughts dwelt upon the behaviour of the late incumbent of St Joseph's, Langwith Junction, he might descend from the state of grace necessary for a priest who was about to say mass and administer the sacraments.

After the formal mass was over, he would have to return to the unfortunate subject of the unforgivable betrayal. But for the moment he would dwell neither on the awful sin which the young priest had committed nor his responsibility for what had happened. As recently as the First Sunday in Advent, he had told the bishop that he had never known a man who was more devoted to the Church.

The Church, which rarely provided spiritual guidance to more than a dozen parishioners at one time, was almost as full. And when the service was over, the whole congregation sat tense and expectant on the hard wooden pews. A sensation was expected. Monsignor Payne was determined to do all in his power to deny them their anticipated pleasure. It was for this reason that he had chosen to make his announcement not during his sermon but at the moment of anti-climax when the mass had ended. He had spent much of Saturday afternoon – time which should have been devoted to diocesan administration – on drafting as dull a form of words as the message would allow. All he had to do was read it without hesitation or emotion. As he walked to the sanctuary steps, he swallowed hard. 'You will be interested to know the latest news of Father Hattersley. I am pleased to tell you that he is much better. But it will be some time before he's back with you. After a brief stay with Bishop Dunn he has gone home to his family. We hope that he will soon go away for rest and change of scenery. That is why your letters will not, I fear, reach him. He knows that he has your good wishes and that you are praying for him. For the next few weeks Father Fisher, the curate at St Philip Neri, will be *locum tenens*.'

The blessing having been given at the end of mass, the Vicar General shuffled off towards the vestry door without further ceremony. Before he turned away from the congregation, he looked again at the thin young woman in the unsuitable hat who sat demurely by the side of the handsome Irish labourer with the high pink-touched cheekbones of a man from the west of Ireland. He had shouted the responses with an enthusiasm which Monsignor Payne so much admired that the Vicar General almost forgave him for being dressed in clothes which were clearly above his station and probably beyond his means. The woman was, he felt certain, the temptation for which Father Hattersley had fallen. She looked as pure and innocent as Monsignor Payne expected a candidate for admission to the Church to be. It was just as he had imagined. She had rebuffed the priest's advances and that had driven him over the edge into fantasy and madness. Monsignor Payne prided himself on understanding the ways of the world.

★

JACK O'HARA looked up from behind the *Mansfield Guardian* and smiled at the huge Valentine card on the mantelshelf. He was finding it increasingly difficult to keep up the pretence that nobody knew who had sent it.

'Has she nodded off?'

'Like a baby. There's been a big improvement this last six weeks. No pain at all today.'

'It seems unfair,' said Jack.

'She's my mother and it's my duty. Not that I do it for that reason. Cold thing, duty.'

'I didn't mean—'

'Not that I couldn't do without the extra work. You wouldn't believe what she's eaten.'

Enid gave a detailed catalogue of invalid dishes which she had prepared during the day. Each one was made with the best ingredients, loving care and to a standard of perfection which put other cooks to shame.

'I meant unfair to her. It doesn't seem fair that she's had arthritis all these years and now she's got ulcers. I suppose that it's sitting there all day and never getting her inside exercised.'

'It's worry. I've told you. It's worry about where the next penny's coming from.'

Jack put his hand on Enid's arm. She flinched away.

'Can you get the irons out of the scullery?'

Carefully, she began to spread an old blanket on the kitchen table. Jack pushed himself up from the armchair and gripped her wrist in his huge hand.

'I've told you. I've got the ironing to do.' She shook herself free.

'I just want to ask you something.'

'Well, ask me.' Enid opened the scullery door and lifted two flat irons from the floor. 'You don't have to touch me to ask me a question.' She balanced the irons against the fire bars and raked the glowing coals towards them. 'If you want something doing, do it yourself!'

Jack made no attempt to help. Instead he walked across to the sideboard and picked up the horseshoe which acted as a paper weight.

'What are you doing? That's Dad's.'

Jack knew all about the paperweight. It was a relic of Brack's last day as a racing farrier, a relic of his heroic past and a constant reminder that the glory days were over. Instead of putting it back, he took the manilla envelope from the top of the pile of letters and held it out for Enid's inspection.

'Look. I recognized the writing straight away.'

So did Enid. But although the handwriting unmistakably belonged to Rex, she did not even blink.

'Who's it from?'

'You know . . .' He paused for her to enjoy the puzzle and then gave her a clue. 'Think of those poetry books. I looked inside one when you were out with Mick. He's wrote "with love from the Three Musketeers".' He sounded triumphant. 'Just the same writing.'

She could pretend no longer. The books – Palgrave, Wordsworth, Browning and Tennyson – were the present that Rex and his brothers had given her at the end of the glorious summer of day trips to stately homes, tennis and rowing on the Trent.

'Whoever it's from, it's none of your business.'

'I think we ought to find out what it says.'

'It's Dad's letter. He'll look at it on Friday with the other bills.'

Jack put his arm round her shoulder and again she shook herself free.

'I've got to tell you about the Father, love. You'll have to know what happened after Christmas when the poor man went out of his mind. He came here and said things he shouldn't to your father. You know what Brack's like. He told me all about it, trying to cause trouble. I said to him, now the poor man's gone it's all better forgotten.'

Enid was not thinking about her father's malice. The sight of the letter with its instantly recognizable handwriting had disturbed the calm of cold despair. She was trying not to cry.

'Don't upset yourself. Nobody believed what Father Hattersley told your dad. The important thing is to make sure that there is no more room for gossip. We better see what he's written.'

She was trying to think what to do when Jack reached down

and moved the irons from the front of the fire. Then he picked up the kettle from the hearth and pushed it into the hot coals. The inch of water that was left from the last tea-making began to buzz and hum. Enid knew that, in a minute, it would start to boil and steam. She hated gambling. But she was a gambler's daughter and when she feared losing, she lengthened the odds and hoped her opponent would not dare to match her stake.

'So you believe him. You believed all the things that the priest said about me.'

'All I am trying to do is protect your good name.'

Steam had begun to spurt in irregular explosions from the kettle's spout. There was, Enid knew, only a moment before Jack began to steam the envelope open.

'Tell me this, Jack . . .'

Enid was not sure how the sentence would end, but she hoped that another angry question might hold his attention for a moment. She knew herself to be capable of brazening the letter out, of behaving as she would have behaved if Rex had been a lunatic and she had never loved him. But believing, as she did, that the letter concerned her, she would have felt defiled if Jack had read it. The letter came from Rex. It was hers and hers alone, whatever the name on the envelope. Her only object in life was to get Jack out of the house without opening the letter and then read it herself.

'If you don't trust me,' she said, 'how can I marry you?'

Jack paused and Enid pounced.

'Take the kettle off the fire before the bottom burns out.'

'Let it.'

'Don't be so stupid. Take it off. When I think of how much I scrimp and save to get a few coppers together—'

'I do trust you and I want to marry you more than anything. I want to set a date and stick to it this time.'

'I'll talk to Mam about it tonight.'

The promise to discuss marriage dates with her mother was the invariable response to pressure to make firm plans. When Jack was convinced that she was serious – as he would be after more moments of prevarication – she would give him a hug and a kiss and he would go home happy to prepare for the night shift. Then she could read Rex's letter.

'Do you mean it this time?'

'Of course I do.'

Jack moved towards her to claim his farewell embrace and Enid waited with open arms, ready to take the letter from him as she told him that trust and love went hand in hand.

The door burst open and Brack, home early from a disastrous night at Cobbler Jack's, smiled maliciously at his daughter.

'What you two up to then? Good job I got back in time.'

Jack, the pink patches on his cheekbones turned pinker than usual by shame, lost the few doubts he ever had about how Brack would react to Rex's ravings. Turning his back to the grate, he dropped the letter into the fire.

HAD IT not been her mother's birthday, Enid would have gone to Nottingham the following afternoon. But everything had to take second place to the celebration. Even Brack gave her an amethyst brooch before he drove off on one of his mysterious business expeditions. Anne and Lottie arrived in mid afternoon to prepare the anniversary supper. Katherine Fox came with them.

Katherine was the head seamstress at Brook House, having been recently promoted to replace an ingrate who, after ten years of care and kindness, had left to get married. She had been apprenticed to Lottie Harthill when she was sixteen and, from the first moment of her indenture, she had been treated as if she were an orphan: patronized, exploited, dominated, protected and indulged in turn. In fact, Miss Fox's parents lived in Newark. Lottie, on the other hand, had been an orphan when she had been bound apprentice to William Allen of Bridge Street, so she behaved as if all apprentices were similarly afflicted and treated them accordingly.

The head seamstress was dark and round with black curls, dark eyes and a smile that had survived at Brook House. She had a capacity for happiness which transcended the dull monotony of her daily life and a grace which enabled her to survive Worksop's eccentricities by laughing at them without anybody ever noticing. She was regarded as a suitable friend for Enid and sometimes, when her employers visited their sister at Langwith Junction, she was allowed to bring a Victoria fish-head tennis racquet and play a set at the club. Enid always beat her six games to love.

Seven places were set around the kitchen table. But at half past six, when the meal was due to begin, Jack O'Hara had still not arrived. There was much discussion about whether or not they should sit down without him and a good deal of implied criticism of his discourtesy. Then he appeared, massive, shamefaced and incapable of causing offence for long. Eamon was with him.

'I couldn't stop him, Mrs B. He got you a little present.'

Agnes asked Eamon if he was better, said how poorly he had looked when last she saw him, insisted that nobody should have wasted money on an old woman and wondered why everyone was so kind.

Jack had to interrupt to say that Eamon would not be stopping for supper. Nobody argued, but it was somehow agreed that, unless he had something better to do, he must eat with the family. Eamon was emphatic that nothing in the world could be better than celebrating Mrs Brackenbury's birthday. He pulled up a chair into the only gap in the close circle round the table and, as a result, sat between Enid and his brother, Jack. There was a long silence, then Uncle Ern announced that a man he knew had told him the real truth about the crash of the R101.

For a time, the conversation turned happily to air disasters: terrified passengers in the gondola beneath the blazing gas, twisted metal and worse spread across miles of countryside, grieving relatives. Ann was the first to say, 'They'd never get me up in one of those things.' Ernie, Agnes and Jack all repeated the sentiment and Jack repeated the actual words.

Then Katherine Fox announced, 'I'd love to go up in an aeroplane.'

'You can do it,' said Eamon O'Hara. 'Pilots from the war fly planes at fairgrounds. You can fly for two bob. I did it at Sligo.'

Katherine Fox giggled appreciatively and Jack wondered if he should expose the lie or let the fantasy ripple on.

'Would you like to go up in an aeroplane, Miss Brackenbury? I bet you would.' Eamon emphasized his confidence in Enid's daring by squeezing her knee under the table. 'You're the sort that doesn't mind taking a risk.'

Enid only suppressed a scream by emitting a gurgle. Everybody looked at her. She coughed. Jack offered to fetch a glass of water. She begged him not to leave the table. To his delight, he felt her legs pushing against his.

It was Eamon O'Hara who broke the spell of embarrassment. He had half turned in his chair and was looking straight into Enid's eyes.

'My brother tells me that you're interested in politics, Miss Brackenbury.'

'Yes.' Enid half turned away.

'Are you going with Mosley? Are you leaving Labour?'

She turned back towards him in astonishment. It was her habit to assume that nobody else knew anything about the subjects about which she knew a little.

'How do you know about Mosley?'

'For sure it's all in the papers. And I'm an Irishman, aren't I? All Irishmen are politicians. All of 'em except brother Jack, that is. But you've not answered my question. Are you leaving Labour and going to the New Party?'

Enid, whose interest in politics had declined since the high point of emotion during the glamour and passion of the General Strike, had only a vague idea of what the New Party was. She knew that Oswald Mosley had resigned from the Labour Government, and she had an uneasy suspicion that A. J. Cook, the miners' leader and her one-time hero, had supported him. But she had nothing of interest to say on the subject and she knew it.

'It's none of your business,' she told him, trying to soften her answer by sounding skittish.

'This government will be out in a month,' said Katherine Fox, leaning over and touching Eamon's hand in order to attract his attention. 'My dad voted Labour last time, but he says never again.'

There followed a conversation in which Eamon O'Hara made a series of political assertions about the partition of Ireland, the gold standard, unemployment and free trade to which Katherine Fox responded by saying 'I do so agree'. Throughout the dialogue, his hand rested on Enid's knee.

The conversation was brought to an end by Uncle Ern who,

having moved on from the R101 to the *Titanic*, was about to introduce the subject of the Tay Bridge disaster when he heard what was being discussed at the other end of the table.

'Now, now. No politics. No politics at the table.'

Enid seized the opportunity to stand up.

'Mick needs his walk,' she said. 'Come on, Jack.'

'Why don't all you young people go?' Agnes asked. 'You don't want to stay here all night with us.' Agnes believed in safety in numbers.

Enid had never felt so happy to take Jack's hand and, when they got into the road gladly agreed to turn one way whilst Eamon and Katherine turned the other.

'My little brother been getting at you, has he? On about politics. He's a great talker, is Eamon.'

'He knows a lot.'

'He's mad. Not stupid. But he means no harm.'

'That's what he said.'

Fortunately Jack could not think to ask why he said it.

'There's no way of stopping him showing off to the women. Especially if they're as pretty as you.' He kissed her.

'He's just a silly lad.'

'And you,' said Jack, 'are mine. I know that. I'd trust you with Clark Gable.'

'That's wonderful.' For a moment Enid felt real gratitude. 'I do love you.'

When they got back to the yard, Eamon and Katherine Fox were climbing out of the Ford van that Brack was trying to sell for thirty-five pounds. Enid bit her lip with alarm. Fortunately Eamon's behaviour did not put any unpleasant ideas into his brother's head.

HERBERT HATTERSLEY was impressed. The young lady who stood in his shop was what, in his gallant youth, he would have called 'a looker'. His visitor was not the sort of woman to whom he had been attracted in the years before he settled down with the round and religious wife who had made him reluctantly respectable. She was too thin for his half forgotten taste and, in the old days, he had always avoided 'airs and graces', an attribute which the young lady obviously possessed to excess. But that did not mean that he failed to appreciate a more remote sort of beauty when it walked into his ironmongery. He was not surprised that his son had lost his head as well as his heart. There was more to the lad than he had once thought.

'You're welcome to wait, but . . .'

'Thank you.' Enid pretended to inspect the special offer of dusty gas-mantles which stood on the corner of the counter. The slogan above the faded cardboard display case betrayed its summer origins. 'The Longest Day Has Passed Away. Prepare for the Longest Night.'

'I doubt if he'll see you. He's avoided everybody since the first priest came to see him after Christmas.'

'He'll see me.'

It was always the same. Women who looked like that fancied themselves. His resolve to avoid an afternoon in her company hardened.

'He didn't see the two priests. And they'd both been his friends in Rome. One called Wilson. Roy said he'd been in the war. Great big man. Big enough for the guards.'

'We call him Rex, now.'

'He was christened Frederick, after his grandfather. But his mother liked Roy.' It was exactly the sort of conversation which Herbert had intended to avoid. 'Another priest came, Hugh Atkinson. I knew him when he was only a lad. Used to come home from school with Roy. But he wouldn't see him. I had to come out here and pretend that he'd gone to Beeston.'

'Why Beeston?'

During the summer – when August had barely begun and the gas mantles in the special offer were clean and new – Rex and his two brothers had taken Enid to Beeston. They had hired a boat and Rex had rowed until the palms of his hands were too blistered to hold the oars. Enid wanted him to have gone back to Beeston to relive happier days.

'I suppose it was the first name that came into his head.'

Enid could barely believe that the portly ironmonger with the florid complexion and insensitive reactions was Rex's father. Nevertheless she spilled out the torrent of explanation and argument which she thought necessary to preserve her dignity and justify her determination.

'I got a letter from him. Otherwise, I wouldn't have come here, though I might have come because I was worried about him. Sooner or later. But I came straight away because I got the letter.'

'You'd better come through. He's got a bit of a job clerking at Morley's. He used to stamp stockings with their trademark before he went to Ratcliffe College. We've got connections at Morley's, so he didn't have to give any references.'

It was Herbert Hattersley's last attempt at conversation. After Enid had perched on the edge of the rocking chair, there was no further need for him to do more than nod and grunt agreement, astonishment and admiration as he thought necessary. There was a brief moment, after almost an hour passed, when he half hoped and half feared that his visitor was running out of breath and ideas. But then she switched the subject of her diatribe to dogs. Mick was the hero of every anecdote.

Each time that the bell on the shop door rang, Enid patted her hair into a more precise position and smoothed down her skirt. But when Rex walked in, he was wholly unprepared for the confrontation.

'Oh God!' He spoke in a whisper.

It was not the reaction which Herbert had expected. He had anticipated either the elation of hope restored or the bitterness of dreams destroyed. Grief took him totally by surprise.

Rex was always what his mother had called fair. At the end of a summer spent at Palazzola he retained the pallor of the English urban poor. But that afternoon, at the moment when he first saw Enid, his face turned so white that his father – whose mind always turned to irrelevant detail – wondered whether the blood had really drained down to his feet or if it had, itself, changed colour.

Enid, from whom words had cascaded without remission or respite for the previous hour, stood silent and still. In the few moments which it took Herbert to escape across the room and into the shop, he recognized, in her sudden incapacity, the anguish of genuine but hopeless love. It would, he suspected, not be hopeless for much longer. After a brief weep and a quick recrimination, she would regain her poise and confidence. Then Rex would become a willing prisoner. Herbert, who was a romantic, closed the door behind him in the belief that they would soon be in each other's arms, swearing that they would never part again.

'I'm sorry. I didn't expect to see you.'

Enid did not reply. Although the living room was warm and airless, she was shivering. Rex feared that she was about to cry.

'But I'm very glad that you came.'

'Are you?' Enid spoke at last. 'Are you really?'

She was right to doubt him. For a second, the sight of her sitting in the living room behind his father's shop had given him more pleasure than anything that he could remember. But the joy had quickly turned to anguish. Whatever she had come for, it was not to ask him to marry her. He could only think of one plausible reason for her visit. She was going to marry Jack O'Hara and she had decided – either to spare his feelings or to avoid later scandal – that she would tell him herself. Perhaps Jack had insisted upon it. Whatever the reasons, he was looking once again upon the promised land and, once again, he would have to turn away.

'I came,' she said, 'because of the letter.'

'What letter?'

'Your letter to my father.'

Enid was still shaking, but she shook with anger not anxiety. Rex had written to her father and the letter must have been about her. It was inconceivable that he had forgotten. For some reason he was trying to deceive her, trying to go back on whatever the letter had offered or promised.

'I didn't write to your father. It's all a—'

'What? I saw it for myself. Don't treat me like this. I saw it. I saw the letter.'

'It was a postal order, a postal order for two pounds, seventeen shillings.' He hoped that, by adding the extraneous detail, he would give his story the veracity which a bald statement lacked. 'I owed it him for the work he did on the car. It wouldn't start.'

The anticlimax was more than Enid could bear. She had travelled the slow twelve miles from Shirebrook to Nottingham in a
mood of high emotion which increased with every mile of bumpy
track. The truth was intolerable. She had made herself ridiculous.
Rex chose to say exactly what she wanted least to hear.

'I don't understand how you could have thought it was about
you.' He felt that, somehow, he was being blamed for a crime
which he had not committed and offered the reasonable man's
defence. Enid was not prepared to be diverted by reason.

'Are you trying to pretend that you didn't write?'

'I didn't. I wanted to but I didn't.'

'How can you tell such lies? How can you do this to me?'

Enid was barely conscious of what she said. She needed to be
locked to Rex by the expression of a passion which was too strong
to resist. She had come to Nottingham expecting the undeniable
emotion to be love. But, as love was out of the question, she chose
anger as the only alternative.

'Do you know what you've done to me? Do you?' She was
shaking again. 'I hate you.'

'You know that's not true.' Rex was too frightened to think of
anything else to say.

'It is. You've humiliated me. You've lied to me – lied and lied
and lied. You've deceived me and made me look ridiculous in front
of everybody. Why have you done it to me? Tell me why.'

Before Rex had the chance to reply, she answered her own
question.

'It's something to do with your Church. You hate women.
That's why you humiliated me. You think that it's dirty to get
married. You're disgusting. Do you hear me?'

'I don't hate you and you don't hate me. I've loved you from
that moment I saw you. Why do you think I'm here in my
brother's old jacket? I left the Church because I loved—'

'Don't blame me. I never asked you to. I told you not to do it.'

She slammed the living room door behind her, and Rex heard
the flap in the counter bang back into place as she ran past his
father. The bell on the shop door was still ringing when Rex
reached the pavement. He paused for a moment, worrying in case

running in pursuit down the road would only make her hate him more. As always, delay was damaging and doubt fatal to his determination.

Herbert sucked at the shaggy edge of his moustache, scratched his ear and shifted his weight from foot to foot.

'She's gone, then?'

Rex did not reply. His father tried a different tack.

'There's a do on at the Grove tomorrow.'

When he failed a second time to attract his son's attention, Herbert tried a question.

'Do you remember the old Grove?'

Rex remembered it very well. Although he had never been into the long tap room, he thought of the public house with nothing except affection. It stood at the end of the road in which he had been born. The Grove Hotel was part of the old days, the real home which he had left for Ratcliffe College and the real family in which he had lived before his adoption by the Church of Rome. But it was not the moment for silent nostalgia. Rex was vaguely aware that his father was trying to be kind by making some sort of suggestion about how he might pass the time.

'The landlord's leaving. He was only there for a couple of months when I was a regular, but he'd heard of me. Heard of the war and the singing. Would you like to come? It would take you out of yourself.'

'I'd like that, Dad.'

At that moment he would have agreed to anything that Herbert had suggested.

CHAPTER FIVE

FATHER AND son sat in the corner of the tap room so far away from the doors that they could barely make out the complicated pattern of rosebuds, oak leaves and bulrushes on its glass panels. Rex – ill at ease in the blue serge suit which he had bought to impress prospective employers – found it difficult to fit his knees between the elaborate wrought-iron legs of the marble-topped table. The half-pint glass in front of him was almost empty. Like most casual drinkers, he had swallowed almost all of his beer as soon as it was set before him. He was left with half an inch of dregs which he dare not even sip.

Herbert – magnificent in bold-striped worsted which had only just gone out of fashion – lolled on the red velvet banquette which ran the full length of the wall. His jacket was longer than any other jacket in the room and his waistcoat more extravagantly double-breasted. The silver chain which looped across the curve of his stomach had half-inch links. He smiled benignly as the barman approached.

'Compliments from Mr Chapman. Will you join him in something?'

Herbert looked at the two full pint glasses which stood on the table, waiting for him, then consulted the almost full glass which he held in his hand. After a moment's thought, he gave his grave answer.

'I'll just have a half, Percy. Half of bitter. A bottle of Blue Label for my lad here.' He leant forward and asked, in a confidential whisper, 'Which is he, Percy? I can't quite place him.'

'Since your time, Mr. H. Comes from somewhere the other side of the Boulevard.'

Mr Chapman, who had noticed that Herbert had asked for him to be identified, raised a whisky glass in salutation. Herbert nodded a gracious acknowledgement and the benefactor edged his way across the room.

'I'm much obliged,' said Herbert. 'So's my lad here.'

Rex half rose from his seat, struck his knee on one of the table's flying buttresses and sank back in horror as beer, from each of his father's full glasses, spilt on to the grey marble. Mr Chapman took no notice.

'Are you going to give us a song, Mr Hattersley?'

'It's a year or two since I sang in here.'

Rex feared that his father was both anxious to be persuaded and impatient to begin. Mr Chapman seemed genuinely afraid that Herbert believed himself to be past public performance.

'From what I've heard the voice is as good as ever it was.'

'And who, may I ask, told you that?' Herbert sounded wounded by what Rex had regarded as a compliment.

'A lady.'

'And who was this lady who talked to you about me and my singing, if I may make so bold as to enquire?'

'Mrs Chapman used to work with her at Players. They're both Navy Cut.'

In the silence that followed, Mr Chapman acknowledged Rex's existence. He held out a chubby hand. Rex grasped it without daring to rise for fear of another collision and consequent flood. The table was now almost covered with full glasses of Blue Label Bass, bitter and whisky.

'I don't think we've met,' Mr Chapman said.

'I've been abroad for seven years.'

'Abroad?' Mr Chapman was impressed. 'Where abouts?'

'Rome, most of the time.'

'What took you there?' Mr Chapman was more impressed still.

Rex was ready to answer. The lie had been practised in January and perfected in February. He had lied his way into the accounts office at I. and R. Morleys and he had lied to the men who shared with him the onerous duties of filing clerk.

'Cooks. Thomas Cook and Sons. I ended up at the office in the new Terminal Station.'

'It sounds a marvellous opportunity for a young man. You

wouldn't have got me back to Nottingham, not in a thousand years.'

Rex answered the unspoken question. 'I wasn't too well.' He tapped his chest.

Mr Chapman looked at Rex's white face and sunken cheeks and assumed tuberculosis. But he did not have time to wonder why a consumptive should move from the warmth of Italy to the damp chill of a Nottingham winter. Before Rex had finished his fit of simulated coughing, the glass doors swung open with a crash which attracted the attention of the whole tap room and two middle aged ladies, wearing identical fur fabric coats, appeared from the dark of Grove Road.

Herbert stood up, without touching the table or spilling a drop of beer. He remained regally upright, beaming with pride, as the two women pushed their way, arm in arm, down the length of the crowded tap room.

Rex knew that he had met one of them before. Her face was certainly familiar to him and, for a moment, he was afraid that she might be a parishioner who would expose his true identity to Mr and Mrs Chapman. Then he remembered. The lady had no doubts.

'This is Bert,' she told Mrs Chapman, kissing Herbert on both cheeks in the manner of a French general awarding a medal. 'And this is his son. This is the one I told you about.'

Rex had never heard his father called Bert. That was the name of his elder brother who had been killed with the Sherwood Foresters in the Battle of the Somme. In normal circumstances, that in itself would have made the hairs on the back of his neck stand up in embarrassment. But on that evening it was of no consequence. He was in the presence of Mrs Nicholls, the woman who had once almost accepted his father's proposal of marriage and, according to Syd, intended to move into the house behind the ironmonger's shop. She had sat next to his father during his ordination in St Barnabas's Cathedral. He knew all about Mrs Nicholls and Mrs Nicholls knew all about him.

There was much ordering of beer, whisky and sweet sherry for the ladies. Mrs Chapman asked if she was going to hear 'one of the

songs which she had been promised' and Herbert, who had
become suddenly benevolent, asked, 'Is there a pianist coming?'
Mr Chapman, who had become Henry, consulted the barman
who said that a pianist was expected at half past eight, and added,
to Herbert's delight, that 'it wouldn't be like old times without a
song from Mr H.'. Mrs Chapman, who had become Nellie, swore
that she would leave at that very moment if Herbert did not
promise to sing 'The Old Superb' before closing time. Mrs Nicholls, who had not demanded to be called by her Christian name,
squeezed Herbert's arm and said, 'He will. I know he will.' Then
she turned to Rex.

'Doesn't your dad look well? Even after all this time on his
own.' Her tone changed from triumphant to apologetic. 'I've been
away since Christmas with my daughter in Bristol.'

'I thought you worked at Players.' Rex could not think of
anything else to say.

'Yes, duck. I did till Christmas. Then I gave up. Alice lost her
baby and was real ill. I didn't like to leave him on his own, but I
had to.'

The hairs on the back of Rex's neck rose up again. Mrs Nicholls had him pinned in the corner with her face almost touching
his. There was a large mole embedded in the crease where her left
nostril joined her artificially pink cheek and he stared at it rather
than look her in the eye. The smell of her perfume was very
different from the odour of sanctity. But, because he had lived for
a month in the world where there were no smells at all, it reminded
him of the mass.

'He needs looking after. He's been on his own too long.'

'Don't be surprised if I'm round to do a bit of baking for the
pair of you. I know that you've been in a bit of trouble.' Her voice
sank to a conspiratorial whisper. 'But you don't have to worry
about me.'

Mrs Nicholls nodded and winked in the direction of the Chapmans who, believing the grimaces to be a salutation rather than
their identification as victims of a conspiracy, nodded and winked
back. Rex smiled weakly to confirm his confidence in Mrs
Nicholls' discretion. He had no doubt that, by the end of the

following day, embroidered accounts of her meeting with the renegade priest would be common currency amongst her old friends in the Players' factory.

Rex had always accepted that if he stayed in Nottingham he would become notorious, but he had hoped to postpone facing up to reality until his life had changed. He had no idea how the change would come or what the change would be, for he had no fixed points by which he could steer into the future. He had no wish to drift, but he lacked the self-confidence to navigate. Whenever he thought of a way in which he might go, he was afraid. Mrs Nicholls was living proof of the importance of moving out of Nottingham and starting a new life. In the shadow of St Barnabas's Cathedral he would always be ex-Father Hattersley. Yet the thought of living on his own, far away from the family into which he had been born and estranged from the Church which had adopted him, was unbearable.

The pianist, unnoticed behind the old upright piano, began a musical comedy melody. When he thumped out 'The Indian Love Call' Rex wanted to cry. He had been with Enid to see *Rose Marie* at the Lyceum Theatre in Sheffield. At the time, cramped in the upper circle and uncomfortable in George's old clothes, he had longed for the evening to end. A year later it seemed the most wonderful night of his life. It was when a stout lady in purple velvet emerged from the women's lavatory and began, without announcement or obvious preparation, to sing that Rex first considered the possibility that Mrs Nicholls – cloche hat no longer square on her head and fur-fabric coat open to allow knees and feet to be spread wide – might become part of the family which kept him in Nottingham. Mrs Nicholls mouthed the words and gazed at Herbert.

> When I'm calling you; ou, ou, ou; ou, ou, ou.
> Will you answer too; ou, ou, ou; ou, ou, ou?

Herbert, who was explaining to Henry Chapman the way in which high-quality scissors were ground in the good old days, did not immediately notice the grotesque mime which was being performed beyond his son on the red plush banquette. So Mrs

Nicholls sang her silent song with added emphasis, contorting her mouth in a manic determination to attract his attention.

> That means I offer my love to you, to be your own.
> If you refuse me I will be blue and waiting all alone.

Stepmother, thought Rex. Syd was right. This woman might become his stepmother. Mrs Nicholls turned back towards him and, once more pinning him against the flock wallpaper, confirmed his fears.

'You mustn't mind. He needs looking after. And he deserves it after working hard for your mam and you all this time. He needs a bit of comfort.'

Rex wanted to defend the memory of the years when his mother had looked after her family with a single-minded and suffocating devotion. Whilst he was still composing a defence which was both firm and courteous, Mrs Nicholls elaborated on her theme.

'He wants a bit of spoiling. And only a woman can do that. It's not natural him living on his own. He's still a young man.'

Before Rex could say that his father was more than sixty years old, the stout lady in purple velvet had moved on to 'Roses of Picardy'.

> She is watching by the poplars.
> Colinette with the sea-blue eyes.

Herbert abandoned his description of the way in which scissor bowls are forged and concentrated all his energy on being sad. Picardy, being in France, brought back memories of the war and the son who had died for King and Country. Tears began to form in his pale blue eyes and were ostentatiously wiped away with a gleaming white handkerchief which, its work being done, he carefully folded and returned to his breast pocket.

> And the years fly on for ever.
> Till the shadows veil their skies.

The handkerchief was flourished again as Herbert blew his nose with an explosion that reverberated around the tap room.

'Cheer yourself up with a song,' Mrs Nicholls suggested.

'I couldn't,' Herbert told her, with a look which meant that he could and would. Rex wondered which would cause him most shame, his father singing or his father in tears.

The pianist was told that a volunteer soloist was waiting to perform and, when he discovered that it was Herbert Hattersley, walked the length of the long bar to greet his old partner and escort him to the place of honour by the side of the keyboard. Herbert, who had miraculously recovered his composure, struck up a heroic pose and announced 'Drake's Drum'.

Herbert sang well, not only for a sixty-year-old man who had not sung in public for a year, but well by comparison with any singer who had sung in the Grove Hotel in living memory. Rex, who was incapable of understanding that he was the only person in the room who did not enjoy his father's performance, listened in a paroxysm of shame which drove from his mind all thought of the betrayal of his mother and his own exposure.

The calls of 'encore' had barely begun when Herbert began 'M'Old Shako'. He did not even wait for the applause to end before he moved on to 'Trumpeter, What Are You Sounding Now?' Even the young drinkers, who had never heard either the songs or the singer before, were impressed. The 'old days' of which their fathers had boasted and their grandfathers bragged were being re-created before their eyes. They remained entranced throughout 'The Holy City', 'The Absent Minded Beggar' and, the grand climax, 'The Old Superb'.

> Eastward Ho to Trinidad
> And Westward Ho to Spain
> With Ship Ahoy! A hundred times a day.

To Rex's relief, Mrs Nicholls and the Chapmans caught a bus on Castle Boulevard and left him to walk his father back to Alfreton Road. Despite his elation Herbert walked in silence, like a man who feared that if he spoke he would lose the joy of the evening. Even when they passed the Gunn and Moore's factory, he neglected to tell his usual tales about the day when he shook hands with William Gunn – the founder of the firm and the greatest batsman of his time – during a cricketers' smoking concert and benefit at the Black Boy Hotel. They were inside the ironmonger's shop before he spoke.

'There's no disloyalty in it. No disloyalty to your mother, I mean. It wouldn't be the same. Nothing like it. I wouldn't pretend it was. I want a bit of pampering, that's all. I don't like living on my own. It's not natural.'

'I know, Dad. Mrs Nicholls said just the same.'

MONSIGNOR PAYNE always prepared for meetings with his bishop by silently repeating the vows of obedience from start to finish. Monsignor Payne despised Bishop Dunn, whose ignorance and superficiality were only excused because he had been born into the English middle classes. For twenty years attempts to suppress the feelings of contempt had only succeeded in hiding them behind the appearance of resentful servitude. Father Ellis, the bishop's secretary, feared that the Vicar General was envious of Bishop Dunn's success and the bishop himself attributed the boorish behaviour to Irish origins and education at Maynooth, where scholarship was regarded as more important than good manners.

'My lord, I know that it is not easy for you to put yourself in the position of a parishioner. But, with all due respect, I ask you to try.' He leant forward in his chair and stared at the bishop on the other side of the fireplace. 'What are they thinking in Langwith Junction?'

The bishop tried.

'Priests are mortal. Priests fall ill. They know that even in Langwith Junction.'

'That is the other danger, my lord. What few unpleasant rumours there were have died down. But I don't know how long we can go on without saying something more definite. They keep writing to him asking how he is and saying that they are lighting candles!' The Vicar General was dangerously near to displaying outrage. 'They're praying for his recovery and he's not ill. And you and I, may we be forgiven, know it.'

'They are praying that he is restored to his former self.' The bishop spoke in the slow, consciously reassuring voice which he knew infuriated Monsignor Payne. 'So am I; praying for his restoration to his former state of mind. Are you still sending the letters on, Bill?'

'I delay them as long as I decently can.'

'Tell the Vicar General how he replies.'

'He has not replied to very many. But those that we've seen just say that he's grateful for their prayers.'

The bishop waited for the Vicar General to grasp the full implication of Rex's conduct and then decided that, since he could not rely on Monsignor Payne's powers of perception, he would have to explain its significance.

'He never says that he's left the Church. Never burns his bridges. He's not lost yet, Frank.'

Frank was the name by which the bishop called the Vicar General when he wanted to punish him. Monsignor Payne had been baptized Francis, but since his brother died in 1920, nobody had even dared to call him by his proper Christian name. Yet, from time to time, he had to endure Frank, an intentional insult and calculated reminder of the gulf in status which separates bishop and monsignor.

'This trouble is what comes from invention.' It was the only form of retaliation which came into the Vicar General's mind. 'Lies and invention are closely related. We're bearing false witness.' He mopped his red face with a red handkerchief.

'Goodness me, Frank. And I thought that I was acting on your advice. Wasn't the idea of a nervous breakdown yours? We believed you because we thought you knew what sort of man he was.'

For a moment Father Ellis believed that the Vicar General was about to have a heart attack. His face changed colour from puce to purple and the veins in his neck began to swell. He was the last priest in the diocese to wear the frock coat which, before the war, had been the standard uniform in presbyteries all over England and – despite the cheeks and brow which seemed to burn with fever – he pulled it round him like a man caught in a sudden draught. Bishop Dunn prepared himself to withstand the avalanche of indignation.

'I truly believed it at the time,' Monsignor Payne said. 'If I hadn't I would never have suggested such a thing.'

'Bill and I believe it still. He's not behaving normally now.'

The Vicar General turned to the bishop's secretary and asked him the offensive question which he would have liked to direct towards the bishop.

'How can you possibly know that?' Monsignor Payne's occasional attempts at irony were rarely a success. 'Have you had him followed? Is it paid informers we rely on now?'

'We've kept an eye on him, Frank.' The bishop, knowing he was the Vicar General's real target, retaliated. 'Not paid informers. Bill wouldn't stoop to that. That's very nasty. Reminds me of the civil war in your part of the world. Wasn't that great hero of yours, Michael Collins, sold by his friends?'

'No, he was not. He was ambushed.'

'It doesn't matter, Frank. It doesn't matter at all. Let me tell you what's going on. You have a right to know. We just asked his sister to keep an eye on him.'

'She lives in my parish.'

'One of them does, Vicar General.' Father Ellis felt that the time had come to give Monsignor Payne the message which he had been summoned to receive. 'I've talked to the one who worships at English Martyrs. She's called Muriel.'

'Muriel Moon,' the bishop interrupted. 'That's her real name.' He enjoyed the sound of the words so much that he repeated them. 'Muriel Moon.'

'With a name like that,' said the Vicar General, whose soul had no room for poetry,' 'it must have been a mixed marriage.'

'She married just after the war was over. Both sisters did.' Bishop Dunn seemed to be making excuses for their disloyalty. 'The other one married a soldier who lost a leg at Ypres. Used to be a postman. But they put him in the sorting office when he got back.'

Father Ellis waited for the bishop's digression to run its natural course and then continued his concise account.

'I've seen both the sister and the brother Leslie.'

'He's a baker now,' said Bishop Dunn. 'You'll remember him.'

'They all say that Father Hattersley is very unhappy.'

'Well,' the Vicar General looked impressed. 'That's a start in the right direction.'

'Unfortunately, he's not unhappy about the right things. His sister says that his father is going to marry again. Rex doesn't like the idea of it.'

Bishop Dunn stretched out his long legs so far across the length of the hearth that his huge shoes almost touched the Vicar General's neat boots. He closed his eyes and placed the tips of his fingers together like a man in prayer.

'But it's all helping. It's all making him think of the consequences of his actions. Let me explain, in simple language, what we're going to do, Frank. There's his aunt. Clare Martin. She's a parishioner of yours. You must know her very well.'

Monsignor Payne's reaction was predictably sympathetic.

'I certainly do. She was an actress for years. Then, when she settled down, she more or less lived with a man called Tom Cross.'

'Charity, Frank. Charity.'

'I accept your reproof, my lord.'

'It's not a reproof, Vicar General. I just want you to understand that I'm not prepared to slam the door on Rex. Not yet.'

Bill Ellis judged that the time had come for him to use his talent for reconciliation.

'His lordship wants to protect the parishioners' innocence. If we have to tell them that their priest has run off because of a woman they'd begin to wonder about the strength of their own faith. We're protecting the Church.'

'That's not it, Bill. The parish would get over it soon enough. I'm not going to push Rex out into the cold until I have to.'

The bishop corrected his secretary but the moral of the message was intended for the Vicar General.

'Whatever you say, my lord. I take my instructions from you. I need no reminding of that.'

'Frank. Frank. I didn't mean to cause you offence. Quite the opposite. The reason that I'm telling you all this is that you'd have a real grievance if you heard that I'd been wandering around your parish and you'd not been told about it.'

'Wandering about my parish, my lord.'

'I'm coming to see Clare Martin. Unless you want to see her for me.'

'I will do as you wish, my lord. But I cannot pretend that I would enjoy visiting Miss Martin. She chooses to walk half way across Nottingham rather than worship with me in St Paul's. She drops in to my church from time to time when she has some advice to pass on to the Cardinal Archbishop or His Holiness.'

The Vicar General was not alone in finding Clare Martin infuriatingly certain. She had been certain that she wanted to become an actress with Mr Wilson Barratt's touring company, certain that she wanted to remain single and independent from Tom Cross, certain that she was called back to Nottingham to look after her sister Augusta and her numerous nephews and nieces.

She had arrived back home too late to influence the lives of the two older boys. But on the day Rex was born she had decided that he was destined for the priesthood. And she had decided the same about his younger brothers. Whilst their mother had told them about the honour of entering the Church, Clare had described the glory. She had talked to Rex about the mysteries as if they were magic and had described the great feast days as if they were festivals of colour and light, rather than celebrations of redemption. She made the Church of Rome the romance in Rex's early life.

'I hope,' said Monsignor Payne, 'that you'll forgive me, my lord, if I speak my mind.'

Monsignor Payne waited for the bishop to reply and when he was met with an uncharacteristic silence, almost lost his nerve.

'I find it almost impossible to go on with this play acting. Father Hattersley has sinned grievously. We must all face up to the truth sooner or later. God bless us and save us. We ought to do it now.'

'That, Frank, is exactly what I intend. When I see Clare Martin the day after tomorrow, I shall not spare her the full consequences of Rex's conduct.' The bishop pushed hard on the arms of his chair and, when he was levered upright, took a letter from behind the clock on the mantelshelf. 'For example, I shall show her this letter from the President of Ratcliffe. The precedents probably require him to expel Sydney. We may not be able to prevent it for very long. Rex had better learn how many people he's hurting. His aunt is the person to tell him.'

'I DIDN'T mean you to trail up here. I would have gladly called on you in Clarence Street.'

'It was very gracious of you to suggest it, my lord. But it would have caused more trouble than it was worth. I would have been up at half past six black-leading the grate and cleaning the windows.'

Clare Martin sat at the bishop's dining table, calmly stirring her coffee. She had arrived twenty minutes before her appointed time and Bishop Dunn, who saw the trim figure through the window, had insisted that she be brought straight in for her audience. Some of his flock would have found the experience an ordeal. Clare Martin, he knew, would only pretend to be over-awed.

'I can remember visiting your sister in Grange Road, nearly fifteen years ago. I hope that didn't cause too much trouble.'

'Oh, but it did. That was the great day. We'd thought of him becoming a priest for years. After your visit, we believed it was possible. It started all the trouble that I've been summoned here to discuss.'

'Not summoned, Clare. I was coming to visit you, if you remember. But you wouldn't have it.'

'I've told you. Clarence Street would never have forgotten about it. I've got my reputation to consider. Anyway, Father Ellis's letter made me sound too old to crawl along Lenton Boulevard. I had to prove him wrong.' Encouraged by the bishop's indulgent smile, she elaborated on her theme. 'If you tell the Vicar General that I felt unworthy of your visit, he may absolve me of the sin of pride.'

'He'll only do that if you go to lunch at St Paul's. Do you know, he has the same pudding every day. It's a sort of blancmange made out of seaweed. It's Irish seaweed, of course. English seaweed doesn't taste the same.'

'Kelp,' said Clare. 'Kelp.'

'What?'

'Kelp. That's what it's called. You forget, my lord. I've trav-elled. It grows in America as well as Ireland.'

'The Vicar General will be devastated. Do you know that he puts peat on his fire.'

Bishop Dunn led the way into his study. He noticed, to his annoyance, that whilst he spilt coffee into his saucer, Clare Martin's hand was steady.

'How old would your sister be now, if the Lord had spared her?'

'The same as me. We were twins, even if we looked like chalk and cheese. She'd be sixty-one. No age at all when she died.'

'And Father Atkinson tells me that you devoted your life to looking after the boys.'

'Father Atkinson, a sweet man, but he gives credit where it's not due.'

'So you're not like a mother to Rex. He won't necessarily take your advice.'

'He wouldn't even see me when I went round to the shop. Pretended to be out. But I knew. His father's a terribly bad liar. Always was. I've known him a long time. Did you know that he came calling on me before he got to know Augusta. That's how he got to meet her.'

'Is that why you never married?'

'You know very well why I never married, my lord . . .'

She had never married because Tom Cross – with whom she had fallen desperately in love – was already married and the wife from whom he was estranged, stubbornly refused to die until the idea of marriage meant only hopes disappointed. Clare believed that, once upon a time, she had understood about love – love that transcended all other emotions and set her aside from men and women who had never suffered for love as she had suffered. She believed that no one else was capable of understanding how she had felt or of feeling as she had once felt.

'It was a scandal when I taught at your school and it remained a scandal until my Tom died. I suppose it's still a scandal since I live on what he left me. What do you want me to say to my poor old nephew?'

'Tell him we want him back. Tell him that it won't be easy but that it is possible. Tell him to come home. I hear that he isn't very happy living with his father.'

'His father wants to get married again. If he'd taken my advice he'd have done it years ago.'

'And Rex hates the thought of it?'

'He did when I talked to him about it. But that was a long time ago when his dad first had the idea. It's not just his mother's memory. Father Hattersley has become a bit of a snob. Mrs Nicholls is just what his dad needs. But she's a rough diamond. She used to work in a cigarette factory. Not quite Carmen, mind you.'

'Talk to him for me. It's the last chance.'

'He thinks that his last chance has gone. This minute, all he can think about is that young woman.'

'That will pass. I don't think that he'd ever forgive himself if he really left us.'

Bishop Dunn stood up and reached for two letters which were propped against the clock on his sideboard. First he handed his guest the agonized enquiry from the President of Ratcliffe College. It did not quite propose Syd's expulsion, as he had pretended to the Vicar General, but it did include a reference to a Victorian apostasy which had set the unhappy precedent. Then, with what he believed to be a tragic flourish, Bishop Dunn handed Clare Martin a confidential note from Hugh Fisher, curate of St Philip Neri in Mansfield, parish priest *pro tempore* of St Joseph's, Langwith Junction. Father Fisher had to take a decision which he felt unable to face without the benefit of the bishop's advice. The problem, once again, was Enid Brackenbury. She had asked for instruction in preparation for becoming a Catholic.

AT ONE o'clock on Saturday afternoon, the men and women who worked at I. and R. Morley Limited always ran across the factory yard in the first stage of a crazy competition to be first out of the gate and into a weekend of freedom from socks, stockings, gloves and ladies' underwear. The girls who fed the knitting machines for eight pence an hour jostled with the designers who copied the latest fashions from the London magazines and even the under-managers (who never took off their long brown dust coats until the factory siren had faded into a puff of steam) sprinted along at the back of the mob. By ten past one the street beyond the wrought-iron gate was empty and the fish and chip dinners, the football matches, the cinemas and the allotments were changing from anticipation into reality. But for the few minutes which followed one o'clock, the same patch of road was a swaying mass of liberated humanity which was far too preoccupied with hopes of the afternoon to notice the elderly lady who sheltered behind one of the gate posts and stared intently into the haze of faces that swarmed her.

On Thursdays a dozen or more women stood at the gate at half past twelve and waited for their husbands to come out with their new wage packets and hand over enough cash to buy food for the evening. But Thursday's women were poor and downtrodden. Saturday's elderly lady was elegant, well dressed and as confident as it was possible to be whilst trying to pick out a nephew from amongst a horde of strangers.

Even when the crowd had gone and the nephew had not been found, Clare Martin did not lose her poise. She straightened her hat, pulled the buckle of her belt back into its proper position and turned towards the bus stop. Then she saw Rex. The last to leave the factory, he walked slowly across the empty yard in a way which left no doubt that he was a man with time to kill and nowhere to go. She smiled at him but did not speak.

'What on earth are you doing here?'

'I came to see you, of course.'

'Why didn't you come to the shop?'

'Because you don't see people who come to call. You pretend to be out. And I needed to talk to you about things that can't be dis-cussed in the street. Where were you going, before you met me?'

'I was going to Meadow Lane.' He shrugged his shoulders hopelessly. 'Just hanging about till the kick-off at three o'clock.'

'Well, hang about with me.'

Rex showed no enthusiasm for tea and toasted teacake at the Kardomah. But he did not have the energy to challenge Clare Martin's determination.

'The booth,' Clare commanded the Kardomah manager. She pointed to the empty alcove.

'No service, at the moment. No service until two o'clock.'

Clare consulted the watch that hung down like a fob from the lapel of her jacket. It was half past one.

'We'll sit there until you're ready.'

Before the supervisor could object, Rex was shepherded into the pen. His aunt slid in after him.

'Bet you they serve us before two o'clock. I want you to get to the match on time. You look as if you need all the pleasure that you can lay your hands on.'

'Is it about Syd?' Rex asked, too anxious for any more small talk.

'Why all the concern for Syd, all of a sudden?'

'He doesn't like Mrs Nicholls being about all the time.'

'What would he do if he had to leave Ratcliffe now, next month or next week?'

'But he won't, as you know full well.' Rex was impatient with silly speculation.

The idea that Syd was in any sort of trouble was so preposterous that Rex never even considered it. Other parts of his world had crumbled and most of what was left might fall apart. But Syd was safe and secure for another two years.

'Rex, listen. They're going to expel him.'

'I don't believe it.' He meant 'I don't believe you', but he could not bring himself to call his aunt a liar.

'It's true. Bishop Dunn told me. That's why I was hanging about in the street outside Morley's.'

'What on earth has he done?'

'He hasn't done anything, not Syd. It's what you've done. They treat you like the plague. They think you'll infect him and all the school will catch it.'

Neither the priest's instincts nor the priest's training had been totally submerged under the few weeks of apostasy. So he noticed, although he was almost overcome with guilt and remorse, that

Clare was talking about the Church of Rome as if it was an alien force. He had never heard her speak like that before and he felt an irresistible compulsion to defend the institution which, until the previous year, had been his whole life.

'They wouldn't take it out on him. Dozens of priests leave. Baldwin left a month after he was ordained. But he's got a little brother at the English College. What's the difference with Syd?'

'There are ways of doing things, Rex. The others did it properly. They talked to other priests. They listened to the bishop's advice.'

'I went to the bishop and what did he tell me?'

'If he was worth his name and title he told you to go back and pull yourself together.'

'I went back and I didn't pull myself together.'

'Then you should have gone gracefully.'

Clare's definition of grace would have been unacceptable to most theologians. She believed in the splendour and majesty of the Church – the Church Beautiful as she called it in an artistic improvement on the Church Triumphant. By grace she meant the calm order of the mass and the serenity of Gregorian chant. The processes by which a young man became a priest were part of the Church's mystic elegance. Rex should have ended the romance with dignity.

'When the others lost their vocations, they went to retreats at Ushaw or Spinkhill or somewhere. They agonized. Then they decided it was right – right for the Church – to return to the world. You just ran away. You're still a priest.'

'Do I look like a priest?' He pulled at the lapels of George's old jacket.

'I'm telling you. You're still a priest. You're a priest who got infatuated with a woman and ran away. You're a priest living in sin.'

'Don't be . . . I never . . .'

'I don't mean that, for heaven's sake. You're still a priest but you don't say mass. You haven't renounced your vows, you've just broken them. You're still breaking them.' Her voice rose. 'Do you believe in hell, Rex? Hell and damnation?'

His response suggested that hell had lost its terror. He put his fingers to his lips and pointed to the tables outside the booth.

'They can't hear a word. I was having secret meetings in here with Tom Cross before you were born. And I'm not going to be put off. You're breaking your vows every minute that you live and breathe. If you wanted to leave, there was a proper way of doing it.'

'And that's what you want, is it, an orderly retreat instead of a rout?'

There was a pause and Rex was about to ask if there was still time to save Syd when Clare laid her hand on his.

'That's not what I want. I want you to go back.'

'They wouldn't have me.'

It was not the reply which Clare Martin had expected, for it was very nearly the reply for which she would have prayed, had many years not passed since she last expected her prayers to be answered. She had feared that he would swear that he had finished with the Church for ever. But, instead, he had gloomily predicted that the Church had finished with him.

'They'd have you back tomorrow. You'd have to pay a price. I suppose that they'd send you away for a bit.'

'Rome? Do you think that they'd send me back to Rome?'

The campaign was progressing far more successfully than she had anticipated. Rex was on the point of surrender.

'You're still a priest at heart, aren't you? You still have your faith.'

'I don't know.'

'Well, I do and I'll tell you the answer. You're a priest from head to toe. Your mother and I saw it in you when you were a little boy. But priests are human. You made a terrible mistake—'

'How can you say that?' Rex no longer worried about being overheard. 'I fell in love. That's not a mistake. It's a glorious thing to happen. You ought to know that. You trailed around after Tom Cross all those years, without marrying him.'

'That was my decision. He asked me often enough. At first, I wasn't sure that I wanted to. Then it was too late. Now it's too late for you. You're not a daft lad who's going to fall in love again next week with the first girl who smiles at him. Men have become priests because the woman they loved married somebody else. That's not very different from what's happened to you.'

It was five past two and the waitress had not appeared even to clear the debris left over from the previous meal. Clare turned, smiled at the cashier behind the glass screen and tapped her watch. The cashier took no notice. Charm having failed, she scowled at the manager who scowled back in Clare's general direction without actually looking at her. Clare began to rattle a dirty spoon in a cup which was still half full of cold tea.

A waitress with a pad and pencil had appeared at the entrance to the booth. She picked up the used crockery with such ill-tempered vigour that a shower of cake crumbs fell on to Clare's shoulder. Clare did not turn round, to relax her grip on Rex.

'A pot of tea for two. Two toasted teacakes and two Jap fancies.' After the waitress had gone, she asked Rex, 'Is that all right?'

'I don't mind what we eat. I just don't want to talk about it any more.

'You're going to whether you like it or not. Perhaps you won't talk, but you will listen. After your mother got ill, all she thought about was you becoming a priest. It kept her alive for that year. The last thing that she said to me before she died . . .'

'I know what she said.'

'Well, live up to it. You've nothing to lose, my lad. You're not exactly happy, are you? Be sensible. Go back.'

The waitress reappeared, bearing a tray which she dropped with a bang and a rattle on to the table. Clare wrapped a paper serviette round the hot handle of the gleaming EPNS teapot and began to pour.

'Another thing you ought to know. That young lady's become a Catholic. The bishop told me. She wants a proper wedding. She's going to get married in June.'

CHAPTER SIX

ENID GAVE up hope of marrying Rex and, gradually and reluctantly, began the preparations for her marriage to Jack. The more she prepared, the more reluctant she became, but she could not bring herself to break off the engagement. In the storms of her emotional life, Jack was the only port available and she was not ready to face the rough seas alone. She needed someone to talk to. She chose a man with whom she had discussed everything under the sun except love.

Once she had decided what to do, she could not wait to reach Shirebrook market place. Mick wanted to loiter at every lamp-post and urinate where other dogs had urinated before him. Every time he stopped, Enid pulled on the leash, jerked his head forward and led him on towards the little huddle of stalls. He was not allowed to linger for a satisfying sniff until they reached a barrow from which second-hand books were offered for sale. Behind it, the proprietor – six feet four, twenty stones and totally bald – was reading a tract with the aid of a magnifying glass.

'Look what the wind's blown in.' The bookseller spoke in the accents of a repertory company aristocrat.

'What's got into you?' Enid asked.

'A couple of years ago, you'd have known without asking. Haven't you read the *Herald*? Snowden wants a "spirit of national unity". He wants a compromise – Labour government and Tory policies. Went on about the national interest. But you're not bothered about politics these days. You're a tennis player now.'

'Don't be stupid, Percy. Anyway, I've not come to see you. Where's Owen?'

'He's poorly. He's not coming today. Go and see him if you feel inclined. We're still in Austin Street. Me and Owen haven't got on and moved out.'

The Ford brothers had come down in the world. When Enid

first knew them, Percy rented a book and foreign stamp stall in Chesterfield market hall and Owen was a full-time official of the Nottingham Miners' Association. In those days, the house in Austin Street was rented by Arthur Ellis, who lay under the front room window in a long, low, wicker bath chair and thought of nothing except the compensation which was owed him for his broken back. Owen Ford and Ernest Brackenbury, who then lived four houses away, called in from time to time and read to him; Brack from the *Sporting Life* and Ford from Fabian tracts and Independent Labour Party pamphlets. Enid (then 'little Enid') joined in, reading in her piping voice and absorbing the politics of the coalfield. After the Brackenburys moved on and away, Arthur Ellis died and Owen Ford married his widow. When Mrs Ford came to the door, Enid was staring through the front window at the place where Arthur used to lie.

'Hello, stranger. He will be pleased to see you. He had a bad night. Cough, cough, cough. But he'll want a talk with you.'

Owen Ford looked up, put a handkerchief to his mouth, coughed and spoke from behind his hand.

'You'll forgive me not getting up.' He seemed less pleased to have visitors than his wife had suggested. 'I know why you've come. Jim Wright came round from the *Guardian* office ten minutes after your young man gave him the notice. Good news travels fast.'

'Aren't you at least pleased that I've made up my mind?' Owen Ford had been the intellectual in Enid's young life. She desperately wanted his approval.

'I'm delighted. I'm always delighted when somebody takes no notice of my advice.'

'Come on, Owen. It's nothing to be bitter about.'

'Don't flatter yourself, young lady. I'm too sick to work. All three of us is living off what we can sell off that barrow. If I'm bitter about ow't it's not about you marrying a paddy.'

'It's the best thing, Owen. All the rest was just talk. I never had a chance of doing the things I dreamed about.'

'I don't understand why it had to be Ruskin College or nothing. You could still have made something of yourself. You didn't have to choose between a baby a year and queening it with a striped blazer on.'

Sally Ford bustled in, carrying the pot of tea which was the real sign of a warm welcome. She was a big raw-boned woman, not yet forty, and although her first husband had died and her second was dying, she remained insufferably cheerful. To her, love was indistinguishable from looking after. Owen bitterly attributed her composure to a Catholicism which he envied but could not emulate.

'Can I take the dog into the kitchen? They're not very good for Owen's chest.'

The leash was reluctantly handed over and the dog heaved in the direction of the kitchen door. It growled, choked on the collar and splayed out its feet in an attempt to anchor itself to the floor. But it was dragged, half walking and half sliding, into the kitchen. Enid, without looking in its direction, addressed Owen on the subject of the dog's fidelity. She wanted Owen to feel sorry for her and hoped that his sympathy would be a first step towards the renewed assertion that she should not throw her life away.

'Mick's the one I have to rely on. I can't afford anything or anyone coming between me and Mick.'

'I hope that you've explained all that to Mr Jack O'Hara.'

'Jack understands me.'

'Well, he doesn't understand much else, by all accounts. Nobody in the Welfare has ever heard him talk about anything except you and cards.'

'That's not true. He's a wonderful tennis player.'

'They don't talk much about tennis at the Welfare. But they do talk about miners who dress up as if they've just come out of Burton's window.'

'I'm going,' said Enid. 'I just came to see how you are and you're nasty.'

'You didn't come to see how I was. You haven't been near the place for six months. You came to hear me say that you're throwing yourself away by marrying a bog Irishman. Well, I've said it. You can feel flattered and go back home.'

Owen struggled up from his chair.

'This little row has fair set me up. I'll walk back with you to the stall. Percy and me will give you a book for a wedding present. It's likely to be the last one you read.'

As Sally Ford first protested and then carefully buttoned up his coat against the spring wind, Owen described his vision of Enid's bookless future.

'If I live long enough, I shall come to visit you in Colliery Row. You'll be standing on the pavement, talking to the woman next door. I'll have to look twice before I can tell which is which. You'll both be wrapped in one of them flowered overalls and you'll have big aprons, with pockets on the front, on top. You'll scrub the doorstep every morning and whiten the edge to keep out evil spirits.'

'Don't, Owen.' Enid was pretending to laugh.

'You'll be late with Jack's dinner and late with the kids' tea. You'll be behind with the sewing and the washing will still be on the clothes line. The woman next door will be fed up of listening to you, but you'll not stop for half an hour because it's the nearest you get to intellectual activity. Six to four, you'll be telling her how clever you are. And one thing's certain. You won't be doing any reading.'

'It won't be like that.' Enid was suddenly serious. 'Jack'll look after me.'

They finished the journey in silence. Owen coughed because they walked too quickly for his failing lungs and Mick coughed because they walked too slowly for his liking and as he strained on his collar the leather cut into his windpipe. As soon as they reached the barrow Percy Ford pulled out an old chair from between its wheels and his brother sank down on to it.

'Pick her out a book,' Owen gasped.

There was much picking up and putting down, rummaging amongst slim volumes and careful examination of imitation gold leaf on fake leather. To Enid's relief, the final selection was not a collection of Fabian tracts, but an anthology of poems by Ella Wheeler Wilcox. Owen had denounced the *Poems of Cheer* when she had told him that her mother had enjoyed them. Pretending to herself that he had chosen the book as a tribute rather than rebuke, she walked resolutely towards home.

★

OWEN FORD having failed her, Enid decided that the advice that she so desperately needed could only come from a woman. Her mother, she knew, would respond to her cries for help by veering wildly between announcements that love conquers all and demands for reassurance that her own future was secure. Neither Anne nor Lottie would understand what she was talking about. The only other possibility was Katherine Fox, the nearest thing to a friend that inclination and opportunity had allowed.

After some weeks of desperate doubt, she suggested to Jack that they invite Eamon and Katherine to a tennis club social. Jack agreed with the warning that he could take no responsibility for how his brother behaved.

Eamon behaved impeccably, dancing each dance with Katherine and showing a real reluctance to be parted from her even during the gentlemen's 'Excuse Me'. Jack had to be persuaded to take him into the bar whilst Enid shepherded Katherine into the ladies' lavatory for their talk.

They stood side-by-side, in front of the single wash-hand bowl, staring at each other in the mirror and listening to the sound of a woman being sick in one of the cubicles behind them. Enid came straight to the point.

'I don't know what to do.'

'You don't want to marry him, do you?'

'Can you tell?'

'He can't,' said Katherine. 'But I can. So can Eamon. Eamon's tried to tell him but he won't listen.'

'I want to break it off. But I daren't. It would break his heart.'

'Better to break his heart now than later.'

Enid wanted to say that her heart was broken already. But Rex had to be kept a desperate secret. There was a pause whilst a middle-aged miner's wife pushed past them into the second cubicle. Fortunately, when she came out, she did not want to wash her hands.

'Are you going to marry Eamon?'

'I shall if he asks me. But he's not the marrying sort. He says that men where he comes from don't settle down until they're fifty.'

'He'll be a handful.' Enid, who resented being alone in her unhappiness, grasped the opportunity to make Katherine companion in misfortune.

'I know that. But he makes me happy most of the time. And that's what matters.'

'Happiness isn't everything.' The years spent under the influence of Lottie and Anne had taken their toll.

'Oh yes, it is. And if you've got any sense you'll not give up hope of finding it. I know all about you and that priest. But you're a young woman. Life's not over. You'll never be satisfied with Jack. Break it off tonight. It isn't fair to him and it isn't fair to you. Do it as soon—'

Before she had finished, the door burst open. The interval had begun and the tiny lavatory was suddenly filled with jostling, impatient women.

For the rest of the evening, Enid danced with Jack in silence. As always he concentrated on helping her follow him through the complicated steps in which he took such pride and hardly noticed that she seemed preoccupied. To his delight she did not agitate about going home early, but gladly stayed until the lights were turned down for the last waltz. They walked back to Langwith Road more slowly than usual.

She made her first attempt as soon as they got out into the road.

'Jack, we need to have a serious talk.'

'What about?' Instead of sounding nervous – as Enid had hoped – he seemed barely interested. The shock would be as great as she feared.

'About the wedding.' She knew that she should have told him there and then that she no longer wanted to marry him. But she played for time. 'We've hardly talked about it at all.'

He put an affectionate hand round her shoulder.

'It's all right, love. If you don't want to join the Church . . .'

'It's not that, Jack.'

'What then?'

'Tomorrow night. Come round tomorrow night and we'll have a real talk.'

Enid spent a sleepless night planning how she would break the news to Jack. She knew that the best, and possibly the only, way to end the agony was the simple and forthright statement that she no longer loved him. But she wanted to spare his feelings and she needed her own moment of drama. She constructed, in her mind, a moving but meaningless speech about duty and destiny. She spent most of the day of decision rehearsing. Once, her mother complained that she had developed the habit of talking to herself.

Jack arrived punctually at seven o'clock, the earliest time that he was welcome, but he showed no signs of expecting to be engulfed in tragedy. Eamon had seen *City Lights* at the Regent Cinema in Chesterfield. Jack wanted to tell Enid all that his brother had told him about the film.

It was nine o'clock before Enid forced herself to say, 'What about our talk, Jack? We said we'd have a talk.'

'All right,' he replied, smiling, but not moving from his seat next to Mrs Brackenbury.

'Come into the kitchen.'

Enid hoped that the impatience that she felt with Jack's insensitivity would harden her heart.

'Jack, we've got problems and we better face them.'

'Enid!' It was her mother from the living room.

As always, Enid responded at once. Agnes's book had fallen from her grasp. She returned to the kitchen with most of her courage intact.

'Did you hear what I said, Jack?'

'Yes.'

It was not Jack's intention to make Enid's task difficult. He simply had no idea what to say.

'There are real problems.'

'All young couples have problems. As soon as I get back to five full shifts—'

'Enid, quick!'

Before Agnes's cry for help was answered, Enid walked across to Jack and, holding her hands in his, put her face close to his.

'It's not just money, Jack. We've got to have a serious talk.'

For the first time, Jack seemed to take her seriously.

'It's half past nine, love. I'll miss my shift. It'll wait until tomorrow.'

'Tomorrow then. Tomorrow afternoon. We'll go for a walk so we can be on our own.'

She felt relieved that the burden was to be lifted from her conscience. But she also felt afraid. She was about to become what her mother called a confirmed spinster – Anne without a Lottie to look after her.

A T FIRST, Enid believed that she had been woken by a cry from her mother's bedroom. She boasted that she slept so lightly that she could hear the faintest cry for help from across the landing and as she gradually came back to life, she believed the myth that she had invented and cried out, 'I'm coming, Mam.' She was out of bed and half way to the door before she realized that the noise which had disturbed her was the colliery siren. There had been an accident at the pit.

There had not been a disaster in the Derbyshire coalfield for more than fifty years and all that she knew of floods and explosions she had learned from folklore, Brack and a short story by D. H. Lawrence which Percy Ford had persuaded her to read. But she knew that when the siren sounded, the friends and families of the men who were working underground all rushed to the pit. She pulled on the clothes which were scattered about the bedroom and, when she was ready to leave, held the alarm clock in the pool of watery moonlight that shone through the gap in the curtains. It was still not midnight. Barely two hours had passed since Jack had left for the night shift. She thought of him dead or, worse still, slowly dying under a pile of rock and coal.

Her first emotion was a mixture of affection and compassion. The second was guilt mixed with relief that she had not, after all, ended their engagement. If her nerve had not failed, he might be lying trapped and maimed with nothing to think about except the bitter memory of rejection. Then she felt lonely. Living without Jack, because she no longer loved him, would be easy enough – not least because he would always be within easy reach. Living without Jack because he was dead frightened her. If Jack had been killed, she would have no choice. She would be alone.

Agnes was sleeping so soundly that Enid was tempted not to wake her. But she recalled stories of grieving women standing all night in the shadow of the winding gear and gently shook her mother's shoulder.

'What's happened? Is it your dad?'

'It's the pit, Mam. Can't you hear the hooter? I'm going down to see if Jack's all right.'

'Be careful,' Agnes said, as if Enid was going underground with the rescue team.

'I'll leave a note for Dad in case he's back first.'

'What do you think did it, love?'

Enid had no doubts.

'It's the pit props, Mam.'

She had a vague memory of her father telling Jack that, in the old days, the Federation would never have allowed wooden pit props to be replaced by steel. Wooden pit props creaked when the earth moved and gave early warning that the roof might collapse. Jack had told him not to be old fashioned and went on to say that the pit props dispute had been no more than a pay demand, the refusal to modernize without an increase in the hourly rate. Neither of the men had listened to the other. Brack spoke of miners in the romantic language which was common amongst men who had escaped from the mines. Jack was less concerned with working-class solidarity than with a secure job. Enid, who had only half listened to the argument, had instinctively sided with her father and stored a fraction of the information in her memory.

'It's the pit props, Mam.'

Enid repeated her explanation with absolute certainty as she hurried downstairs and out into the night air.

She had taken it for granted that she would be one of the first to arrive in the colliery yard. But a crowd of more than a hundred had already gathered: miners from other shifts, wives and sweethearts, volunteers of every sort who hoped that they could help with prayer, first aid or tea and sandwiches, men who remembered Parkhouse in 1852 and the forty-five men who died, sightseers who did not want to miss the sensation. They stood in little bewildered groups, throwing long shadows across the pit yards and asked each other questions which nobody could answer. She had expected a frenzy of desperate activity. But, except for the shouts of the men who were pulling the arc lights into place, everything was still and silent. Half of the rescue team had already gone down. The rest were waiting, tense and nervous, at the pit head.

Enid pushed her way towards a man in a Homburg hat, confident that someone respectably dressed would know what had happened.

'Gas,' he said. 'Hundred yards from t'bottom of shaft. We don't know how big t'fire is. Deputy's just gone down.'

The great wheel above the pit head began to turn and the crowd fell almost silent. But one voice could be heard amongst the creaking of wooden spades and the grinding of metal. Enid's father – Brack no longer but Councillor Brackenbury of the ILP – was laying down the law. He was careful to keep well clear of the little group which surrounded Fred Hall, President of the Derbyshire Mineworkers' Association. The check-weighman and lodge officials were paying their respects. He had no intention of attending anyone else's court.

'They care now't for safety, now't,' Brack said.

His cronies from Cobbler Jack's nodded their agreement.

'Nationalization will end all this nonsense.'

They nodded with less certainty, trying to recall the details of the Labour Government's failure fully to implement the new Coal Mines Act.

The man in the Homburg hat edged towards him.

'It's all the electrics,' the man said. 'You know that as well as me. Sparks from the electricity.'

'What about Ringrose lamps?' Brack asked as if he had trumped an ace. He was not sure what the Ringrose lamp was or what it did, but he felt certain that it had something to do with gas and safety.

As the cage clanked up to the surface, Enid ran across to her father.

'What the bloody hell are you doing down here?'

'Jack's down there.'

For the first time in years, Brack took his daughter's hand.

'It might be a long job, this. They've got to put the fire out before any of the men come up. Best wait at home.'

'I'll wait here.'

The waiting ambulance backed up to the cage and two stretchers were dragged out. The men who lay on them were burned but alive. They called out encouragement to the crowd. There had been an explosion and there was a fire. But nobody was dead.

'Thank God,' said Brack, 'that I'm not down there.'

'And thank God,' said the man in the Homburg hat, 'that I'm not going down to put out that bloody fire.'

For the next half hour, there was nothing to do except wait. Then, with horn hooting and headlights flashing, a motor car pushed its way through the crowd, causing the more nervous of the onlookers to jump back and the more aggressive to hammer in protestation on its windows. The men who leapt out, as if they were afraid that they had missed all the excitement, were the reporter and photographer from the *Derbyshire Times*. Someone at the back of the crowd noticed them and a murmur of resentment began to ripple through the pit yard. There was a shout of 'Bloody ghouls' and another of 'Scabs'. The *Derbyshire Times* had published a daily denunciation of the miners during the desperate days of 1926. The bitter memories had not faded in five years.

'I'm going home,' said Brack. 'What about you?'

'I'll wait,' Enid told him. 'Tell Mam not to worry.'

'You must be freezing. You'll get your death of cold.'

'I'm waiting.'

Brack, who was determined that he at least would escape pneumonia, stamped his feet to revive his circulation and edged his way through the crowd, talking loudly about the mistake that the miners had made when they agreed to load with forks instead of shovels.

'That's when t'rot set in. That's when Markham knew he had them beat.'

The Deputy came up at one o'clock, bringing with him an injured member of the rescue team. A rush of miners volunteered to take the burned man's place. Only one could claim that he was a trained fireman and even he seemed uncertain about how often he had spent an evening in the Miners' Rescue Centre at Mansfield Woodhouse. But he was given the breathing apparatus and sent down. Then the Deputy addressed the crowd.

'The fire's nearly out. They've done marvels down there. We'll soon be able to start shifting the rock. They deserve a medal. Everyone of them.'

'What about the men?' somebody shouted from the back of the crowd.

'I can't tell you because I don't know. I don't think anybody got crushed. There was nobody working under the fall. It all depends on what we find on the other side.'

Nobody said it, but everyone thought gas. Not just a pocket of gas that had caused the explosion, but gas all along the seams, gas choking the miners to death.

'Have you a man down there?'

Enid had never seen the woman before. But she replied with the camaraderie of muted fear.

'My fiancé, Jack O'Hara. We're engaged.'

'You looked starved. It'll be an hour before we know ow't. I'd go home and get a warm if I was you.'

'Are you stopping?'

'My husband's down there.'

'I'm stopping as well.'

The first men came up at half past three. They were still coughing when they got out of the cage but they managed to reply to most of the questions that were shouted at them from beyond the pool of light. A great cheer echoed through the crowd when one of them said there was no gas, but it died away when another added, 'It's the air. There's no air down there. It'll be a miracle if nobody's suffocated.'

'Any dead yet?' asked the man from the *Derbyshire Times*.

None of the rescued men knew the answer and in the silence women began to call out names.

'Did you see Tommy Walsh?'

'Anybody working near Bob Taylor?'

'Jim Pearson. Anybody know about Jim Pearson?'

Enid could not bring herself to ask for news of Jack, so she waited as cage after cage of rescued miners were brought to the surface, wrapped in blankets, and hurried off by their families to home or the ambulance hut.

Five men came up on stretchers and the crowd pressed so anxiously towards them that Enid was almost swept away. But she caught a glimpse of each face and felt both relieved that Jack was not injured and devastated not to find him injured but safe. She only began to feel really frightened when she noticed the crowd was beginning to drift away. Most of the miners had been rescued.

Jack came up at half past five. She had never seen him black from the pit before and that night there were rivulets of sweat running through the grime. She ran towards him, shouting his name, and hurled herself into his arms.

'I thought you were dead.'

He could not speak for surprise.

'Nearly everybody else came up hours ago. I thought you were dead.'

'I'm fine. That's why I stayed down. Our stall wasn't touched. We stayed to help shift that stone. Biggest fall I've seen.' He proudly showed her his torn palms and bleeding knuckles. 'I've been lifting rocks as big as beer barrels for the last two hours.'

'And what about me standing here and frightened you were dead?'

'I never thought you'd come. I didn't even think that you'd know that it had happened until morning.'

'Oh Jack,' she said, wiping away her tears with a grimy hand. 'You mustn't say that. What would I do if I ever lost you? I'd be all on my own.'

BROOK HOUSE did not boast a telephone. There were times when Anne Skinner and Lottie Harthill, High Class Ladies' Dressmakers and Tailors, would have found it immensely convenient to speak directly to a cloth warehouse in Leeds or to a customer whose coat was ready for its second fitting. But Worksop did not believe in convenience. Telephones – like electric lights, gas ovens and wireless sets – were part of the strange new world which the partners were afraid to inhabit. When Agnes Skinner needed to send an urgent request for help, it arrived at Newcastle Avenue by telegram.

Telegrams, in the partners' experience, were always bad news. Indeed, bad news was the best sort of information which telegrams conveyed. Often the news inside the yellow envelope was terrible. Sometimes it was tragic. Occasionally, catastrophic would not have been too dramatic a description. It was, Lottie and Anne believed, best to prepare themselves for the shock by speculating about the nature of the calamity before they read the words on the buff form and discovered exactly how desperate the news really was.

'It's the ulcer,' said Anne. 'It's burst.'

'I'd be relieved if it was,' Lottie told her. 'I think it's Brack. He's run off for good and left them without a penny.'

'Or just turned them out into the street.'

'No, it can't be that.' Lottie failed in her duty to escalate the horror with every new suggestion. 'If he'd turned them out, they'd have come straight here.'

The competition for the most distressing invention having been completed, Anne ran a scissor blade along the inside of the flap.

'It's Enid,' she gasped. 'She's getting married. It's definite.'

It was more definite than Anne Skinner realized. Jack O'Hara had, at last, been offered a pit cottage. A letter – on the official paper of the Staveley Coal and Iron Company – had promised the tenancy of the next vacant property in the romantically named Colliery Row. The check-weighman had said that he happened to know that one of the houses would be empty by Easter. Anne had remained sceptical even after the sixpenny notice had been placed in the Births, Marriages and Deaths column of the *Mansfield Guardian*, naming the day as June 5th, the Friday after Corpus Christi. But she was totally convinced by the twelve word telegram. Neither Enid nor her mother would have wasted even more money on announcing anything which was less than certain.

Lottie sat down on the *chaise longue*. She had aged ten years in ten seconds.

'Can you imagine it, little Enid with that great big collier?'

'She's made up her mind, and there's nothing that we can do about it.' Anne would have said that she had made her bed and must lie on it, but the metaphor seemed distastefully appropriate to the situation.

'Are we going to lock up and go?' Lottie asked.

Anne did not even bother to reply.

The routine was well established. The years when the two women could cycle between Worksop and Langwith Junction were long past, but a regular train chugged between town and village. Lottie consulted the timetable. Anne pulled out a wicker basket from under the kitchen table and started to fill it with the basic requirements of a mission of mercy. They caught the twelve-fifteen train.

Much to the distress of other passengers, Chum was combed and brushed in the compartment. Lottie, suspecting that the pickled onion jar was leaking inside the wicker basket, emptied it on to the seat. Her fears were unfounded and the relief expedition arrived in good order at Langwith Road, where they were greeted with great pleasure but no surprise.

'Does she really mean it this time?' Lottie was still hopeful. 'It would be awful if we bought all the material . . .'

'She means it all right. Ask her yourself. She's just down at the shops. They're going away for a week at Cleethorpes. She decided everything last night.'

The three women began to decide it all again on Enid's behalf. It was taken for granted that Agnes would spend the honeymoon weekend at Brook House.

'Why doesn't Ern come to us instead?' asked Anne. 'Then they can be on their own in his house at Overend Road. It would save them money and they'd be near by if anything went wrong.'

A Worksop honeymoon was agreed.

'Katherine will make a lovely bridesmaid,' Lottie said, breaking the rule of the day with a cheerful comment. Katherine Fox, although still in the employment of Skinner and Harthill, was *persona non grata*.

Nobody approved of Katherine Fox's association with Eamon O'Hara. Jack believed that it was preventing his brothers in Langwith from looking for a job outside instead of pretending to wait for a job in a pit which was laying off colliers. He took it for granted that the talk of five years in the Irish Guard, followed by the Metropolitan Police and a pension was simple fantasy. And Jack did not hold with fantasy. Anne and Lotte were bitter that Katherine had betrayed them. They had saved her from imagined poverty, taught her a real trade and encouraged her friendship with their only niece. She had repaid them by forming a relationship with a man.

The telegram announcing Enid's wedding date had arrived on Katherine's day off so there was a real risk of their meeting her in Langwith Junction – hanging about, as Anne would put it, with those brothers. But they determined to face the shame as bravely as they could. While they talked to Agnes about their niece's wedding they felt a continued fear that Katherine would appear at the door, hand-in-hand with Eamon O'Hara.

Anne and Lottie were safe, at least until dinner time, for Katherine was where there was no chance of a meeting. She was spending the morning in bed with Eamon O'Hara at his lodgings in Hucknall. She had lurked amongst the shops until she had seen Jack's landlady haggling over the price of vegetables in the market place in front of the church. Then, knowing that all the lodgers were on the morning shift, she had allowed Eamon to smuggle her up to his attic. It was only when she heard Mrs Ferguson return that she began to develop scruples.

'You are going to marry me, aren't you, Eamon?'

'Of course I am,' he said and meant it.

'I wish we could get on with it.'

'You know very well that we've got to let Jack sort himself out first.'

'But you said there'd been an announcement.'

'And so there has. Are you blind, woman? Those two will

never marry. There's no joy in it. Whatever they say now it won't happen. She doesn't love him.'

'She more or less told me so. But now, they've set the date . . .'

'They'll never do it. I'm telling you the truth. That night at the old woman's birthday, she was eyeing me all the time. But it was you that took my fancy.'

Eamon, who his brother had rightly explained was mad but not stupid, believed that he had fought off Enid's advances and turned instead to Katherine Fox, who had become the love of his life. His feelings for Katherine were neither pretence nor invention. She made him happy and he wanted to be happy for the rest of his life. It was only with great restraint that he prevented himself from arranging the wedding there and then.

'A week or two more won't matter,' he said, trying to convince himself that virtue would be its own reward. 'Jack will look daft enough as it is.' He turned towards her.

'Not again?' said Katherine incredulously.

'Again,' said Eamon. 'Then you can creep out and go and see the bride.'

Lottie was in the road outside Brack's coal yard, looking so desperate that Enid took it for granted that Chum had escaped and was missing, presumed run over.

'Thank goodness you're back,' said Lottie, showing the strength of her feelings by speaking first and using the strongest language in her vocabulary.

'We wouldn't have waited,' Anne announced. 'We'd have gone straight back rather than stay in the same house as him, but we didn't want to leave her on her own.'

'When did you get here?'

'Half an hour ago. We were having a nice talk when he walked in.'

Brack sat defiantly on a hard chair, leaning back in a way which he knew would make Agnes fear that its legs would break. It was one of the Grove Cottage chairs, a relic of the Eden which the Skinner sisters had inhabited before the Fall. The sound of cracking oak would signal not damage but desecration. Brack looked at his daughter, half mocking and half serious.

'Perhaps you understand, but it beats me. I come home. They're all talking about you and your mother moving out. And when I say that suits me very nicely, hell breaks loose.'

'Don't you use that sort of language in front of my sisters,' said Agnes. Then she turned to Enid. 'He's going to live with that woman. That's the truth of it. He came in and told us, as calm as you please.'

'I just walked in and found Miss Skinner acting the lady bountiful with a half eaten piece of meat. This other one comes in from out the back and asks what I think about you marrying Jack.'

'It was a civil question,' Lottie insisted.

'And I gave her a civil answer. I said that nobody had asked my opinion and what I thought didn't matter.'

'That's not all.' Anne came to Lottie's defence. 'He said that you wouldn't like it in a pit cottage.'

'Nor will you. You've talked enough about having the bathroom built on. You've talked about it more than you've used it. Some men might have complained.' Brack seemed genuinely hurt. 'Might have asked how it was that his wife had planned to move out without mentioning it to him.' The resentment deepened. 'Might have felt bad about being deserted. Not me. I told 'em I've been thinking of selling up for years and that I'd move out after the wedding.'

'You see!' Agnes sounded almost triumphant. 'He admits it. He's going to live with that woman in Mansfield.'

'It so happens,' said Brack, speaking directly to his wife for the first time, 'that I am.'

Agnes, although still hunched in her wheelchair, managed to lift her head to an angle at which she could look her husband in the face.

'Don't think there'll be any divorce, June, July or ever. You can live with her but you won't marry her, I'll see to that.'

Agnes, whose senses had been dulled with the years of pain and infirmity, was astonished by the violence of her own reaction.

At that moment, she hated her husband with such violent emotion because once she had loved him so much. She had forgotten the man that once he was and the joys which she had shared with a husband, who although never honest and honourable, had been handsome and dashing. The marriage had begun with half a dozen years of romance and passion, punctuated with occasional desertion and casual violence. But until that moment when he announced that at last he was going to leave her for ever, Agnes had either loved Brack or convinced herself that she loved him. Her sudden hatred was, not the least, the result of the despair which she felt from the discovery that she loved him no longer.

Brack waited for the shock waves to subside.

'This row is none of my making. I didn't come home looking for trouble and I'm sorry that I found it. None of this is any of their business.' He waved dismissively towards Anne and Lottie, who bristled and cowered simultaneously. 'But as usual they poked their big noses in, so they might as well know what's what. Yes, I am going to live with her. Sooner the better. Probably before June now. And you might as well all understand why. I'm getting on for sixty. I've got ten or fifteen good years. And I'm going to enjoy them. I'm going to have some comfort and some respect and I'm going to live like a man again.'

Lottie gasped with outrage and Anne drew in her breath in horror at the thought that her partner understood Brack's meaning.

Then Agnes had one of her shuddering fits and her husband returned to the supervision of coal bagging in the yard. Enid rubbed her mother's back and Anne said that she would not leave until she was sure that her sister was safe. Everything having returned to normal, Lottie fell asleep on the horsehair sofa.

CHAPTER SEVEN

THE IRONMONGER'S shop in Alfreton Road was shut and dark but Clare was not in a mood to be ignored. So she felt her way down the dark entry which led to the yard and banged on the back door. To her relief, Herbert made no attempt to pretend that Rex was not at home. He asked her in, took her coat and suggested, as a good brother-in-law should, that she sat in the most comfortable chair.

'Where is he?'

'Down the yard. He'll be back in a minute.'

'It's about time you told him, Herbert – told him what his mother hoped for him and told him what she must be feeling now.'

All that Clare said was acutely painful to Herbert. Because he was incapable of being miserable for more than a few minutes, the pangs of conscience did not trouble him for long. But whilst the regret and the remorse lasted he felt profound resentment towards his sister-in-law. She had no right to impose such burdens upon him, especially when they reminded him of the failings and failures of his own past which he had worked so hard to push out of his mind.

He did not even consider telling Clare to mind her own business. That was not his way. For, although she had offended him, he was anxious not to cause her any offence. He had based much of his life on the conviction that it is difficult not to love, at least a little, a man who is desperate to be loved without limit. He knew that his need for affection made him vulnerable and that sometimes people rallied to his cause out of compassion – a victim who could be exploited or rescued according to taste. But it was better than no affection at all.

'When did you ever sit him down and talk to him about anything serious – anything except cricket and football and the old times. For God's sake, Herbert, he needs your advice.'

'He's a grown man, Clare. He's got himself an education. He's not likely to do what I tell him.'

'It's your duty to try.' Clare reached for her coat with a gesture of absolute moral certainty and pushed the hat pin into the bun at the nape of her neck with a single thrust, which suggested that she would return and hold him to account for continued failure to play the father's part.

'I'll see you to the end of the entry,' Herbert offered as a conciliatory gesture.

'No need. I'm going with Muriel to the Regent. It's *Congress Dances*. You ought to come. You'd enjoy it.'

It was a genuine attempt to soften the parting. But the invitation did nothing to improve Herbert's spirits. He hated the cinema. It was the Al Jolsons and the Charlie Chaplins who had destroyed real entertainment – the smoking concerts, the musical soirées and the public house performances which had once lightened his life. He had triumphed over the gramophone and held his own with the wireless. But talking pictures were too much for him. If they had not been invented he would, at the very moment when Clare disappeared into the yard, be lathering his face in preparation for an early evening shave – the shave which once was the prelude to submerging his sorrows under a melody of patriotic songs.

'Not me,' Herbert told her.

Clare left without condescending to argue or persuade. Herbert could barely wait for Rex to return.

'I think she's right. I should have had a talk, after you came home again.'

'You've been marvellous, Dad. You've left me in peace. That's what I wanted.'

'That's as may be. But it may not be what was best. What you want and what is best aren't always the same. As I know to my cost.'

Rex felt so sorry for his father that he began the conversation that Herbert believed must take place but dare not initiate.

'Just tell me, Dad. What do you think I should have done?'

'I'll tell you one thing. You don't have to worry about what's happening here. Stay as long as you like. It's your house as much as mine. Just yours and mine. I've made up my mind about Mrs Nicholls. She's a nice woman, a very nice woman. But there'll be no marriage. So you needn't go on that account.'

'That's not . . .'

Rex began to lie. For in the emotion of the moment it seemed right to reassure his father with comforting inventions about his admiration for Mrs Nicholls and his hope that she would become his stepmother. Then he looked at his father – for whom life had been a combination of minor pleasures and major disappointments – and wondered if he had decided against her or if she had decided against him.

Rex made his last plea for help.

'So what do you think that I should do?' he asked.

'It depends what you want to do. I never knew what I was really after. Do what makes you happy.'

'I can't do that, Dad. She won't marry me.'

'There's more than one fish in the sea. I wanted to marry your Aunt Clare and she wouldn't have me. But I've no regrets. Marrying your mother was the best thing I ever did. God knows what would have become of me if I hadn't.'

The conversation was moving back towards Herbert's decision not to remarry and Rex knew that, despite his horror at the prospect, there was no way of preventing his father embarking on a mawkish account of his reasons for staying a grieving widower. Rex had been educated to believe that emotions should be felt rather than described. He did not want to hear an account of his parents' complicated relationship.

'You know how much I relied on her.'

'I do, Dad. I do very well.'

The heartfelt assurance was not enough for Herbert. Indeed, nothing that his son might have said could possibly have prevented him from embarking upon a long and perilous voyage of self-justification. He reminded Rex that 'he had always done his best and that if he had ever let her down, it was not for want of trying'. He described the indignities of a time-served scissor maker working as a navvy on a building site and in the enamelling shop at the Raleigh cycle works but insisted that he 'would have done anything rather than let her worry about the grocery bill'.

As always, the dramatic monologue ended with an account of the happy times which he and Augusta had spent together: day trips to the banks of the Trent, afternoons in the gardens of Woolaton Hall and evenings in the upper circle at the Theatre Royal. None of the pleasures which he recalled with such sweet sorrow had taken place after they married.

'So you understand why I don't see me and Mrs Nicholls . . . It's not sentimental, like your aunt Clare says. I just can't see it. I couldn't get used to somebody else being Mrs Herbert Hattersley. I'm not saying that it wouldn't be right. It just wouldn't feel right.'

'It would after a bit. You'd get used to it.'

'God almighty!' Herbert, moved by a lofty emotion which, since it was unusual, he did not wholly understand, was horrified. 'What sort of a way to get married would that be? You get married when you can't bear the thought of anything else.'

'I think you're wrong,' said Rex, neither knowing or caring if it were true.

'Can you see me, or her for that matter, walking down the aisle? I'm a bit too old for having confetti thrown at me. She'll still come round. We'll have a drink together and she'll cook Sunday dinner. But none of that need make any difference to you.'

'Sooner or later, Dad, I'll have to move on.'

'Where to?'

'I don't know. There aren't many adverts in the "Situations Vacant" that say, "Wanted ex-Catholic priest". The nearest thing I've got to a trade is clerking.'

Rex's thoughts, which first wandered over the possibility of making a joke about being *clericus* no longer, began to concentrate on what it would be like to be a clerk outside holy orders. His experience of the world beyond the Church was limited to his adolescence at Ratcliffe, the few months since his desertion of St Joseph's and books. His ideas of life as a clerk were based on the work of Dickens, Trollope and H. G. Wells. He imagined himself spending the next forty years on an uncomfortable high stool in a dingy office which he left each evening for a cold garret and a solitary supper.

'You've got a trade,' his father told him. 'You served a seven-year apprenticeship same as me. And they'd have you back tomorrow. Clare said so.'

'Did she tell why I should want to go back?'

'You can't always do exactly what you want. I've found that out in my life. My goodness, I have. So you have to decide what's second best – what gives you least trouble and what gives you least pain. Sometimes you just have to ask yourself what's easiest. Being a priest must be easier for you than anything else. Didn't you feel somebody when you were there in Langwith Junction?'

'Sometimes.' Rex was thinking of how much more confident he felt as a priest than he did as a man.

'And didn't you enjoy it?'

'I did parts. I loved parts of it.'

He loved the sights and sounds of Catholicism: the white and gold vestments on high days and holidays, the altar draped in black during Lent, the racks of candles flickering to heaven, the bell at the moment of transubstantiation and the colours of the painted vestments on the plaster statues. He loved the liturgy and the language, the certainty of the responses chanted in absolute unison, the rustle of a whole congregation kneeling down to pray, the smell of the incense as it swirled out of the swinging thurible and, above all, the Latin. He had come late to Latin, and at first had struggled hard to follow the lectures in Rome's Gregorian University. But, by the end, it was the dead language which made the Church live. It was the Latin which reminded him that all over the world men and women were offering up the same prayers in the same words and that, for almost two thousand years, Christians had worshipped the same God in the same way. It made the Church timeless and boundless and him, as part of it, immortal.

'I remember,' said Herbert, 'you writing from Rome to say how much you enjoyed visiting churches.'

'I did and I still do but there's a little problem about believing in it all, a little problem about faith.'

'I can't help you there,' said his father. 'I can't help you about faith. I was brought up a Methodist myself.'

WHEN HE sent the postcard to Bill Ellis, Rex knew that – in his heart, if not his head – he had already taken the decision to go back. He asked for no more than to see the bishop, but although at first he pretended (even to himself) that he intended no more than to clear his mind, by the time that he wrote the address he had no doubt what conclusion clarity of thought would dictate. The postcard itself was evidence of his intention. It was his last green and white picture of Palazzola. He had brought half a dozen back from Rome and had used them only in moments of great emotion. The picture of the crumbling monastery on the shore of Lake Albano was part of his message.

He wanted to remind Bill Ellis that they were brothers, bound together by the Liber Ruber which bore their names. Together, they had looked out towards the Appian Hills, watched the fireflies in the dusk after dinner and rowed on the lake which the local fishermen said was as bottomless as the pit of hell. The postcard proved that he was going home.

It took Bill Ellis three days to respond. Then, so early on a Sunday morning that he must have come straight from mass, the bishop's secretary came to the shop door and told Herbert – as bishops' emissaries had told fathers for a thousand years – that his son must go at once to the cathedral. Rex, both frightened and excited by the drama, walked down Alfreton Road in silence, waiting for Father Ellis to speak to him, but waiting in vain. He waited for another half hour in the secretary's office and, for every second of the thirty minutes, Rex's anxiety increased. When, at last, he was led into Bishop Dunn's study, he was no longer quite sure what he was anxious about. He was, however, certain that his anxiety was justified.

'Well,' asked Bishop Dunn. 'What have you been up to?'

Rex who, a second before had felt nothing except apprehension, was affronted by the flippancy of the bishop's greeting. He was a renegade priest returning to the Church and he was entitled to be treated with the seriousness appropriate to that status. He had expected, at best, to be met by profound disapproval and he had feared that he would be received with the contempt which the constant feel for those who betray them. Yet he had been welcomed to Bishop's House in language which would have been more appropriate to an indulgent grandfather warning a boisterous child about complaints from the neighbours. Traitors on Dante's last circle of ice, had been treated with more respect.

'My lord.'

Rex thought the two words demonstrated appropriate reticence. He bowed his head and prepared to kiss the bishop's ring. When he was almost down on one knee the bishop walked towards the door and, instead of offering his hand for the obeisance, peered out into the corridor and shouted.

'Bill. Go and see if you can find someone to kill the fatted calf, or at least to make a pot of coffee. Rex looks as if he could do with a hot drink. He's white as a ghost.' He turned to Rex. 'Are you sure that you're all right? You don't look very well.'

Rex wanted to reply, 'Of course I'm not all right', and go on to ask what else the bishop expected. Instead he said that he was more than grateful for the interest in his health, but no concern was necessary. During the last week or two, he had spent less time than usual in the fresh air. No doubt that accounted for his pallor.

'Perhaps it's because you look strange in those clothes. I haven't seen you in civvies since you left Ratcliffe. You're sure that you're eating properly.'

'Yes, my lord.'

'You'll stay for lunch, won't you?'

Rex could not bring himself to reply. He had come home to stay for the rest of his life. It was only on Father Ellis's insistence that he had agreed to leave Alfreton Road without packing his clothes and wishing his father a grateful farewell. He had anticipated a period of penance in Bishop's House or one of the Nottingham presbyteries, followed by a long retreat in a religious house somewhere far away. His aunt had convinced him that he would not be allowed to return to Rome. So he had fantasized about Dormodossolla and the monastery of the Rosminians who taught at Ratcliffe. Because it was obvious that the bishop would regard him as unworthy of a pastoral vocation, he thought of volunteering to teach until he could be trusted with a parish.

Bill Ellis pushed the door open to allow Mrs Griffiths, the housekeeper, to enter with a tray.

'Tell him he must stay. Tell him what you're cooking for dinner.'

'Lamb,' said the housekeeper without trying to understand why it was so important that the young man ate at Bishop's House.

'What do you want to do, Rex?' Bishop Dunn had perfected the disarming change of subject and mood.

'I want to come back, my lord.'

'Back to St Joseph's?'

'I meant back to the priesthood.'

'You've never left it. What did they teach you at the Collegio Inglese, for heaven's sake. You're a priest. Improperly dressed and, if I'm any judge, not revelling in the joy of salvation. But you're a priest. And it's time you went back to work. There are, however, a couple of things that we have to talk over.'

This is it, thought Rex, the mental thumbscrew and the moral rack. He prepared himself for questions about the strength of his faith and the depth of his conviction.

He had come to Bishop's House intending to ask for help and guidance and had expected to be given an opportunity to agonize about his doubts. During the walk from Alfreton Road he had silently recited the creed and convinced himself that he still believed in each of its assertions. The catechism had been more difficult, for he could no longer separate it in his mind from Enid, whose refusal to learn it by heart had ended her first flirtation with Rome and marked the beginning of their mutual infatuation. Rex had decided, before the end of that anxious journey, that he was a genuine Catholic of the casual sort – temperamentally inclined to perform the minimum observances with a zeal which was as real as it was infrequent. His intention, right up to the moment when Bill

Ellis ushered him into the bishop's study, had been to tell the simple truth. He had imagined himself saying, 'My lord, I am a true Catholic but I fear that I am unworthy to be a priest. I need your guidance.'

Bishop Dunn's manner had forced Rex into changing his approach. He could not bare his soul to someone who might respond to his agony with dismissive amusement. When he was asked the crucial questions he had replied with absolute certainty. The call was as loud and clear as it had been on the summer Sunday in Santa Maria Maggiore, when all his doubts had been dazzled away by the idea not of the Church Triumphant, about which he was taught in the Via di Monserrato, but the Church Beautiful.

'Who knows about what's been going on?'

'Enid, her mother and father. The man she says that she is going to marry. My Aunt Clare. My father, of course. I told him and then he met her when she came to the shop.'

'Make a big public fuss did she, when you broke it off?'

'I didn't break it off.'

'Quite. Anyone else? It's the people who might gossip that I'm thinking about.'

'I think that her father said something at the beginning. But he'll say no more. Now that she's definitely getting married, he'll want it all respectable.'

'Good. That's good. We all want that. We've done remarkably well in keeping it out of the newspapers. There's not been a single word except that little story about you being ill in the local rag. That's the main thing now. To keep it out of the papers.'

The main thing now, for Rex, was to decide what he wanted and what he believed. He knew what he was going to do. He could not afford to let doubts about his vocation prevent his life from coming to rest. He would become a priest again and live and die within the comfortable, if no longer comforting, confines of the Church. After a period of punishment and the demonstration of real remorse, he would return to the routine of confessions, baptisms, sermons and last rites. His black suits would soon become shiny with wear and he would develop the habit of visiting his most generous parishioners at meal times. If he was truly forgiven he might yet be given a large parish with a splendid church – perhaps even Pugin's masterpiece, St Mary's in Derby. He would die in the Convent Nursing Home in Nottingham and would be buried in the cemetery behind Ratcliffe College. He knew what he was going to do.

'That relates to the other question. What are you going to tell people who ask you what happened?'

'I hadn't really thought about it, my lord. I thought that I'd tell them the truth.'

'That goes without saying.' Bishop Dunn sounded as near to irritation as his reputation allowed. 'But truth comes in a variety of shapes and sizes. I take it that you've no great desire to re-live the last few months. You don't feel a particular compulsion to describe it all in detail, do you?'

'The very opposite, my lord. I hate talking about it – even to you, my lord.'

'Quite right. Say exactly that. Tell people that it's all too painful to discuss.

'Bill tells me that you haven't managed to answer all the letters. We'll take the burden off your back. Somebody here can knock out a standard note on a typewriter and rattle off as many as you need. Just a brief message of thanks . . . if that suits you, of course. Now, is there anything you'd like to ask me?'

'I thought that you'd want to talk to me about where I stand now. About my mistakes and about how . . . they can be redeemed.'

'No doubt you'll want to make a confession soon. See Monsignor Payne. Wasn't he your parish priest when you were a boy? He'll tell you what the Church expects and requires of you. But don't let it upset you. This is a day for rejoicing. That which was lost – almost lost – is found. I'm not welcoming you back because you've never really been away. I'm just very pleased to see you again. And, of course, to tell you what I've decided.'

Rex prepared himself for the worst – a period of intense prayer in retreat or at Cardinal Newman's college at Oscott, followed by a penance in a missionary station on the Yangtse or amongst the lepers of Africa. He was ready to do whatever was necessary for his return home. He even looked forward to submerging himself in the pursuit of spiritual redemption and putting the word, the flesh and the devil behind him for ever.

'You'll want to spend tonight with your father – packing up, saying your farewells, that sort of thing. Come back here tomorrow. We've got some of your stuff from St Joseph's stored somewhere in the house. Bring whatever else you like. There's plenty of room. There's a job I'd like you to do for me.'

'I really am most grateful. It's not easy to find the right words . . .'

'Then don't try. Just remember what I said to you when all this trouble started.'

The bishop, although sure that Rex had not forgotten, gave himself the pleasure of repeating his moving words.

'I told you that you had to go back and face the temptation, not run away from it. And I was right. And I told you that I was proud of you. Do you remember?'

Bishop Dunn held out his hand and Rex, falling to his knees, kissed the great episcopal ring.

'IF YOU can just tip the chair back a bit.'

Father Hattersley was afraid that the emaciated child would slide from the wicker seat of the bent wood chair and bounce down the steps on to the platform below. Rex placed a protecting hand on her shoulder. She flinched and screamed. The scream turned into sobs.

'Don't be silly, Eileen.' Her mother – almost as thin and pale as the child – was not sure whether her daughter should be scolded or comforted. 'You'll be on the big train in a minute and on your way to the place where you'll get better.'

At the bottom of the steps, a portly nun in the grey habit of a Sister of Charity consulted a list.

'Are you St Vincent de Paul?'

'No,' said Father Hattersley, waving vaguely in the direction of the stretcher-bearers. 'These gentlemen are Catenians.'

'Then you're in the front two coaches. It's Sisters of Mercy down there. They'll give you seats.'

The Catenians struggled on, arms and backs arching in a way which seemed wholly out of proportion to the size and weight of their burden. They longed to set the crying child down. But they longed, even more, to end all responsibility for the bundle of frightened misery. Rex located and opened the door of the third-class carriage to which the girl had been allocated. As the exhausted volunteers wrung their crushed hands and flexed their atrophied muscles, Eileen was arranged in a corner seat.

Rex lowered the carriage window and shouted his thanks and blessing to the disappearing backs of his two helpers. As the whistle blew and the train pulled out of the station, he feared for an uncertain moment that he had left his suitcase on the platform. As he stepped back in instinctive horror, Father Keogh, parish priest of St Philip Neri in Mansfield, caught him as if he were about to fall.

'I only just heard you were coming with us.'

Father Keogh sounded as if he believed that the information had been intentionally withheld from him. He was holding Rex's suitcase.

'That's mine, Father.'

'I know. I saw it often enough in the old days. It's a disgrace. It's time you got a new one.'

The false joviality was familiar enough. Rex had served for a year as assistant priest at St Philip Neri with mixed feelings. After he was promoted to Langwith, Father Keogh developed the habit of calling him the best curate in the history of the diocese. But during his time in Mansfield, the parish priest had treated him with amused contempt. Rex held out his hand but Father Keogh did not relax his grip on the suitcase handle. It seemed more unseemly to wrestle for its possession than to abandon the right to carry it.

'It's very kind of you, Father. I'll join you in a minute. I want to have a word with the people I haven't met yet.'

'There's no need for you to bother with that.' Father Keogh was insistent. 'We'll do that. I've got a young man from the cathedral.'

When the bishop had asked Rex to join the Easter pilgrimage to Lourdes, he had told him that his old friend Michael Eagan was in charge of all the arrangements. But Rex knew that it was best to allow Father Keogh the power that comes from knowledge.

'I'd still just like—'

'Then don't be too long about it. You need something warm inside you. I've got a vacuum flask – and a little something to liven up the tea.'

Rex slid open the door of the nearest compartment. A boy, his head on his mother's lap, lay absolutely still along the four seats which faced the engine. His eyes were open, but he stared sightlessly at the ceiling. Rex sat down on the seat opposite the boy's feet.

'I'm sorry, Father. I should have put something under his shoes. I don't think they're very dirty. He was carried to the train.'

'It doesn't matter,' said Rex.

The Sister of Mercy who sat opposite the boy's mother, took a handkerchief from the depths of her habit and moved in the direction of the perfectly clean shoes.

'It doesn't matter.'

He was less concerned with the suffering he might witness than with the horror of witnessing it. He tried to remember that the boy's paralysis was God's will.

'*Omnipotens sempiternes Deus, salus aeterna credentium: exaudi nos pro famulis tuis infirmis, pro quibus misericordiae tuae imploramus auxilium; ut, reddita sibi sanitate . . .*'

The nun, hearing the Collect from the mass for the sick, stood up in preparation for kneeling down. Deciding either that the place was inappropriate or the space inadequate, she sank back in her corner seat. His poise and authority having been restored, Rex turned to the mother.

'How old is he?'

'Fourteen, Father.' Rex noticed the broken heel in the woman's left shoe. 'He's fourteen. Exactly the same age as Saint Bernadette when she saw the first vision.'

'She's not a saint yet,' Rex told her. 'Though I'm sure that she will be soon.'

'She will be if she cures my Paul. He's just got worse, all year. Last summer, he could sit up and he understood most things that we said. Now he just lies asleep most of the time. We have to wake him up to feed him. A right job that is. Not that we mind . . .'

The child began to twitch and Rex fled without giving even a perfunctory blessing.

A man with the gaunt cheeks and hollow eyes of terminal cancer, stood in the corridor outside the lavatory door. He was struggling to button his flies, but when he saw Rex he abandoned the attempt and flattened himself against the wall to allow the priest to pass.

'God bless you.' Rex knew that he should stop and offer to help, but he squeezed past with the promise that they would talk before Lourdes. In the next compartment, the portly Sister of Charity was holding the head of a middle aged woman who was vomiting into a large brown paper bag. Opposite them, a man with a purple growth covering one side of his face was saying his rosary.

By the time that he reached the sanctuary of his own compartment Rex feared that, like the unconscious boy further down the train, he was unlikely to survive the journey. He was astonished to find that Father Keogh, instead of being submerged in gloom, was happily reminiscing with Father Eagan. He looked up and made a conscious effort to drag Rex into the conversation.

'You've never been to Ireland, have you?'

'No.' Rex held out his hand to the dark young priest who had been pretending to enjoy Father Keogh's stories of Dublin at the turn of the century. 'Just Rome. That's where I met Michael, here.'

'Offer the man a drink,' said Father Keogh.

Father Eagan opened the wicker hamper to reveal Bakelite cups, tin vacuum flask and a half bottle of Irish whiskey.

'Just tea, please,' said Rex. 'No whiskey.'

The four pilgrims who were waiting at Leicester had been told to stand at the wrong end of the platform and, since one of them was on a stretcher, there was momentary panic at the thought that they might not be installed in their reserved compartment by the time that the train began to rock and shudder south. Michael

Eagan rushed out to lend his strength and enthusiasm to helping the newcomers aboard. Rex prepared to follow.

'Sit yourself down,' Father Keogh commanded. 'Silly to get excited. Best for you to keep calm. Finish your tea. We'll be off again in a minute.'

The train pulled away slowly.

'I'm locking the door,' said Father Keogh, taking a key out of his waistcoat pocket. He held it in the air, like an object of veneration. 'It's one of the railway company's little courtesies. We can pull down the blinds and get a little privacy . . . For our devotions, of course! I thought we should pray together. Just you and me.'

Father Keogh took out the prayer book which he had thoughtfully left ready in the hamper. A piece of folded newspaper marked a page at the back of the missal.

Exaudi, Deus, orationem meam, et ne despexeris deprecationem meam . . .

It was Psalm 54, the Introit to the mass for the sick.

Omnipotens sempiterne Deus, salus aeterna credentium.

Rex's mind wandered. When he dragged his attention back to the prayers, he tried to maintain his concentration by mouthing the words himself.

Exaudi nos pro famulis tuis infirmis, pro quibus misericordiae tuae imploramus auxilium.

'God bless you, Rex.' The formal prayers were over. 'God knows, my prayers are with you. All my parish is praying for your recovery. You're a good man. It's one of the mysteries why good men like you . . .'

Even then, it took Rex some time to understand the significance of what Father Keogh was saying. Only when a medallion was pressed into his hand did he realize the full extent of the old priest's confusion. He held the medal in his open palm, and stared at the crude engraving of a featureless saint. He could just make out the name 'Jude' embossed alongside the holy man's indistinct left arm – Jude the patron saint of patience and resignation.

'Damn and blast!' Father Keogh snatched the medallion back. He began to feel in his jacket pocket. 'That's the wrong one, Rex.

That's for pilgrims who come home no better than they went out.' He transferred the search to the other side of his coat. After much grunting and heavy breathing, he pulled out another medal with all the triumph of a greedy boy finding a silver sixpence in a Christmas pudding.

'This is the one. God bless you and may Our Lady of the Immaculate Conception intercede for you.'

The second medallion was smaller and even cruder than the first. The rubric around the figure of the Virgin was written in French. '*Marie conqus sans poene priez pour nous qui avons recours à vous.*'

Rex, who was afraid of losing his self control, spoke very slowly.

'I'm not a patient, Father. I'm here to help you and Father Eagan.'

Father Keogh took a step back as if he feared assault. Rex, suspecting that his denial was taken as confirmation of his disturbed condition, reached up to his suitcase on the rack.

'I have the bishop's letter telling me to come.'

As he struggled to open the rusty locks, Rex wondered if even the letter would provide sufficient proof of his sanity. He could imagine Father Keogh, who did not easily change his mind, believing that it had been written to spare the madman's feelings and guarantee his co-operation. He lifted his spare suit from the top of the case, dropped it on the carriage floor and made a frenzied search amongst the socks and shirts for the letter which he hoped would provide proof of his robust health.

'It's here somewhere.'

And as he burrowed amongst the handkerchiefs and pyjamas with increased desperation he began to fear that the evidence of his sanity had been left behind in Nottingham. He decided to telephone Bishop Dunn from London and ask for confirmation of his status to be telegraphed to Lourdes.

'Calm yourself, Rex.' Father Keogh was not a naturally sympathetic man and his advice sounded more like the result of irritation than the product of compassion. 'For goodness' sake sit down and have a cigarette.' He took out a packet of Player's Weights.

'Look.' Rex pulled the letter out of a shoe and waved it in Father Keogh's face.

'I believe you. If you say that you have a letter from the bishop, I have no doubt that you do.'

'Read it.'

Father Keogh was not a quick reader and it took him several minutes to absorb the single paragraph. To Rex's relief the Maltese cross on the side of the signature worked its magic.

'You must excuse me, Father Hattersley. I had heard—'

'You'd heard that I was half mad.'

'I fear that I was told something of the sort.'

'Well, I hope that you did not repeat the gossip. It's called bearing false witness.'

Rex was surprised by his own anger and astonished that instead of suppressing the rage he turned on his tormentor. In Bishop's House the hints and half suggestions about attributing his conduct to a nervous breakdown had seemed unimportant; no more than a convenient contrivance that smoothed his passage back into the heart of the Church as well as spared the Church an admission of his conscious apostasy. But face to face with the idea that he had lost his mind, he felt nothing but bitter resentment. He could not remember experiencing the feeling before.

There was a tap on the compartment door and a key turned in the lock. Michael Eagan, sensing the atmosphere, retreated.

'Where's mine?' It was clear that Rex was making some sort of accusation.

'Your what?' asked Father Keogh.

'My key. Since I'm not a lunatic and have a letter to prove it you can trust me not to lock myself in whilst I cut my throat.'

Rex could tell from Michael Eagan's expression that, behind his back, Father Keogh was making frantic signs. He feared that the priest's nicotine stained finger was being tapped against his brow or rotated at the side of his head.

'Father Keogh got the idea that I was ill. He was wrong. I'm here to work just like you. If you have a key, I should have a key.'

'Have mine,' said Michael Eagan. He lobbed it towards Rex who dropped the catch. 'We give them back at Marylebone.'

'Don't patronize me, Michael.' Rex was bent double retrieving the key from the floor. 'I'm not off my head, whatever you heard.'

'I heard that you'd given up and then come back. That's all.'

Rex threw his spare jacket into the suitcase and fastened the one rusty catch that snapped into place without coaxing. As he turned to lift his single piece of luggage back on to the rack, he prepared to shake himself free from an unnecessary helping hand. No help was offered. He needed the fresh air of the corridor. The compartment door, which Father Eagan seemed to have opened so easily, was stuck. He struggled alone until it slid back far enough for him to squeeze out into the corridor.

'Well, Father. What do you make of that?' said Father Keogh.

'I wouldn't have believed it. In Rome he wouldn't say boo to a goose. All he did was look at churches. Meekest chap I ever knew.'

THE CROSSING was worse than the Nottingham pilgrims had expected and the Société Chemins de Fer du Midi far less accommodating than they had been encouraged to believe. The train dawdled through France at little more than walking pace and made long stops at every station. New passengers, festooned in Lourdes medals and rosettes, jostled each other in the search for seats and had to be told, in Michael Eagan's hesitant French, that the compartments labelled 'Nottingham' were reserved and fully booked.

The new travellers, few of whom showed signs of affliction, clambered aboard weighed down with food. Baguettes stuck out from their bags like antennae. Bottles of exotic pickles were prised open whenever the train came to rest, and their contents extracted on the sharp point of murderous looking knives. Pieces of cheese were eaten like slices of cake and giant tomatoes cut up and shared between whole families. As the train travelled south, the tomatoes changed from red to yellow and were eventually replaced with onions. Despite the heat, all the English on board kept their corridor doors shut tight. The smell of French peasants *en fête* was too much to bear.

Before the train reached Lourdes, the smell transcended nationality. By the time it reached Paris the lavatories were blocked and full. They overflowed at Limoges and at Toulouse the urine ran under the doors and across the corridors. It combined with vomit and sweat to produce a stench that seemed to thicken the air. Most of the sick were comatose and silent by the end of the first day. But the more quiet the hopeful patients became, the greater the noise that was made by their friends and families as they roamed up and down the train in search of remedies for their own minor illnesses. Father Keogh and the nuns issued Aspirins, Beecham's Pills, Fenning's Fever Cure and a thick white medicine which had been bought by the pint from Boot's Pure Drug Company.

Michael Eagan sat in the corner of the priests' special carriage and fought in vain to prevent his aching shoulders from shaking with a convulsive nausea. Father Keogh, because of his indomitable constitution, remained free of all infection. Rex avoided illness, at least in part, because of the nausea he felt whenever he saw evidence of his companions' various ailments. He dared not visit one of the fetid lavatories, and terror kept his bowels and bladder under rigid control. With every muscle tense, he counted off first the hours and then the minutes before he could enjoy the benisons of bath and bed.

He was not homesick until the train arrived at Lourdes and the tourists, first off the train, reminded him of the jostling crowd which surged out of Meadow Lane at the end of a Notts County home match. When they had pushed their way off the platform and out into the town, the local volunteers moved in to take command. There was a long wait in the sun whilst a search was made for the man with the purple carcinoma sprouting on his cheek. When he was found and seated next to Rex, the quartet set off for the cheap pension which was to be their hospice.

The missing pilgrim, speaking with obvious difficulty, identified himself as Paul Knox, a gas fitter from Ashfield. With even greater effort, and the obvious acceptance of considerable pain, he complained to the three priests about the sores on the horse's withered flanks and urged them to stop the driver from slashing its bony ribs with his long whip. They pretended not to hear or not to understand.

An unshaven young man in a battered sun hat and dirty white sutane, who sat next to the driver, assured the pilgrims that the evening and the following morning were for resting. Nothing was expected of priest or layman until three o'clock the following afternoon. Rex, free at last, was violently ill in the earth lavatory. He washed in cold water and went to bed without eating.

When he woke at six o'clock he almost rushed, unshaven, into the bright sunlight, but habit restrained him and, in his hurry, he cut himself twice on the blunt, rusty, safety razor blade, so he went out with his face dotted with little scraps of bloody paper. The great basilica of Notre Dame would have been easy enough to find, for its spire pointed high to heaven above the houses. But he was not interested in anything which had been built so recently. He went in search of old churches, dark, mysterious and smelling of time and dust as well as of incense.

Rex was not a sophisticated man and he assumed that Lourdes, being Latin and Catholic, would be a replica of Rome. It was more like Nottingham early on the day that the Goose Fair began. All along the Boulevard de la Grotte, traders were setting up their stalls and piling them with tawdry ornaments and cheap mementoes. Priests were notorious bad customers so the hawkers made no attempt to sell him their plaster madonnas, replicas of Bernadette's handkerchief, framed portraits of Christ with His Sacred Heart exposed in lurid anatomical detail, pictures of the Pope, coloured glass rosaries, sandalwood crucifixes, brass candlesticks and sealed bottles of water from the holy spring.

One particular display was entirely dedicated to the Blessed Bernadette Soubiroux. He looked at the representation of the homely, peasant girl, bland in her plump innocence, and thought – before he had time to suppress the sacrilege – that it was impossible that such a person could have seen an apparition of the Virgin. Saints, to Rex, were gaunt men with beards, or haggard matrons whose faces bore the mark of Roman ravishing. Yet he was

expected to believe this sallow adolescent had seen eighteen visions
and discovered the mysterious fountain that cured the sick, healed
the afflicted and saved the dying. He turned into a side street. Long
ago, when his faith had almost failed in Rome, belief had been
reborn in the restrained magnificence of Santa Maria Maggiore.
He hoped to find a similar inspiration and the same stimulus to
faith in Lourdes. He looked all morning for a genuine Romanesque
church or Gothic chapel. He found greasy cafés, grubby houses
and dubious exhibitions which were more concerned with super-
stition than religion. He walked back to his lodgings.

Father Keogh stood in the dingy hall, mopping his face with a
spotted handkerchief.

'Father Eagan's still not well. It's a good time for a word.' He
pushed open the door of the dining room. Pots littered the table,
most of them still clean.

'I'm sorry for my stupid mistake. Though I must say, if you've
been depressed, this place is only likely to make you worse. God
forgive me, this town's a truly terrible place. I promise you, it will
all be different at the grotto. You'll see how the sick are affected.
I'm not saying there'd be miracle cures – cripples throwing away
their crutches, and so forth. Not at all. But there'll be miracles of
faith. Dying men and women who had lost all belief, returning to
the love of God . . .'

The sight of Father Keogh embarrassed was almost too painful
to bear.

'Look at the people, not the buildings. We've got a better
church in Mansfield. Not bigger but better. Better, at any rate,
inside. What I mean is, I know that it's not easy for you.'

'Thank you, Father.' Rex reached forward and shook Father
Keogh's hand as if they had met for the first time. He wanted to
show affection as well as gratitude. The old priest smiled at last.

'We're not going up to church this afternoon. They're not up
to it. Most of them will stay in bed. If you'll take my advice, you'll
go for a walk outside the town. There's an old castle on the other
side of the river and a couple of hills you can walk up easily
enough. I've done it and I'm nearly twice your age.'

'Will you come with me?'

They walked together along the bank of the Gave de Pau and climbed to the ramparts of the ancient fortress. From the Tour de Garnabie they looked out over the elaborate spire of the basilica.

'It's going home that worries me.' Rex was not in a mood for churches. 'If I'd come here with cancer, and had to go home just as ill as when I came, I'd feel—'

'You simply do not understand, my son. It's your strange state of mind. They'll go home renewed in spirit if not in body or mind. It's a wonderful experience they'll have tomorrow. Elating. You can share it, if you choose to. They'll feel close to God and His saints. They may not be cured by a miracle, but they'll feel touched by one. They'll go home in joy.'

The salt throbbed in Rex's wound. The Church was still a refuge. But although it provided comfort, it no longer offered contentment. It was not that he did not believe in the miraculous spring and the sallow saint. His life was dedicated to regret and he would go home believing not that he had been touched by a miracle but that he had once held happiness in his hand and he had let it escape.

'Anyway,' Rex hardly heard Father Keogh's announcement. 'You'll not have to face it for a little while. The bishop wants you to stay and look after the pilgrims until Whitsuntide.'

BISHOP DUNN held the letter at arm's length as if it were contaminated by the germs of a lethal disease. The envelope had been marked 'Personal. Private and Confidential', but Father Ellis had opened it in the honest belief that it contained no more than another message of goodwill. The first paragraph was enough to convince him that providence had delivered it into his hands. He gave it at once – the rest unread – to his bishop, who was equipped neither by temperament nor experience to understand its purpose and meaning.

It began as an apology, continued as justification for unspecified mistakes and went on to emphasize the regret with which those errors were remembered. The bishop recognized the sadness, but he did not understand that it represented Enid's last desperate attempt to persuade Rex to return, save her from marriage to Jack O'Hara and claim her as his own.

The letter ended with what he believed to be a statement of firm intention but was meant, by Enid, to be the last spur to dramatic action.

'I plan to marry Jack O'Hara in June.'

The bishop was rarely afflicted by agonies of indecision, but it took him several seconds to decide what should happen to the letter. He detected a finality about its tone which made it unlikely that Enid would either write to Rex again or speak to him about a message to which he had not replied. Since she was so clearly concerned with Rex's welfare, even she would accept on reflection that Rex's best interest was served by allowing nothing to disturb his intention to return to the priesthood. The letter was of no importance and would only serve to induce another bout of melancholy. Bishop Dunn hesitated. Then he tore the letter into a score of tiny pieces and dropped the fragments into his wastepaper basket.

CHAPTER EIGHT

EVERYONE AGREED that it should be a quiet wedding, but the more they talked about it, the louder the noise became. The noise was usually the sound of argument and the most frequent arguments were about clothes, although Enid – who had been expected to be difficult about every detail – was strangely silent.

Anxiety about Rex replying to her letter had grown into an obsession. At first, she had merely waited anxiously for the postman. But when, at last, she was convinced that he would not come, she was preoccupied with a single question. Why had Rex ignored her? All the talk of pattern books and samples of material washed over her.

'It's not like Enid,' Agnes said to Anne whilst her daughter was out in the kitchen repelling Mick's sexual assault on a table leg. 'She's usually so definite about things.'

'She's not like her normal self at all,' said Lottie. Enid was so unlike her normal self that, after another desultory hour of half-hearted interest, she accepted a pattern that she had rejected out of hand at the beginning of the discussion.

Katherine Fox agreed to be the bridesmaid but assumed that the bride's family would buy her dress. Lottie offered to use all her talents to make her one which did justice to the occasion but was not 'unreasonable'. Worksop defined reason as saving money.

Agnes and Anne agreed that it was not reasonable to expect Lottie to put her talents at the disposal of the second bridesmaid. Gwendoline Ferguson, the youngest daughter of Jack O'Hara's landlady, had been invited to participate in the ceremony at the last minute, after an intemperate intervention by her mother.

A week before she was due to sail, Jack's ancient grandmother had decided that crossing the Irish Sea was too dangerous to risk. The letter explaining that she would be present at the wedding only in her thoughts, ended with the hope that one of the bridesmaids would 'represent her'. Mrs Ferguson treated the suggestion like one of the dying wishes which she so frequently passed on to her young men. The request was irresistible and the landlady naturally took it for granted that the principal beneficiary should be a member of her family. Gwen was nominated second bridesmaid. Jack bought her a ready-made dress.

The purchase of Jack's own suit provoked almost as much anguish as Mrs Ferguson's suggestion that Enid should buy the second bridesmaid's dress. When he announced that it was to be tailor-made in Nottingham, Agnes asked him if he could afford such extravagance and he replied that he would get it on 'the never-never'.

'Jack,' she entreated. 'Don't do that. Promise me you won't start your life in debt. I know what it's like worrying where the next penny is coming from. Don't begin with debts round your neck.'

'It's not debt. 'It's HP,' Jack told her.

Neither the nice distinction nor his matter-of-fact manner calmed Agnes's fears, so he told her that he would draw his savings out of the Penny Bank and pay cash.

'Promise me you won't do that. Promise me you won't start married life with nothing to fall back on.'

Agnes's total collapse was, paradoxically, averted by the arrival of Brack who, hearing that the groom was to have a tailor-made suit, said that the father of the bride would do the same.

'And what's more, I'm going to pay them two sisters of yours for her dress. I'll not be beholden to them two.'

It was clear to Enid that her father had recently enjoyed a winning streak. She was reassured to remember that Worksop would provide her dress whatever run of luck he endured in the week before her wedding day.

Agnes, who seemed to find menace in her husband's decision to buy a bespoke suit, asked him, 'Why do you have to spoil everything?' Brack told her that she 'got dafter by the minute'.

The final argument concerned the best man's clothes. Jack said that his brother Eamon would need a completely new outfit – 'shirts, shoes, the lot' – and Agnes told him that there was no reason why he should pay for it. Jack won her round with a simple sentence.

'It's the only way to do justice to Enid.'

The disputes about the wedding breakfast were trivial, all of them concerned with the place in which it would be held. At first, Jack took it for granted that the reception would be held in the Miners' Welfare but, because of its association with alcohol, Agnes ruled the venue unsuitable. Lottie, Anne and Ernest would certainly refuse to be guests at any reception held on its premises. St Joseph's parish hall was then suggested, but Agnes expressed her surprise that anyone would expect her brother and sisters – having endured a Roman Catholic wedding service – to endure a Roman Catholic consumption of sweet sherry, pork pie and tinned salmon sandwiches. Once again, Brack intervened in the discussion in order to offer his help. Cobbler Jack's main room was available free of charge. Agnes asked him why he enjoyed torturing her, and the groom – denounced by Brack as too stupid to defend himself against the monstrous regiment of women – sat silently in the corner. He had already decided that the Brackenburies were arguing for arguing's sake and that next day on his way home from the pit, he would book the back room at the Miners' Welfare.

The longest and most passionate argument went on inside Enid's heart and head. A decision had to be taken about whether or not she joined the Catholic Church. For her status – true believer or member of a disparate cult – would determine the form of the wedding ceremony itself. Jack, who had no stomach for theology, had announced himself content with a mixed marriage. All he wanted was a decent wedding.

Enid did not like the idea of becoming a Catholic, for she still felt an emotional sympathy for the rationalists of the Independent Labour Party who had encouraged her to believe that she possessed an intellect of such transcendental glory that only the wickedness of the capitalist world prevented her from achieving her prodigious potential. On the other hand, she was about to marry a Catholic in a Catholic church and she was instinctively opposed to going through that process as a spiritually poor relation. She wanted to travel first class into marriage. But, more than that –

more than almost anything – she wanted to do what Rex would expect of her.

Enid was quite sure that she was in love with Rex; in love with him in every way in which a woman can be in love with a man and incapable of ever loving anyone else with the same complete and all encompassing intensity. She was also sure that she would never see him again, at least in circumstances which allowed their old relationship to flicker into a moment's life. She might catch a glimpse of him across the road in Nottingham or watch him bend over a bookstall in Chesterfield. But it would never be the same. She spent desperate hours wondering whether or not she wanted suddenly to be confronted with the sight of that slightly stooping figure, the carefully combed-back hair and the *pince-nez* spectacles that always seemed about to fall from his nose. She was not sure if she longed for the brief sight of him or feared that – once she saw him again – her whole, precariously constructed world would collapse.

She was, however, sure that she wanted to behave as he would have her behave, particularly in her relationship with those things which she believed to be of greatest importance to him. Most of all, she wanted to treat his Church in the way which, were he to know of it, would make him understand that his high opinion of her was justified. Her problem was that she did not know what he would want her to do.

Sometimes she thought that he would want her to become a pious Catholic, to kneel in St Joseph's before the chipped statue of the old man with a lily in his hand and swear that she believed all that the Church had taught her. But, just when she had convinced herself that she could at least pretend that the Pope was infallible, she began to wonder if that was what Rex really wanted. He had fallen in love – if he had fallen in love at all – with the young woman who chose to argue with the catechisms rather than learn them unthinkingly by heart. He had always known that she found the idea of the stigmata repugnant and the notion of purgatory absurd. If she became a meek Catholic with a lace mantilla and theatrical genuflections whenever she walked in front of the altar, she would be (or pretend to be) a different person – hardly recognizable as the woman who had cycled with him through the dukeries, rowed with him on the Trent at Beeston and, above all, argued with him about every subject under the sun. Although she wanted to embrace the Church which she thought was again Rex's whole life, she also needed to remain the woman he had loved. It was a dilemma which Father Fisher, during her renewed instruction, did nothing to resolve.

'You can't pick and choose. It's as simple as that.' He was making his last desperate attempt to concentrate Enid's mind on the real issue that she faced. 'And you have to make up your mind today, at least about the wedding.'

'Do I have to believe it all?'

'If you were only sceptical about the Roman soldiers being instantly converted by the sight of St Catherine shattering the wheel—'

'Were they?' Enid asked. 'I didn't know that. How did she shatter it?'

'I only gave that as an example of the minor—' The adjective was a mistake and Enid pounced on the error. 'What are the major things? Make me a list and I'll tell you how many I believe.'

'I can't possibly do that. The whole body of belief is so large.'

'Then how can I be expected to believe it all in a few weeks? It's all right for you. You were born a Catholic. You could announce tomorrow that you had doubts about baptism of desire.'

'Where did you learn about baptism of desire?'

'Father Hattersley and his brother – his brother George, the older one who's in Spain – not Syd, that's the younger one at Ratcliffe College, though he was there too. I got on very well with Syd. I got on with George as well. Rex and George discussed it. It made no sense to me.'

Enid instantly regretted her admission, but it was too late. She had said it without thinking and by saying it probably sacrificed whatever chance she ever had of joining the Church of Rome and Rex. All she could do – all that temperament allowed and her reckless instinct prompted – was to justify her heresy.

'I can't see how you can possibly say that a baby would have chosen to be a Christian if he had known about it. You might as well say that I'd choose to be a Catholic if there wasn't something inside my head that . . . that . . .'

'That stopped you believing in the baptism of desire.'

'You can catch me out if you try to. I left school at fourteen. That was an extra year, of course. Most people left at thirteen. I've not had your education. You don't have to rub it in.'

She had said much the same to Rex when he argued with her about the catechism. It had happened in the same room less than a year ago, but it seemed like part of a dream – the dream in which they had first admitted that they were in love. Rex's dog – the collie that he had not wanted but had been forced upon him by Enid Brackenbury – had been killed in the road. And Rex had cried. Until then she had thought of him looking after her. At that moment, she had wanted to look after him for ever. Her eyes filled with tears and, in order not to make an exhibition of herself in front of the priest, she turned towards the window.

For the first time during their unhappy relationship, Father Fisher felt sorry for her. He was not a compassionate man but when the thick seam of insecurity showed through the top dressing of arrogance, it was clear how unhappy the life that lay ahead of Enid Brackenbury would be. She would grow old defending herself against imagined slights and demonstrating that she possessed unacknowledged talents.

'I was more helping you out than catching you out.'

'But I'm not as stupid as you think.' Enid hated being patronized far more than she disliked being contradicted. 'I understand about these things. You can pick and choose because you were born a Catholic, and that isn't fair. For all I know, you don't believe in baptism of desire either.'

'For heaven's sake forget about baptism of desire. It isn't important.'

'Then why do I have to believe in it?'

Father Fisher decided to try just once more.

'Just listen for a minute. Don't interrupt. Just concentrate. Make sure that good mind of yours is taking it all in.'

The reference to her good mind did the trick. Enid furrowed her brow and stared into the priest's face. He built on his success.

'I know it's more difficult for you than it would be for some people. Some of the young women round here – the girls in service, the shop assistants – would just agree to everything without thinking about it.'

'What good would that be?'

'Listen, Enid. Listen for once in your life. You think about things. So, of course, you have doubts. What we need from you is the will to believe. The desire to accept what is good and true—'

'How do we know that it's—'

'Listen! If you want to become a member of the true Church, you will believe in its teaching. Remember the casting out of the dumb spirit . . .'

It seemed a particularly inappropriate miracle to use to illustrate Enid's condition.

'Remember. "Lord, I believe, help thou my unbelief." You've started to believe. "All things are possible to him that believeth." You're half way there. You believe in God already. That's why you don't have to be christened. Your parents have already dedicated you to God and you confirmed it at your first communion.'

'Not first communion. That's a Catholic idea. I confirmed it myself at confirmation in Steetly Chapel where my grandfather, my mother's father . . .'

'Exactly. You confirmed it when you learned the creed.' He added 'more or less' when he remembered their recent argument about the Catholic habit of leaving out the final reference to kingdom, power and glory. 'Take any line of the creed. You believe in the life everlasting.'

'And if God chooses we'll but love each other better after death.' Enid misquoted Elizabeth Barrett Browning with a passionate certainty.

'There you are then. All you have to do is decide what you want. If the voice inside you tells you that it's right, all the rest will follow. I'm sure Father Hattersley told you that.'

Enid could not remember.

'Yes, he did.'

'And I'm sure that he thought that you had the capacity for belief. Otherwise he would not have wanted—'

'Do you think that he wanted me to become a Catholic?'

'Of course he did.'

It was not a subject that the two young priests had discussed, but Father Fisher felt totally justified in asserting his predecessor's enthusiasm for Enid's conversion. Father Hattersley was, after all, a product of an institution which had been founded to train priests for the specific task of reversing the great Tudor apostasy. Father Hattersley wanted every soul in England to find comfort and consolation in the Church of Rome.

'I will,' said Enid. 'I will. I've been thinking about it and I will. Yes, please.'

'Then we had better get to work straight away. Have you still got your copy of the catechisms?'

'It's still a month to the wedding.'

'It's only three weeks before I go back to Mansfield. I'd like to present my successor, whoever he is, with a brand new parishioner.'

Enid walked slowly home. She was to become a Catholic because she believed that Rex wanted her to join his Church. Yet she was marrying Jack although she knew that Rex – like almost everyone else she knew – thought that the marriage would be a disaster. She had never before felt so confused. The idea of becoming Mrs Jack O'Hara in four weeks' time seemed ridiculous and nothing frightened Enid more than the risk of looking absurd. So did the notion of conversion to Catholicism. If her only wish was to do what Rex wanted, it was better to leave Jack than to join the Church.

The idea that she would be breaking off the engagement because of her love for Rex added so much emotion to the enterprise that she felt ready to face both Jack and the neighbours who had read the announcement in the *Mansfield Guardian*. It was the essential romantic justification for doing what she wanted to do for the most prosaic of all reasons: the certainty that marrying Jack would be marrying beneath her.

She did not even think of how wrong she had been to accept Jack's proposal. Nor did she regret losing her nerve so often that the rejection and parting had been postponed until a month before the wedding. She did not even feel remorse that she was about to cause such pain. Escape was all that concerned her – and the joy of believing that it was all done out of love for Rex.

Jack was sitting on the wall outside her father's yard, swinging his legs and throwing pebbles at the lamp-post. He had become the epitome of all that Enid despised about miners.

Instead of walking down the road to meet her, he took aim and let fly again. There was a clang of metal on stone as he hit the target and he let out a yelp of joy before he even acknowledged Enid's arrival.

'Your dad's just gone out. In a terrible hurry by the look of things. Never even spoke.'

He tried to put his arm round her waist but she sidestepped him.

'Why didn't you go in?'

'I was waiting for you to come. I wanted a word on our own.'

Enid had no doubt that Jack chose to sit in the cold rather than talk to her mother. She had even overestimated his kindness.

'Well, let's go in now. Mam's on her own.'

Jack gripped her by the wrist whilst he took a metal crucifix out of his pocket. It was suspended on a rosary like a locket on a chain.

'If you're going to be a Catholic, I wanted to give you this. I gave one just the same to Eamon at his first communion. Mam got it for me.'

Enid took it from him and held it at arm's length. The cross with its tortured figure swung like a pendulum from the string of cheap glass beads. It was not the image of Rex's Church which she cherished. Indeed, she felt nothing but horror at the thought of living with that memorial to grief and suffering for the rest of her life – in her handbag most of the day, over her bedhead at night and, horror of horrors, slipping through her hands during the mass. She could not even bring herself to thank Jack for the gift. Instead she gave him a forced smile. It was enough to make him happy.

Breathless with pleasure, he followed her through the kitchen and into the half-lit living room.

He heard Enid scream before he saw her mother slumped over

one arm of her wheelchair. At first, he feared that Mrs Brackenbury was dead, but as he rushed towards her she lifted her head. A
purple bruise swelled under her eye and a trickle of blood ran from
the corner of her mouth. As she turned towards him her open
handbag fell from her knee to the floor.

'You shouldn't have tried to stop him.' Enid knelt by her
mother's side and dabbed at the blood with her handkerchief. 'You
should have let him have it.'

'It was for your wedding present. He took every penny.'

'It doesn't matter, Mam.' She turned to Jack and told him, 'Get
her a drink of water. Let the tap run for a bit.'

Jack obeyed her instruction. When he returned to the living
room Agnes Brackenbury, much recovered, was telling Enid,
'You've got to get me away. I can't stand it any longer. You've got
to get me away.'

'It's all right, Mam,' Enid said. 'We'll all be gone in a month.
That's what I've just been to see the priest about, isn't it?'

AT FIRST Herbert Hattersley chose not to believe that Syd really
wanted him to visit Ratcliffe, although he had been once before
and had enjoyed his afternoon. Everybody that he had met seemed
anxious to make him feel at home and the monks had all congratulated him on fathering so clever and athletic a son. Syd had been
attentive and introduced him to all his friends with what seemed to
be genuine pride and pleasure. It had been a good day, even allowing for the two-hour journey at each end and the necessity of
keeping his shoes laced and his collar fastened from start to finish.
But he had a special reason for not wanting to see Syd for a week or
two. He had a decision to take and Syd would not help him take it,
so when he got the postcard from his son asking him to come to
the opening cricket match of the season, he tried to persuade
himself that the invitation had been sent out of duty or on instruction. He convinced himself that Syd did not really want him there.
Mrs Nicholls thought different.

'You'd enjoy yourself no end. Day in the sun, watching Syd
play cricket. It'd be a real treat. You'd be so proud of him.'

'Not if he was hit all over the ground, I wouldn't.'

Mrs Nicholls knew nothing about cricket. Her late husband had not been a sporting man and she had never learned the strange language of the game. But she understood from Herbert's tone that he was talking about the possibility of Syd failing in some way. Anticipating disaster was so alien to Herbert's character that she wondered if he was sickening for something.

'But I thought Syd was a champion cricketer.'

'Nobody talks about champion cricketers. Champion boxer, but not champion cricketers. You know nothing about it.'

The bad temper was even more unusual. He was obviously upset, but Mrs Nicholls was not the woman to let things rest. She was determined to talk him into a better mood.

'Is something the matter, Bert? You'll feel better if you get it off your chest. You can tell me. You can tell me anything.'

'Nothing's the matter. I just don't want to go traipsing off to Ratcliffe, that's all. There'd be something wrong with me if I did.'

Herbert had no intention of prolonging the argument which was disturbing his reading of the *Sunday Empire News* and preventing Mrs Nicholls from preparing the dinner. There was only one way to ensure that life returned to its normal state of tranquillity and that his bottle of brown ale was placed by the side of his chair at one o'clock.

'You know I'll go in the end.'

He rustled his paper as a sign of his wish to retreat into the privacy which it provided. Mrs Nicholls was merciless. She took Syd's postcard from the mantelpiece and held it at arm's length. After several attempts to read the tiny handwriting she tapped on the newspaper as if it were a door behind which Herbert sheltered.

'Right. I'll make sure that your best suit's had an iron on it. You can't go amongst all those clergymen looking anyhow. Can't let young Syd down. Got to do your best.'

Herbert set off with exactly that intention.

The journey was, like all journeys, tedious and uncomfortable. But the train pulled into Leicester on time and the bus to Ratcliffe trundled along the Fosse Way with such meticulous respect for the Trent Traction Company timetable that Herbert arrived a quarter of an hour before Syd expected him.

It was a warm spring day and Herbert, having consulted his pocket watch and confirmed that he was early rather than abandoned, sat on the grass verge which separated the wide college lawn from the tarmacadam. He was half asleep when Syd tapped him on the shoulder.

'Did I make you jump?'

'I think I just nodded off for a moment. Clear conscience, that's what it is.'

He held out his hand as if they had just been introduced. Mrs Nicholls had told him that Syd would not welcome a show of affection. Syd hugged his father in exactly the way which Herbert had been told to avoid. In the violence of the embrace, his cricket cap – green and white rings with the college's winged cross crest above the peak – fell on to the gravel drive. Herbert bent to pick it up, but his son moved more quickly.

'Give it here.' Herbert beat it against his leg to remove the dust. 'What time do you start?'

'Not for an hour. We've got to go and see the President first, he wants to meet you.'

Herbert's heart sank. 'Is that why you wanted me to come? You should have said.'

'No. Honest, Dad. I wanted you to see the cricket. It was when Father Cremonini heard you were coming that he said he'd like a talk.'

'Your brother didn't get on with him. He's a foreigner.'

'It's a different one, Dad. It's the other one's nephew. And they are both English.'

Everything about Syd impressed his father: the broad shoulders, the striped cricket blazer, the canvas boots which (from a distance) were almost indistinguishable from the buckskin worn by real professional cricketers and, most of all, his lordly self-confidence. 'If I didn't know better,' Herbert said to himself, 'I'd think that he's been born and bred a proper gentleman.'

Father Cremonini's study fascinated Herbert. He had inherited his father's passion for what, in his home town, was known as 'quality': oak, iron and brass transformed by time-served craftsmen into objects of complicated, though slightly heavy, beauty.

The President of Ratcliffe had a quality desk which the college servants had polished until the dark wood glowed a burnished brown and the locks and handles shone as if they were made of pure gold. Herbert ran his finger along the bevelled edge like a man making sure that the dusting had been properly done.

'Sit down, Mr Hattersley. You too, Hattersley. Sit down.'

Herbert, although momentarily confused by the instruction, sank gracefully into the armchair which faced Father Cremonini. Syd sat erect on the high stool by the door.

'You must be very proud of him.'

'Yes, sir. I am. And if his mother were still alive, she'd be prouder still. It's thanks to her that he's here.'

'He's going to be a credit to both of you, whatever he does. The problem is, Mr Hattersley, that he's finding it difficult to decide.'

Father looked at son in the hope of help. Syd, who was staring into the half distance, did not change his expression. But he twisted his cap in his hands in a way which made Herbert fear that he would break the peak.

'I'll recommend him for Rome if he wants to go. But it's his decision. If he's lost his vocation – or never had it – we've got to start thinking of how we can get him into a university. I don't think that he'll get a scholarship. At least not one that will keep him. And I doubt if you can afford to send him unless you get some sort of help . . .'

Pride prevented Herbert from nodding his anxious agreement. But Father Cremonini had no doubt that what he said was true.

'It's for him to say, sir, not me.'

Herbert resented his day being spoilt by difficult questions about his son's future. But Father Cremonini was as remorseless in pursuit of the subject as Mrs Nicholls had been in her insistence that he should make the journey to Ratcliffe.

'I understand, very well, Mr Hattersley that you can't give your son spiritual advice. But you can help him to be settled in his own mind. He seems very . . . very insecure about home.'

Herbert would have found it difficult to discuss such questions at the easiest of times, but he was quite incapable of responding to

questions about Syd's state of mind with the disturbed young man
sitting silent and immobile by Father Cremonini's study door. He
looked at his son and then he looked in turn at his feet and his
fingers. Father Cremonini took pity on him.

'Think about it, Mr Hattersley. Think if there's anything you
can do.'

The President rose majestically behind his desk. Herbert stood
up with matching dignity. Syd slid silently off his stool and followed his father through the door.

'Don't take any notice of that stuff about being unsettled,' said
Syd. 'I don't know where he got it all from. I suppose it's because I
don't want to be a priest any more.'

They crunched across the gravel which separated the school
from the cricket field. Syd waited for his father to reply, but
Herbert had nothing to say.

'I expected him to say something about Roy.' Syd knew that
his father had never quite accepted the name that his brother had
been given at Ratcliffe. 'That's what's behind it. He thinks that
Roy's persuaded me to give it all up. But he's wrong. I just don't
see myself as a priest.'

'I don't blame you. It wouldn't do for me at all.' Herbert was
thinking of discipline and celibacy.

'Look, Dad. If you go off before the match is finished I might
not get another word. I'll have to have lunch with the team. You
can get yours in the marquee. It'll only be sandwiches and ginger
beer.'

Syd hugged his father so hard that his cap fell off for the second
time that day. As a mark of respect he dusted it before he put it
back on his head.

'Wish me luck. I'll see you soon.'

Herbert sat on the nearest bench and watched his son run to the
pavilion. He took off his jacket and folded it with loving care
before he carefully laid it on the seat beside him. Other parents and
friends, applauding Trent College coming to field, woke him at
five minutes to eleven.

There was Guinness as well as ginger beer in the lunch tent.
Syd, batting number seven, scored nineteen not out and, when

Trent College batted, took five wickets for forty runs. After he had run half way round the boundary to take a skied catch, an elderly gentleman in a straw hat announced, 'That young man will play for Nottingham one day.'

'That's my lad,' said Herbert.

'You must be very proud of him,' the elderly gentleman replied, echoing the words of Father Cremonini. 'What a happy day this must be for you.'

Herbert was very proud of Syd. But it was not a happy day. He had travelled to Ratcliffe determined to tell his son that he was, after all, going to marry Mrs Nicholls. But he had lost his nerve. He returned to Nottingham wondering if he should write with the good news or if he should arrange the wedding and worry about Syd finding out when the summer holidays began.

REX SPENT a desultory month in Lourdes. On some days he did nothing to help the sick pilgrims and on others he did very little. His frustration was intensified by the feeling that he ought to be enjoying himself. Most of the time he lived the life of a tourist. Had he been told, before he left England, that he would spend four sunny weeks visiting the valleys of the Gavarnie and Heas, he would have regarded the prediction as too good to be true. But, as was so often the case in Rex's life, realization did not live up to expectation. He worked hard at seeing all the sights. But the sightseeing brought him little joy.

He could not afford the price of a seat on the funicular railway, but he walked up the steep slopes of Pic du Jer and Le Beaut and gazed up to the high peaks of the Pyrenees. He knew that he should marvel at their majesty. But all that he could think of was Spain and his brother George on the other side of the mountains.

Anything called a museum attracted him. So on the days when he had duties to perform in the town, he spent his spare hours in the Musée Pyrénéen. It was a profound disappointment. Souvenirs of the early mountaineers – all of whom were Victorian Englishmen – stimulated a passing pride. But the lithographs held no attraction and the local fauna little charm. Rex wanted armour and weapons, cannonballs collected on the fields of battle and fragments of parchment maps which had once marked the lines of heroic rearguards and the paths of reckless cavalry charges. He was the least warlike of men, but he thought of history as a catalogue of kings and wars, the subjects to which the museum in Nottingham Castle was devoted.

At Saint-Pé-de-Bigorre he found at least ruins which had once been fit to compare with the churches that glorified every street in Rome. He stood in the shadow of the crumbling tower and thought of the Cluniacs guarding the road to Compostella and tried to convince himself that their history was his history, that he was heir to the Knights Templars and Knights Hospitallers who had once passed that way. But every picture of crusaders that he painted in his mind had Richard Coeur de Lion at its centre. He was, he feared, becoming incorrigibly English.

During his third week of virtual inactivity he walked each afternoon to one of the little towns which were recommended on the tourist map – Barèges, Argelès-Gazost and Luz San-Sauveur. Each one was wildly different from anything that he had seen before, but on each visit he saw something that reminded him of England. The Grottes de Betharram were twice as high and three times as wide as the Blue John Caves at Castleton which he had explored on one of his days out with Enid. But he thought the Laverd in every way inferior to Derbyshire.

Rex had been taught to believe that his home was the Church, where even the common mass was spoken in the common language. And for years he had struggled to believe it. At Lourdes he felt dispossessed. It was, he told himself, the penalty of growing old. He was twenty-nine and he possessed nothing except a spare set of clothes, a rolled-gold cigarette case, a dozen books, two battered brass vases and a painted Buddha that he had left on his father's sideboard. When he received the telegram that called him home, his first thoughts concerned not what he would be told to do but where he would be expected to live. The bishop had told him that the leatherette armchair, the fake Jacobean dining table and the four almost matching chairs which he had left in the presbytery in Langwith Junction, were stored safely in Bishop's

House. If he reclaimed his property, he could begin to put down roots.

The journey home was better than Rex had expected. There were no English pilgrims travelling that day and the sick and dying from the north of France returned to their homes and hospitals as cheerful as Father Keogh had promised that they would be. The Blessed Bernadette had wrought no miracle for them. But, as far as Rex could make out, they did not even ask themselves why she had chosen not to intercede on their behalf. They had seen the spot where the Holy Mother of God had appeared in a vision. They had drunk the blessed water which had suddenly flowed out of the barren rock. They had been closer to God than ever before and whilst His mysteries remained mysterious, they had felt His presence and, in consequence, would die with grace. Rex feared that when he saw Bishop Dunn he would be expected to describe the marvel of unquestioning faith which he had witnessed. He rehearsed his lines. It was, he knew, a sin not to believe that what he said was true and an even greater sin to pretend that he believed it. But as he walked across Nottingham from the station to Bishop's House, he was not in a mood for theological niceties.

'My dear boy, welcome!' said Bishop Dunn as the housekeeper showed Rex into the study. 'We didn't expect you for another couple of days.'

Bishop Dunn had a talent, unique in Rex's experience, for disconcerting warmth. His greeting might have been intended either as a reproof or celebration. The only possible response was an apology.

'I'm sorry, my lord. I thought that you wanted me home at once.'

'I did, Rex. I did. But I didn't expect you. I'm delighted to see you. Lord be praised, you got here just before Mrs Griffiths left. She won't mind staying on to get your room ready. We can't have you sleeping in sheets that haven't been aired.'

It was summer and even Rex – innocent and unsuspecting – could not believe that sheets straight out of the linen cupboard would pose any great danger to his health. He decided to play the bishop at his own inconsequential game.

'I thought of staying with my father tonight. I simply came to tell you that I am back as instructed. There's really no need to trouble Mrs Griffiths. I shall go home.'

'You'll do no such thing.' Bishop Dunn had turned unequivocally jovial. 'It's worked out very well. It's a perfect opportunity for our talk.'

Rex told himself that he could live till dinner time. But it would not be easy. It was four o'clock and he had to survive until eight without knowing what the bishop wished to say in private. He was sure that he had done nothing wrong in Lourdes, for he had hardly done anything at all. The conversation was certain to concern his future and the parameters of pain and pleasure – the boundaries of the best and worst that could happen – were not so far apart as to justify much real anxiety. But he worried as he washed and changed his socks, and worried even more as he tip-toed towards the dining room.

Waiting did nothing to ease Rex's anxiety. There was no clock in the room and he had sold his pocket watch during the desperate days of January, so at first he feared that he had arrived ridiculously early. Then he was afraid that he should not be in the dining room at all. He was just about to edge towards the study door when Bishop Dunn appeared.

'When did you last have anything to eat?' He seemed genuinely concerned.

Before Rex had a chance to answer, the bishop began to describe the difficulties which he was facing in his heroic attempt to redecorate the Lady Chapel. He dwelled at length on the unreliability of monumental masons, the avarice of painters, the sloth of architects and, finally, the incompetence of Canon Hunt, the Cathedral Administrator. It was another half hour before he rang for the supper to be served.

They were well into mutton and boiled potatoes before the bishop put the question which Rex had assumed was the reason why they were spending the evening together.

'What do you want to do now?'

It was asked so casually that Rex could barely believe he was being invited to describe his hope of spiritual rehabilitation. He almost answered that he would like to walk round to the shop in the morning and see his father.

'Whatever you think best, my lord.'

Bishop Dunn did not hesitate.

'I'm sending you back to Langwith Junction.'

Jumbled words of protest ran through Rex's head.

'I can't face them. How can you expect . . . ? Half the village think that I went mad. Don't you understand that I need a fresh start? I can't just walk back as if nothing has happened. It isn't fair.'

But all he said was, 'She's still there.'

'Exactly. You'll have to face it, as you had to face it last year when I sent you back.'

'I failed you last year.'

'You went back and you tried. This time you must go back and succeed.'

'I can't.'

'You must. It's the only way. Do you remember what I told you last year? *Tu ne cede malis, sed contra audentior ito.*'

Rex remembered only too well. 'It is not by running away from evil that we overcome it, but by going to meet it.'

'It wasn't evil,' said Rex. 'It was good and pure.'

He had never argued with the bishop before. Indeed, he had hardly ever argued with anybody, and he did not enjoy the new experience. But whilst he was prepared to admit his own transgression, he could not allow even the faintest suggestion that Enid had behaved badly.

'Everything that you say makes it all the more important for you to go back. Rex, you'll go with my love and blessing. You know that already. You'll also go with my absolute confidence. I know you'll pull through.'

'I won't.'

'Won't?'

'I won't pull through.' It was not what Rex had meant but, despite his new independence, he was not ready to escalate his reaction from disagreement to defiance.

'Of course, you will. It won't be easy. But it will be easier than last time. You know about the young lady and this Mr O'Hara?'

'Yes, my lord. I do.' The thought of Enid's marriage had sobered him into submission.

'They're getting married quite soon.' The bishop spoke almost casually.

It took Rex some time to grasp the implication of what Bishop Dunn had told him. Even then he could not quite believe it.

'When am I to return to Langwith?'

'Straight away. Father Hugh leaves on Saturday. That's why I brought you back from Lourdes so quickly.'

'So I will . . . ?'

'Yes, Rex. You will. It will be the first wedding after you go back. Once that's over, the air will be properly cleared.'

CHAPTER NINE

PRIESTS LIVE solitary lives. Some enjoy being protected from the world by a shroud of mysticism. Others are destroyed by their isolation. Most accept their lonely state as an unavoidable consequence of their vocation for which they have been prepared by the strange social paradox of their training.

In Rome, Rex had spent seven years in a closed community of isolated individuals. He was not allowed to eat alone but forbidden to entertain a friend in his room. The rules required that he walked in the city each day with a group of seminarians but he was not allowed to choose his companions. As a result he left the English College without having made a close friend. He admired Frick Wilson, liked Hugh Atkinson and envied William Ellis, but he did not feel able to confide in any of them. Were he to ask them what he should do, they would – he had no doubt – give him the answer that the Church required of its faithful children.

There was no older priest to whom he could turn for advice. The bishop – who had once been, or seemed to be, his avuncular patron – had callously caused his agony. He was, Rex had no doubt, loyal only to Rome and its reputation.

Rex felt little more confidence in his family's capacity to guide him back to comforting certainty. Syd was too young to understand, George was a thousand miles away in Spain. Leslie and his sisters had all written to express their joy at his return to righteousness. If he went to them, they would treat him with appropriate deference, but they would not be able to disguise the anguish which his conduct had caused them. Aunt Clare, if asked her opinion, would reply with reminiscences of her own great love and homilies devoted to the beauty of sacrifice.

Rex was reluctant to make a second attempt at serious conversation with his father. But there was no one else to whom he could go. Herbert would, he knew, desperately try to avoid giving his advice, for responding to that request required him to face the harsh reality of his responsibilities – the notion that his son might be profoundly miserable and the idea that he might have a duty to help him find the way in which his happiness might be regained. But, at least, he would be sympathetic – unthinkingly and super-ficially sympathetic – but sympathetic nevertheless. He would be a kindly sounding board. And a sounding board was exactly what Rex needed.

He set off for the ironmonger's shop in Alfreton Road, after a sleepless night, an unwelcome breakfast and a brief conversation with a shamefaced Father Ellis. The bishop's secretary gave him a five-pound note, a single third-class railway ticket to Langwith Junction and the message that Bishop Dunn hoped he would return to his parish that afternoon.

The shop, and the room behind it, were somehow different. In the weeks whilst Rex had been away they had changed in a manner which he could recognize, but could neither describe nor under-stand. There was a new atmosphere which, since there was no sign of customers, could not be described as commercial bustle. But the counter was clean and the floor tidy. The glass in the showcase gleamed.

'Business going all right?' asked Rex, expecting his father to tell him of an anticipated surge in demand for two-inch nails and glue.

'It's been better. But we're managing. We've not sold a pair of scissors or a saw since you went away. It's the little things as keeps us going. Carpet tacks, stair rods, gas mantles. And electric light bulbs now. They don't last long . . . thank God . . .'

Herbert, remembering his son's calling, stifled the profane laugh. Rex wondered why his father had begun to use the royal plural.

'But how are you?' Herbert asked. 'That's the important thing. You didn't say much on those French postcards. For which, thank you very much, by the way.'

'There wasn't much to say, Dad. Not much of a place, Lourdes. I'm glad to be back.'

'And about to settle down again, if what I hear from Clare is true?'

Whilst Rex was working out whether the news of his future had reached his aunt three or four days before it was vouchsafed to him, Herbert began to fidget with his watch chain. Talk of his son's future was clearly an unwelcome diversion from the only subject that interested him.

'I think it's all sorted out, Dad.'

'That's all right, then. I'll make a pot of tea and then I'll tell you my news. You might not like it, mind. But best to get it over and done with.'

It took what seemed like an hour for Herbert to carry the teapot, a half empty bottle of milk, a bowl of damp and coagulated sugar and two cups and saucers out of the kitchen. Then he went back to search for a spoon which, when it was found, he used to dig pointlessly at the sticky mess in the sugar bowl.

'All right, Dad, you first or me?'

'Me.'

Rex should have known that his father was a changed man. Normally Herbert, who had never heard the Legend of the Salamander, had no fixed view about the best way of overcoming trouble except the importance of running away from it.

'I'm going to get married again. I've decided once and for all. I'm going to marry Mrs Nicholls. You know Mrs Nicholls. You've met her.'

At that moment, his father's intentions were supremely unimportant to Rex. For Herbert could not love Mrs Nicholls. At least he could not love her as Rex loved Enid. Nobody had ever been in love as he was in love. If his father wanted a housekeeper, that was his father's business. Rex's only concern was not to admit, by word or deed, that his father's search for comfort and companionship had anything in common with the great passion which he had felt and been forced to deny.

'What do you think?' Herbert asked.

'Whatever you want. It's up to you.'

'I told you. It won't be like your mother. But I do need somebody to keep an eye on me. You see what's she done to this place. Came in yesterday and went through it. She's done it every weekend. I get a hot Sunday dinner.'

'I understand, Dad.'

'So you'll come to the wedding?'

'Of course I will.'

'Even if it's at a registry office?'

'Yes. I've told you. I'll be there.'

'And you'll tell Syd for me, won't you. I've wrote to George. And I've told your sisters. Leslie is coming round tomorrow night. I reckon the girls will have told him and Dorothy already. But I'd be obliged if you told Syd.'

'Come on, Dad. You've got to do that yourself. I don't mind telling him. But what will he think? What will he think of you?'

'I tried the other day. I went all the way to Ratcliffe College to tell him. But the headmaster told me that he wasn't happy. So I couldn't. Not settled, he said.'

Rex was about to take responsibility but Herbert would not allow him even to share the guilt.

'And you know what's unsettled him? He doesn't want me to get married again. You tell him. Explain that it's only natural and that it won't be like his mother.'

'Saturday, Dad. I'll go down on Saturday.'

Herbert expressed his gratitude by opening his heart to Rex. He knew that he had been a bad husband – well, not a bad husband exactly but thoughtless. He had always made sure that nobody in his family ever went short, even when he had to give up his real trade and work as a labourer. The worst that he had done was stop off for a drink on the way home from work. He had virtually given up the singing by the time Augusta got ill. Just a song or two in the Grove Hotel on a Saturday night. Anyway, she had always admired his voice. If only she had told him how ill she was. How could he be expected to know? He was not a doctor. There were genuine tears in Herbert's eyes.

'I've been lucky in one thing. I've had wonderful children. I'm proud of you all. As proud as any father in the land. And poor old Bert would have been the same. He'd have made something of himself. Not a priest like you and George. But he'd have done all right, poor little bugger. Only eighteen . . .'

'Yes, Dad. I know.' Herbert's maudlin moods were not new to

Rex, but he was not used to seeing his father in tears and sober. The sobriety added to the embarrassment.

'And you will tell Syd. Explain to him why it's all right.'

'I promise. When's the wedding?'

'Next Monday.'

'That's before my wedding.'

'Your wedding?'

'The first wedding at Langwith Junction. The first wedding is Enid . . . Enid Brackenbury. I'm not sure that I can stand it, Dad.'

'Good Lord. You marrying her!'

It was not meant as a joke. To Rex's relief, his father had no idea that his intention might have been misunderstood, so he made no apology for his unhappy choice of words and there was no need to pretend that the pain it caused did not matter. He had given his father the little comfort of which, on that day, he was capable. It was his turn to ask for help.

'That's it, Dad. I wanted to marry her and I'm going to marry her.'

'You shouldn't joke about such things.'

'It's only because I don't know if I can go through with it.'

'She might like it. She might like the idea of having your—'

'Having my blessing.'

'I was going to say having your good wishes. I suppose it's more or less the same.'

'Yes,' said Rex. He had given up his attempt to find comfort in talking to his father.

REX WAS not sure what he expected to find in St Joseph's presbytery, but he was astonished to discover that the bishop had instructed that it be prepared for his return. The leatherette armchair with the ashtray fastened to the arm was back in front of the fireplace and the imitation Jacobean dining table had the same book under one short leg. The living room curtains, which had always hung precariously on their sagging wire, were still half drawn across the window. There was, he thought bitterly, no Mrs

Nicholls to come round on Sunday mornings to clean the house and cook his dinner.

The pile of books which he had left on the living room floor was undisturbed and he added the dozen he had brought back from Nottingham to the top of the heap. There were new saucepans hanging on the kitchen wall. None of them looked as if they been used. He was relieved to find something different. He remembered that he had taken the old saucepans when he made his escape and the memory gave a reality to the extraordinary events of the winter. Had everything been in its old place, it would have been difficult to believe that the last six months had ever been anything except a dream. Reassured that the world had really changed – and then changed back again – he climbed the stairs to investigate the bedroom.

The blankets were folded neatly on the bed and the wardrobe door was open. It was Rex's first moment of real panic. When last he had slept in that bedroom, George's old sports coat had hung in the wardrobe and his flannels – left behind after his brother's last visit to England – had been hidden under the mattress. They had been the disguise which made his escape possible and they had been left at Bishop's House, to be given to a beggar at the back door of the convent. He was trapped and he would remain a prisoner until Enid's wedding.

For the first few days he spent each morning mass staring out bleakly into the church as if he was searching amongst the dark pews for a familiar face. When the service was finished he stayed in the vestry until he was sure that all the congregation had left and then, when he had locked the door, tiptoed along the corridor that linked church to presbytery. A dozen parishioners called to welcome him back and wish him well. When he felt even reasonably confident that they thought he was at not home, he did not answer the door. Then he worried why they had not left him friendly notes. The few that he feared had noticed a light or heard a noise, were offered the priest's gratitude for their interest and, if they did not leave at once, were invited into the cold living room. Father Hattersley then thanked them for a second time and listened patiently to their expressions of concern in a way which made clear that his mind was on other – they hoped higher – things. On the mornings when the cleaning woman came, he took refuge in the church without even leaving her written instructions. As a result, there was no bread or milk for his Saturday morning breakfast and he left for Ratcliffe fortified by a single cup of black Camp coffee. He missed the train to Nottingham and the bus to Leicester was late. But Syd was still waiting. Rain had stopped play.

'I knew something was up when Dad came out last week.' The rain showed no sign of stopping and Syd seemed more concerned about missing the afternoon's cricket than his father's impending wedding.

'You mustn't mind. He's lonely sitting there at home. Wants to have his tea ready for him when he closes the shop. It's only natural.'

'Don't you mind it not being natural for you?'

'That's nothing to do with it. We're different.'

'I'm not. Didn't Dad tell you?'

'He told me you were unhappy. Father Cremonini said you were unsettled. Dad thought that was because of him getting married.'

'It's because I don't want to be a priest. That's what Father Cremonini told him, but he wasn't listening. He was just thinking about that Mrs Nicholls.'

They walked out together into the damp morning. On the cricket field, Syd groaned as his feet sank into the wet turf.

'We won't play today. Do you want a walk into the village?'

'Too wet, but I wouldn't mind a cup of tea.'

They squelched together up to the music room which boys of Syd's seniority were entitled to use for the entertainment of guests. The grand pianos inside the strange wire pens which Ratcliffe called the chicken coops, were Rex's first memory of the school. He had thought as he waited, new and nervous, for his tour of the building of his mother's sad stories about the piano which she had owned before she was married. He tried not to let the memory prejudice him against his father's plans to marry Mrs Nicholls.

Syd went to the scullery to make the tea and Rex switched on the little electric fire that stood against the wall. Then he took off

his shoes and socks and arranged them on an orchestra chair which
he had put near enough to the fire for the wet soles to feel its heat
but far enough away to make sure that the gold paint did not
blister.

When Syd came back, already eating a chocolate biscuit, Rex
asked. 'Got any cardboard?'

'I can find some.'

'And scissors?'

Rex took his still wet shoes and, holding them like a template
on the cardboard, drew a line round the welts. Then he cut out the
shape he had drawn. With the shoes back in front of the fire, he cut
out a second pair of soles.

'They'll not be dry this morning,' Syd said.

'They'll be drier.' Rex leaned over to the orchestra chair and
pulled two pieces of soggy cardboard from inside his shoes. 'This
wasn't thick enough.'

'Mine's not much better. Beer mats are the best.'

'I didn't know you were an expert,' Rex told him. 'I hoped
you'd never needed to find out about these things. Since you're so
wordly wise, there's something else you need to know . . .'

Rex had decided to make one last plea to Syd's better nature.
He could imagine his father's delight at the sight of his younger
son – splendid in the uniform of Ratcliffe College – arriving at his
wedding.

'I know what you're going to say. But it's no use. I never
wanted to be a priest. That was Mam's idea. At least that's what
everybody told me after she was dead. Anyway, nobody asked
me.'

'It's not that . . .'

'What is it, then? If it's not my duty to Mam, why should I
become a bloody priest? Don't you try to tell me that it's the voice
of God speaking inside me. It hasn't spoken inside you. And look
what a mess you've got into by pretending that it has. It's not
going to happen to me.'

Rex was overwhelmed by the violence of Syd's reaction, and
by the implied accusation that he would condemn his brother for a
life as miserable as his own.

'I'm not talking about Rome. All I want you to do is come to the wedding on Monday. It would make Dad happy. That's all.'

'Oh, is that all? I'll come to the wedding. But not to make Dad happy. If I understand anything about what's going on, you're going to feel the flames of hell. Your little brother had better be there to take some of the heat.'

The shoes were not dry, but Rex pushed the cardboard soles inside them and pulled on his damp socks. He had Syd's exeat to arrange. He felt loved again and he needed to make sure that the feeling lasted until the new Mr and Mrs Herbert Hattersley left the Nottingham registry office on the following Monday morning.

THE WEDDING, although bearing no resemblance to a real marriage, was not the ordeal which Rex had expected. Indeed, with Syd one pace behind him, he felt gratifyingly secure from the prying and the pressures of Langwith Junction. His brother, Leslie, although conscientiously unwilling to bear witness at a pagan ceremony, headed the gaggle of family guests and gave strength to his pious wife who had declared, on her way to the registry office, that it would be a miracle if she survived the ceremony without fainting. Rex and Syd, on the second row of hard chairs, were separated by their sister Muriel and her husband Bill, who, for some reason which Rex tried not to guess, found the whole occasion immensely amusing. His profane jollity infected Syd, who joined in the suppressed giggles when Herbert repeated his secular vows in his best baritone voice.

Aunt Clare, all religious scruples put aside, acted as one of the witnesses. Henry Chapman, the husband of Mrs Nicholls's friend, was the other. To Rex's relief his father's bride appeared to have no relations except the daughter and son-in-law who had lost their baby at Christmas. One stepsister was enough. Syd wanted to go back to Alfreton Road for the celebration that the new Mrs Hattersley had prepared, but Rex, fearing that his father would sing, reminded him that the exeat ended at three o'clock. They walked together to the station and ate meat pies in the railway buffet.

'It wasn't so bad, was it?' Syd sounded almost triumphant.

'Look here. There's no point in me being older and wiser if you keep improving on my fireside philosophy.'

'Older I grant you. Wiser I doubt.'

'To tell the truth, so do I.'

Syd grinned and then wiped his hand down his face as if to rub off the smile. He spoke slowly to match his solemn appearance.

'Can I come to Langwith on Friday? It's half term.'

'Of course you can. You don't need to ask.'

Rex felt the special guilt that comes from taking credit where no credit is due. Syd asked to come to Langwith Junction as if he were begging some sort of favour when, in reality, he was offering his brother the hope of remaining sane for the next awful ten days.

'You don't ever need to ask. You know that.'

'I was just being courteous, like what I was telt at that posh school. You know why I'm really coming. I'm coming to look after you.'

Rex was so elated by the proof of Syd's affection that on his way home he bought a newspaper for the first time since his return from Rome and turned first, just like the old days, to the cricket score on the back page. He had no interest in politics and the pages of debate about Philip Snowden's budget (all prophesying even greater austerity before the summer was over) had no relevance to his impecunious life. It was impossible for his existence to become more austere. He had read all that concerned him by the time that the train arrived at Langwith.

It was a warm afternoon and he enjoyed his walk from the station to the presbytery. Unknown colliers tipped their hats as they passed. The butcher slowed down his van, blew his horn and waved as he drove past. For a few minutes, the parish priest of St Joseph's felt that he could survive the wedding and might one day live in peace again. The key was, as always, under the brick on his front step. Inside the door lay a folded sheet of paper. It was a badly written note from Jack O'Hara delivered to remind him that Father Fisher, before his sudden departure, had agreed to spend that evening discussing the details of the impending nuptial mass.

★

JACK ARRIVED at the Brackenburys' half an hour before he was expected. A note in his pay packet had announced, in the most peremptory of terms, that the long promised house in Colliery Row would not be available until the end of August. If the wedding went ahead as planned, they would have to spend more than two months in Langwith Road. It was, Jack knew, only right to pass on the bad news to Enid before their meeting with the priest.

Enid greeted him with the friendly irritation which he expected. She hated him to be late but also reacted to his early arrival as if she had allocated him a specific part of her life and resented him taking more than his proper share. Before he had the chance to begin his story, she told him, 'Mam's been bad all day. You'll have to go on your own.'

'I can't go on my own. He wants to talk to both of us. That's what the meeting's for.'

To Jack, the switch in tactics was imperceptible.

'I meant that it's only polite for one of us to get there on time. You go first and I'll get down as soon as I can.'

'Shall we put it off altogether?' Jack tried to edge his way into the living room to see the invalid for himself, but Enid stood firm.

'Please, Jack. Don't be difficult. I've had a bad day and I need a minute or two's peace. Then I shall be all right.'

'I thought you said . . .'

Enid wiped the back of her hand across her brow in a theatrical gesture of exhaustion.

'Why can't you do what I ask without all this fuss? It's awful. All I'm asking you to do is get to the presbytery on time.'

She spoke with a finality which would have made it difficult for Jack to continue any sort of conversation. He did not even consider telling her that they would have to lodge, until the late summer, with the increasingly restless Brack.

Jack walked through Langwith as slowly as he could, but he still arrived at the presbytery long before his appointed time. He stood uneasily in the road and waited for seven o'clock.

He had kicked his feet in the dust for less than five minutes when the door opened and Father Hattersley called out to him in a voice which was so loud that it was almost unrecognizable.

'What you doing out there, man? Come in for heaven's sake.'

Startled by both the sudden invitation and its tone, Jack almost stumbled as he turned round. How did the parish priest know that he was there? He could not have been watching for him out of the window. That was not the sort of thing that parish priests did.

It was a balmy summer's evening and Jack was sweating inside his waistcoat. Father Hattersley grasped his hand in a greeting which was ferociously jovial and then slapped him on the back. The priest's face was redder than he remembered. Recalling that he had been to Lourdes, Jack wondered if it was tanned by the French sun.

'It's good to have you back, Father.'

'Thank you, Jack. Thank you very much. That's very nice. Very nice indeed. It's good to see you. It really is. Did you write to me whilst I was away? I can't remember. Come in, for goodness' sake. I can't have an old friend standing in the hall.'

They were only half way towards the living room when host suddenly turned on guest again.

'Where is she? She should be here. We can't do the job without her here. There's no show without Punch. Come into the living room. How many times do I have to ask you?'

Jack followed obediently before he started to answer the question.

'Her mother's not very well. She'll be down directly.'

'What's her mother coming for? She should be here herself.'

'I meant Enid. She'll be here any minute.'

'Well, let me get you a drink whilst you're waiting. Tea or something stronger? I've got some whisky left over from last Christmas. Blame Father Ellis. I opened the bottle for him.'

'Whisky,' said Jack, feeling that never in his life had he been more in need of a strong drink. 'Whisky, if you're having one.'

'I never touch it, but you must have a drink with me to celebrate.' Father Hattersley began to giggle.

The bottle and a glass were fetched from the kitchen. There was barely a measure left and Rex poured it all into the tumbler. Jack, who liked his whisky with ginger beer or lemonade, longed to ask for water, but was afraid of how the priest would respond.

They sat in silence until Jack had finished his drink. Then Rex walked over to the window, parted the lace curtain and looked up and down the road.

'Well, we'd better start without her. It's nuptial mass, isn't it?'

'Yes, Father. Father Fisher admitted her last week.'

'I'm not sure that we can get any choir boys on a Tuesday.'

'Friday, Father.'

'That's just as bad. Difficult enough getting servers.'

'We thought of only having one hymn. Mrs Ferguson, my old landlady from Mansfield, will play the organ.'

'Who's your best man?'

'My brother, Eamon.'

'Is he a Catholic?'

'He's my brother. I said.'

'Good. Her witness won't be a Catholic. Did Father Fisher take you through the mass?'

'No, Father. That's what we've come for tonight.'

'But you haven't, have you? You haven't both come.'

'I'm sure that she'll be here any minute.'

'When I left. Did she ever ask . . . ?'

'She got very mad when they said you were ill.'

Rex bowed his head, but not quickly enough to prevent Jack from seeing that his pale blue eyes had filled with tears. He shifted his feet, coughed, began to search for his handkerchief, found it and blew his nose. The effort seemed to restore him to the calm condition which all the parish had once admired. His face was no longer flushed. Indeed his old pallor had more than returned. He had turned a sickly green and he seemed about to speak but, instead, emitted a huge and uninhibited belch. Jack could not help gazing, open mouthed, at the spectacle in front of him. Rex spoke with difficulty.

'I don't think there's much more we can do, not without . . . without her being there.'

Why, Jack wondered, does he never call her by name?

'I think we know what to do at the mass, Father. It's not all that different, is it? Father Fisher just thought that you'd want to give us your blessing and—'

174

'You have my blessing . . .'

Jack did not take the hint and move towards the door. Despite the pain behind his eyes and the nausea which washed up from his stomach, Rex remembered that something more was expected of him. A terrible fear formed within his head around the words 'Catholic Men's Society'. If Father Fisher had given Jack the pamphlet, like a good Catholic, he would certainly have taken every word literally. The last paragraph promised that, in the weeks before the nuptial mass, the priest would tell the celebrants about the obligations of a Christian marriage. Perhaps Jack expected to be reminded that the object of marriage was procreation, that birth control (apart from the natural method) was a mortal sin and that carnal pleasures, enjoyed for nothing more than physical gratification, were an offence against the Holy Ghost – even in holy wedlock.

'A word about a Catholic marriage, Jack.' Rex belched again. 'You're to love her and look after her. Look after her. That's the important thing. Don't get annoyed when she's awkward. She's not as sure of herself as she seems. Look after her . . .'

'Yes, Father.' It sounded as if he was saying 'Is that all there is?'

'If you'll excuse . . .'

Rex rushed out of the living room. As Jack pulled the front door shut behind him, he heard Father Hattersley being sick into the kitchen sink. His walk back to Langwith Road was disturbed by fears that perhaps the priest had not, after all, recovered from his madness.

He tapped on the back door of number eleven and, as was expected of all visitors, lifted the latch and walked in. Enid was sitting in front of the kitchen fire, legs wide apart and her hands, which were holding an open book, between her knees.

'Why didn't you come? I felt a right idiot. I kept saying that you'd be there in a minute.'

Enid barely looked up.

'Well, you shouldn't have done. I told you that I might not be able to come. It's been awful. Much worse.'

'Who? You or your mother?'

It was a genuine enquiry. He could not totally suppress his

anxiety about Enid. There was a possibility that she was unwell and he did not want to appear unfeeling about her distress. He did not feel much genuine sympathy. Women, by their nature, were often ill and God had given them the power to accept pain without complaint and inconvenience to others. But he did not want Enid to think of him as an unfeeling Irish collier.

'Both of us.'

The answer was so recklessly dismissive that even Jack – simple and trusting – knew that the honest answer would have been 'neither'. It confirmed his worst fears. Enid was afraid to meet the priest again.

Jack knew that it was his duty – to the Church and to his manhood – to insist that another appointment be made and that, together, they receive the advice and blessing of their parish priest whatever Father Hattersley's state of mind. But he also knew that, even if a second meeting were arranged, somehow Enid would avoid the ordeal. So he prepared to be ruled by her will.

'Perhaps you were well out of it. He's not better yet, if tonight's anything to go by. He didn't half act peculiar. Red faced, stuttering. Half of what he said didn't make sense.'

'There was nothing wrong with him.' She closed her book as a sign that she was taking the conversation seriously. 'He is as sane as you are.'

'Then,' said Jack, incredulously, 'he was drunk.'

JACK HAD expected Enid to say that if they could not move into Colliery Row before August, the wedding would have to be postponed. To his surprise, despite all the talk of needing to get her mother away from Brack, she accepted that she must begin married life as her father's lodger with a resignation for which Jack was profoundly grateful.

'I shan't really feel married until we're in a place of our own. But it can't be helped. We'll both have to be understanding with each other.'

Gratitude for the sympathy of her reaction drove all other

feelings out of Jack's mind, so he did not even wonder what she meant by the need for understanding.

'What do you think your dad will say?'

Only Brack's objection to their sharing the attic now stood between Jack and his dream coming true. As he asked the question, a new gloom descended on him. Brack wanted them all out of the house so that he could live with the Mansfield widow.

'Dad will be all right.'

Enid understood her father and knew that he was not yet ready to choose between the respectability of marriage and the pleasure of setting up home with Mrs Wood. It was not that Brack found it hard to make up his mind. What he wanted, and what he intended to retain for as long as possible, was the best of both worlds. The postponement of Enid's departure gave him another two months' equivocation. In her mind, she could hear him explaining to the bookmaker's widow that he accepted her ultimatum and that as soon as Agnes moved out she would move in, but unfortunately Agnes could not move out until the summer was over.

Her cynicism was justified. When she told him that the pit cottage would not be ready until August, he made a crude joke about the creaking floor boards in the attic and offered to telephone the Mansfield Co-op to make sure that the hire purchase charges on the furniture did not begin until it was delivered to Colliery Row.

AT WORKSOP, the partners faced a moral crisis. Lottie, with a spare afternoon on her hands, had measured Katherine Fox for her bridesmaid's dress almost a month before the wedding day and been surprised by how thick her waist had become. When, three weeks later, the dress was fitted, the signs were unmistakable. Katherine was pregnant. Naturally, Lottie consulted Anne before she confronted the expectant mother.

Anne behaved like a saint and martyr, promising Katherine forgiveness as if the girl had done her a personal injury. She would remain in their employment for as long as her health and the baby's safety allowed. And she would be welcomed back, without recrimination, as soon as the child was safely in a home and she was fit once more to earn her living. In the period in between, they would help her all they could, including seeing the miscreant father and reminding him of his obligations. Katherine Fox was to be smothered in forgiveness and understanding.

'Then we needn't mention it till after the wedding?' Lottie asked.

'Of course we must,' Anne told her. 'You don't think that she can be bridesmaid do you? Not like that!'

Lottie did not try to work out the logic of Anne's morality but simply enquired which one of them was to break the news to Katherine. Anne said that it was a task for both of them, meaning that she would talk and her partner would nod in agreement where appropriate.

Miss Fox, as she automatically became when she stepped inside the fitting room, stubbornly refused to be pitied rather than blamed. She did not possess sufficient courage to contradict her employer, but she renounced all claim to being treated with the sympathy appropriate to a victim.

'Everything will be all right.' Katherine was flagrantly undowntrodden. 'We're going to get married. We decided to let Enid get hers over first. Though Eamon thought of a double wedding with Jack—'

'Eamon!' Anne was horrified. 'You don't mean *that* Eamon?'

'I do. And it will be a special licence next week.'

'How could you?' Lottie asked.

'Because I love him and he loves me.' She patted her belly with a fine disregard for her employers' sensitivities. 'You don't think I'd have allowed this to happen if I didn't?'

Anne was furious, and Lottie, naturally enough, copied her mood. Both women prided themselves on being friends in times of trouble, the sort of women who rallied round the deserted and the betrayed. They would both have gladly comforted Katherine in her hour of need and told her that, although she might be ostracized by all respectable people, they would stand by her. But they were not sure how to deal with a pregnant employee who seemed to be rejoicing in her pregnancy.

'How could you?' Lottie asked.

'He makes me happy!'

'Happy!' said Anne. 'Happiness. Huh! See where happiness has got you.'

LOTTIE WAS so upset by Katherine Fox's reckless determination to live a happy life that she could not properly concentrate on finishing Enid's dress and it was not ready until three o'clock on the morning of the wedding day, three hours before the hire-car was to arrive. The sisters were determined to be in Langwith well before seven.

At first they had hoped that Ernest would not accompany them, for in the war between the sexes, he was less reinforcement than walking wounded. They had never quite forgiven him for his unsuitable match. And although he had been released by the providential early death of his young wife, Anne was not sure that even after a gap of nearly thirty years he was ready for exposure to a blatant display of normal behaviour. But he insisted that he must support the partners. So the partners accepted that they would have to support him.

His house in Overend Road was on the route from Brook House to Langwith, but Ernest walked to Newcastle Avenue to be fitted into the hire-car together with all the other luggage: Enid's dress in a long flat cardboard box with tissue paper sticking out from under the lid, the inevitable baskets of fresh eggs, cooked meats, bottled fruit and home-made jam and a bulging hessian bag. It bulged with a box of dog biscuits, a basin of cooked offal and a bottle of gravy. If Chum was to be left alone for most of the morning, it was essential that, in his loneliness, he was properly fed.

Lottie and Anne were waiting in the hall, coats buttoned, hats on and gloves in place. As soon as they heard Ern's footsteps on the path, they left the house and walked resolutely towards the car.

Both were fiercely determined not to show the fear they felt at the prospect of a fifteen-mile car journey. Anne, majestic on the back seat and Lottie, indomitable by her side, looked perfectly composed.

'Where's Chum?' Anne asked.

'Good Lord!' Ernest emitted the most violent expletive of which he was capable. 'You haven't left the poor beggar in the house!'

'No, we haven't,' said Lottie, wounded by so serious an allegation. 'I let him have a little run in the garden before he got cooped up in the car.'

'Go and get him,' Anne commanded in a manner sufficiently regal to have been copied from Queen Mary. 'He can go on Ern's knee in the front.'

Lottie did as she was told. But Chum was not in the garden to be got. Dock plants stood a foot high and rose bay willow herb, not yet in flower, clustered in little clumps with the Queen Anne's lace. Sycamore seeds, which had blown in from the churchyard over the wall, had grown into saplings. Rhubarb, which had turned wild and gone to seed, flapped its great flat leaves in the early morning breeze. But although the garden was a jungle, it was not so dense that the foliage could hide an obese Old English sheepdog. Chum, normally so docile and domesticated, had escaped.

'He's gone,' Lottie shouted as calmly as she could.

The wedding dress was abandoned on the back seat of the hire-car and the hessian bag was kicked over on the floor between the seats as Anne – regal demeanour forgotten – scrambled out into the road. Lottie emerged from the undergrowth and, together with Ernest, stared theatrically along the course of the brook.

'He's gone down the stream, dang him,' Ernest said.

'Not Chum, he's frightened of water,' said Anne proudly.

It was Lottie who made the sighting.

'He's lying on the bank, kicking his legs in the air.'

All eyes were focused on a flat patch of grass in the bend of the river. Chum, for a moment still, lay like an upturned table. Then the kicking and rolling began, again.

'Writhing in pain,' said Anne, who was an expert on suffering.

'Injured and writhing in pain.' Lottie liked to agree with her partner.

'He's probably got caught in one of those danged rat traps.'

Ernest scrambled down the soggy bank and balanced, for a precarious moment, with one foot on a flat stone round which the stream flowed. For a few agonizing seconds, as one leg waved in the air, it seemed that he would lose his balance. But, with great presence of mind, he plunged the carefully polished boot into the water and stabilized himself by sinking his foot into the brook's muddy bottom. The only way forward was with the tide. He squelched resolutely towards what still seemed to be a dance of death.

'It might be a convulsion,' Lottie shouted after him, though whether that was a warning or a consolation, nobody was sure.

'Thank heavens we've got the car,' said Anne. 'At least we'll be able to take the poor thing to the vet and have him put out of his misery.'

Ernest made slow progress and when he reached the soggy ground on which Chum lay, climbed out of the stream with both difficulty and caution. He took a tentative step in the dog's direction, anxious to avoid a rabid bite and intending to roll it over with a waterlogged boot. Hearing, or sensing, the approach, Chum stood up and shook himself. Blood and worse flew from his matted coat and dappled Ernest's sodden trousers. A gobbet of putrefying flesh and mangled bone was matted into the long fur on his back. On the grass between his feet, the rotten head and fore-legs of a long-dead rabbit lay crushed almost out of recognition. Chum, excited by the smell of corruption, had rolled on it in orgiastic ecstasy.

'Dang you, sir!' said Ernest. He could not remember ever swearing so much in one day.

Lottie accused Chum of being a naughty boy and Anne suggested that since her brother had so little left to lose, he should wash and dry the dog ready for the journey. After twenty minutes a clean abut apparently unabashed necrophile was led out of Brook House. On examination the fur was found to be still damp.

'He'll get his death of cold,' said Anne.

Ernest agreed to improve on his first relative failure. The job was done in another ten minutes and the hire-car moved off. It took another half hour for Ernest to change into his second-best suit and clean his second-best boots.

There was a false start from Overend Road. Ernest Skinner never travelled anywhere without taking a spare collar with him as a precaution against the ravages of sweat and razor cuts. In his hurry, he had left his reinforcement lying on the kitchen table. He remembered it just before the car moved off and hurried back muttering, 'More haste, less speed.'

Anne and Lottie sat impatiently in the car outside his house in Overend Road, pretending to be angry with Chum and escalating each other's anxieties about the consequences of arriving in Lang-with Junction only four hours before the wedding. The journey was a nightmare of fear that they would arrive late and terror that they were going too fast.

The streets of the little town were deserted. As they passed St Joseph's church – at which they looked in frightened anticipation of horrors to come – the wedding guests did not notice a man hammering on the presbytery door. The man was Jack O'Hara.

CHAPTER TEN

FATHER HATTERSLEY, bleary eyed from lack of sleep, asked Jack in. He anticipated the worst, which was really the best. Enid, he was sure, had run away. Then, before Jack had time to speak, he considered the possibility that she was dead, that she was ill and that she had simply refused to go ahead with the ceremony.

'I've got a bit of a problem, Father.'

That, Rex felt sure, meant that Enid had announced a change of mind. It was of little consolation to him. By ten o'clock, she would have changed it back again. For the rest of his life, he would wonder if, during the time of her doubts, he should have claimed her as his own. But priests do not persuade brides to abandon their bridegrooms – any more than brides kill themselves or run away. Priests persuade brides to go ahead with the ceremony. He steadied himself against the hall wall.

'How can I help you?' He could hear the tremble in his own voice.

'It's my brother, Eamon.'

Rex was so relieved that his knees almost buckled as the tension dissolved inside him.

'What's happened to him?'

'He had a real skinful at the party last night and he can barely walk this morning. I've dosed him with everything I can think of, but I can't risk him in the church at twelve.'

The feeling of relief did not survive the explanation. Enid was, after all, going to be married. She did not even need to be persuaded. She had not locked herself in her bedroom and cried all night. He made another brave attempt to do his duty.

'Are you sure he can't just stand there?'

'I daren't risk it, Father. I know what he's like. He'll likely as not be ill in church. So I don't have a best man.'

'Another one of your friends must do it. It isn't a difficult job.'

'None of them are Catholics, Father. I talked to you about witnesses and you said we needed Catholics. That's why Gwen Ferguson is going to be a bridesmaid.'

'One will do, Jack.' Rex did not add – for he was ashamed of the truth – that his witness was the only testimony that mattered. He would be the instrument of Enid's marriage.

'I'd like a Catholic best man, Father.'

'Isn't there somebody else you could find at the last minute?'

'No.' Jack looked totally dejected. 'Only a few of the lads are coming. Enid said it had to be a quiet wedding. There's not a left-footer amongst them.'

Rex thought, with a complicated mixture of pain and pleasure, of the determination with which Enid would have invented excuses to avoid being surrounded by colliers.

'I wondered if your little brother . . . Enid always liked him. She's always talking about the good times you had together last summer.'

'I'll ask him.' Rex had lost all will to fight.

'You'll make him do it, won't you?'

'I won't have to. If I ask him, he'll agree.'

All that Rex wanted was for Jack to go away and Jack was just as anxious to return home triumphant and begin his complicated toilet. But the two men stared silently at various points on the ceiling, each one waiting for the other to initiate a new conversation.

'Big day for you,' Rex said.

Jack was spared the necessity of working out an answer. The front door rattled.

'I better see who that is.' Rex waved his hand in a way which he hoped conveyed his wish for Jack to precede him into the hall. Jack took no notice.

A brown manilla envelope lay on the hall floor below the letter box. Since it was unaddressed Rex took it to be a business circular. He picked it up with undisguised disappointment. A parishioner in distress would have convinced even Jack O'Hara that it was time for him to go.

'One more thing, Father. You are coming up to the Welfare afterwards, aren't you? It's nothing very big. But we hope you'll be there. And your brother too. I know that Enid would be disappointed if you didn't. Mrs B. as well.'

'I'll try to, Jack.' The time for niceties had passed. Rex opened the front door. 'I'll try to, I promise.'

It was several minutes before Rex remembered the letter. There was anguish to be exorcised and he walked into the kitchen, walked back into the hall, stood in the living room with his brow resting on the cool un-papered wall and then went back into the kitchen. He needed company. Syd would be woken with a cup of tea and prepared for the duties which he had to perform. Whilst he waited for the kettle to boil, he opened the brown envelope. The letter inside was from Enid.

It was not a declaration of undying love or a call for him to come to her. It was, at least in form, no more than a note of polite apology.

I am sorry that I did not come with Jack the other night. I just couldn't face it. Please don't think me rude.

Enid had given up all hope of sharing her life with Rex. His failure to reply to the letter which she had sent to Nottingham had ended that dream for ever. But she could not bear to think that she had lost all power over him. The note was intended to give a tug on the string by which they were still bound together. Its real message was that they were not, and never would be, free of each other.

Rex read it twice and hurried upstairs to waken Syd.

Syd groaned. 'Not yet. I get up in the middle of the night at Ratcliffe.'

'I need your help. *Praesentibus* or *testibus*, I don't mind which. But I need you to perform at the wedding.'

'What the hell are you talking about?'

'I want you to be best man. Best man at Enid's wedding.'

'For you then.' He was still half asleep. 'I wouldn't do it for everybody.'

Syd reached out for the cup of tea and knocked it over. Rex

began to mop the bedclothes with his handkerchief as his brother sat up and stared at him through his horn rims.

'It's not for me,' Rex told him. 'It's just helping out the bridegroom.'

'You don't have to pretend with me. Aunt Clare told me all about it. That's why I'm here.'

At first, when he found out that Syd knew everything and was not censorious, Rex felt immense relief. At last there was one person in the world to whom he could show his true feelings. He had bitterly resented having to suffer in silence. But once Syd was part of his secret and he was able to show his feelings he was no longer sure that he dare say what he really felt. He wondered if he had been more secure inside the walls of his solitary sadness.

'It's not worth talking about.'

'It is, if it makes you feel better. That's what Aunt Clare says, anyway.'

'I'm not sure it will. It's probably better bottled up. That's why I don't turn to jelly and bring up my breakfast.'

'Well, I'm here if you want me.'

'I do. But not to talk about it. I need a friendly face. I certainly need you there for the mass . . .'

'I'll be there, won't I? Holding the ring.'

'Don't look at me. At least don't look sorry for me.'

Rex leaned towards his brother and Syd, although uncertain about what he should do, took him in his arms. Both men wept and neither of them was embarrassed by the weeping.

'WHERE ON earth have you been?' Agnes was near to collapse. 'I thought you must have had an accident.'

'I've just been taking Mick for a walk,' Enid told her without mentioning that it had taken her to the presbytery. 'I knew he'd have to be locked up all day.'

'Let's not waste any more time.' Anne was opening the suitcase in which she had brought Agnes's new coat. 'You know that it's half past eight?'

Ernest, fearful that the talk was going to turn to women's

clothes, said that he would 'get a breath of God's good fresh air' and Lottie began to prepare the table for the last ironing of the wedding dress.

Enid managed to avoid putting on the dress until nearly eleven o'clock. But when her father came in from the yard and announced that it was time for him to wash and change, she knew that she could procrastinate no longer.

She dragged the long dress up the stairs and dropped it in a heap on her bed. Then she slowly unbuttoned her cotton washing frock, pulled off her lisle stockings, and sat morosely on the bed, looking at herself in the mirror. What she saw improved her spirits and, buoyed-up by the sight, she began to ease herself into the tight dress. She enjoyed the feel of the silk stockings and, having chosen to put them on after the dress, had to rearrange the skirt and smooth down the creases that she had made when it was pulled up to fasten the suspenders. Immensely satisfied with the result, she was about to try on her circlet of orange blossom when there was a heavy knock on the door. It must be, she decided bitterly, Anne come to disturb her last few minutes of peace.

It was her father, handsome in his new tailor-made suit and unusually diffident.

'Am I pushing in where I'm not wanted?'

'Course not, Dad. I'm nearly ready.'

'You look lovely.'

She blushed. Enid and Brack were in constant conflict. But she longed for his admiration. Had he told her that she was wasted on marriage and ought, instead, to read for the bar or stand for Parliament, she would have been more gratified. But, on this morning, she was prepared to rejoice that he thought she looked lovely.

'You look marvellous too. A real gentleman.'

'Well, I'm not. And don't ever think that I am.'

He took a roll of pound notes out of his back pocket and pressed them into his daughter's hand. She took them without showing either surprise or gratitude.

'That's for you. Keep it quiet. Just in case you ever need it in an emergency.'

Enid wrapped the money in the discarded lisle stockings and bundled them up with the cotton washing dress.

'I can't think what it might be.'

The only emergency she could imagine was one which her father had created and she was determined not to be patronized.

'Neither can I. Jack's a decent chap. He'll look after you as best he can. I suppose it's conscience money.'

'No need, Dad. We've had our rows.'

'I've got no conscience about that. You asked for everything you got. But we should have had a word. I should have talked to you during the last few weeks.'

'About what?'

'About getting married.'

Enid blushed again and Brack, for the first time that his daughter could recall, blushed .

'I didn't mean *that*,' he said. 'I meant getting married at all.'

'Bit late for that.'

'That's why I should have talked to you before.'

'Too late now, Dad.' She tried to sound as if it were all a joke.

'Not if you want to call it all off, it isn't.'

'What makes you think I do?'

'Everything. Everything does. Look how you've behaved today. Brides are supposed to have doubts, run about crying and shouting that you can't go on with it. You're as cool as a cucumber. And the way you've treated those two old women from Worksop. Usually you behave as if they were little tin gods. This morning you were as rude to them as you are to me.'

'They just got on my nerves a bit.'

'So you have got some feelings.'

'Course I have.'

'For him?'

'I'm getting married, Dad.'

'To get away from me? To get some peace for your mother?'

'No, Dad.'

'I tell you, Enid. I know what it's like to be tied to somebody you can't stand. I've had it for thirty years. It would be better to walk out of here now, better than to have the life I've had with your mother.'

'Don't say it, Dad. It's too late.' She was crying. 'I'm going to make the best of things. Jack's a good man, He'll do his best to make me happy.'

'Just because you've got a fancy wedding dress you don't have—'

'I do. If I don't marry Jack, God knows what will become of me.'

He took her in his arms as if she was a child who had fallen and grazed her knee and she put her head against the hard cloth of his lapel and sobbed as if they had always loved and trusted each other.

'It's all our fault,' Brack said. 'Your mother's and mine. We set you the wrong example. You don't know what love is.'

'I do,' she said, pulling away. 'I do. I'm in love and don't you ever dare say anything different.'

She began to rub her nose with the back of her hand and, because she looked as she had looked when she was five, her father smiled.

'Keep tight hold of me,' she said, 'all the way to the altar.'

MRS EDNA FERGUSON's talents as a musician were best displayed at Irish Night in St Philip Neri's church hall. When her troupe of Gaelic dancers – saffron cloaks flying and kilts swirling above their chubby knees – moved forward and back across the bare boards of the stage, their coach and accompanist kept immaculate time on the old upright piano. No matter how brutally she thumped out the music, it brought sentimental tears to the eyes of her audience. Some cried at the sight of the children dancing in such determined unison. Others wept at the memory of the old country which they had been so desperate to leave.

At the keyboard of the organ in St Joseph's, Langwith Junction, she performed to less advantage. Her style was essentially *fortissimo*. But the congregation which anxiously awaited the appearance of the priest and the arrival of the bride, expected *pianissimo* entertainment. Her problems were compounded by the pedals, one of which was stuck and one of which was missing. Despite the need to accustom herself to the special circumstances of her performances, she had been able to practise for only ten minutes before the first, and absurdly early, wedding guests had arrived. But life as a landlady had made her indomitable, so she played a series of chords as quietly as her technique and the keyboard allowed.

Ernest Skinner looked at Anne and Lottie out of the corner of his eye and wondered if he had been wrong to expose them to such depravities.

Below the altar steps, the statue of Joseph had been surrounded by so many sweet peas and wild roses that the old plaster saint seemed to be standing in a flower bed. It reminded Ernest of his father, once head gardener to Squire Hodding at Harness Grove. He longed for the old hymns which he had once sung in Steetly chapel and for the old certainties of his boyhood. The painted walls – decorated in exotic patterns by the band of itinerant Italian artists who once travelled through Catholic England – confirmed his fear that he was about to take part in a pagan ritual. He kept telling himself, 'when in Rome', without fully appreciating how apposite a cliché he was repeating. From time to time, he reassured himself with the thought that he was half way through the day's ordeal. It was five hours since he had arrived at Brook House. When another five hours had passed, he would be home in Worksop and the warmth of his sister's admiration. He had a well-developed talent for surviving the frequent unpleasant passages in his life.

The pews behind Worksop were occupied by Enid's acquaintances from the tennis club, Brack's friends from Cobbler Jack's and various trades people who, it was hoped, would be flattered by an invitation to the wedding into buying more coal or booking a hire-car. Further back was the usual clutch of spectators: widows with memories and time on their hands, young girls with romantic aspirations, the church cleaners who would have to sweep away the confetti and the old men with coughs who had chosen to sit huddled at the back of the service rather than sit hunched on their own doorstep or outside the Miners' Welfare. In the very last row Percy and Owen Ford sat so close together that their knees touched. When they whispered to each other – in astonishment at the sights around them or in contempt for the rest of the congregation – Sally Ford, separated from her husband by several feet of wooden seat and a chasm of belief, hissed that they must behave with respect and stop showing her up.

Agnes, her wheelchair in the aisle, craned her arthritic neck in the hope of catching the first possible sight of the bride sweeping, in glory, down the aisle. All that she could see was the sad rows of empty pews behind the bridegroom and his best man.

Syd, respectable in his grey flannel Ratcliffe suit, tried not to look over his shoulder. Mrs Ferguson had told him to keep the ring safe in his waistcoat pocket but, fearing that it would disappear into the torn lining, he clutched it in the palm of his hand. From time to time he touched it with his finger-tips to confirm that it had not disappeared like fairy gold. Jack, splendid but uneasy in bespoke navy serge, sat motionless. The stiff collar of his new white shirt was too tight and he longed to ease the pressure on his neck. But he did no more than cough and swallow hard. He had heard Agnes tell her brother that blue suit, white shirt and spotted tie was 'the Paddy's Sunday uniform'. He had always prided himself on not looking like an Irish collier and he was determined not to behave like one by pushing his thumb between stud and Adam's apple. He believed that respect for the occasion required him to remain straight and still. He did not even turn his head when Father Hattersley appeared at the vestry door.

When Syd had been at his side, Rex had managed to remain calm. Over breakfast and during the brief walk from presbytery to church, he had done more than counterfeit composure. He had been unhappy, but he had not been afraid. He had become reconciled to the long years of loneliness spent in the joyless pursuit of a dubious vocation. He had even convinced himself that he could survive without Enid Brackenbury – survive the forty bleak years of regret and reproach to which, because of his folly, he had been condemned.

Rex felt proud of the way in which he had prepared himself for the difficult days which lay ahead – prepared himself like a man who sucks on a hollow tooth in the hope that a sudden brief agony would prevent a long dull ache. He had even rehearsed his response to the news that Enid was about to become a mother. In his imagination, he had congratulated Jack O'Hara on the birth of what, he was sure, would be a son and gone on to baptize the child Ernest after its grandfather. Relying on nothing except the strength of his own character, he had made himself ready to face anything but the first ordeal. But he had not prepared himself for the trauma of the service itself.

Until the morning of the nuptial mass, thought of the ceremony was so painful that he had chosen to drive it out of his mind with brave decisions about how he would behave next week and next year. When Syd left him at the vestry, he had to force himself to push the heavy door open and contemplate alone the horrors of the next hour. He was about to lose both Enid and his soul.

Before he prayed for grace, Rex made a determined effort to find, from within himself, the strength to say the mass from start to finish. First he smoked a cigarette, something that he had never done in the vestry before. Then, resting his head on the cool windowpane, he stared out at the tangle of bushes which grew against the church wall and spoke to himself in what he hoped was the voice of courage and responsibility. He had learned at Ratcliffe that, when the mind wanders from prayer, concentration and composure can be restored by mouthing a silent conversation with God.

'Of course I'll do it. Got to. I can't let her down. Can't shame her. Can't let Syd down either. I've got to do it. I know that. And I will.'

By the time that the talk had finished, he was still not sure that he could survive from Introit to Blessing. But at least he had given himself enough courage to try. He pulled on his vestments, said his prayers in thoughtless haste and walked into the church, steadying himself as he went by running his hand along the smooth, painted wall.

The worst moment would, Rex knew, be the first sign of Enid as she came round the screen that protected the congregation from the open church door. Waiting at the foot of the sanctuary steps, he felt an almost irresistible desire to stoop like a man with stomach pain. Instead of bending forward, he leaned back against the polished brass of the altar rail. Then a sudden wheeze from the organ so startled him that he momentarily forgot the fear that he was

about to fall. Mrs Ferguson had heard the crunch of a car on the
gravel path and was poised to welcome the bride. It took Rex a few
seconds to concentrate on what was happening and he was still
staring at the volunteer organist when she struck the first belated
chord. When he turned back towards the nave of the church, Jack
O'Hara had sprung to his feet and was standing at something
approaching attention. Syd, by his side, was staring anxiously at
the wedding ring which was stuck by sweat to his palm and Enid –
radiant on her father's arm – was already well on her way down the
aisle.

Rex's first thought was how small she looked. Ernest Brackenbury – massive in charcoal grey – seemed to be twice as broad as
his daughter. Beneath his carefully clipped moustache, his mouth
was set in a thin theatrical smile. But despite the discrepancies of
size, Brack was overshadowed by his daughter.

The Worksop wedding dress was simple, simpler than Enid
herself would have chosen. But together with the veil, (which was
worn, swept back from her face) and the circlet of artificial orange
blossom which held it in place, the whole ensemble combined to
make the bride look like a not quite respectable elf. Rex, who
thought that he remembered every detail of her face, was surprised
that the chin was quite so pointed and the eyes were so big and
blue. He watched her walk towards him – gangling awkwardly in
comparison with her father's stately progress – and told himself
that he must carry on through the whole service. He would take
each line as it came and, having survived one, move on with
greater determination to the next.

'*Deus Israel conjungat vos: et ipse sit vobiscum, qui misertus est
duobus unicis: et nunc Domine, fac eos plenius benedicerete.*'

Every prayer seemed to convey a personal message for him.

'*In te speravi, Domine: dixi Tu es Deus meus, in manibus tuis
tempora mea.*'

He had to force himself to say 'my trust in Thee, Lord, is not
shaken', and he felt nothing but apprehension about the assertion
that 'my fortunes are in thy hand'. God had led him into temptation and, when he had fallen, the Church had not delivered him
from evil.

'Propitaire, Domine, supplicationibus nostris, et institutis tuis, quibus propagationem humani generis ordinasti, benignus assiste . . .'

For a moment, standing at the Epistle corner of his altar and staring above the heads of Jack and Enid who knelt before him, he feared that he could not go on. He did not want God's design for the continuance of mankind to be furthered by that morning's communicants and he feared that if he prayed for the preservation of their union, the congregation would tell from his demeanour and tone of voice that he was lying to the Father, Son and Holy Ghost. But somehow he finished the prayer and told the congregation that it was never lawful to put asunder that which was fashioned from a single substance.

Back in the middle of the altar, with the hollow feeling in his stomach again making it difficult for him to stand upright, he felt the first tear run down his cheek.

'Five minutes and it's all over,' he told himself. 'Five minutes and you've done your duty to her if not to God.'

'Ecce sic benedicetur omnis homo, qui timet . . .'

He brushed the tear aside as if he was scratching his cheek.

'Quaesumus, omnipotens Deus . . .'

The space in his stomach seemed suddenly to be filled with fire and he feared that he was about to vomit.

'Benedicamus Domino . . .' He swallowed hard.

'Deus Abraham, Deus Isaac, et Deus Jacob sit vobiscum . . .' He reached for the aspergillum. Sixty seconds and the blasphemy would be done *'. . . adjuvante Domino nostro Jesu Christo, qui cum Patre et Spirito Sancto vivit et regnat Deus, per omnia saecula saeculorum.'*

Rex sprinkled the married couple with holy water. It was all over. He was damned on earth and damned in the life hereafter. But he had done his duty, he had sacrificed his soul for her convenience. He felt sick no longer and stood erect without difficulty. Back in the vestry, he opened the parish register with a steady hand.

'Where do we sign?' Brack was determined to sound businesslike and even more anxious to assume his role as host at the reception.

The registrar squeezed into the vestry between the half open door and Agnes Brackenbury's wheelchair and spread his forms out on top of the vestment chest.

Ernest Skinner – behind his sister's wheelchair and nearer to incense than he would have wished – was confirmed in his belief that the marriage was bogus. A clerk in the Holy Order of the Church of England needed no secular registrar to make the wedding legal.

The witnesses signed and Brack paid the fee with a flourish. Rex sat alone in a corner with the parish register on his knee. A corroded inkwell was on the floor beside him. From time to time, he leaned down and scratched about in the gritty black dregs with the rusty nib. He made his entry with meticulous care.

> *Ego Fredericus R. Hattersley . . . in matrimonio*
> *confunxi Joannem O'Hara*
> *filium Joannis O'Hara*
> *et Enidam Brackenbury*
> *filiam Ernesti Brackenbury . . .*

He wrote on without looking up from the lined page.

Brack ushered the family out of the vestry and led them through the church to the front door where a small crowd had gathered to greet the happy couple. Sally Ford opened her bag of confetti, but before she could throw the first salvo, Anne Skinner, looking over her shoulder, said to nobody in particular, 'At Steetly they don't allow confetti. It makes such a mess on the graves. At Steetly, they only allow rice. The birds eat it, poor things.'

Sally's hand dropped to her side.

A noise from within the church, just distinguishable as Mendelssohn, gave warning that the bride and groom were on their way. Mr and Mrs Jack O'Hara appeared in the porch to gasps of delight and incredulity that such a handsome pair were to be found in Langwith Junction.

The photographer prepared each picture with infuriating precision, choosing the right background with meticulous care, insisting that no suggestion of shirt appeared between waistcoat and trouser and inviting the ladies to straighten hats. Whilst the guests grew increasingly restless, Enid co-operated with a good temper which surprised everyone who knew her, smoothing out the creases in her dress as instructed and adjusting the angle of her orange blossom circlet on request. She would have gone on posing all afternoon – on her husband's arm, gazing up at her father in gratitude as he looked down at her with pride and bending tenderly to embrace her crippled mother – had Brack not insisted that it was time to go. There was one more picture – Enid looking wistfully at her bouquet – before the three hire-cars moved off in procession, with the less important guests hurrying behind on foot.

It was almost an hour before everyone was satisfactorily seated at the trestle tables. The meal went on for so long that Anne crept out half way through the main course and hurried across Langwith to the coal yard. To her surprise neither of the dogs had died of starvation, heat stroke or loneliness. When she returned to reassure Enid that Mick was safe, her niece accepted the news with a perfunctory nod and an inquiry about how she could get the grass stains out of her white satin shoes. There was no time for a reply before Brack – host and master of ceremonies – rose to introduce the groom.

Jack struggled his way through a few good-natured sentences and, as always, particularly endeared himself to the middle-aged ladies who were present. Brack then declaimed a long speech on the joys of parenthood, the satisfaction of knowing that a father's duty had been properly done and the pain of losing a much-loved daughter. Although uninvited, Mrs Ferguson made a speech on behalf of Jack's absent family, and two collier friends of the groom – who had hurried to the wedding breakfast straight from the pithead baths – applauded so loudly that a startled Percy Ford spilled shandy on the previously spotless white tablecloth. The guests took the consequent commotion as a sign that the time had come for them to leave. It was only then that Agnes noticed that the two chairs, opposite Mr and Mrs Owen Ford, were empty.

'The priest didn't come,' Lottie told her. 'Nor did that nice young brother of his.'

'Very rude,' Anne replied. 'Very rude indeed.'

CHAPTER ELEVEN

THE HONEYMOON was not a success.

During the drive from Langwith Junction to Worksop, Enid was sick out of the car window and Jack had to help her down the passage at the side of the house. He could not remember her ever being sick before.

Uncle Ern's living room was normal enough in its dilapidated way. The pendulum which hung down from the clock on the far wall was still and the mercury behind the mirror over the fireplace had corroded into a dull grey blur. The shelves in the china cabinet were empty except for a silver goblet and a cream jug, both of which, to Jack's surprise, shone as if they had been polished that morning. They were gifts given to Ernest's father on his retirement as gardener at Harness Grove and were kept burnished bright in memory of the better past. Nothing else in the room seemed cared for or loved. The sofa on to which Enid collapsed was so worn that the pattern on the moquette had worn away.

A folded gingham cloth covered half of the heavy oak table. On it two places – cups and saucers, plates and cutlery – had been set. They were the host's gesture of welcome. Behind them on the part of the tabletop which had been left bare, were the fretwork rocking chairs, windmills, wheelbarrows and pen holders which Ernest Skinner had made with loving care in his youthful spare time. The complicated curves and angles were thick with dust. A tarnished brass handle, which had fallen from a sideboard drawer, lay on the base of the pipe holder which Uncle Ern had once offered Jack as a sign of good will. Even at that fraught moment, Jack wondered why a man from the wood trade had not screwed it back into the dry mahogany.

'Make us a cup of tea.' Enid looked distraught.

Jack walked over to the dull black-leaded fireplace and lifted the soot-encrusted kettle from the empty grate.

'You'll have to make a fire first.' Enid's voice was faint with thirst.

'What? It's a warm night.'

'It's the only way to boil the water.' She sounded impatient with his ignorance. 'Uncle Ern doesn't believe in gas. He can taste it in the food.'

Jack was half way into the yard to look for sticks and coal.

'I'd get the water from the pump, if I were you. Uncle Ern thinks that water that's stood in the pipes—'

'You drink it at home.'

'Show a bit of concern, Jack. Don't shout at me when I feel like this.'

There were no sticks in the coal house and Jack had to lay the coal on twisted rolls of old newspaper. As he knelt in front of the hearth, worrying about the knees of his new suit and trying to keep his snow-white cuffs free from the dust and ashes, Enid recovered enough to remind him of the debt which he owed to her uncle.

'I've never known anybody else stay here.'

'We're probably the first people to sleep here. Apart from him, that is.'

'And his wife,' said Jack, striking a second match and attempting to light the stubborn paper.

'She died before he came here. That's why he never bothered to get the gas. There's no paper on the walls upstairs. He didn't have the heart.'

Trying to push out of his mind all thought of the comfortable Cleethorpes boarding house at which he had hoped to spend his honeymoon, Jack struggled on. At last the coal – encouraged by a sprinkling of sugar – caught light and, anxious to encourage a real blaze, he held a sheet of paper in front of the grate to create a draught. It suddenly turned brown and burst into flame. The burning front page of the *Worksop Guardian* disappeared up the chimney.

'Look at the smoke,' Enid shouted. 'It's blowing back. It'll mark the ceiling.'

Jack looked up, past the dusty fireplace, and the corroded

mirror, the loose picture rail and the cracked moulding which joined wall to ceiling. Above his head, two wires hung from a jagged hole.

'Was he going to have the electric?'

'Of course he was. This house was built by his father-in-law, Mr Sweeting. He owns property all over. This house was to have every modern . . . every modern luxury.'

'Then your Uncle Ern lost interest?'

'Because his wife died. Lucy. That's what she was called.'

Jack, concentrating hard on fanning the coals into flame, asked the question without thinking.

'What did she die of?'

'Having a baby,' said Enid.

She was sick three more times during the night.

THEY STAYED in Worksop for three days and nights, each of them longing for the other to suggest that they should go back to Langwith Junction and both of them preparing to be offended when it was suggested. Inevitably it was Jack whose nerve snapped first.

'I can't see much point in stopping. You being unwell and all.'

'I'll be better tomorrow.'

'We'd still be better off in Langwith. At least we've got a wireless there.'

'That's an awful thing to say. You told me that it would be like an ordinary holiday.'

'I'm only saying—'

'I know what you're saying. You've thought of nothing else.'

Jack thought of how some of his friends would have reacted to the three days of unconsummated marriage. He thought of quoting the Catholic Men's Society on the duties of a Christian wife but, in the end, simply decided to reassure her of his good intentions.

'I just thought you'd be more comfortable, that's all.'

Enid called him ungrateful and asked him to consider the sacrifice which her uncle had made in moving out of his house and to remember her aunts' kindness in accommodating the pair of them in Brook House. Then she agreed that it would be best to go back to Langwith Junction.

It took most of the day to arrange for their departure. The hire-car had to be booked. Agnes, at the other end of town, had to be prepared for the journey. Uncle Ern's house had to be restored to the exact condition in which they found it. And, most important of all, Langwith Road had to be telephoned in order to give Brack the warning that was necessary to make sure that he was not caught *in flagrante*. When Jack got back from making the call, Enid was in tears.

'I can't help thinking about what my dad will say. All those coarse jokes. He'll be horrible to me and horrible to Mam. You won't leave me with him, will you? You know what it will be like.'

Jack knew exactly what it would be like. He would sit in front of the fire with a pot of tea and the daily paper and when Brack went out, as surely he would, the house and everything in it would seem like his. Enid knew exactly what it would be like for her. It would be almost identical to life before the wedding, except that Jack would be under her feet every night of the week.

The drive back to Langwith was uneventful, at least by the standards of the outward journey. Agnes groaned in pain every time the car lurched over a hole in the road and Mick – still hysterically excited by his reunion with Enid – growled, whimpered, and barked in turn. To Jack's relief there was no reoccurrence of the sickness which had made the drive to Worksop so memorable.

'You look a lot better, love.'

Enid's spirits had been visibly improved by the discovery that Brack was not at home to welcome them back.

'I've got to be, haven't I? Who'll look after Mam if I don't? I can't see you feeding her and rubbing her neck. And all the washing's waiting. Were you thinking of getting out the tub and dolly peg?'

The reproach wounded Jack. He had spent the three days of his honeymoon poaching eggs and helping his new wife hobble down the garden path to the lavatory. And she was treating him like a heartless stranger.

'I've looked after you as best I can.'

'I know you have.'

For a moment her mood changed. She put the slice of toast which she was buttering with concentrated precision and, leaning forward, kissed him.

'I'm sorry. I know I'm not easy. Thank you for being so understanding. You're a good man.'

'And you love me,' Jack said.

She leaned forward and, without a word, kissed him again.

SYD STAYED in Langwith for almost a week and did his best to make his visit seem like a holiday. Each morning, whilst Rex was at mass, he made the breakfast and when his brother sat, silent and absent minded at the table, he listed the delights that they could enjoy during the day. None of his suggestions was original. He simply proposed that they should re-live the joys of the previous summer – the summer which they had spent with Enid.

Rex did his best to keep Syd happy. His old bicycle was made, more or less, roadworthy and a more respectable model was hired from the shop in Main Street which Brack had once rented. Together they returned to the cathedrals and castles which they had visited a year before. Sometimes Rex talked obsessively about happier days and sometimes he changed the subject when Syd began to talk about them. The harder Syd tried to make him happy, the sadder he became.

After five days, when half term was over, Syd forced himself to ask, 'Are you all right? I could come back next weekend.'

'Time,' said Rex. 'Time will put it all right.'

'But I could come back.'

'Better not. Better for me. If I act sensibly for long enough, I'll begin to feel sensible again. After a month it won't be so bad.'

Rex did not believe it. But after a month, although he was still desolate, he no longer despaired. Life was no less meaningless, but he again hoped that he would find the meaning of his life in the

Church. He tried his best to become a parish priest again, but at first he was a parish priest who hardly dared leave his presbytery. He sat in his living room staring at his books in an unsuccessful attempt to persuade himself that he was reading. Between every line he thought of Enid.

He was constantly distracted by the fear that if he left the house he would come face to face with the new Mrs O'Hara. Neither she nor her husband had been to Sunday mass, but he had failed in his duty to find out why.

He greeted every knock at the door as if it was the crack of dawn or Enid come to reclaim him. So, when the boy who cleaned and polished Brack's secondhand cars, rang Rex's doorbell as if his life depended upon an immediate response, Rex pulled his jacket on with one hand as he opened the door with the other. The boy spoke with the breathless urgency that Brack had made him practise and perfect before he left the yard.

'Mr Brackenbury said can you come straight away.'

'What's happened?'

'I don't know. Mr Brackenbury wouldn't tell me. He just told me to run down here and get you quick.'

Agnes was the most likely candidate for sudden collapse and imminent death. But Rex could not believe that she was also a candidate for deathbed conversion to Catholicism. The time made it unlikely that Jack had been carried home broken and bleeding from the pit. When he prayed 'Please God don't let it be Enid', he was as much concerned with the trauma of behaving towards her as a priest as he was about the injury or illness from which she might be suffering.

'Come on,' said the boy. 'He said quick as you could.'

Rex ran so fast down Langwith Road that he did not notice that the boy was laughing. He ran on through Brack's yard and into the kitchen without pausing to knock on the door. Rex followed him, braced for the bad news.

Brack sat at the kitchen table. He was reading the *Daily Worker*.

'What's happened?' Rex wiped the condensation from the lenses of his *pince-nez*.

'What do you mean, what's happened?'

'The boy said you wanted to see me.'

'So I do.'

'But he said it was urgent.'

'Did he say that? Silly little bugger. Wait till I see him tomorrow.'

'So nobody's ill or injured?'

'You sound disappointed, Father.'

Rex sank down on the other side of the table. Brack turned the pages of his newspaper.

'Listen to this, Father. "The Pope And The Working Man. Some people will rejoice that the Pope has chosen to speak out about the dignity of Labour".'

'You sent for me to discuss that?'

'I didn't send for you, Father. I just said I'd like to see you.'

'Well, perhaps some other time.' Rex, who had at first felt relieved, only felt ridiculous.

'Busy tonight, are you, Father? Pity. It would have been an ideal moment. They're all round at the tennis club . . .'

Rex stood up and edged towards the door.

'It beats me,' said Brack. 'If somebody was interested in a Labour Party pamphlet we'd want to talk to him about it. Doesn't your Church want new recruits?'

'Thinking of joining, are you?' Rex asked.

'No. Not that.' Brack noticed that the priest was unusually belligerent and made a tactical retreat. 'I didn't mean to cause you any inconvenience. I just like to keep up with things.'

'Well, you haven't done. His Holiness published the encyclical more than two months ago.'

'Would you believe it? Just shows that the *Daily Worker* isn't what it was. Old Harry Pollit's just found out about it. "It is all very well for the Pope suddenly to discover the dignity of labour . . ." Old Harry Pollit's suddenly discovered the Pope's discovery!'

Brack began to laugh at his own joke, but the laughter died away when all the sounds that Rex dreaded hearing echoed in from the yard. Mick yelped. The wheels of the bathchair crunched

through the gravel. Enid, voice loud with excitement, was describing the day as one of the happiest of her life.

The back door swung open and Jack backed in as he eased the
wheelchair over the threshold. Sensing that there was a visitor in
the kitchen, he turned round and revealed the silver cup on Mrs
Brackenbury's knee. A terrible silence fell over the whole room.

Enid, still in her tennis dress, stood in the doorway with her
head bowed. Rex, white faced, clasped and unclasped his hands.
Jack's expression combined surprise, pleasure and respect in equal
measure. Brack surveyed the scene with obvious satisfaction. He
turned to each member of his family in turn as if he was honestly
surprised to see them.

'I didn't think you'd be back this early. A young man who
came in for petrol told me you were celebrating. We were having a
bit of a talk.'

'You knew we wouldn't stay,' said Enid. 'Not with Mam.'

'What about your manners?' Brack asked. 'Aren't you going to
say good evening to our guest? We were just having a bit of a
discussion.'

'It's nice to see you, Father,' said Jack.

'It is,' said Agnes. 'And it's been such a long time. Not since
you were ill. And we saw so much of you last summer. How are
you?'

All that Rex wanted to do was walk half a dozen paces across
the room and escape into the warm summer night. But he was
paralysed by anguish. Suddenly everybody began to talk at once.
Through the hubbub of questions about whether or not he was
going to buy another car, when they could expect to see George
and if he was looking after himself properly, Jack's apology
sounded strangely artificial.

'I'm sorry that you haven't seen us at early mass since the
wedding, Father. We haven't missed. We've been going to your
old church at Mansfield in the evening.'

Brack gave a huge wink.

'Can't get them up in the morning, Father. You know how
newly-weds are. Perhaps you don't. But take it from me. You'll
not see them at early morning service for a week or two.'

Rex was paralysed no longer. He managed to stutter 'good-night' as he took the half dozen steps to the door. Jack stepped aside. Agnes flinched as if she thought that he was going to brush against her aching shoulders. As he pulled the back door closed, he heard raised voices in the kitchen behind him.

'What's up with him?' asked Brack. 'Funny way for a priest to behave.'

'You arranged all this,' said Enid. 'You arranged it to spoil my evening.'

'HE REALLY isn't very well,' Bill Ellis was developing the court-ier's talent for understatement. 'You better be prepared for a shock. He's really gone downhill during the last couple of weeks. That's why he asked you to come. Wants to talk all the time. Can't bear lying there thinking.'

Rex had hoped that the visit to Nottingham would take his mind off the terrible events of the previous evening. Unfortu-nately, one sort of anguish does not drive out another.

'What is it?' Rex, who still felt sick whenever he thought of the patients on the road to Lourdes, hoped that it would be nothing visible.

'It's his stomach. We're trying to persuade him to go to St Mary's. We can't look after him here properly. But you know what he's like.'

The failure to specify the bishop's illness confirmed Rex's fear that it was cancer. As he climbed the steep stairs, he rehearsed reassuring comments about swift return to duty and imminent convalescence.

The bishop's bedroom was not what Rex had imagined it would be. He had imagined oak panelling, a stone fireplace, a four-poster and a chandelier. It was exactly like the whitewashed cell in which he had spent the night of his first flight from Langwith Junction – the same picture of the Pope, the same plain wooden washstand and the same low bed under the narrow window. Bishop Dunn, propped up on two pillows, was barely recogniz-able.

'It *is* me, dear boy.'

He held out his hand. Rex knelt to kiss his ring. The fingers were so emaciated that the ruby hung loose above the knuckle. Rex closed his eyes. He could feel the bones under the skin and feared that, if he looked, he would flinch away.

'Before you ask, I'm very well. Far better than this Jeremiah makes out.'

Rex knew that the bishop was asking for reassurance. He wanted to hear that Father Ellis had confirmed that complete recovery was certain and imminent. The bishop was afraid of death and wanted to be told that he was not going to die.

'I didn't even know that you were ill, my lord.'

'I haven't been for very long. Bit of indigestion, started about six weeks ago. But I've been keeping an eye on you. I'm very proud of you.' He eased himself on to his elbow. 'I wanted to tell you about my letter from Valladolid.' He reached with difficulty into the locker by the side of his bed. 'It's a fascinating letter. Sit down. These days I don't take up much room.'

Rex, terrified of crushing part of the withered frame, lowered himself on to the bed with ponderous caution.

Bishop Dunn picked out the nugget of news from each page. 'Henson, the new rector says that all's quiet now. He's not even sure if the fire was arson. He hasn't seen a Republican for months.'

Rex would normally have been fascinated by a first-hand account of the upheaval in Spain since, unlike domestic politics, it was the stuff of which history books are made. But he had to counterfeit interest. He assumed that the letter contained news of George and George was more important than an incipient Civil War.

'Henson's full of contempt for the king, running off like that.' He gave a forced laugh and then turned suddenly serious. 'They've treated Henson very badly. Ought to have been made rector years ago. At least he's in fashion with Rome now.'

'There's a bit about your brother, later on.' Bill Ellis had noticed Rex's anxiety.

The bishop turned to the last page.

'Your brother will be ordained in Valladolid. Despite all the trouble, they're not coming home. I can tell you that for certain now. Cardinal Bourne's going over to show the flag.' He laughed at his own joke before explaining it. 'He's taking a Union Jack to fly over the college. He thinks it will frighten the anarchists off.'

Bishop Dunn seemed to have drifted off into a half sleep. 'Come and see me again, Rex.' The last word was spoken in a long sigh.

'I'd better tell you what he meant to say.' Bill Ellis was well out of earshot of the bishop's bedroom but he still whispered out of fear or respect. 'He wants you to go to Valladolid for the ordination. Likes the idea of family being there. He's looking at ways of buying you a ticket. I thought he would manage to get it out. But he frightened himself by talking about the rector. He thinks that Henson will come here after he dies. I don't know where he got the idea from, but he's got it. And he's terrified of dying. It's ridiculous. He's a bishop and he's so afraid of death that he wouldn't even admit he was ill for weeks. That's why he didn't have any treatment. Now it's too late.'

'Really too late?'

'No hope. We're talking about weeks. God rest his soul.'

'God, Bill, you're talking about him as if he was dead already.'

'I've lived with it for nearly a month. And I've lived with his fear. It's not easy to feel much respect. How many Easter Day sermons has he preached? He's supposed to welcome death as a victory. Now he wakes me up in the middle of the night because if he lies awake on his own he thinks about being in the vault under the cathedral.'

'You're a hard man, Bill.'

'I'm a priest, Rex. I get up at three and I pray with him and I listen to his ramblings until he drops off. I'm sorry for him. Then he tells me what he's thinking. The pain of the world going on without him. The sadness of thinking of this house without him in it. The fear that he won't be remembered. It's pagan, at best. Not a word about forgiveness or redemption. Nothing about resurrection. But the last few weeks he's . . .'

'Unnerved you?'

'Not a bit, Rex. The very opposite. I've never been more

certain of God's love.' It was clear that Bill Ellis had practical matters on his mind. 'There's another bit of the letter he hasn't told you about.'

'Tell me.'

'George is supposed to be worried about your father. When he heard the ordination was definitely in Spain, he was very upset. They think that he wanted to come home early to keep an eye on him. George seems to think the marriage isn't a success. Says your father isn't happy.'

'That,' said Rex, 'shows how little George knows about his dad. He's been away too long. I can put his mind to rest with a single postcard. I'll write to him today. If that's all it is he won't come home.'

'His lordship will be very grateful.'

'My father has never been unhappy for more than half an hour in his life. If he had, he might have taught us how to deal with it when it comes. It's like poor old Bishop Dunn. When you're told that everything will be all right in the end, you're not prepared for real life.'

THE NEXT Sunday, Enid insisted on going to early mass at St Joseph's. Jack had wanted to stay in bed, for during the previous afternoon his little brother had married Katherine Fox in a godless registry office and after Enid had left the Miners' Welfare to look after her mother, the brothers had drunk away their sin and sorrow until the newest Mrs O'Hara – who had seemed happy enough – fell asleep on her husband's shoulder. But despite Jack's aching head and dry mouth, Enid had him out of bed by half past six.

The change of routine caused Agnes Brackenbury great distress, for it meant that her daughter was out of the house at the time when she needed to get up and wanted to come down. But although Enid had previously been prepared to meet her mother's convenience, on the Sunday after Rex's visit she was obdurate. The O'Haras arrived at the church so early that it was empty apart from them. With twenty rows of pews to choose from, Enid led the way to the front row.

Rex, instead of being reassured by the sight, thought only of

Brack's crude joke. He looked at Enid in anguish and, for a moment, she dropped her guard and looked at him in a way which left no doubt about her feelings. She felt that she was still in love and would be in love with him for ever. She felt it so strongly and showed it so clearly that even Jack understood what, for so long, he had not even suspected.

He tried hard to concentrate on the mass, but he could think of nothing except his wife's infatuation. Shame made it impossible for him to confide in his brother, and he dared not speak of it to Enid herself in case she admitted it to be true. Nor dared he ask Father Hattersley for advice. The burden of his wife's foolishness could not be heaped on to the priest, against whom she sinned almost as much as she sinned against her husband. They walked home in silence.

It was one o'clock before Jack spoke.

'I'm nipping out for a pint,' he told his wife.

Nipping out for a Sunday pint typified all that Enid hated about Langwith Junction. It was how other colliers behaved. Jack had not taken a Sunday drink since they were married.

'You can't,' she said. 'Dinner's almost ready.'

'I can,' he said, 'and I am. Who's going to stop me?'

The unusual aggression made Agnes gasp with fear. It evoked too many memories of a brutality from which she hoped to have escaped.

'Take no notice of him, Mam. He's just upset because his precious Eamon has joined the army.'

'Not at all,' said Jack, reassuringly unprovoked by Enid's reckless and intentional provocation. 'I'm glad to see the little madman on his way. Katherine's welcome to him.'

'Irish Guards,' Enid scoffed as if Eamon's pretensions were his brother's responsibility. 'I should say Irish Guards. After all that talk, he ended up in the Service Corps.'

She looked up from the beans she was slicing so that she could enjoy his hurt reaction. There was no reaction at all. The jacket of his best suit was still on the back of his chair, where he had left it since he got home from mass. He pulled it on with defiant deliberation, crossed the room and walked out into the yard.

Despite her father's impatience to be on his way to Mansfield and the regular Sunday afternoon *rendezvous* with Mrs Wood, they waited to serve dinner until almost three o'clock. When Jack got home, the joint, untouched except for Brack's portion, was surrounded by a cold sea of coagulated gravy. To everybody's surprise, Jack was sober.

'Where have you been?' Enid asked, having no doubt about the answer.

'A walk.'

'And drinking,' Enid added.

'I had a couple of drinks. Then I went for a walk. I wanted to think.'

Jack, who was unaccustomed to careful thought, had done no more than allow ideas which had rattled around inside his head all morning, to drop into place. He could not bear to speculate, even in his own mind, about what his wife really felt about the priest and what that revealed about her feelings for him. But he knew that they could not remain in St Joseph's parish. Pride, respectability and the hope of happiness all demanded that they should move. He took Enid by the hand and led her into the living room.

'I hope,' he said, 'that you're not going to argue. Because there are things that are best not said. But I'll say 'em, if I have to.'

Enid did not even try to interrupt.

'You and I are going to move out of Langwith.'

She asked where to, not why, and he told her that he could get a job in any of the three great coalfields of middle England and that she could choose whichever pit village took her fancy as long as it was more than twenty miles from Langwith Junction.

'What about Mam?'

'She'll come with us.'

'We can't be too far from Worksop.'

The concern was genuine. She had grown to rely on Anne and Lottie and she was afraid of dealing alone with her mother's deteriorating health. But Jack did not believe her.

'The time for all that sort of rubbish is over.'

'It's not rubbish. When Mam's really bad I need some help.'

Jack knew what she said was true. He prided himself in helping as much as a man could. And Mrs Brackenbury had often thanked him for being so kind and considerate. But there were some things that only a woman could do and Enid was notably short of female friends. Being a decent man, his determination – although not undermined – was temporarily subdued. He played for time.

'Think about it.'

She thought about it all afternoon and evening and for most of the night and decided that marrying Jack had been the greatest mistake of her life. As he lay beside her snoring his way through another untroubled night, instead of counting sheep she counted a balance sheet of his qualities.

His unfailing courtesy and endless patience had begun to annoy her. But she had the grace to admit that those gentle virtues had once been part of his attraction. He was gentle – particularly with her mother – and unfailingly reliable. The pay packet, which had once remained in his back pocket until it was empty, was handed over unopened every Friday night and he received, in return, the few coppers necessary for him to hold up his head in the Miners' Welfare. Gratitude for his generosity had turned into contempt for his subservience.

Jack was also the cause of constant small embarrassments. She recalled one incident which had caused her particular distress. On the day after Ellsworth Vines beat Fred Perry in the American Open Tournament at Forest Hills, Enid and Jack had played tennis together at the Langwith club. As usual they had won and, as usual when she was victorious, Enid had been happy. One of their vanquished opponents had compared Jack to the American champion and Jack had said that he would prefer to be Fred Parry. There was, Enid knew, nothing intrinsically wicked in mispronouncing the name of England's greatest tennis player, but she felt ashamed of her husband's ignorance – an ignorance that made the other tennis players giggle and was totally typical of the man she had married. Jack never got things quite right.

But one attribute, above all others, convinced her that she and Jack were incompatible. He was too concerned with what, even in her own mind, she called 'the physical side of marriage'.

In fact, Jack was remarkably undemanding. He was by nature a warm and affectionate man, but he was also far more sensitive than either his wife or his workmates would have allowed, and he found the idea of forcing himself on an unwilling wife so repulsive that even the thought of it made him incapable of behaving in so detestable a fashion. So he suffered in virtual silence and consoled himself with the hope that one day – when they were in their own house, when Mrs Brackenbury was sound asleep, when Enid felt more confidence in him or when Mick was dead – he would be part of what, even in his own mind, he called 'a proper Catholic marriage'.

The conclusion to which Enid came, during her long and sleepless night, had a natural and inevitable corollary. She should have formed a more spiritual sort of union. It did not take her long to decide what the union should have been. She knew – and slowly came to admit that she had always known – that she should have married Rex. Of course she blamed him for the end of their strange relationship. Rex had failed her. He had not even acknowledged the last desperate letter which she had sent to Nottingham. But she still loved him, faults and all.

Initially, she felt only regret. Then, as the night dragged on, her predominant feeling was every sort of frustration. Frustration led to fantasy. She began to dream of a dramatic reunion, followed by a close platonic friendship. Slowly, the idea of Abelard and Eloise faded. She was not sure and dared not fully consider what she wanted their relationship to be, but she grew obsessed with her need for a relationship of some sort. At half past six she crept silently out of bed and stole downstairs. For the first time in her life, she was going to a weekday mass.

REX DID not even see her until the service was over. Then, after the mixture of pleasure and pain which made him feel too weak to stand, he prayed for strength to go on behaving sensibly.

That he was acting sensibly had become his greatest consolation. It was not possible for him to forget Enid. Indeed she filled his thoughts for far too much of his time and crept into his mind at the most inappropriate moments. But although he could not prevent himself from thinking about her, he could resist the temptation to act in the foolish way which his thoughts encouraged.

For months he had steadfastly not walked where he thought that she might be walking, not called round to enquire after Mrs Brackenbury's health, not visited the tennis club and had not invited Jack O'Hara to bring his wife to one of the social evenings arranged by the Society of Mary. And because he had behaved so responsibly, responsible behaviour was gradually becoming second nature to him. He was beginning to face his bleak future with equanimity which even the awful confrontation in Brack's living room had not completely destroyed. Common sense encouraged calm and calm bred composure. Then, for no apparent reason, Enid had come alone to early morning weekday mass.

As he stood in the dusty vestry and pulled off his cassock, he told himself that he had behaved sensibly when he had come face to face with her on the night of Brack's practical joke and that he could behave sensibly again. Then he rushed down Langwith Road. When he arrived at the gate into the coal yard, he had still not decided what excuse he would give for his unexpected call on the O'Haras.

The back door was ajar, just as it had been on his first visit to Langwith Road. When he knocked – just as timidly as he had knocked on that fateful morning – again there was no reply. He knocked a second time and then a third. From deep inside the house, through the kitchen, and somewhere beyond the hall in the living room, Brack called 'Come in'. He sounded as impatient as Agnes Brackenbury had sounded when, not understanding the conventions of the invalid's house, he had waited on the step. Brack, his back to the door, was leaning over the dining table which, since Rex's last visit, had been pulled under the window. Hearing the tentative footstep in the hall, he shouted, without straightening his back: 'Come in if you're coming.'

Rex walked in.

'Sorry, Father. All the Catholics are upstairs. Jack's still asleep and Enid's in the middle of doing what she does for her mother.'

He returned to the examination of the various pieces of machinery which were spread across the table.

'I called in to apologize for being so rude last week.'

'What do you take me for, Father? You didn't come here to say you were sorry. You came here in case you could get a word with her. You're still trailing after her.'

All the proper remonstrations came to mind. But Rex did not even have the heart to imitate outrage. He backed towards the door.

'I'm not blaming you. I just don't like being taken for a fool. You saw her in church and you came running after her.'

Rex turned into the hall.

'And it's no use getting on your high horse. I'm the only friend that you've got in this family. She'd have been much better going off with you than marrying that great Irish lump. I told her as much on her wedding day.'

Brack feared that Rex, still and silent in the hall, had not yet been provoked beyond endurance. He did not wait to see if the desired explosion was on the way, but lit another fuse.

'That's assuming of course that you really wanted to marry her. For all I know—'

Before the provocation was complete, Rex was back in the living room, deathly white, his fist clenched and a pulse throbbing in his forehead.

'You know very well that I did.' It was almost a whisper.

Until Rex spoke, Brack assumed that the priest was going to hit him and had decided that, notwithstanding spectacles and vocation, he would have to defend himself. He was rather looking forward to telling the tale in Cobbler Jack's. 'I'm old enough to be his father and I could have managed him with one hand tied behind my back.' But the reproof was delivered with more measured self-control than was natural. Brack had wild fears of suicide under one of the coal lorries that thundered past the end of his yard or even a quick return with the carving knife from the kitchen drawer. He made a strategic retreat.

'You're right, I do. And I'm sorry that it didn't happen. So is her mother.'

It was total invention. Brack had no information about his wife's current view on that or any other subject, though he understood that Jack O'Hara could not have looked after her better if she had been his own mother. But he hoped that Rex would be comforted by news of his general popularity.

'She misses you, does Mrs Brackenbury. Used to enjoy your talk about books and that sort of thing.'

'But Enid doesn't?'

Sympathy was not an emotion which often burdened Brack. But looking at Rex – smaller and more bent than he had seemed a moment before – he felt only sorrow that a man should suffer so much in such a bad cause. There was no feeling of regret at having increased the pain, only a mixture of pity and contempt which he thought of as human kindness.

'Sit down a minute.'

Rex obeyed instantly.

'It's none of my business, Father. But, if you take my advice you'll put all thought of our Enid out of your head. I don't know – and I don't want to know – what went on between you. But it never would have come to anything. She's not one for a scandal. And she wants somebody who she can put-on. That's what she's got.'

'Is she happy?' It was not a question but a challenge.

'I'd be the last one to know that. She'd put it on with me whether she was or not. She reckons not to think much of me. But it's not right. She wouldn't like me to think that she'd made a mess of things. Enid wants me to think that she's special. And so I do. Too bloody special for him that she's married to.' He feared that he noticed a glimmer of hope in Rex's eyes. 'But put her out of your mind. I don't know why you came back here to torture yourself. I'll call her downstairs if you want me to. But I don't advise it. Get them to move you to another church. I tell you that she wouldn't have done it before and now that she's married, there's no chance.'

'She came to early mass this morning. You don't want to believe it, but it's the only possible reason. Whatever you say, I know why she came. She came to see me.'

'I don't doubt it for a minute. The question is why. I know her. You don't. She came to see if you were still on the end of her string.'

It was only by a mighty effort of self-restraint that Rex prevented himself from saying 'I am'.

Brack leaned back in his chair and launched into one of the homilies which had become a feature of his late middle age.

'If you take my advice, you'll find something to occupy your time instead of just sitting and brooding. You've not enough work to do. Father Froes, now. He had it all worked out. He had a hobby. But you're not interested in horses, are you, Father?'

Rex looked guilty.

'Strange that most Catholic priests are. Father Froes used to say that the Irish ferry was black with 'em on the day before the Grand National. We had some good times together, me and Father Froes. But if you're not interested, there's no help there.'

'No.' Rex agreed. 'No help there.'

'Me, on the other hand, I never waste a moment. I know now't about armatures, but because they're putting 'em in motors these days, I'm finding out.'

If Rex had replied, Brack would have gone on expounding the gospel of hard work and enthusiasm. But Rex had endured almost as much improving advice as he could tolerate.

Brack did not see his guest out. Instead, he returned pensively to work on the electric motor. He was still trying to put it back together when Enid came downstairs.

'Who was that?'

'Father Hattersley.'

'Why didn't you tell me?'

'He didn't come to see you. He came to see me.'

'I don't believe you.'

'I'll tell you straight. He says you're pestering him. If you don't stop he's going to have a word with Jack.'

CHAPTER TWELVE

Bishop Dunn died in the Convent of Mercy Nursing Home, late on a hot August night. He was alone.

He had received the blessed sacrament in the early evening, soon after Dr Coogan had whispered that it was 'only a matter of time'. The Mother Superior felt sure that a bishop's last rites should be administered by the Vicar General or the Cathedral Administrator. But when the shouting and kicking – which had made the day terrible – subsided into a deep and smiling sleep, she feared that time did not allow for observance of the proper procedures, and the curate, who was making a routine visit to less exalted patients, was enlisted to speed Bishop Dunn's soul on its way to purgatory, Paradise and heaven.

The funeral service more than made up for the inadequacies in the way in which Bishop Dunn's last sacrament had been administered. Cardinal Bourne preached the sermon and spoke with episcopal eloquence of forty years' service to the Church. His account of Bishop Dunn's ministry included, at Father Ellis's suggestion, a description of how, during his last visit to Rome, he had insisted on prostrating himself before the Pope. The cardinal was not altogether convinced that such a theatrical gesture was entirely to the bishop's credit. He turned with more conviction and enthusiasm to the 'restoration of all things Pugin' which had been the abiding theme of Bishop Dunn's renovation of the cathedral. Finally, he gave thanks for the many 'splendid young men' who had entered the Church because the 'most gentle of teachers' had drawn their attention to 'God's urgent call'.

The priests of the diocese sat in the Lady Shrine in memory of Bishop Dunn's habit of kneeling there each evening and reciting the rosary with the cathedral clergy. Rex wondered if the shrunken old man, whose sick room he had visited in July, had remained afraid right to the end.

As the service ended with the choir crying 'Fiat Voluntas Tua' in unison, and then repeating 'Thy Will Be Done' to make sure that all the congregation knew that the bishop's motto was a pun built round his name, Father William Ellis handed Rex an envelope. To his relief, identical envelopes were passed along the rows to other priests. Whilst officers of the Guild of the Blessed Sacrament – which Bishop Dunn had founded – escorted the coffin to the crypt, Rex picked furtively at the wax seal which held down the flap of the envelope. He was still in the porch when he read the letter. It was an invitation to visit Bishop's House immediately the service was over but, since it had been written by the Vicar General, it was written in the language of a command.

The handful of young priests who assembled at Bishop's House were all members of what Monsignor Payne would have described as the 'junior clergy'. Rex was the only guest with a parish of his own. It was generally assumed that the senior incumbents were being refreshed more lavishly elsewhere.

When the door burst open it was not the housekeeper with food and drink, but the Vicar General himself with a folded sheet of foolscap.

'Please sit down.' His courtesy had the intended effect of causing visible embarrassment to those young priests who had not stood up.

'Bishop Dunn, having renounced material pleasures and all that wealth can buy, set up a trust some years ago to dispose of the legacy which he had inherited from his father. As you know, much of the capital was used, in his lifetime, for cathedral restoration. But a considerable sum remains. Some weeks before his death he made recommendations about how part of the money should be spent. The trustees were pleased to agree with his recommendations.

'The largest part of what is to be now distributed will be divided between the Accademina de Nobili Ecclesiastici and the further restoration work which his lordship had commissioned Mr Frederick A. Walters, FSA, to supervise. The trust is also to make half a dozen small payments to individuals. I must emphasize to you, the recipients, that you are not the beneficiaries of a will.

Bishop Dunn possessed nothing except a few personal effects. Those have been bequeathed to his sister and are no concern of ours. You will hear from Canon Hunt, the secretary to the trust, during next week. Thank you.'

Monsignor Payne held up the hand of a man who was, *pro tempore*, the head of the diocese.

'God bless you.'

It was a fortnight before the letter arrived. Folded inside it was a cheque which promised to pay Frederick Roy Hattersley fifty pounds.

More than the size of the bishop's benefaction made Rex's hand shake. He was afraid to read the letter – afraid that it would congratulate him on returning, like the prodigal son, to his true family and afraid that it would express his patron's pride in the way in which he had withstood the temptations of the flesh. Judas, having been paid thirty pieces of silver for betraying Jesus, hanged himself. A gift of fifty pounds for abandoning Enid put the same idea into Rex's head. He opened the letter.

The first page, which had clearly been written during Bishop Dunn's last days, was covered from top to bottom in an uneven hand that the dying man had scrawled at an angle across the whole sheet of paper. Sentences usually possessed a legible beginning, but rarely went on to a legible end. The opening paragraph began clearly enough to make Rex's life worth living again.

> I am making small gifts to each of the young men on whom the future of the diocese depends . . .

He worked his way through the meaningless references to the wisdom of Pius XI, the sudden asides on the importance of a good education and the garbled reflections on the nature of the Trinity to the last paragraph which, as the result of supreme or superhuman effort, was easily read and understood.

> No doubt your instinct will be to spend the money on something connected with your church – but please, no memorial. No candles. No masses. I have a better suggestion . . .

Bishop Dunn was reaching out from the grave to determine how his gift was to be spent. In death – as in life – he wished to impose his will on those around him, if possible without taking the blame for the problems which followed.

> It would give me great pleasure, dear Rex, to think during my final days of you doing something which you would really enjoy. Please use my little gift to pay for a visit to Valladolid at the time of your brother's ordination. I know how strong your family feelings are . . .

The sentence ended abruptly at the bottom of the page and Rex turned to the second sheet. It was not, as he had imagined, the conclusion of the bishop's last message, but a note written by Bill Ellis.

> I know that the bishop's letter is almost impossible to read. It was difficult to write. It was the last of all, written two days before he died, God rest his soul.
>
> He was very keen that you go to Valladolid. Wanted to keep you three brothers together.
>
> In haste now. No idea for months who's coming here. Be ready for something better. Something different anyway. V.G. talks of you being p.p. at Heanor.

Rex put the cheque inside his missal. Forty-eight hours earlier he had longed to leave Langwith Junction. As soon as his wish seemed to be granted, he wondered if he could bear to live anywhere else. He tried to put Heanor out of his mind and think only of George and Valladolid.

TO REX, the visit to Valladolid seemed like a miracle. Even the date was providential. He would be in Spain whilst Syd was on Ratcliffe's cricket tour: Downside, Appleforth and Stoneyhurst. And two days after his return to England his brother would join him in the presbytery and help him through his last summer at

Langwith. He would still be lonely, but he would not be lonely on his own. The bishop's gift seemed like a God-given chance to put the parish behind him for a week without having to face leaving Enid's village for ever. He knew in his heart that it would be best to make a clean quick break. Then, the pain would not end but it would at least be dulled with time. But he had not the strength to visit Bishop's House and beg for an immediate move. Valladolid would keep him sane for a few more days.

The picture postcards, which George had sent him during his seven years in Spain, were pulled out of the cupboard and propped up on his bedroom dressing table. He rejoiced at the thought of even a temporary reunion with cloisters and paintings of English saints and martyrs. News of the political upheaval in Spain, previously barely noticed and never read, became the story for which he most avidly searched his newspaper. Bill Ellis, who offered to send him information on the English College, found nothing more exciting than an article in *The Month* for December 1894. But Rex read 'Jesuits and Benedictines in Valladolid, 1599 to 1604' from start to finish. In his mind, the Spanish seminary became a temporary refuge.

Enid searched desperately for similar sanctuary, or at least a decent excuse to avoid moving out of Langwith Junction. For weeks Jack did not even mention his determination to leave the village. But when she recklessly shook him awake and suggested early Sunday mass at St Joseph's, all the suppressed resentment exploded in a single brutal sentence.

'Mansfield tonight. I've told you. That's definite. Get back to sleep.'

She was so startled by the ferocity of his instruction that she did exactly as she was told. But after a few moments of tossing and turning she gently swung her legs over the side of the bed.

'I'll not tell you again. We'll go tonight. Get back in bed.'

'I'm just going to look after Mam.'

Jack rolled on his side and squinted, through eyes still filled with sleep, at the alarm clock.

'Don't let me find you've been down at that church.'

'I'll go if I want.' She had no intention of going, but fear as much as pride made her react against his attempt to keep her prisoner.

'Very well, my lady.'

He half sat up and, turning towards her, grasped her wrists in his hands.

'I've seen it all before in Ireland. I should have caught on months ago. I thought the Father had gone off his head when all the time he was . . .'

Jack dare not finish the sentence.

'If there was anything wrong with him he got over it. And you've got to get over it as well. Usually, it's young girls and they grow out of it. Well, I'm not prepared to wait. First, unless you change your ways I'm going to tell him. I'm going to tell the priest that you've got a daft schoolgirl crush on him —'

She gasped with outrage and tore her hands free. Jack seized her by the shoulders and shook her so hard that her head rocked backwards and forwards and her hair fell into her eyes.

'I'm going to tell him that's why we're moving out.'

'We're not. We're not moving out.' She cried with pain and fear. 'We're not.'

He shook her again.

Both of them shouted. Neither even attempted to listen to the other. Enid begged her husband to have pity on Agnes. Jack insisted that he would be master in his own house. She was sure that he was going to hit her, but just as she felt certain that he could not contain the anger, he began to reason, rather than threaten.

'Can't you see, it's ruining everything. It's not a proper marriage and it won't be until we get away from here.'

Enid began to cry with shame and pity. She was married to a gentle and loving man who wanted nothing more than a gentle and loving marriage. But she could not provide it. She wanted to tell him that she was sorry, but she could only sob.

'I'm not going. I'm not going.'

Jack lay back, near to tears himself. He had attempted to be reasonable and his attempt had been rebuffed. It was less than three months since his wedding and his marriage had already failed. He felt ridiculous as well as rejected, for he feared that most of the blame lay with him. It was not his way, but he should have put his foot down from the first day. He turned towards her again and put his great arms round her shoulders. There was only one way to make her see sense. She sobbed and she shouted but he did not let her go. He was a simple man and he told himself that the blessing of children would make her settle down.

Twice she told him that she heard her mother shouting and twice he took no notice of what he believed to be an invention. By the time that she got into the back bedroom Agnes had been so sick that Enid, who prided herself on not being squeamish, had to turn away as she changed the sheets.

When the bed was remade and Agnes lay white and shaken but at last comfortable, she announced that she would not get up that day. Enid tried to persuade her that she would feel better downstairs, but her mother, speaking faintly and finding it diffi-cult to choose the right words, said that it would be nice for the two young people to have the house to themselves. When Enid remembered that Brack was going to spend all day in Mansfield, she shuddered.

AGNES WAS sick again just as Enid and Jack sat down for dinner. It had been an uneventful morning. When Jack heard that Agnes was comfortable he had turned and gone back to sleep. Two hours later, when he came downstairs, braces dangling and feet bare, he behaved as he had behaved on the other Sunday mornings when they decided to miss early mass. As always, he sat in the living room with the *Sunday Empire News* and called to Enid in the kitchen every time he saw an item of particular interest. At one o'clock, when all the work for the dinner was done, he asked if he could be of any help.

Jack was on to his second helping when Agnes shouted. She had slept so soundly for most of the morning that Enid had not even woken her with a cup of tea, but suddenly a spasm of pain knotted her stomach and ran, in a dull ache, down her loins. Before she could shout for help she began to cough. She could tell from the taste in her mouth that she was vomiting blood.

Enid arrived in the bedroom a pace ahead of Jack, whilst her mother was still spluttering as much with fear as because of the convulsion inside her. Her head and shoulders lolled limp over the side of the bed.

'Help me sit her up before she chokes.'

Jack pulled her back on to the pillows. Enid put her arm under Agnes's head and, lifting it up so that Agnes breathed more easily, she began to make the comforting noises that a mother makes to soothe a frightened child. She was, Jack thought, the picture of tenderness. Even at that moment, he wondered why she was so rarely tender with him. Blood from the haemorrhage smeared her face and the front of her dress. Jack wanted to retch, but told himself that, if Enid was brave, he must be brave too.

'Shall I get her a drink of water?'

'The ulcer's perforated.' In a single sentence Enid dismissed his suggestion as absurd, emphasized the seriousness of the situation which they faced and established her authority. 'Get a wet flannel and a towel. Then get Dr MacDonald. Quick as you can.'

Whatever doubts Jack felt about his mother-in-law's condition were immediately removed. Mrs Brackenbury must be near to death. Nothing else could justify disturbing Dr MacDonald on a Sunday afternoon. Yet Enid remained calm and in majestic command. He knew that he should think of nothing except obeying her instructions, but he could not stop his mind from wandering to thoughts of how lucky he was, despite the little temporary difficulty, to be married to such a paragon. As he ran down the road, love – which he had always confused with admiration – swelled up inside him.

Dr MacDonald took what seemed an age to come to the door. He then refused, point blank, either to fetch his car from the garage down the road or run to Langwith Road. Jack had little doubt that Mrs Brackenbury would be dead by the time that he returned with help and no doubt at all that he would be blamed for it. He ran up the stairs, with the doctor several paces behind and burst into the room.

'Shush,' Enid told him. 'She's just dropped off again.'

The scene – daughter holding mother in her arms – was almost exactly the same as the one which he had left, except that (by some miracle) Enid had washed her mother and changed her nightdress in preparation for the doctor's arrival. She herself remained heroically bloodstained.

'You've not given her anything have you?' Dr MacDonald asked cryptically.

'No, doctor.' Enid replied with a deference which Jack thought wholly inappropriate in a woman who had just saved her mother's life. 'Not even water.'

Before Dr MacDonald left, Enid made a long and obviously unwelcome speech of thanks. During the peroration, she actually blocked the doctor's escape route to the road and home. She explained that her mother would wish to be associated with her expression of gratitude. Jack waited anxiously to hear the doctor's prognosis. He only received instructions.

'You'll have to take it in turns to sit up with her. If there's any more blood, she'll have to go into hospital.'

'Perhaps she ought to go now.' Jack was genuinely only interested in Agnes's welfare.

Enid was scandalized.

'It's best for her if she stays with me. Nobody will look after her like I do.'

At first they sat together by the bedside. Then Jack, full of guilt, went downstairs and stared at the paper without reading any of the news. When he took Enid tea and toast upstairs, she declined both with thanks.

'Are you going to manage through the night? I can't see Brack being much help. I can miss the shift.'

'I can manage. Aunt Anne will be here in the morning. I'll sleep then. We can't afford to lose a shift's money.'

She pushed herself off the bed and went downstairs to make his usual snap – cheese and pickled beetroot sandwiches – and fill his bottle with cold sweet tea. Brack was not home by the time that he left. Walking to the pit, he thought of Enid fighting to keep her eyes open until Worksop arrived.

At the end of the shift, the bath, as always, invigorated him. It was less fatigue than the formidable sight of Aunt Lottie already sitting in the kitchen which made him announce that he would have a lie down.

'Anne's with Aggie and Enid's having a sleep,' she told him without making clear if her comment was intended as a deterrent or an accusation of ulterior motives. Blushing, he climbed the stairs to join his wife in bed.

The room was warm and dark. Enid lay on her back snoring and Jack's half hearted attempts to roll her over on to her side only made the snoring louder. He climbed under the sheets beside his wife and because he was so tired not even the sound of her rebellious adenoids kept him awake. It was more than an hour before Mick pushed the door open and leapt on the bed.

Enid, exhausted by her long night, only half woke and Jack, both arms under the sheets turned on his side to push the dog away. As the dog snarled and jumped down, Jack's hand fell on to his wife's bare stomach. He left it there for the few seconds before a sudden convulsion made Enid's knees spring up and trap his arm as she rolled into a ball. She screamed.

'It's me, love.' He knew that she was still half asleep.

'Get off. Get off me. How can you when Mam's across there ill?'

He shook her awake.

'In the name of Jesus! Everybody will hear you.'

There was a moan from Mrs Brackenbury's room on the other side of the landing. The moan brought Enid back to life. Pulling down her nightdress she half fell and half rolled out of bed, and ran out of the bedroom and across the corridor. Anne, by the side of the invalid, lifted her finger in warning. Agnes groaned but did not wake.

Jack lay in the darkened room staring up at the ceiling and wondering how he would face the two old ladies who would, he knew, be sitting stone faced in the room below. He had no time to think about the void at the heart of his marriage. All that concerned him was the humiliation which awaited him in the kitchen.

'You didn't half make me jump then.' Enid began to dress. 'Mam only half woke up and she's dropped off again. Get some sleep. I'll wait to eat with you at tea time. Those two won't want anything. Not anything that's cooked on gas.'

WHEN JACK came downstairs after his fitful day's sleep, Aunts Anne and Lottie had left for home. Brack was, however, in command of the living room. He stood in front of the fireplace, legs apart and hands behind his back, like the lord of the manor. He showed no sign of concern about his wife's health.

'You look tired out,' he told his son-in-law.

'We're in a terrible seam,' Jack told him. 'Four foot at the most. Swinging the pick kills you.'

'Is that it?' Brack asked. 'I heard all that shouting from upstairs. I thought that you might not be getting your proper rest.'

Jack tried to pretend that he had either not heard or not understood.

'Never mind,' Brack told him. 'You'll be out of here in a couple of weeks, if what I hear is true. The agent says that your house will be ready next week.'

'What's that?' asked Enid who had appeared, dishevelled and bleary eyed, from the kitchen.

'That's not the only news,' Brack told her with obvious pleasure. 'The priest's leaving. He's going to Spain.'

BRACK SORTED his bills into three piles. A few he had no need to pay immediately, if at all. The doctor had written a curt little note on the bottom of his most recent account, but he would not dare to refuse his services. Anyway Enid boasted about her powers of persuasion. She could use them down at the surgery. Half a dozen of the larger creditors could, he was sure, be persuaded to give him more time. If Shell closed him down, they would lose the income from oil and petrol supplied for over more than a year. Brack, who knew about bankruptcy, having experienced it twice, was sure they would give him time. The council might be more difficult. In Brack's estimation, the Treasurer was quite unreasonable in his unwillingness to bend the rules for serving councillors. It would be difficult to postpone the payment of his rates for much longer without being summonsed. But he would try.

The bills in the third pile could not wait. He owed nearly seventy pounds in rent and the landlord was waiting for an excuse to transfer the tenancy to his daughter and son-in-law. A farmer in Cresswell, who had sold him a secondhand car in June, had already sent him a solicitor's letter threatening action if payment was not made in full by the end of the month. And there were the wages. They were not a bill at all, just dates and figures scrawled on a scrap of paper, but they were the most pressing debt. Fool that he was, he had persuaded the two men who worked for him to join a trade union. It had been almost a month since either of them received a full week's pay. Soon the union would start to make trouble.

It was not his fault. The country was in crisis. Everybody knew that. Philip Snowden said it everyday. The Prime Minister himself had insisted, 'It is not we who are on trial. The system is on trial.' The system had let Brack down. He had not sold a second-hand car since Whitsuntide. Marriages, when they took place, were conducted without the benefit of sleek, black Humbers. And the funeral trade, which never flagged, was monopolized by the Co-op. Coal sales, always bad in summer, had been terrible. It was not his fault. But he still had more than a hundred pounds to find within a week.

The real total was more, but he tried to push the last fifty out of his mind. That had been lost in a card school in Nottingham on the previous night. The evening had started with a hand of bridge at Cobbler Jack's and he happened to mention that he needed a winning run. Somebody had said that a player of his ability could make a fortune in a single night in a room at the back of the Black Boy, so Brack had talked his way in and lost fifty pounds. The gentleman who took his IOU did not look as if he would wait long for payment.

Brack examined his possible sources of income. With Jack in the house, it was more difficult to search for the small sums that Enid saved and hid, but he had found a total of seven pounds between the pages of books and hidden under clothes in her dressing table drawers. It was only a little, but it was a beginning.

Jane Wood could clear off his debts and never notice that the money had gone out of her bank account, but she would exact a terrible price for his salvation. The nearer he got to the date on which he promised to move to Mansfield the less appealing Mansfield seemed. He had developed a limited but rewarding relationship with the wife of an unemployed railwayman and he was not ready to settle down into what, marriage certificate or not, would be a more or less respectable union. Worksop had always helped in the past. They had set him up in the cycle shop, bought him out of bankruptcy, set him up again and bought off the girl who claimed – wrongly, as it turned out – that he had made her pregnant. But he could not see Worksop helping him out of another crisis. They knew it was only a matter of time before their precious Aggie moved out with Enid into Colliery Row. He would have gladly endured another lecture from Ernest Skinner and the reproachful glances of Anne and Lottie. But, they had never liked him and would not come to his rescue. It was, Brack felt, an unfair world.

He was still thinking of possible routes of escape when Jack came home from the late shift. Enid came down from her mother's bedroom to finish the supper and her husband immediately began to tell her the gossip of the day.

'You know, Father Hattersley's going to Spain.' He crinkled his eyes as he concentrated on gauging her reaction.

'Dad said last night.' Her attention did not waver from the loaf and butter.

'Well, it's only for a holiday.'

Enid and her father were united in their incredulity.

'It's true. He's been left money in Bishop Dunn's will. So have all the young priests in the diocese. Father Keogh told Mrs Ferguson and she told the lads she has lodging there now.'

'And he's spending it on a holiday?'

'He's going to see his brother. Father Keogh says that all the other priests are painting their churches or buying new altar cloths in the bishop's memory. But Father Hattersley is going on holiday to Spain.'

Brack, who usually ate his breakfast with ponderous care, left half the bacon untouched on his plate. Enid heard the back door slam shut. Her father had, for the first time she could recall, left for the day's work without a second cup of tea.

Rex was neither startled nor surprised to find Brack on his front doorstep, for he was no longer startled or surprised by anything that the Brackenbury family did. But it was not a welcome visit. Rex, having discovered that there was no way of thinking about Enid without feeling a dull immobilizing pain, was trying not to think about her at all. The sight of Brack put the thought of everything else out of his mind.

Normally, Brack had no time to waste on civilities. But, sitting in the priest's living room, he made a flowery little speech about not seeing Rex as much as he would have liked, complimented him on the number of books which he possessed and added that it was nice to think of him living so comfortably. It was the reference to comfort which aroused Rex's suspicions. Brack immediately confirmed them.

'I'm in a bit of trouble, Father.'

'How can I help?'

'I need to borrow a pound or two.'

'I'm hardly the man for that.'

'I'd heard that you'd come into a bit of money.'

Rex decided to tell the truth, since the truth was conclusive and therefore would end the conversation more swiftly than high-handed refusal to discuss the subject at all.

'The late bishop, God rest his soul, made me a small gift for a specific purpose. I am going to my brother's ordination in Spain. The ticket is bought. Money has already been sent to the seminary for my board and lodgings. I have kept a few shillings for the journey. The rest has already gone back to Bishop's House.'

Brack changed tack.

'But you must know where a pound or two can be borrowed.'

'How many pounds, Mr Brackenbury?'

'Two hundred.'

'I couldn't raise twenty. Anyway, why should I?'

'To help our Enid.'

Inevitably, Rex had momentarily thought of Enid sick or

dying, but he could tell from Brack's manner that it was not so. He stood up. Only another month and he would have a break from all this madness. He opened the living room door and waited for Brack to leave.

'I'm desperate, Father, and you're nearly my last chance.' Brack waited for a reaction. Rex neither moved nor spoke. 'I'll tell you why you should help me and why it will help our Enid. If you're any sort of a man, it's worth a few pounds to make sure that I keep quiet about what's been going on between you two. And still is, if I'm any judge.'

It was surprise, rather than the strength of the blow that made Brack fall off the chair. He had been a great fighter in his youth and had often brawled in middle age. But fighting always began with threats and challenges, the folding of coats and the rolling up of sleeves and the combatants grappling with each other before either of them struck a blow. He had never in his life been hit behind the ear whilst sitting in an easy chair.

When he got up, he kicked over Rex's pile of books. Then he picked up the poker and smashed the glass in the picture of the Sacred Heart. Rex assumed that it was his turn next. He backed towards the door.

'Don't you try to stop me leaving,' Brack shouted, 'or I'll break your bloody back.'

Rex stood aside. The proper relationship had been resumed. Brack was the aggressor, Rex the victim.

In the hall, he turned and, purple with anger, made his promise. 'You've got till Sunday. A hundred pounds by Sunday or everybody knows. Think how your bishop will feel about that.'

AGNES LAY white and still for almost a week. Lottie came out from Worksop every day, bringing with her all the food the family needed and a good deal more that no one in Langwith Road would eat. Jack, fortuitously on nights, kept vigil for most of the day, whilst Enid stood guard from dusk till dawn. Brack twice looked into the bedroom and once asked his daughter if the doctor believed that it would be 'a long job'.

When Agnes began to speak, all the talk was of Jack's goodness and her hope that Enid properly appreciated what a treasure he was. She told him that, for the first time in ten years, she felt part of a family again. 'As soon as we move into that little house . . .' Jack told her that they 'would talk about that after she was better'. She took it as a further sign of her closeness to her son-in-law.

For Enid, the hours spent at her mother's bedside were continual torture. Unlike Rex, who longed to put all thought of their times together out of his mind, she wanted to remember and re-live every detail. But memories of a true but star-crossed love could not survive the news that he was going on holiday to Spain. The idea that he might enjoy himself was intolerable. When at last her mother was well enough for Mick to be taken a proper walk, she almost walked down to the presbytery and confronted him with his betrayal. It was only because she dare not risk being told that he had recovered from his broken heart that she chose instead to walk in Scarcliffe Wood.

When she saw Rex standing by the gap in the hedge through which they had pushed their way so often during the previous summer, she almost turned and ran away. She had no doubt that he was waiting there in the hope of seeing her, and she was afraid that what he had to say would only add to her misery. His grave manner confirmed her fears.

'I need to talk to you.' He spoke more slowly than usual for he was finding it difficult to speak at all.

'Is there very much to say?'

'I'm afraid there is.'

Rex had worried and wondered whether or not he should tell Enid of her father's threat. Had he believed that Brack was only bluffing, he would have spared her feelings, but since he could not be sure, he felt he had a duty at least to warn her. He had waited until the day before the ultimatum ran out. Giving thanks that he had been spared the necessity of running Brack's gauntlet in Langwith Road, he apologized, told her the whole story and then apologized again.

'Do you think he'd do it?' he asked.

'I wouldn't put it past him,' Enid answered.

'Then we're in trouble. I can't possibly raise the money.'

'That wouldn't work anyway. He'd never leave you alone. Leave it to me. I'll get the money from Worksop.'

She knew exactly what she would do. Brack would be told that they wanted to move into Colliery Row as soon as her mother was well enough to face the exertion. She would announce that she had discovered – from a telephone call from one of the creditors – that he was in debt and would offer to avoid the risk of shame by borrowing the money from her aunts and uncle. But Worksop would not even know what had happened. The hundred pounds which Brack had given her as a wedding present was locked away for safety's sake in Owen Ford's sideboard. She would sacrifice it for the sake of her father's silence – at least she would sacrifice fifty pounds. Fifty pounds would buy time.

'Won't he still want to blackmail us?' When Enid took charge, Rex always lost all initiative.

'Not for a bit, he won't. I know him. He'll just be happy to have escaped. In a couple of months . . .'

In a couple of months, she thought, the world will be different.

She had seen Rex again – seen him alone and spoken to him. And once again the old obsession had returned. There was still a chance. But for the chance to be taken she had to convince Jack that their future lay in Langwith and the pit cottage in Colliery Row. She was sure that, if she gritted her teeth and really tried, she could persuade her husband that he had nothing to lose by staying in the parish.

'I'm sure that's best,' said Rex.

Enid turned away to complete her walk to Owl Spring.

'Enjoy your holiday,' she said without a trace of bitterness.

As he walked back to the presbytery Rex gave thanks that, in barely another week, he would be on the boat train. So he picked up the letter, which had come by second post, with great joy. George's writing and the gaudy Spanish stamp combined to make him give thanks for the one good thing that had happened to him for months.

Greetings and salutations!

I'm coming home. No final vows for me. I've thought and thought and decided that I don't want to be a priest. So no ordination. At least you won't have to trail to Spain.

I shan't be back for a couple of months. I've promised a long retreat and then I'm going to come back here for a bit. I'm going to do it but I want to do it properly. The rector has been very decent . . .

Rex did not even ask himself why his punishment never ended. He knew that the penance was eternal, for he had never repented his sin.

THE COTTAGE in Colliery Row was small and designed in a way which made it seem even smaller. If the coal owner's architects had been instructed to emphasize, by steep stairs and low ceilings, the inferior status of the company's employees, the house into which Enid and Jack moved with Agnes would have discharged that duty down to the last detail.

They moved out of Langwith Road on a still and airless morning in early August. As soon as Jack began to load the van with odds and ends of O'Hara property, particles of sweat began to dapple his shirt. When the wet cotton stretched from shoulderblade to shoulderblade and flapped uncomfortably against his back, he thought for a moment of working bare to the waist as he did in the pit. Then he remembered how offended his wife would be at such a show of vulgarity. Enid – all nerves and urgency – kept warning that unless they hurried, the Co-op van would arrive at Colliery Row before them and return to Mansfield without delivering their hire-purchase furniture. She had developed her Aunt Anne's habit of extending her bottom lip and blowing on to her face in order to cool her brow and disperse stray hairs that hung in her eyes. Brack steadfastly refused to change his routine. He lingered over breakfast and the *Daily Herald* and occasionally stopped Enid and Jack as they hurried past him with bags and parcels.

'Have you seen this, then? Bloody May Committee . . .'

Jack had never heard of the May Committee, Enid only vaguely.

'Twenty per cent off unemployment pay! Christ almighty.'

They were all too busy to be offended by the blasphemy.

Colliery Row suited Agnes. The special narrow bed which Ernest had made for her was put up under the window. She no longer spent half the day in exile upstairs. The ulcer improved, as Dr MacDonald had promised that it would, after the first few weeks of the rigorous diet which he had prescribed. Unfortunately the recipes so absorbed Enid's attention that she had no time to cook normal meals. Jack became the only collier in the coalfield to prepare for a day underground on poached plaice and semolina pudding.

But Jack was at first contented. During the last weeks in Lang-with Road, Enid had convinced him that at least a proper marriage was in prospect. They did not make love as often as he wished or in the way which he would have chosen. But he believed that by acting like a man on the day when he had first suspected her infatuation, he had driven all thoughts of the priest out of her head. Once away from her father's baleful influence, she would become the wife he wished her to be.

He was understanding, patient and tolerant in turn. But she was colder in the home of their own than she had been in her father's back bedroom. He reasoned, cajoled, persuaded and in the end forced himself upon her. For a week, they barely spoke and for all that time, his shame was greater than her anger. The gulf grew so great that there was only one thing for a God-fearing Catholic to do.

The church was empty at six o'clock, but it was Rex's duty to wait until seven, so he sat in his box and pulled the curtain closed and stared at the dead moth that lay on the floor between his feet. His mind wandered from cricket to politics and back again. Nottingham had a real chance of winning the County Championship. With any luck there would be a coalition government by the end of the week, men of good-will co-operating in the national interest. He had begun to wonder if there would be any communicants at all when, on the other side of the shabby velvet, there was a rustle, a swish and the smell of camphor. An old lady who was a stranger to the parish confessed that the Co-op grocer had given her too much change from her half crown and she had kept it.

'Give it back,' the priest told her, adding impiously, 'You don't have to tell him that you knew all along. Tell him you found out when you got home. And say two Hail Marys.'

A young man who began by confessing that he was a railway guard embarked on a confused account of something that had happened in Mansfield on the previous Saturday night. He got through the preliminary apologies and admission of guilt easily enough but the narrative spluttered to a halt when he left the Cavendish Hotel at ten o'clock, as far as Rex could make out, without committing any more serious a sin than spilling his beer.

'What happened then?'

'It's difficult for me to say. I feel ashamed.'

'Together we can end the shame. It's all secret between you and me.'

After several more unsuccessful attempts to identify the young man's devil, Rex gave up.

'Try to sort it out in your own mind. Then come and see me again. You don't have to wait till next Friday. Call round at the presbytery. I'm usually there.'

The curtain rustled again.

'Good evening, Father.' It was the soft Irish brogue of Jack O'Hara.

'When did you last come to confession?' Rex was surprised by his own composure.

'To tell the truth, Father, I'm not sure if it's a confession I'm wanting. More like a bit of advice. Could we sit in the church?'

'I've got to stay in here. I can't see the people who are waiting. I'm not supposed to know who they are.'

Rex was fighting against the horror of talking to Jack O'Hara, man to man.

'Just tell me what you want to know.'

'Father, I'm not living a Christian life.'

'Why not?'

'I'm not living a Christian marriage.'

The empty feeling returned to Rex's stomach. Jack's reply was a well-known euphemism which he heard at least once a month. It was the decent way of confessing to artificial birth control.

'How long has this been going on?'

'It was bad when we were first married. I thought on the honeymoon that it would be different after. But it's got worse. Then it got better for a bit and I thought that when we got a place of our own. But now . . . At least we . . . Now she screams if I . . .'

As the great weight was lifted from Rex's heart and mind, he began to worry not about the success of Enid's marriage but the consequence of its failure.

'Do you talk to her, try to persuade her?' He dare not add 'force her?'.

'She won't listen to reason, Father.'

Rex knew, with a certainty which he had not felt for years, that he was about to take a decision which would alter the course of his whole life. He was afraid, but he had no doubt what he should do.

'Ask her to come round to see me. Sooner the better. Tonight, if she can. It will be less painful for us all if she comes on her own.'

CHAPTER THIRTEEN

ENID PUT her head in her hands and wept.

When Jack told her that he had been to see the parish priest and described – with agonized integrity – the reasons for his visit, she had looked at him with a speechless hatred which was far more frightening than the scream of rage which he had expected. Then, to his relief, he was deluged with the flood of anguish which he had anticipated.

'Do you really hate me as much as that? Have you got a scrap of decency in you? How do you think I can ever show my face in the street again? Would any decent man even think of talking about such a thing? Why did you marry me if all you wanted to do was humiliate me?'

The suggestion that she herself should visit the priest, which he had blurted out right at the beginning of his carefully prepared but badly delivered speech, was first ignored and then denounced as a combination of cruelty and perversion.

'I wouldn't talk about that sort of thing to my mother, let alone a man who's a stranger.'

Jack, remembering that she was a convert, forgave her for not understanding that priests, though sometimes strangers, were never men. He retreated to bed, slept on the edge of his mattress and prayed that, by the morning, she would have forgiven him. His prayer was granted. Next day, she sent him off to work with her usual brisk efficiency.

As soon as he had left, she asked her mother if she was well enough to be left whilst Mick was taken for his early walk. Agnes Brackenbury thought, long after the door banged shut, that she heard the dog barking in the kitchen. But she concluded that it must be her imagination and drifted back off to sleep. Wearing her best coat and the hat which she had bought for her honeymoon drive to Worksop, she walked as fast as she decently could to the presbytery.

Enid had no idea what she was going to do or say, for she had no idea what Rex was going to say to her. They had not met since the anguished conversation in Scarcliffe Wood and, in the months which had passed since her wedding, she had been to evening mass in Mansfield more often than the morning mass at St Joseph's.

The woman she would have liked to be – and still dreamed of becoming – would have boldly announced that she was in love and nothing else mattered. But she had a real fear that Rex, locked again in the Church's tight embrace, had sent for her to preach a sermon on Christian marriage. She was not sure if she could survive him telling her to go home and behave like a proper Catholic wife. Indeed she was not sure that she should be going to the presbytery at all, but no power on earth or authority in heaven could have persuaded her not to go. As she opened the gate, she feared that her knees would buckle under her and when she knocked on the door, she felt sick. If only, she thought, he tells me that he loves me, I shall feel whole and well and happy in a second. But she knew, in her heart, that such a deliverance was impossible.

Rex silently opened the door and, taking her hand, led her into the living room. Then she bowed her head and wept.

'There's nothing to cry about now,' he said, crying too. 'It's all right now.'

'How can it be?'

'Because we're going to be together. Always.'

'No, we're not.' She was crying inconsolably again. 'We can't be.'

'I love you and you love me.'

'That doesn't mean anything.'

'It means everything.' She had not ever heard him sound so determined.

'I don't know what to do. I can't stand much more, but I don't know what to do.'

'Come away with me. We need never be apart again. Not for a minute.'

'That's just ridiculous. And it's cruel. I want that so much and it can never happen.'

He pulled her towards him and they stood for a moment with their bodies touching for the first time. Rex could not help thinking about what Jack O'Hara had told him. With me, he thought, it will be different. He pulled himself away.

'Of course we can. And we will. This time, I'm going to make it happen. What time does Jack get home?'

'Two o'clock. He's on mornings. Why? We can't just run away. What about Mam?'

'I'm going to tell him. I'm going to make a clean breast of it. He's a decent man. He'll—'

'It will kill him,' Enid said, still crying.

'It will kill us if we lose each other. What else can we do?'

It was meant as a rhetorical question but, offered the opportunity to command, Enid's spirits visibly improved.

'We can't do it like that. I can't sit there whilst you tell him that we were going away together. I can't do it. There's only one way. You go away somewhere. Nottingham or Sheffield. Get a place and a job. Then Mam and I will come to you.'

He pushed himself to his feet and stood over her. She looked up at him, smiling at her own ingenuity and because she again felt in charge of her own life.

'Unless we do it now, we won't do it at all.'

'Rex, I can't. I can't leave Mam and I can't face Jack.'

'*The Statue and the Bust,*' he said.

'What are you talking about?'

He took her in his arms again.

'I love you.'

'You're laughing at me.'

'I suppose I am. But it's the first time that I've laughed for months. You're the one who's supposed to know about poetry, not me. Don't you remember? It's Browning. In the book I gave you.'

' "A sword filled up the empty sheath of a man." '

'That's the good bit. And that's what's happened, but the rest of the poem's not so encouraging. They keep putting it off. They love each other but there's always a reason for not going away together. In the end it's too late.'

'Life's not always like poetry. I've got Mam to think of.'

He had never heard her say a word against poetry before.

'I think you like all this agonizing. We don't have to go through days of torment. All you have to do is pack a few things in a bag, I tell Jack and we leave.'

'There's Mam, I tell you. She's all that's stopping me. She's been ill again all week. We can't move her yet. And I can't leave her.'

Rex was suddenly incapacitated by debilitating reasonableness. He could not think of any argument to justify abandoning Mrs Brackenbury. He imagined the message sent to her relatives in Worksop and Jack keeping guard until his relief arrived. It would be wrong – as wrong as running away without facing Jack and telling him the truth.

'Do you really want to do it?' he asked.

'Of course I do. How can you even ask?'

'Then don't argue. It's this way or no way at all—' He thought that she was about to interrupt him. 'If we fail now, we fail for good. I'm going to find a place. I'm going to start looking today.'

'Have you got any money? I've still got a bit. If you knew what it took to save that.'

Rex – certain that, at least until the plan was laid and executed, Enid's excursions into personal anecdote had to be curtailed – put his finger on her lips. She looked coyly down at her feet and gently subsided. But when he moved to take his hand from her face, she grasped it and held on tight whilst he set out his terms of surrender.

'I'm going to Nottingham here and now—'

'Not to tell them at the cathedral!'

'To look for a job and somewhere to live. And I'm going to see my father.'

He was testing her and, when she did not reply, he put her to the test more directly.

'We both need to feel that it's real, that it's not just a dream that we hide in. We need to talk to somebody about it so it's not just our fantasy. It has to become part of our ordinary lives. We want to behave like an ordinary couple.' He did not add, 'One of whom happens to be married to someone else.' 'Anyway, we need some friends. Are you going to tell your mother?'

'If I do, she'll tell Jack. She'll be sure that she's going to be left on her own and she'll want Jack to write to Worksop. She'll not keep a secret.'

'I'm going to tell Jack. I'd never forgive myself . . .'

The sentence was too stupid to finish. He was the parish priest who had joined them together in holy matrimony. When the marriage had begun to collapse he had been asked for help and he had responded by persuading the unhappy wife to run away with him. Yet he was talking as if breaking the bad news to the wronged husband was a moral obligation which honour required him to fulfil. It was only pride, the sin for which Lucifer was cast out of heaven.

'I'd like to tell Owen Ford.'

Rex, Enid knew, would be suitably reassured by the offer to tell anyone, but the idea of talking to Owen had real attractions. She could rely on his discretion. As a free-thinking radical, he would be sympathetic to her decision. Most important of all, by confiding in Owen she would convince herself that she really meant to run away with Rex.

'Tell him today.' Rex, for the first time in their relationship, was giving orders.

'I will. Today.'

In a second, the weight that had passed so heavily on Rex's life was removed. Relief turned into elation and elation into pure joy. It was really going to happen. He knew it. Taking Enid in his arms seemed the most natural thing in the world. To cry at such a moment seemed ridiculous. But she was crying too.

'I'll come back,' she said. 'Tonight, I promise.'

It was time for an act of pure and selfless love, the greatest commitment and the most complete act of dedication of which she was capable. She opened her handbag and took out the roll of pound notes which she had been left after her father was bought off. She handed them to Rex.

'You might need a deposit or something.'

Much to her surprise and almost equally to her disappointment, neither Mick nor her mother seemed to have noticed that she had been away. The dog was stretched out asleep in front of the fire and, in her narrow bed, Agnes, with her head down on her chest like a sleeping sparrow, was snoring softly.

It took Enid less than half an hour to clean out the fire, make the bed and shake the rugs out in the back yard. Then she gently shook her mother awake.

'I didn't want to wake you, but I've got a bit of shopping to do.' She looked down at the bedpan which was only partly hidden under the counterpane which hung down from the bed. 'Can you wait for your lift until I get back?'

Agnes was not sure that she could. So the lift was provided before Enid set off on her odyssey. As she carried the bedpan down the yard to empty it in the lavatory, she thought of what she would say to Owen Ford. She decided on the high romantic. 'I love him, Owen, and he loves me. It would be wrong to stay apart.' She left her mother staring at the *Daily Herald* headline: 'Cabinet Meets Again Today. Crisis Deepens.'

The market was almost empty and as she looked along the lines of stalls, Enid could see Percy Ford's bald head bobbing over his books. He greeted her as if she was expected.

'Do you know if your dad's signed? He never comes to Ward meetings these days. Jack isn't a member, is he? Never mind. There'll be another petition at the lodge meeting tonight.'

He handed Enid a sheet of paper headed 'Humble Petition to Charles Duncan Esq., Member of Parliament for the Clay Cross Division of Derbyshire'. When she hesitated to take it, he put a reassuring hand on her arm.

'I know you've not paid this year's subs, but you're still a member all right. You can sign.'

She took the pencil and wrote her name.

'Owen's down at the post office sending him a telegram. He reckons that Ramsay will do it today, the bastard. No stopping him now. But at least there's a chance.'

Enid wanted to tell him that the formation of a National Government was of no consequence to her – that Ramsay Mac-Donald's long awaited betrayal and the anticipated destruction of the Labour Party were trivial issues compared with her decision to live with Rex and be happy ever after. She tried to assemble enough courage to challenge his news with hers.

'We're all going into Derby tonight to Jimmy Thomas's meeting. Do you want to come? Thomas will go with him all right. Anyone who stabbed the miners in the back . . .'

'I'm busy tonight, Percy.'

Percy Ford barely heard her. He was denouncing the bankers' ramp which had destroyed the Labour Government.

'I'll be off, then,' she said.

'Don't lose faith,' said Percy. 'Never give up.'

BETTY HATTERSLEY was serving in the shop and, when Rex pushed open the door she went on weighing out nails as if he were just another customer. Then, when the bell on the shop door had rung shut and they were alone, she said, 'Your dad's not here. He's gone down to the Royal Oak for his dinner-time pint. You've only just missed him.'

'I'll walk down.'

'I wouldn't if I were you. He'll be with all his cronies, singing and telling his soft stories.'

Rex was about to reassure her that he had been in a public house before when he remembered the night in the Grove Hotel. His stepmother – for like it or not that is what she had become – was not worried that he would feel uncomfortable in the hearty atmosphere of the saloon bar. She was afraid that his father would not feel comfortable with him. It was the penalty Rex paid for being the child of a mixed marriage. Catholic fathers, with priests for sons, introduced them to their friends with undisguised pride. If he went round to the Royal Oak, his peculiar status would demand an explanation which sounded distressingly like an excuse. Rex had grown weary of feeling lonely.

'You're right. Can I come through?'

They sat for a few moments in the back room, staring uneasily at each other. Then the shop bell rang and Betty hurried back behind the counter. The customer was clearly a friend. The sound of animated, and occasionally agitated, conversation drifted through the half-open door. Betty was, he felt sure, describing the alien presence that sat in her living room.

It was more than half an hour before his father returned and embarked on a wholly unnecessary apology for his mid-day visit to the public house.

'Just passing through?' he enquired.

'Sit down, Dad. I've something to tell you. Don't look so worried. It's good news. At least, I think it is.'

'Promotion!' He was genuinely pleased. 'Your aunt Clare's been going on and on about you getting a proper parish.'

'Resignation.'

Herbert sank into a chair. Change always worried him. He had not wanted his son to become a priest, but when Rex became one, his father did not want him to be anything else. Change meant trouble and trouble was something that Herbert had devoted his life to avoiding.

'What's happened this time?'

'I'm going to get married, sooner or later.'

'God almighty! So you really are giving up. I don't envy you telling your aunt Clare. I should have said that I'm very pleased for you. And so I am, if it's what you want. We ought to have a drink to celebrate.' He opened the sideboard door. 'Not got much in the house.' He pulled out two bottles of Magnet pale ale and a bottle of Guinness. 'Better than nothing.'

'That's fine, Dad. Magnet for me.'

Two glasses were brought from the kitchen and Herbert poured out the beer with meticulous care. Betty in the shop was forgotten.

'Here's to you both, then. And who, if I may ask, is the lucky lady?'

'You've met her, Dad. She came here to see me when you were putting me up.'

'I remember her. A real looker. Do you know, Clare told me that she'd got married.'

'She did, Dad. I told you. I married her.'

Rex found a strange satisfaction in describing the full horror.

'I said the nuptial mass. I performed the ceremony. She married a collier called Jack O'Hara.'

Herbert wanted to warn his son about the perils of such a union, but the best he could manage was an anecdote.

'A man at the Raleigh went to live with married woman.'

'First of all, we need a place to live.'

Rex, who listened with endless patience to his father's reminiscences was not in the mood for parables.

Herbert tried to hide his anxieties. Rex, he was sure, was about to ask if he could move into the room over the shop and it was a father's clear duty to offer his son shelter. Yet he could not imagine how he would explain to Betty that his lodgers lived, not in married bliss, but in sin. Nor could he visualize himself explaining to his neighbours that his son had left the Church with a parishoner's wife. He wanted to say 'My home is your home and all I have is yours to share', but he could not face the prospect of telling Betty, 'Whatever he has done, we must help him as best we can.' He played for time.

'When are you going to tell the cathedral?'

'Not until we're all fixed up. I'm going to look for a place, this afternoon.'

Encouraged, his father asked him, 'Anywhere in mind?'

'No. I'm just going to go out Lenton way and look in newsagents' windows. I want to be out of town but near enough to cycle in to Morley's. I'll try to get my old job back.'

'If you need a bob or two, I'm not doing badly at the moment.'

'Money's all right, Dad. What we'll need are friends. I don't want Enid to feel an outcast. Come and see us.'

'Of course, I will,' said Herbert with tears in his eyes. 'Just let us know where you are, that's all.'

'And another thing.'

It had all been difficult, but Rex had left the most difficult part until last.

'Syd was coming to stay with me. I'm meeting him off the train at four after the cricket tour.'

His father did not help, as he had hoped, by making an immediate offer.

'I don't think that's possible now.'

'Do you want him to come here?'

'It's here or Clare's and this is his home.'

'It's a home that he won't want to come to. But he'll be more than welcome.'

Rex knew that what his father said was true and realized that Herbert was only reluctant to say how much he looked forward to seeing Syd because he feared his son's rejection. He longed to say, 'It's not you, Dad. It's your wife', but he had been as brave as was within his power on a single day. He tried to look reassuring as he walked towards the door. For the first time in his life he was knowingly doing Syd a disservice and not feeling guilty about it.

Betty, who had sensed that some sort of drama was being played out in the back room, hovered near the shop door as Rex left. But, notwithstanding her alien presence, Herbert embraced his son and told him that he could always rely on his father. Then he asked his wife if she could manage on her own for the rest of the day and, without even waiting for her to reply, hurried off to the bus stop. Clare, he knew, was always in her house during the early afternoon.

'I'm relying on you not to let him know. He'd never forgive me if he knew I'd come straight round here. But I don't know what to do for the best.'

'Of course I won't tell him, Herbert. What do you take me for?'

'I don't understand these things, not being a Roman myself. I just want to do the right thing for him. I can't think what his mother would say. Do you think we should stop him?'

'Lord bless us and save us, he's your son, Herbert.'

'He's a son who, thanks to you and your kind, I barely know. How much have I seen him in the last ten years?'

'It's no use getting ratty with me. I want what's best for him as well. Though if what you tell me is right, he's doing a terrible thing. There's no two ways about it. And if you won't tell him so, I will.'

'He won't take any notice.'

'Then he'll need my practical advice. He won't get any from

you, that's plain enough. He hasn't got the sense he was born with, talking about living in Nottingham. Can you imagine what it would be like bumping into Monsignor Payne in High Pavement? Has he got any money?'

Herbert did not answer. He was thinking about the great service that he was about to do his son. The solution to all Rex's problems lay, he was sure, in Sheffield – the city which, since he was exiled from it at the age of eighteen, had assumed in his mind the characteristics of Eldorado, the Promised Land and the Garden of Eden.

'He ought to go to Sheffield. I'll send a card to his uncle Joe.'

'He ought to go to London. He could get lost there easily enough.'

Chilled by the blast of her cold logic, Herbert sank back into depression. He could see nothing but trouble ahead. At such moments he always needed to be reassured that he was surrounded by friends.

'I'm sorry if I was nasty. I'm just a bit bewildered. Don't know what to think.'

'Let me tell you this. If he really means it . . . If he really does it, I shall have a new respect for him. I know it's wrong and I'll tell him so. But going off will take some doing.'

The unpleasantness having passed, Herbert agreed to sit at the kitchen table and write to Rex. Clare made humble suggestions about what he should say. After brief arguments he accepted all but one of her corrections and improvements, agreed to them as if they were his own ideas that he had imposed upon her. He did, however, insist on recommending Sheffield rather than London and he argued for the town of his birth with persuasive passion. Rex had relations in Sheffield who, *in extremis*, might help him out. It was far enough away for the pair to live in anonymity but near enough to Nottingham for Rex to keep in touch with his father and family. Clare knew that it all added up to Herbert's obsession with the past, but in the end she agreed. As long as Rex was persuaded to move outside the diocese, she could not be forced to live in perpetual shame as he lived in continual sin.

'That's it, then,' she said wearily.

'I've still got to finish it.' Herbert added, without any prompting from Clare, 'Let us hope that this serves to bring us closer together.'

When the envelope was sealed and addressed, Clare told him that he should post it straight away to make sure the letter was not left forgotten in his pocket. He kissed her on the cheek with lightened heart and a feeling of deep satisfaction that he had behaved with such responsibility.

REX WAS an hour late at the station. Syd, disconsolate, stood at the barrier. He had performed badly on the cricket tour and dreaded having to report the failure to his brother. It was almost a relief when Rex launched, at once, into his account of the latest drama in his life. His immediate thoughts were for his own comfort.

'I could still come to Langwith, until you left,' Syd told him.

'I'm leaving tomorrow.'

'Do I have to go to Dad's?'

'That or Clare's. There's nowhere else.'

'If you'd got ten quid, I'd go early to Ratcliffe. I could do with the chance to swot, changing to science. And the nets will still be up . . . if you'd got ten quid for board, that is.'

It was a bitter joke, so Syd's relief in miracles was almost reborn when Rex felt in his back pocket and took out the roll of pound notes.

'You've got Enid to thank for this,' he said, trying to imagine what Enid would say when he told her.

THE SIX o'clock reunion was not the joyous occasion for which they had both hoped. Rex was tense. Enid knocked on the presbytery door at five minutes past six, but he had been counting off the seconds since half past five and when she did not arrive by exactly the appointed hour he was convinced that she had changed her mind or lost her nerve. Enid had been nervous, but there was no thought of turning back. She had left home so early that she arrived at the church almost twenty minutes before she intended and had waited amongst the gravestones, feeling blatant and conspicuous.

'Owen was awful,' she said. It was impossible to describe what really happened, so she invented a story which raised the question that she most wanted to ask. 'Said you'd leave me sooner or later.'

'I won't. You know that.'

'I do now.' She looked into his eyes and, to her distress, he half turned away. 'I do now. But up there in the market with Owen, I wasn't sure . . .' She sensed that he was about to protest. 'Just wait a minute. I want you to know what I thought. I thought that I'd rather have you for a year than not at all.'

'For ever,' said Rex.

He felt neither guilty nor absurd – the bespectacled priest kissing his married parishioner – whilst her ridiculous dog barked in protest and ran round them with such neurotic determination that the lead, which Enid still held tightly in her hands, bound them together.

Rex took his mouth from hers for what he hoped would only be a moment. 'For ever?'

'You know for ever. I mean it more than I've ever meant anything in my life.' The spell was broken. 'I've not got very long. Mam's on her own. Tell me what you've been up to.'

'Not much. I've been to a dozen shops and I went through all the cards in the window. There's nothing. They're all cheap enough, but nothing I'd let you live in. They wouldn't do for you and Mrs Brackenbury. Filthy old attics at the top of houses, mostly.'

'That's not the way to do it. You decide on an area and you go looking for "To Let" signs outside houses. Then you go and see the landlords. Shall I look for some tomorrow?'

'Could you get away?'

'If I brought Mick I could. Till dinner time anyway. What was your dad like?'

'I was sorry for him. I felt I had to help him instead of him helping me. You could tell that he was thinking about what would get into the papers. He could see himself walking into the Royal Oak and them all sniggering. We're on our own, love.'

Enid, who was thinking about the newspapers and the sniggering, did not answer.

He held her in his arms and would have kissed her and said that being on their own did not matter, but he suddenly felt a deep reluctance to prolong the drama. It was marriage, not courtship, that he wanted. Moments of brief passion – either physical or emotional – had no attraction for him. Yet he feared that they would go on with their furtive courtship for weeks, not sharing long moments of contented silence, but snatching brief meetings. The feeling of now or never, which he had only counterfeited that morning, became the central reality of his life.

'Let's get it over with now. Let's go and tell Jack and your mam.'

'How can we? Where would I go? Let's both go and look for a place tomorrow. Let's look together.' She put on her practical look knowing that it would reassure him. 'What are you going to wear?'

'This.' He shook his arms like an animated scarecrow. 'It's all I've got. I left all George's stuff at the cathedral.' He saw her look anxious and her anxiety worried him. 'It's too late for play-acting. Buying something will take another day. If we mean it, we'll have to get on with it.'

'I mean it. You worry me by keep saying that I don't.' Before he had time to calm her fears, she heightened his. 'I've got to get back. I've been gone an hour. Will half past eight do?'

She did not wait for a reply but, back in command, gave her detailed instructions. It was best to meet at the station. She happened to know that the eight-forty Worksop train went on to Nottingham. She would be outside the booking office at half past eight. When he opened the front door, she took his hand and held it for a moment against her face. Then, having glanced furtively up and down the road, she ran down the path without looking back.

By midnight, Rex felt sure that she would not be at the station next morning. At two o'clock he began to understand why it was unreasonable even to hope that she would share a life of poverty and shame. As he fell asleep at four, he was seriously considering getting up, dressing and going round to Colliery Row to claim his bride. Then he remembered that she had been Jack O'Hara's bride three months earlier and that he had performed the ceremony. Fortified by almost two hours' sleep, he said mass out of habit and with his thoughts of Enid driving all other ideas out of his head, returned to the presbytery to wash, shave and worry. His father's letter lay on the hall floor.

The hope that they would grow closer served only to make him feel more lonely and the frank advice about living in Sheffield – which he knew to be wise – only added to his suppressed hysteria. Herbert, under his sister-in-law's supervision, had faithfully reproduced Clare's injunction to imagine how he would feel meeting Monsignor Payne in High Pavement and he remembered the night in the Grove Hotel when he had feared that he would never feel safe in the diocese. He was intimidated by the idea of looking for a house in a town he did not know but the thought of the confrontation was enough to convince him that he could not set up home in Nottingham. Yet he dared not admit his fears to Enid that morning. He had seen her turn pale at the mention of newspapers and he was terrified that if she understood what horrors faced them, fear would triumph over love.

A knot of some sort had to be tied that day. If Enid kept her promise, they would go to Nottingham and look for a house. It was, Rex told himself, a sort of betrothal.

The station forecourt was deserted except for a stray mongrel that was urinating against the front wheel of an empty Ford lorry. Rex divided his time between reassuring himself that she would come and thinking what he would do if she did not. As the station clock struck half past eight, the train from Mansfield pulled into the platform. Still praying that she would come, he walked down a side street so as not to be seen by the early morning travellers. Half way along the narrow pavement he turned back, just in case by some miracle, Enid had appeared outside the station.

The forecourt was still empty, but a plump matron sat incongruously in the passenger seat of the dilapidated Ford. Through the windscreen, Rex could see the fur which curved across her back and ended with a fox's head peering nervously over her shoulder. Her face was vaguely familiar and Rex, fearful that she was a parishioner, was about to retreat again into the side street when Brack appeared from behind the lorry. He was resplendent in the suit that he had worn to give his daughter away. The same starched collar, only slightly less stiff than on Enid's wedding day, once again cut into his jaw. He was carrying a starting handle.

'Well.' He looked at Rex with his usual amused contempt. 'This is a bit of luck. Would you like to do an old gentleman a favour?' He held out the starting handle. 'It's a young man's job, this is.'

Rex would have taken him at his word, but he was not sure that he could turn the engine over. Brack, who would have been disappointed if the priest had started the engine for him, bent down in a fine show of muscular agility and slotted the handle under the radiator.

'What brings you here, Father?'

Despite the arrival of the Nottingham train and the end of all his hopes, Rex managed to construct a plausible explanation.

'I came for the Sheffield train.'

'You missed it. Mrs Wood and me got off it.' He swung the handle. The engine did not respond. He stood back. 'Let's see if kicking the bastard's any better.'

The starting handle turned through half a rotation, one cylinder fired and the handle spun back, hitting Brack on the shin. With a cry of agony which must have echoed throughout all of Langwith, he collapsed on to the dusty forecourt. The lady in the passenger seat screamed and began to tap on the window. Rex opened the cab door, left her to climb down unaided and went to Brack's help.

'Don't touch it.' Brack, sitting on the ground, with his damaged leg stretched out before him, was swaying backwards and forwards. 'It's broke. I felt it go. Go to t'pit and get one of the ambulance men.'

'Let me see.'

Jane Wood, despite the fox fur, and at least a stone of excess flesh, was clearly more agile than Rex had imagined her to be. Having clambered down from the lorry, she bent over Brack and began slowly to roll up his trouser leg. He cursed under his breath and begged her to go steady, but he did not argue.

The huge black lump on Brack's shin was bleeding from an inch-long gash that ran across it just below the knee. The swelling stretched down under his suspender and disappeared inside his sock. To Rex's horror, Jane began gently to prod at the purple flesh.

'It's not broke. It's a bad bruise but it isn't broke.'

She had just begun to confirm her diagnosis by manipulating the ankle when Rex heard Enid, invisible on the other side of the lorry but unmistakable.

'Now! You bad boy. Here at once. Here! Come here! Come here this minute.'

It was too late. Mick, lead fastened to his collar but trailing behind him, had seen or smelt Brack and ran at him in joyous reunion.

'Get that bloody dog off my leg.' Brack looked up at Jane. 'Have you no bloody sense, woman? Catch hold of the bloody dog.'

Rex put his foot on the lead and Mick choked to a halt.

Enid stared down at the extraordinary sight of her father, sitting, one trouser leg rolled up, in the road. Despite his obvious distress, she wanted to turn and run. But it was too late.

'I've broke my leg.'

'No, he's not.' The hated Jane Wood, widow and paramour, contradicted him. 'It's bad, but it's not broke. We ought to get a taxi to take him home. Unless you can drive this thing, Father.'

It was the first time since the beginning of the crisis that anyone had acknowledged his existence.

'He couldn't drive it.' Brack looked up. 'We've had enough trouble today, as it is. Help me up.'

It took all three of them to get him on to one foot, then, leaning heavily on Jane and Enid, he hopped into the station. Rex walked a pace behind, dragging Mick, who could smell the mongrel's urine on the lorry's wheel and wanted to prove that he could do as well or better.

Enid telephoned Brack's yard. There was no reply. Her father cursed softly, told her to try again in ten minutes and sent Jane to the fishmonger's for ice to reduce the swelling. He sat with his injured leg stretched along a platform seat.

'Well,' he said, looking up at Rex. 'Where were the pair of you buggering off to?'

It was, Rex remembered, now or never.

'Mr Brackenbury, we're going away together.'

'I suppose you mean this morning?' Brack intended to sound dismissive.

'As soon as we can find somewhere to live.'

The second answer took more courage than the first. Rex braced himself for the blow of Enid explaining that she had changed her mind or that she had never really meant to leave her husband.

'Bloody hell!' Brack turned his attention from his wounded leg to his daughter. 'Does your mother know?'

'We'll tell her as soon as we find a place to take her, Dad.'

'You are taking her, then?'

'Of course we are,' they answered in unison.

Jane reappeared carrying the dripping parcel of ice at arm's length.

'If this leg's not broke, I can drive that bloody lorry. At least I can if the Father here can swing the handle.'

The women protested that he would do himself permanent injury and Rex insisted that he could turn the engine over. Enid ended the argument by running back to the telephone box and returning with the news that the yard had come to life and that help was on its way.

The Humber was already decorated with white ribbon in preparation for the wedding at which it was to be used that afternoon. Jane did not understand why Brack said, 'Anyway, we've got the right car for t'job.' She sat on the back seat with Brack's great bulk lying across her so that he could stretch out his leg. She thought that if only he had shown her proper respect and left a motor car at the station instead of the lorry none of the trouble would have happened.

'You ought to see a doctor,' she told him.

'It's you that said it wasn't broke. Anyway we've a bit of family business to discuss. Enid, the Father and me, that is.'

Jane was not offended. She was happy enough to leave Brack on his sofa with an enamel basin under his leg and melting ice piled on the swelling whilst she made tea in the kitchen. When she came in with the tray, the talk suddenly stopped. But she felt no resentment. Jane knew her place. Brack's daughter was none of her business.

'Is this,' Brack repeated for the fourth time, 'serious or are you just playing at it again?'

'I've told you, Dad. We're going to do it.'

'We've done it, Mr Brackenbury, haven't we?' Rex added, 'We've told you. It's out in the open.'

'It needn't be. Not if you want to keep it quiet. I shan't tell anybody.'

'We both mean it, Dad.' She got up and reached for her coat. 'We're getting a house in Nottingham.'

Rex looked uneasily at her.

'I need to talk to you about that.'

He nervously fingered the letter in his pocket. He could not take part in a long discussion about the merits of Lenton and Arnold when he intended to persuade Enid that they had to settle not in Nottingham but Sheffield. Correcting her in front of Brack was the certain path to conflict.

'I knew it. He's having second thoughts. Won't say it in front of witnesses.'

The memory of Boxing Day's mistakes had made Rex bold as well as wise. He took Enid's hand in his and, before she could say a word, shouted his explanation.

'That's not what I meant, so don't try to cause trouble. I've not had time to talk to Enid about it yet but I don't think Nottingham's the best place. We thought of Nottingham because it was easiest. The easiest place to look for somewhere. But now I think it's best further away. That's all.'

He could not bring himself to say 'outside the diocese' or 'away from the priests'. The admission that fear of scandal forced them to live where they were not known was too much of an humiliation to be faced at the moment. Rex waited for Enid to denounce him for taking her for granted.

'It doesn't matter,' she said. 'As long as we're together, it doesn't matter where it is.'

Rex had never felt so proud of himself. With a single impetuous sentence he had changed the whole world. Had he prevaricated or worried about decency and discretion, Enid would have still doubted his determination and, holding back because of her doubts, she would have made him doubt too. But he had said it – 'Mr Brackenbury, we're going away together' – and her certainty had begun to grow out of his. Rex's delight in Enid's answer was not shared by her father.

'That's all very well. But you've still got to find somewhere to live, you and her mother.'

'My father suggested Sheffield.'

'You could do worse. That's where I went when I left home.' Brack clearly believed that as long as they followed his example, they would not go far wrong.

'Are you off to look for somewhere now?'

'It's too late.' Rex was already trying to be a considerate husband. 'She's left her mother on her own. Enid's got to get back home.'

'What do you need her for?' Brack did not think of thanking them for abandoning their expedition in order to see him safely home. 'Get it over with. Borrow one of the cars from t'yard and get off straight away. No point putting it off.'

Rex looked at Enid and she nodded. Brack noticed.

'If you take my advice, you'll start as you mean to go on. You don't need her permission.' He smiled, leaned forward and pulled at Rex's stock. 'Is there a shirt under this thing?'

'Of course there is,' Rex told him, flinching.

'And that thing round your neck, does it fasten on with a stud?' No reply was expected or given. 'Stop here, and I'll get you a proper collar and tie. Best not to make a show of yourself.' He gave a huge wink. 'You can say goodbye to your young lady whilst I'm gone.'

The thought that Enid was his young lady – acknowledged as such by her own father – gave Rex much pleasure, but Brack's description seemed only to anger her. She walked, without a word or glance in his direction, through the kitchen and out into the yard.

'I could hit him,' she told Rex.

'I thought he was marvellous. I couldn't believe it. We've got what we always wanted. We've got a friend.'

'You don't know him like I do. All he's interested in is making sure that Mam moves out of Langwith Junction. The further away the better. That's all he's worried about. He wants that woman to move in with him or he wants to . . . to . . . to live like a single man. I think it's disgusting. She may be a widow, but he's a married man.'

Rex did not attempt to unravel Enid's moral confusion, even in his own mind. Instead he determined to make the best of Brack's offer without worrying about why he had made it. He pretended to make an expert inspection of the second-hand cars which stood, in varying states of dilapidation, in the muddy yard.

'I shan't be back till late. Can you come round and find out how I've got on?'

'As long as it's before ten. He's on the late turn. I can take Mick out for a bit as long as I'm back when Jack gets home for his tea.'

Enid meant no more than that the deception had to be sustained. But Rex, reminded that she still had a wife's duties to discharge, looked like a man betrayed.

She dared not touch him or take his hand, so she stared into his face in a way which she hoped would make him understand that, in her heart and mind, she was holding him in her arms.

'Get what we can afford. Anything will do. Really. I just want to be with you.'

Enid was half way to the gate when she felt Rex's hand on her arm. When she turned round, he had his *pince-nez* in his hand, a sure sign of nerves.

'What is it, love?'

'You're not going to tell Jack now, before he goes off to the pit?'

'How can I? I have Mam to think of.'

'I'm not saying you should, only . . .' He found it almost impossible to speak the words. 'When Jack came to see me in church . . . You know . . .'

'Of course I do.'

'I knew that you still loved me because of what he told me. It was true, wasn't it?'

'You know it was.'

'So I don't have anything to worry about. I don't have to worry about you staying at home tonight?'

Her exasperation was gloriously reassuring.

'You've got a lot to worry about. Finding a house. Telling Jack. Moving Mam and looking after me for the rest of my life. But *that* you don't have to worry about.'

'I'm sorry.'

They were out by the gate and a coal lorry was rumbling along the potholed road. She kissed him on the cheek and although he looked up to see if the driver had noticed, he took her hand and kissed her again. She held his head against hers. He could feel her trembling with pleasure.

'You're human, after all. I think you really do mean it.'

Brack was watching them. He stood for an impatient moment alongside the Morris Opal which he had decided that Rex should choose and waved a collar and tie in the air.

'Come on, if you're coming. I've not got all day.'

As Rex walked back up the yard to receive his driving instruction, Brack muttered half to himself and half to an uncomprehending world.

'It beats me. You'd think that they want to get on with things, not hang about. You'd think they couldn't wait to be sorted out and settled down.'

BRACK'S COLLAR was several sizes bigger than Rex's neck. The back stud worked loose before he was out of first gear and he drove west out of Langwith Junction with the sharp edge of starched linen beating a tattoo against the base of his skull. For the first ten miles of his journey, he could think of nothing except finding the gears and manipulating the eccentric steering wheel. Then, after he had passed the crooked spire of Chesterfield's parish church, he had time to think about what lay ahead. He counted the times that he had visited Sheffield before. Four visits in all. But, he could list a hundred Sheffield place names. All of them featured in his father's anecdotes.

As soon as he passed the city boundary, he pulled alongside the first pedestrian he saw and asked directions to Heeley where his father had been born. It was from Heeley that his uncle Joseph had run away to Canada and to Heeley that Herbert himself had come back in disgrace after his father had bought him out of the army. For Rex, returning to Heeley was like arriving at the place where, according to the childhood stories, all dreams came true.

He resisted the temptation to search for what his father thought of as the ancestral home and turned instead towards the more humble streets of Heeley Bottom. Not a single terraced house displayed a 'To Let' sign. Higher up the hill, pair after pair of Victorian villas stood empty and neglected. At the end of each overgrown garden, a notice board announced that prospective tenants should contact Walter Clegg and Sons, Solicitor.

The name of Walter Clegg was almost as much part of Rex's boyhood as Bramall Lane cricket ground and the Worshipful Company of Cutlers. Walter Clegg had defended Charlie Peace, the Darnall murderer whose carnage guaranteed Sheffield a place in fairground waxworks. The idea of meeting so legendary a figure gave Rex such pleasure that he almost forgot to be frightened about the interview which lay ahead. He drove into the city centre, parked his car in sight of the town hall and searched for Campo Lane. Although he lost his way twice, it was a joyous journey. He saw both the cathedral and the Cutlers' Hall.

The clerk in charge of Sir Walter's outside office was typing classified advertisements for inclusion in the *Sheffield Telegraph*. As he typed he hummed. He did not regard the arrival of a potential customer as a reason for abandoning either activity. At the foot of the second sheet of paper and the end of the third verse, he looked up.

'I'm interested in renting a house in South View Road.' Rex ran his fingers round the inside of his loose collar.

'Which one?'

Rex had no particular number in mind. Half a dozen apparently identical houses were empty. Each one was slightly bigger than he would have wished. All of them met his needs. He vaguely remembered numbers which ran from three to fifteen.

'I thought of number seven.'

The clerk flicked half heartedly through a tray of cards.

'Seven's gone. Eleven's still available, though there's a lot of interest.'

'Eleven then.'

The clerk pulled open a drawer and took out a form with such casual indifference that he tore it as he shook it free.

'We'll have to take down some details to see if you'll do. Name and occupation.'

'Frederick Roy Hattersley. I'm a clerk.' He did not think it necessary to add 'in holy order'.

'Employer?'

'I. and R. Morley.' It was the first indisputable lie of the day.

'Never heard of them. What's their address?'

'They're a Nottingham firm.'

'So what are you going to do in Sheffield?'

'I'm looking for a job.' He saw the clerk write down 'unemployed' and, thinking a further explanation necessary, he added, 'My wife's a Sheffield woman. That's why we're moving here.'

'You've chosen a bad time. You being unemployed, we'll need two references. And a deposit.'

'That's all right.' Rex was glad of an opportunity to improve his reputation. He had over ten pounds in his back pocket. He took out what was left of the roll of notes with what he hoped was panache. 'I've just come into a bit of money. A relation died.'

'It's eleven shillings a week. We'll need four weeks' rent in advance, two pounds deposit and a couple of references.'

Rex could hardly wait.

'Mr Ernest Brackenbury. Coal Merchant and Haulier. Langwith Road, Langwith Junction, Nottingham —'

'One will have to be local.'

'Joseph Hattersley, the landlord of the Hen and Chickens.'

The clerk's mood changed.

'I drink in the Hen and Chickens every Saturday. Are you related to Joe Hattersley?'

'Nephew.'

'Well, fancy that. I never thought of old Joe having any family. I'll tell him on Saturday that I saw you right. When do you want to look at it?'

'Now, if I can. My car's just down the road.'

The mention of the Morris Opal had an even more dramatic effect than the discovery that Rex was related to old Joe. The clerk swung open a cupboard door with an expansive flourish and lifted two bundles of keys from their hooks.

'Have a look at number nine as well.'

As Rex drove back to South View Road, he counted the lies that he had told within the space of ten minutes. He had lied about his job, his relationship with Enid, his reasons for moving to Sheffield and his legacy. It was not the sin, but its consequences, which disturbed him. Before he returned to Langwith, he would have to turn his lies into an approximation of the truth. The clerk was the sort of man who would make an immediate visit to the Hen and Chickens and boast of his meeting with the landlord's car owning nephew. Rex would have to get there first.

He tramped the bare floorboards of both number nine and number eleven, but he thought less about the condition of the paint and the state of the wallpaper than about what he would say to his Uncle Joe. It was, Rex felt sure, possible to construct an explanation of his status which told enough of the truth without telling too much.

On the way back to Campo Lane he almost convinced himself that he could risk waiting to see his uncle until he was secure and settled in South View Road, but his high hopes of procrastination were first encouraged and then totally extinguished by the clerk's joyous celebration of their reunion.

'There's no need to wait for the references. Not in your case. As soon as you pay the money, you can have the key.'

Rex's attempt to decide between number nine and eleven were hampered by elation at the thought that he might not have to visit the Hen and Chickens at all.

'Will you be celebrating in the Hen and Chickens? I'll be along tonight to tell him that I kept an eye on you. Old Joe'll owe me a drink for this.'

By the time that Rex arrived in Exchange Street, the public house was closed for the afternoon and the back gate was barred and bolted. After much hammering and shouting, the landlord shouted through the locked door.

'Is it the brewery?'

'I'm your nephew, Herbert's boy.'

'Has he passed on?'

It was exactly the question which Joe had asked when Rex had visited him a year earlier.

'Dad's as fit as a fiddle. Got married again since I saw you.'

'The old bugger. Never told me. You just passing through, then?' It was a family phrase.

'I've got a favour to ask.' Rex noticed Joe flinch. 'It's not money?'

'Come inside.' The landlord carefully re-bolted the gate behind his visitor. 'I was just having a bit of a sleep.'

The invitation to sit down was grudgingly given and unhesitatingly rejected.

'All I wanted to say was that I'd given your name as a referee. I've rented a house in Heeley. They wanted a local reference.'

'No bond is there? No guarantee? Just reference.'

'I've paid four weeks in advance.'

'That's all right, then.' It was clear that Joe thought that the business was over and Rex was about to leave him to his sleep.

'Only, there's a couple of questions they might ask. The clerk from Cleggs comes in here for a drink on Saturday nights.'

'I can guess,' Joe said. He looked at Brack's floating collar. 'I take it, from that thing that's hanging round your neck, that you're not a priest any more.'

Rex was grateful that he did not have to speak the words himself.

'Well, you can rely on me. You don't even need to tell me the address. That way, you can be sure that they won't get it out of me.'

The landlord poured himself a drink from the whisky bottle on his sideboard and looked knowingly at Rex with the special contempt that the cynical feel for the innocent.

'When they come, I shan't say a word. I shan't even say that I've seen you.'

'When who comes?' Rex asked.

'The priests,' Joe told him. 'And the monks. You don't have to pretend with me. I've seen it all in Quebec. Are you going to change your name?'

'Of course not.' Rex felt an obligation to defend the Church which he was about to desert. 'They scrapped the inquisition three hundred years ago. It won't be like that. I'm going to live a perfectly normal life.'

Rex was not prepared to allow his uncle to frighten him out of enjoying the hope of at last becoming ordinary.

'Poor sod,' said Joe. 'They won't give you a chance.'

'We'll be all right.' Rex, suddenly desperate to return to Enid, held out his hand. 'I'll tell m'dad I saw you.'

'Tell him to come and see me. Tell him to call in for a drink, if he's ever out this way.'

'When he comes to see me, we'll drop in together.'

Joe Hattersley shook his head in pity and in sorrow at the thought of Rex's life of exile and isolation.

CHAPTER FOURTEEN

THE JOURNEY back to Langwith Junction was filled with new worries, most of them concerned with the acquisition of furniture. Rex had started off methodically enough by making a list in his mind of the minimum requirements, basic goods and chattels which, on the following day, he would have to obtain in preparation for the arrival in Sheffield of Enid and Mrs Brackenbury.

The list was far longer than he had first anticipated. He could not imagine how he would find time to visit the second-hand furniture shops and the cheap salerooms.

Nobody he knew had ever set up house in a day. It normally took months of careful collection. The new householders were usually assisted by their parents and friends and their acquisitions were augmented by wedding presents. Rex was not sure that he could complete the task in time for Enid to join him before her nerve broke.

At the great moment of his life, he was once again required to behave in a way which set him apart from other men. He longed to be at the end of a conventional courtship, with George chosen as a best man and a wedding car arranged to arrive at his lodgings the next morning. He was an essentially respectable man who resented being denied the chance to behave respectably. He drove back from Sheffield overwhelmed with the fear that it was after all, too late for him to become ordinary.

Back in the presbytery his thoughts turned to more material problems. With all the time in the world, he still could not set up a decent home. After he had paid the deposit on the house, his total assets were two suits of clothes, a few items of dilapidated furniture and nineteen pounds, seven shillings and threepence. He thought gloomily of moneylenders.

Enid, sparkling with fear and excitement, knocked on the presbytery door before the promised time and immediately began to cross examine Rex about the house which she took for granted he had rented. He was able to answer none of her questions about the bathroom taps, the size of the garden and the type of oven. Indeed, he could not recall seeing an oven in the kitchen. He was, however, able to confirm the existence of a bathroom with a bath.

'Good.' Enid expressed the genuine satisfaction of a woman who would have been pleased with anything. 'Now. I've been thinking about furniture. What have you got here?'

Rex admitted ownership of an imitation leather easy chair, an imitation Jacobean dining table and four hard chairs. The wireless, he reported with regret, was broken beyond repair.

'The rest of the stuff isn't mine. If I took it I'd be stealing.'

'Then steal it.'

If Enid had asked him to burn down the presbytery, her impatience to start their life together would have guaranteed his agreement. He was so excited that he could not reply. Enid was so excited that she could not stop talking.

'Tomorrow's perfect. It's maintenance tomorrow. Jack's doing a double shift.'

'When shall I tell him?' Rex asked.

'I'm going to tell him, not you.'

'No.'

Rex tried to sound stern. 'It's my job and I'm going to do it. We don't know what he'll do.'

Enid pulled him down next to her on the sofa which, she had already decided, was too big for them to take to Sheffield. It was, she knew, essential that she changed his mind at once. One of Rex's weaknesses was an inclination to see questions of principle embedded in issues which she recognized as simply matters of convenience. And when he imagined that the principle at stake involved her honour and integrity he was inclined to defend it with an even more unreasonable determination. If she was not very careful, he would soon announce that her willingness to make the sacrifice made him both love her more and increased his determination to protect her. She took his hands in hers, stared into his eyes and told him.

'I thought that you wanted to do it properly. You told me that we had to think about his feelings.'

Rex feared that Enid intended to speak tenderly to Jack about the good times they had enjoyed together and promise him that she would never forget him.

Rex had misjudged her. The more Enid thought of how Jack would react to the news of her departure, the more certain she became that a brief letter, containing a lying account of why she had left and where she had gone, was the only sensible way of giving him the news.

'I'm going to live with you for the rest of my life. That's because I love you. Finding you was the best thing that I ever did. And, whatever happens, I'll only regret that we wasted the last years. I'm not going to spend time arguing about Jack.'

Enid felt immensely proud that, thanks to her, the great love story was to have a happy ending. It had become her great achievement, the success that compensated for her failure to make any of her other dreams come true. No matter how hard she tried, she could not help feeling sorry for Jack. But she felt no guilt. For once, she was following her star. She could not be blamed for that.

'Trust me, love.' She leaned forward so that their cheeks touched. 'I've got it all worked out.'

Enid had it all worked out. During the day, whilst Rex had been in Sheffield, Enid had arranged for her mother to make one of the periodic visits to Dr Anderson of Worksop which Aunt Anne regarded as essential to her sister's health. All that was special about Dr Anderson was the location of his surgery. But that was enough to justify a sudden visit. A telegram had warned her aunts that they were coming and hoped to spend the night in Newcastle Avenue. Her father's wedding car had been booked.

She was particularly pleased with herself for insisting on the wedding car, in which a glass partition separated driver from passengers. During the journey, she would explain to her mother that they were never coming back.

'So you'll have to speak to him tonight.' Rex was less pleased with her plan that she had expected.

Enid had not even contemplated speaking to Jack that night. Her plan was not to speak to him on the subject at all, but to leave a note propped up on the kitchen table where when he got home at half past ten, even he would see it. But she knew that Rex would not agree to what she intended. So she had to pretend that his fears were justified.

'I'll have to tell him tonight.'

'And stay in that house afterwards?'

Rex was back to his old irrational – but to her extremely encouraging – fear that Jack would exact a terrible revenge for her betrayal. He was immovable.

'No, you won't. I'll go and see him after you've left. It's the right thing to do anyway.'

To his surprise, Enid agreed and began to tell him what he must do. Rex would borrow the lorry from her father and take his furniture (and various household goods which were the property of the diocese) to Sheffield. He would then return to Langwith, wait for Jack's return from the late shift and tell him the awful news. She spoke with great conviction, even though she was pre-occupied with her plans for doing exactly the opposite of what she promised.

'Go round to the house on your way to Sheffield. The key's in the coal house. Take Mam's bed down after Jack's gone to work and bring it with you. It's the only thing she can sleep on.'

It was, Rex thought, the happiest moment of his life. Enid was at her most practical and determined – her whole mind and soul concentrated on the details of going away with him. He had always know that, once she definitely decided, nothing would be allowed to stand in her way. He felt confident enough to take her over the last hurdle without any fear that she could fall.

'You know it's not going to be easy.'

She knew what he meant and looked suitably solemn.

'I don't know when I'll get a job. There won't be any advertise-ments in the local papers. "Wanted Apostate Priests".'

'I'm not stupid. I know that.'

'And there's another thing. We're going to Sheffield.'

'We're going to Sheffield to hide. What do you take me for? I know that.'

'We're going to become different people.' He thought of his Uncle Joe's advice. 'Perhaps with different names.'

'The same people,' she said emphatically. 'The same people living different lives. Perhaps with different names. Though the only name I want is Hattersley.'

'It might be a long time coming.'

'I know that too. I'm ready to wait.'

'Are you ready for the newspapers, the *Empire News* and the *News of the World*? It will be pretty awful. "Renegade priest elopes with parishioner's wife." That sort of thing.'

'If I'd been afraid to face all that, I wouldn't have got this far.'

He kissed her, holding her tight and pressing her against the rough hall wall. All thought of prying newspapers and prurient neighbours was driven out of his mind.

'I know what it's going to be like,' she told him, her lips close to his face. 'It's all going to be wonderful. It's what I've always wanted. You're just right for me.'

'And you for me.'

He wished that he could have composed something more original, but consoled himself with the thought that he had echoed the beautiful expression of a beautiful sentiment. He kissed her again.

'I've got to go. I've got to get back to Mam.'

'I wish that you didn't have to go at all.'

'Not much longer. Tomorrow. The day after at most.'

Enid edged towards the door and he wondered if he dare delay her progress by attempting to kiss her again. She was fumbling with the latch when she turned towards him again. There was a five-pound note in her hand.

'I got it from Dad. Told him that we couldn't take Mam until we'd paid a deposit on the furniture.'

REX DECIDED to pick up the lorry under cover of darkness. As he struggled to fit the starting handle into its socket under the radiator, Brack, sitting in the passenger seat, watched with malicious amusement. He pushed up the windscreen and shouted down across the bonnet with mock concern.

'I'd climb down and do it for you, but you've got to learn to do it for yourself. I reckon that you'll have to start it four times during this little jaunt of yours. That's if you don't stall the engine. And I reckon that's a big if. It'll probably be ten times, in all.'

Rex, back in a clerical collar in case he was seen walking through the village, sweated with nerves and prodded again at the hole under the radiator. He had told Brack that there was no need for him to hobble across the yard and pull his swollen leg into the lorry's cab. But Brack had demanded a shoulder to lean on and announced that he would not 'miss the show for a thousand pounds'. Rex could not imagine anyone else hopping with menace. The intimidation was intentional and entirely successful. Fear built on fear. He was irrationally afraid that he would never fit the end of the handle into the socket. And he feared, with good cause, that when he succeeded in his first task, the second would be too much for him.

'You might find it easier if you knelt down, Father.' Brack roared with laughter at his joke.

Suddenly, the handle slipped home and Rex, surprised by his success, lurched forward and grazed the knuckles of both hands on the radiator grille.

'Now I'm going to do what you'll have to do for yourself when I'm not here. Gears in neutral. Handbrake tight. Ignition on. Now come on, Father. Swing it!

'Well done, Father.' Brack sounded as if he was really pleased. 'Do you want a drive round the village to make sure that you can manage it?'

'I can manage it.' Rex was already at the side of the lorry, anxious to help Brack back into the house and be on his way. 'I'm very grateful.'

'Don't be. There's no need. Just remember, as far as I'm concerned you hired the bloody van. That's all. I'll lose enough customers as it is. So when Jack comes round asking questions, I know nowt.'

Rex steered uncertainly back to the presbytery and started to pack his few personal belongings in the old pressed cardboard suitcase which his aunt had bought him to take to Ratcliffe. He slept badly, but his night was disturbed only by excitement.

On the other side of Langwith Junction, Enid O'Hara was

talking to her husband about the hope of a summer holiday.

'If Mam settles at Worksop for a couple of days – settles without me – we'll persuade her to go there for a week next August. And we'll go to Skegness.'

'Or, perhaps, I'll take you home to Ireland,' said Jack. 'Or we could go to London. I've always wanted to go to London.'

'At least, we'll have a holiday. A holiday on our own somewhere.'

'On our own.' Jack repeated the idea as if it had mesmerized him. 'That would be wonderful.'

'Yes, on our own. That's why I need to take her to Worksop and see her settled down.'

Jack snored all night dreaming, his wife suspected, of seaside lodgings, public houses on the promenade and swimming in the bathing costume which she would be expected to knit for him.

As always, Enid got up at five to make his breakfast and pack his snap. But when he had left, she did not go back to bed. She packed all the clothes that she and her mother possessed into every sort of case and bag that she could find. Then, as she waited for the hire-car, she wrote two notes. The first was to Jack. She had tried to soften the blow with thanks, apologies and regrets. But however they were written they had always sounded disloyal to Rex, so she scribbled out a curt announcement that she no longer loved him and that she would never see him again. She propped it up on the table which, true to her obligation, she had left set for Jack's supper. The second letter was to Rex. It announced – in language which was as guarded as the message was fraudulent – that 'He knows. No need for you to do anything.' The note to Rex was laid on the counterpane which covered her mother's bed, so that Rex would find it when he called, as instructed, to collect the essential items of furniture.

Enid should have known that a combination of conscience and anxiety would prevent him from making the furniture raid on Colliery Row.

★

IT WAS midnight when Jack O'Hara got home.

Usually, when he finished at ten o'clock he rushed into the pit baths, turned the taps as far as they would go and, without waiting for the water to run hot, blasted himself clean by the sheer force of the deluge. For a fastidious man without a bathroom at home, it was a great sacrifice to make. But when he stood with the other naked men, testing the temperature of the shower until he was sure it would not take his breath away, he wasted half an hour that could have been spent with Enid. She never expressed any particular pleasure at his return. But if, for some reason, he was later than usual, she always complained that his supper was ruined or that her mother had made herself ill with the thought that there had been an accident in the pit.

On the night that Enid was to spend with her mother in Worksop – proving that Mrs Brackenbury could be left with her sister and that the O'Haras could get away together for a week in the summer – Jack luxuriated in the steam. He soaped himself twice and, when the suds were rinsed away, took particular care to dry between his toes. Then he walked slowly home. Life would, he knew, soon be wonderful.

The sight of the parish priest standing at his front door would have disturbed him at any time of night or day – disturbed him because priests must not be kept waiting and because of the fear that the priest brought bad news. Jack noticed the glow of a cigarette in the priest's hand. He had never seen him smoke before. It confirmed all the fears. Nerves were being calmed in anticipation of the horrors which were to follow.

The likelihood, and the best hope, was that something terrible had happened to Mrs Brackenbury. Jack's second preference was the death of his grandmother. But he could not totally rule out an accident to Enid.

'Let's go inside, Jack.'

Jack could not wait for the seconds that it would take to find his key and open the door. Although he knew it was wrong, he grasped the priest by the shoulder.

'Let me know. What's wrong? What's happened. Is it Enid?'

Even at that moment, Rex felt a deep resentment. Whenever

he arrived unexpectedly, it was assumed that he brought desperate news – news about normal men who are allowed to feel the emotions that priests are denied. He led the way into the house and sat down in the dark living room.

'Don't bother with the gas,' he commanded. 'Sit down.'

Jack, who had never intended to fumble with matches and mantles, sat down opposite him.

'Now tell me, Father. What's happened?'

'Enid's gone away, left you.'

'I don't believe it.' There was more incredulity than horror in his voice. 'Saving your presence, Father, I just don't believe it. She's gone off to Worksop. She left me a note about groceries for when she comes back.' He pointed to the unopened envelope on the kitchen table. 'I didn't have time to read it before, but I know what it's about.'

'She's left you and she's not coming back.'

'You're telling me that I'm never going to see her again? I walked off to the pit this morning and she was here. She packed up my snap and made the tea. And you're saying that she's left me?'

Jack was protected by the unreality of all that was happening to him. Ten minutes before he had been at the normal end of a normal day. Now he sat in his living room and, outlined against the pale moonlight that shone in through his window, his parish priest was repeating the details of his wife's desertion.

'It's true, Jack. It's been on the cards for a long time. She thought you might even know. At least suspect.'

Rex wanted to say that he was sorry and then go on to mouth the meaningless hope that it would not be too painful, or that the pain would not last, or that Jack would understand, or that Jack would not blame himself. All the conventional expressions of sorrow and condolence seemed not so much hypocritical as absurd. He was sorry for Jack, but not sorry enough to regret behaving in the way which had caused him such pain.

'We had difficulties.' Jack was beginning to believe it might be true. 'You know that, Father. I came to see you about it. But this . . .'

273

'I'm sorry I can't do more to help.' Rex was bracing himself to finish his story.

'She can't mean it. I'll go and see her tomorrow. I've got to get her away from those aunts. It's them that's behind it. They never liked me. They never wanted her to get married. I bet Mrs Brackenbury spoke up for me.'

'Jack, there's another man.' Rex was slowly working his way towards the awful moment of complete revelation.

'Never. She's not like that. Whoever said that is a dirty liar. Never. Who told you that, Father?' Jack was struggling to maintain the control that was necessary in the presence of a priest. 'You've got to tell me.' He stood up. 'I'm going to see him now. People shouldn't say such things.'

'It's true, Jack. Sit down. I know it's true.'

Being a romantic, Rex took it for granted that when he admitted that he was the man, Jack would hit him. And he was afraid. He dare not stand up and he dare not stay buried in the deep cushions of the old wicker chair. To his relief, Jack sank back on to the sofa. But then he put his head in his hands and slumped forward until he was half balanced on the cracked leather and half kneeling in front of his parish priest.

'Tell me what to do, Father. Tell me what to do. I want her back, Father. Tell me what to do.'

'It's me, Jack.'

'What's you, Father?'

'I'm the man, Jack. She's going away with me.' Rex could feel his heart pounding with every sort of fear. 'That's why I know it's true. I'm the man.'

'You're a priest.' It took some time for Jack to understand. 'You're a bloody priest. You're supposed to help us. You're a priest.'

'I'm also a man.'

'You're not a man like I am. You're supposed to behave different.'

'I can't believe you didn't have your suspicions. There's been enough talk. Why do you think I went away?'

'It's no good you pretending that it's my fault. I didn't know. I didn't suspect. No decent man would suspect a priest. When you told me that she'd gone . . . when you told me just now . . . I was going to ask you to pray for me. I was going to ask you what I should do.'

'We can still talk about it.'

'And shall we pray as well? That's what you're supposed to say, Father. Let us pray. Will you pray for me or shall I pray for you? Because it's you that's going straight to hell. You are going to burn, Father. And I won't pray for you. I hope nobody prays for you. I don't want your soul to be saved. You're going to hell, Father.'

All the things that a priest should say came instantly into Rex's head. God, in his infinite mercy, sent His Only Begotten Son to save the world from sin and open the path of redemption to all those who truly repent. But he was not even tempted to deliver the classic reproof, 'Judge not that you be not judged'. He was a priest no more and he neither repented, nor asked for mercy. Enid had become the beatific vision and it was within the radius of her light that he wanted to live, world without end. Being a man of faith and conviction, he was unable to pretend anything different.

Jack spoke without looking up. 'I fucking hate you. I came to you for help . . .'

Rex had no idea how to deal with Jack's recrimination. The obscenity was, in its way, reassuring, for obscenity was what he had expected. But the passionate denunciation – part personal and part theological – left him speechless. He expected to be knocked down and kicked where he lay, since that was the way in which the colliers of his imagination settled their arguments. He had no weapon with which to defend himself against moral outrage.

'To think of it. I came to you with my troubles. And you must have known . . . known all along.'

'I had no idea, believe me. Not till you came to see me. I thought you were happily married.'

'I don't believe you. I don't believe a word you say. Any road, we're not happily married now. Thanks to you.'

'It's not thanks to me, Jack. I don't know what causes these things, but it wasn't plotted and planned.'

'If you didn't plot it, she did. It couldn't just happen. Not with you being a priest.'

Jack's homely wisdom disturbed Rex. It was, he decided, time to go.

'There's nothing more that I can say.' He began to shuffle across the shadowy room. 'I'm not going to say that I'm sorry, because it wouldn't be true. But I am—'

'Don't leave me.' Jack half turned away, half fell and lay across the sofa with his face buried in the padded arm. 'Don't leave me on my own, Father. I don't know what to do.'

Jack O'Hara was in torment. All his life he had been taught that, at such times, he should turn to the priest for comfort and guidance. Although Father Hattersley was the author of his despair, he was also the route to salvation. Jack's faith was untouched by the discovery that he had been betrayed by the man whom the Church had sent to protect him.

'Will you pray with me, Father?'

'How can we pray together, my son?' Rex slipped, without thinking, back into the language of his vocation. But his faith had not survived the experience of the last few days. 'Soon, a real priest will come to St Joseph's, one that you can talk to and trust. Pray with him.'

'Will I ever see her again, Father?'

'Never again. I can't pretend anything different.'

Jack pushed himself up, first on to his knees and then on to his feet. Then he began to snivel like a bullied schoolboy. When he started to rub his nose on the back of his hand, Rex wanted to pray, 'Don't let him cry. Please Lord, don't let him cry.' Not expecting his prayers to be answered, he ran out of the living room before he witnessed their mutual humiliation.

As Rex pushed the cottage door shut behind him, he heard not the sound of the sobbing that he expected but the noise of breaking glass. The photographs of Enid – Enid in her wedding dress, Enid taking Mick for a walk and Enid at the tennis club – had been swept from the mantelpiece on to the hearth, together with the letter which had leaned against the clock. It was, he knew, a priest's duty to return and offer what help he could. But he was a priest no longer. At last he was free.

Rex was free, but he was frightened and, because of his fear, he had nowhere to go. He had spent the day first writing his letter to the Vicar General and then taking his few pieces of furniture to Sheffield. The lorry was back in Brack's yard before dark and in good time for him to tell Jack and make his great escape.

The plan had been to spend the night in the church, as he had once spent a night in Westminster Cathedral when he had been stranded in London during his sudden journey back from Rome to see his dying mother. Rex had thought of St Joseph's as a sanctuary both from the violence which he feared from Jack and his brother and from the appeals to conscience which he expected would be made by his more sober parishioners in an attempt to revive his better nature, sense of fitness and hope of eternal life. He had planned to sleep on one of the hard wooden pews, wash in the vestry and catch the first morning train to Worksop. But as he walked unsteadily down Colliery Row, the idea of pushing open the heavy oak door and smelling again the mixture of incense, candle grease, damp and human sweat which makes up the real odour of sanctity, terrified him. It was important to avoid thinking about why he was so afraid, for he did not wish to speculate about the nature of guilt, sin and conscience. So, instead, he imagined Enid waiting for him in Worksop. Inevitably, he chose to walk along Langwith Road and past the house where they first met.

A light shone through the gap in the living room curtains and spilled out in a silver line across the yard to where the lorry stood. Rex, watching the front door in case Brack suddenly appeared, tiptoed through the dark and reached down between the double rear wheels. The key was still in the mouth of the exhaust pipe, where he had been told to leave it. The cab door opened silently and closed with barely a sound. Rex climbed into the driving seat and spent his first night of freedom worrying that Jack would find him, worrying that he would not sleep and worrying that he would not wake up in time to catch the early train to Worksop.

WORKSOP TOOK eggs and bacon very seriously. For an acceptable breakfast, eggs had to be new laid, bacon home cured and both fried until they were as hard as stone. Fried bread was thought vulgar, but it was permissible to dip crusts into the bacon fat which rippled across the plate like the sea around an archipelago. Uncle Ern believed in 'starting the day with something warm inside you', and although he ate a solitary breakfast on the other side of town, Worksop respected his views on diet as they respected his views on every other subject.

Enid reached for the pickled beetroot, speared a piece on the barbed pickle fork which had been brought from Grove Cottage, dropped it on her plate and, as she watched the congealing fat turn pink, spoke without looking up.

'I've got something to tell you.'

Lottie looked nervously at Anne who looked disgusted. Agnes looked apprehensive. All three women believed that Enid was pregnant. They waited for the announcement through a silence which, in Enid's presence, was unprecedented.

'I'm leaving Jack.'

'Oh, my God!'

Neither Anne nor Lottie had ever heard Agnes blaspheme before.

'I hope you'll do no such thing,' said Anne as if her niece had announced that she might be late home from a church social. 'You've got your mother to think of.'

Enid remembered bitterly that thinking about her mother was the reason which they had given for opposing her marriage in the first place. Now it had become their argument for the marriage going on.

'I don't understand.' Agnes was crying quietly. Her handkerchief had fallen on the floor and a rivulet of unchecked tears ran down her face. 'I thought you were so happy. Jack's such a kind man. He's so considerate to me. I can't think what's got into you . . .'

'What's he been up to?' asked Lottie, unable to make up her mind between adultery, sadism and normal brutality.

'No marriage is perfect.' Agnes longed to reach out to her daughter. 'But you have to make the best of things. Talk to him. He's always very good to me.' She tried to reach her handkerchief and Anne, ever attentive, picked it up and held it to her sister's nose. 'You can't throw your whole life away because you've had one row.'

'Jack's a nice enough man. It's nothing to do with him.'

Agnes, relying on her own experience, had little doubt that Enid's married life would be interrupted by half a dozen separations and that she would return to her husband as often as she left him, but the announcement of Jack's innocence added a new and more sinister aspect to the potential tragedy. Enid was, she feared, fantasizing about getting herself an education. She had been to see those Fords. No doubt, hidden somewhere in the bedroom was an application form for a place in a workman's college.

'Does Jack know?' Agnes asked. 'Have you told him or have you just run away?'

Before Enid had time to answer, Anne had a suggestion to make.

'You'd better move in with Ern until you come to your senses. Nobody need know what's going on. As far as people are concerned, you're just having a bit of a holiday.'

Enid could stand no more shadow boxing.

'If you'll give me the chance, I'll tell the whole story. I am going away with Rex.' Enid articulated her announcement with the care of an elocution student performing a test piece. 'With Rex Hattersley. I love him. We've got a house to go to and everything. He's coming to get me tomorrow.'

She expected to be engulfed in an immediate torrent of screams and sobs in which her mother's anguish rivalled Anne's anger and Lottie's horror. Instead, she was surrounded by the silence of disbelief.

Agnes's jaw was too atrophied to drop, but one corner of her mouth twitched grotesquely. It was several minutes before anyone dare speak and, in that time, the three witnesses to Enid's shameless declaration all gradually absorbed the fact that what she said was true. What she had told them was, at once, so terrible and so extraordinary that not even Enid would have made it up for effect or said it before she was absolutely certain that what she described would really happen.

'So now you know,' said Enid.

The spell of silence having been broken, it was Anne who spoke first, as always censorious by instinct and sanctimonious in manner. What Enid had told her did nothing to moderate either her temperament or her style. What Enid proposed was wicked and she looked forward to telling her so one day, but the compulsion to be a friend in time of trouble pushed other instincts aside. Her niece had to be saved from self-destruction.

'Have you any idea what you're letting yourselves in for?' It was as near to an expression of sympathy and concern as her vocabulary allowed. 'Have you any idea what it's going to be like?'

'It will be wonderful. We love each other.'

'Don't talk rubbish.' Anne was her usual self again. 'Will it be wonderful when a baby comes along and it doesn't have a father?'

'Rex will be its father.'

'If he stays with you.' Lottie had caught up with the conversation. 'Anne's only thinking of you. It's what Ern calls being cruel to be kind. It's best you should think of these things. The Catholics will get him back, sooner or later. Have you thought of that?'

'I've thought of nothing else ever since Christmas.'

'But you hadn't married Jack at Christmas.' Agnes was still bewildered. 'How long has this been going on?'

'We should have gone away together then. We should have gone on Boxing Day.'

'So now we know. That's why you spoilt Christmas.' Anne's reserves of compassion were running out. 'What if he doesn't come tomorrow? Have you thought about that?'

Enid began to cry and Anne started to feel sorry for her again.

'I beg you – so does your mother – don't just rush off without thinking.'

'We can see why it seems very exciting now,' Agnes told her. 'I can remember when I was young.'

'It isn't like that, Mam. I've never been so serious about anything in my life.'

'Think about it, love,' Agnes said. 'I've had a lot more experience of the world. I'm sure that it seems like a bed of roses now . . .'

'I've got one thing to say to you, Enid.' Anne did not mind

that she sounded menacing. 'One thing to say before this man comes, if he comes at all. When you need help, as you will, don't let pride stand in the way of asking for it. We're always here. It will end in tears. You'll see. But, when it does, don't let pride stand in the way of asking for it. We're always here. Whatever you do, we'll always . . .'

It was a noble attempt and she almost managed to say 'love you'. But she could not quite bring herself to use the word.

REX HAD hoped that by the time he went to claim Enid, Brook House would no longer hold any terrors for him. As the train bumped between station and station, he told himself that he was about to enjoy a moment of triumph which would eradicate from his memory the humiliation of Boxing Day. His only regret was that he would have to meet his destiny unshaven.

Had he not, foolishly, left everything he owned in Sheffield, he would have scraped away at his stubble in the station lavatory and, despite his sleepless night in the lorry, felt a new man. As it was, he had to choose between waiting for a barber's shop to open or facing Worksop unkempt and apparently uncouth. He hung about for an hour in Bridge Street, only to be told that the hairdresser, in whose door he had hidden, had moved with the times and sold his razors. He spent another desperate ten minutes looking for something more old-fashioned and then – remembering the penalty that he had paid at Christmas for arriving at the wrong time – walked on to Brook House, hoping that he looked confident and assured but feeling dirty and disreputable. When he heard the bolts begin to slide, he fingered his jaw to hide the day's growth of beard. To his relief, it was Enid. She was wearing her best coat.

'Thank heavens. I expected you ages ago. It's been awful.' She did not ask him in.

Enid stepped back and Rex followed her. They stood uneasily together, close but not touching, with the front door still open. The years of subservience to her aunts' opinions had cast a spell which she could not entirely break. She was strong enough to leave them, but not strong enough to ignore their forebodings.

'Do you think Jack'll come after me?' she asked. 'It would kill Mam if there's a fight.'

'Of course there won't be a fight. He won't come. You know him well enough.'

'Let's get off anyway, just in case.'

'But I've got to see your mother and talk to her about what's going to happen now. What will she think if I just walk off. We need to talk about her coming to Sheffield, if nothing else.'

'They won't talk to you, Rex. And Mam says she won't come with us. They don't want to see you. They told me not to ask you in. They've telephoned Uncle Ern at work. They've never done that before. He'll be here any minute.'

'Then I better see him.'

'No Rex, please. I couldn't stand it. Let's just go.'

Enid was beginning, in her own mind, to work out the theory of salvation which was to become the pattern of their lives. She had no doubt that what they were doing was glorious. But she also believed that it was so right that it was entitled to be treated as if it was respectable. Anyone who did not accept that truth would be excluded from the little world she meant to build around her new happiness. Enid had begun to live in the fortress of her obsession.

'No, Rex. Let's wait at the station. We can try to persuade Mam later on.'

The temptation to agree was very strong. The thought of a second scene, almost as terrible as the one which he had borne on the previous night, was almost too much to bear. But it was too late. The front door opened and Uncle Ern stood framed in the lintel and jamb like a small and neat avenging angel. Rex waited to be engulfed in righteous anger.

'This is a rum do,' Uncle Ern said.

'We're on our way, Uncle,' Enid told him.

Ernest Skinner seemed unable to find the words with which to reply. Rex attempted ingratiation.

'We know that you only want what's best for Enid. But I'll look after her. And we'll both need you. We'll need real friends.'

'She will.' Anne, who had heard the rattle of the front door, had arrived to support her brother in the work of saving Enid from a life of sin. 'She will,' Anne repeated, 'when you leave her.'

'You have no right . . .' Rex rarely lost his temper. But when he did there was always a risk that he also lost control. He dare not allow himself to finish the sentence.

'Have no right?' Anne shouted. 'Let me tell you, right or not, you two disgust me!'

'Come on, Anne.' Ern did not attempt to hide his distress. 'Least said, soonest mended.'

Rex took Enid's hand. She squeezed hard and he rubbed his knuckles against her thigh.

'You've got to understand.' Ern spoke only with difficulty. 'It's not easy for us. Other days, other ways.'

Enid, to her great surprise, felt sorry for him.

'We tried being apart, Uncle. It didn't work. If we left each other now, sooner or later, we'd come back together. Mam will understand. She was in love once. Given a second chance, she'd do it all over again.'

Her uncle looked like a man who could still remember what it was like to be young and in love.

'What are you going to live on?'

Uncle Ern intended the question to be a bridging passage between the expression of emotion, which he found unbearable, and the considerations of practical consequences, at which he excelled.

'I'll get a job easily enough.'

'How will you manage in the meantime?' Anne asked.

'We've got a pound or two,' Rex told her.

It was time to go. The long reconciliation had begun and it would make more swift and certain progress if Worksop was left to itself and its memories. Whilst she said goodbye to her mother and brought Mick downstairs, her uncle continued to make his peace offerings to Rex.

'Is there anything you need? A bit of help is worth a lot of pity.'

'There is one thing. Is it true that you always carry a spare collar?'

'I do.' Ernest was clearly pleased that his niece had boasted about his meticulous habits.

'What size do you take?'

'Fifteen.'

'This one,' he pulled at his neck, 'is what Mr Brackenbury gave me yesterday. It's filthy.'

'Aren't you too big for mine?'

'I can put a cuff link in the collar where the stud ought to be. I used to do it at school when I grew out of my shirts. Enid will wash it . . .'

For respectability's sake, Rex changed his collar in the fitting room, looking at himself in the cheval glass. Anne and Lottie went out into the garden to find peace with Chum. In the kitchen, Ernest Skinner whispered to his niece that he was glad to be of help.

'Do you know,' she asked her uncle incredulously, 'he's left Mam's bed with Jack. Daren't go round and get it. She'll never sleep properly without it. Can you get another one made?'

She kissed her uncle on the cheek and he blushed.

NONE OF Rex's letters had been explicit about his reasons for leaving the Church, so it took Father Ellis almost all day to persuade Monsignor Payne to take Rex's note seriously. Reinforced by the evidence of the previous crisis, the Vicar General first insisted that after a day or two of wandering the diocese, St Joseph's parish priest would return to his church and presbytery. Eventually, the bishop's secretary convinced him that he had always realized that Rex had gone for good and he began to ponder punishment.

There could be no question of a second reinstatement. Monsignor Payne's only uncertainty was whether or not it was proper for him to write 'unattached' against Rex's entry in the register or whether it was necessary to await the arrival of the new bishop before the vacancy at Langwith Junction was both created and filled.

'I ought to go down there before the weekend and find out how things are,' Bill Ellis said. 'The parish must be in a turmoil.'

'I doubt if the parish even knows that he's gone off again. Even if they've missed him, they'll think he's had one of his turns. They know he's peculiar. They expect this sort of thing.'

Bill Ellis wondered if the Vicar General had convinced himself that Rex was mentally ill or if he found it comforting and convenient to behave, even to a fellow conspirator, as if the lie were the truth.

'The risk, Vicar General, is that the man will talk.'

'The man probably doesn't even know about these ravings. Anyway, he's a good Catholic. A man who loves the Church won't go round the parish shouting that the priest has unclean thoughts about his wife.'

'All the same, with your permission, I'd like to be sure.'

Bill Ellis did not say that it was just possible that the Vicar General might be wrong. Seeds of doubt rarely germinated in the stony ground of Monsignor Payne's mind.

It was dusk when he arrived at Langwith Junction. The railway station was deserted, the winding gear was still, the streets were empty, the coal lorries were parked end-to-end in the colliery yard and even the pit ponies in the field beyond the sidings stood in a motionless line staring into space beyond the thorn-topped stone wall.

On any other day, Father Ellis – who, like so many English Roman Catholics was a sentimental patriot – would have given thanks for having been born in the most tranquil country in the world. But, as he walked up towards St Joseph's he thought only of turmoil – turmoil in the diocese, turmoil in the parish and, most wretched of all, turmoil in the minds of the good Catholic souls of Langwith Junction.

The notice on the church door was difficult to read. *No Mass on Thursday.* The note, added at the bottom in indelible pencil which had run into a purple blur, was just legible. It read: 'On Fridays, apart from Lent, mass will be held at six o'clock in the evening. Confessions will follow.' Another twenty-four hours would pass before there were any formal duties for the incumbent to perform.

He hurried back to the station and the telephone box outside the booking office window.

'Philip Neri.'

It was the parish priest's habit to answer the telephone as if the saint himself was awaiting a call.

Bill Ellis had an unpleasant vision of Father Keogh spitting cake crumbs into the receiver. The long silence which followed his request to speak to the curate, reassured him that the fastidious Father Fisher was swallowing hard, wiping his mouth with his napkin and probably washing his hands.

'Sorry to disturb you, but I've got a little favour to ask. I want a bit of information. Can you tell me the name of somebody at St Joseph's that I can talk to. Somebody reliable.'

'There is nobody reliable at St Joseph's. There's hardly anybody there at all. A dozen ancients and two dozen Irish colliers. Jack O'Hara's as steady as any of them, but you can hardly go and ask him.'

'Tell me his address.'

'Colliery Row. But I'd keep away if I were you. You may have heard. He got married. It caused a bit of trouble at the time, one way and another.'

Father Ellis, impatient with Hugh Fisher's flippancy, decided to ask the booking clerk for directions.

All the houses in Colliery Row were the same. An old man in a greasy cap squatted outside the first front door, tossing a penny in the air and catching it in the palm of his hand. When he saw the priest he bared his head. A long, blue scar ran along his forehead. Bill Ellis told him that he was looking for Jack O'Hara.

'Next door but I doubt if he's in,' said the old man, putting the penny back in his pocket. 'Not seen him or her all day.'

Rex knocked.

A gross woman in a stained apron appeared at the end of the passage which ran between the houses.

'He should be on late turn. But I've not seen him go.'

There was nothing surprising, Bill Ellis told himself, about a miner missing a shift.

'What about Mrs O'Hara?'

'She's gone to Worksop,' said the woman. 'Taken the old lady. Perhaps he's gone with her.'

'I'll try round the back.'

He was making his way to the passage which ran in between the houses and ended in the back yard, when the O'Haras' front door opened and Jack stepped out into the dusty road. He was immaculate in his wedding suit, but he was not wearing shoes. Two toes stuck out from a hole in his left sock.

'Come in this way, Father.'

His calm seemed genuine. Bill Ellis noticed that the living room was immaculate, apart from broken glass and a bent picture frame on the rug in front of the fire place.

'I've been expecting you all day.' Jack pushed his feet into his shoes without bending down. 'I'm sorry about the socks. Father Hattersley said that you'd come.'

'When did he say that?'

'Last night when he came to tell me what had happened.'

Father Ellis had no time to spare Jack O'Hara's feelings.

'Have they gone away together?'

'No. She went early yesterday morning. He went late last night.'

'But are they together now?'

'I think so. He didn't exactly say that.'

'And you haven't been to look for them?'

'What's the use? They're in Worksop.' He said it as if it were a foreign country.

'Have you told anybody?'

'I haven't seen anybody to tell. I've stayed in all day. I didn't feel like going out. I didn't have a very good night.'

It was only then that Father Ellis thought of how Jack O'Hara must feel, deserted by his wife, betrayed by his priest and left alone in his cottage to brood and hate. A priest has a duty to comfort those in distress and to convince them that they will find peace and solace in the love of God. But it was not a task to which he could immediately turn his attention. Sorry as he was for the man, his first duty was to protect the reputation of the Church.

'You are behaving with great bravery, my son.'

'To tell the truth, Father, I'm not behaving at all. I've been in a daze all day. I hardly know what's happened to me.'

'I don't believe it. You're a brave man. Brave by nature. It's very important that you go on facing . . . facing . . . facing it with courage. No rampaging about.'

'I'm not the rampaging about sort, Father. I'm the quiet sort. Quiet and stupid. If I wasn't, I might have seen it all coming. I should have guessed. It was never a proper marriage.'

It was not a moment for subtleties and sensitivity. The bishop's secretary did not find intimate questions easy to ask, but there was still the possibility that Father Hattersley had not committed the sacrilege of putting asunder those who had been joined by holy sacrament.

'Never a proper marriage. Do you mean that it wasn't consummated?'

'No, Father. I don't mean that. If it was that, I'd never have been married in the first place. Father Hattersley taught me that. It was consummated, just about. But she never loved me . . .'

'You understand that it is your Christian duty to do all you can to rebuild this marriage.'

'She'll never come back to me, Father. Never. I've thought about it all night.'

The moment was exactly right.

'Then what do you want to do?'

'I want to go away. Not back to Ireland. I couldn't bear the shame. But get away from here. I want to go somewhere that isn't . . . that isn't all her. I want to put it all out of my mind.'

That, thought Father Ellis, you will never do. However great Jack O'Hara's distress at that moment, over the next few days it would grow rather than diminish. Slowly he would begin fully to understand what had happened. When the shock wore off, he would feel the pain more deeply and the hurt that he was already suffering would be increased by thoughts of the loneliness to come. It was torments like those that made men turn against all that was holy, and – demented by the failings of one of its unworthy sons – denounce and deny the Church itself. The nightmare through which Jack O'Hara was living had at least dulled his senses. It was important, before he woke, to provide him with the care and protection for which he asked.

'That's really what you want, is it, Jack?'

'What I want now, Father, is for you to pray with me. Father Hattersley said you would.'

Simple faith, thought Bill Ellis, simple faith. It is that on which the Church is built.

When the prayers were over, Jack, although the older man, helped the priest to his feet and counted his blessings in a manner which was as false as it was febrile.

'It's a lucky thing that I have the Church to help me. I'll always be grateful to you for coming out here today. It's what my mother always says. The Church looks after its own.'

The expression of such unreasonable sentiments worried Father Ellis, for he feared that he was witnessing the manic phase in a cycle of dementia and that, when it gave way to depression, Jack might behave in a way which made it impossible to keep the scandal secret.

'Would you like me to help you get away for a bit?'

'What if Enid came back to me?'

As the priest had feared, Jack's mood was swinging wildly from emotional pole to pole.

'Then you'd come back too. We'd keep in touch with things here. Send on your letters. That sort of thing.'

'What shall I do, Father?'

Father Ellis had no idea what was possible. He needed time to think and to discuss his idea with the Vicar General.

'I can't tell you now, Jack. But it won't work if people start talking about what happened.'

'I can keep it quiet for a day or two. I can't face going to t'pit tomorrow, anyway. Next door they think she's taken her mam to Worksop.'

'Have you got food in the house?'

'Yes, Father. She left all sorts of things. She's very good like that. Wonderful manager. Looks after us a treat.'

The old man with the blue scar across his forehead was still tossing his pennies when Father Ellis left. The gross woman opened her front door to watch him go.

The Nottingham train was already in the station and Father Ellis sank immediately into the corner seat of a third-class compartment and concentrated all his energy on thinking what could be done with Jack.

He did not notice the young man who rushed past the ticket collector after the guard had blown his whistle and, despite the two large suitcases which he carried, managed to struggle on to the train as it moved out of the station. But the young man had noticed the priest sitting, composed and serene, against the carriage window. Leaving his luggage in the guards' van, he edged along the corridor and stepped into the carriage. Before he spoke, he removed his beret as a sign of respect.

Father Ellis had no doubt that the intruder was foreign. His skin was brown, his hair was black and shiny, his teeth were white and, most revealing of all, he exuded the confidence that seminarians in Rome had come to expect from good-looking and well-connected southern Europeans.

'I wonder if you can help me. I've just come from Langwith Junction, I've been looking for Father Hattersley. But there's no one in the presbytery . . .'

A reporter! The priest blamed himself for not recognizing the signs at once. The secret, superior smile. The counterfeit deference. The man was a reporter! Somebody had sold the story of the scandal.

'And what do you want of Father Hattersley?'

'I'm his brother, George.'

CHAPTER FIFTEEN

FOR THE first two nights, they slept on the floor. There seemed no point in going upstairs, so in the half light of early evening they spread one of their blankets on the bare boards in front of the fire and lay down together amongst their few pieces of furniture. They woke up each morning feeling cold, cramped and elated.

Each night, Rex apologized for having prepared so badly and providing so little and Enid thought that her second honeymoon was even more strange than her first. But both of them were at peace, and the waves of sudden excitement – which frightened them no longer – always ended with an increased certainty that the peace would last for ever. Rex still woke at half past five, warm on one side, because he was pressed close against Enid, and cold on the other because the fire had faded into grey ashes. He could not remember waking up before without worrying even as he struggled to open his eyes, but in South View Road he never wondered where he was or thought that he had early morning mass to say. As long as Enid was there he was at home and happy.

Enid, for all her airs and graces, enjoyed the few days of primitive pleasure. Only the whitewash that the estate agent had painted on the window-panes separated her little kingdom from the world outside. She washed with carbolic soap, cooked in a single pan, used a rolled-up coat for a pillow and ate corned beef for her first Sheffield Sunday dinner, but at last she felt that she was a success. She had wanted Rex for more than a year and Rex was hers. During their first weekend together there was no one else in the world. She was almost sorry when Monday came and they could begin a more normal life.

They started their search for furniture at Coles, a department store which had advertised its 'outstanding value' and 'no-deposit terms' in the *Sheffield Independent*. Encouraged by the promise of 'eight specially laid out rooms', they visited the '7-day Exhibition of Complete Furnishing Schemes'. The cheapest suite – 'available on the first of twenty-four monthly payments' – was called 'second bedroom'. The bed was single, the wardrobe was only three feet wide and only one pillow was provided. The total cost was twenty-two pounds. Rex and Enid moved on to the second-hand shops in Heeley Bottom, half a mile from home.

They spent the afternoon on their knees. Enid scrubbed the living room floor and, when it was dry, Rex stained the bare boards with a liquid which Woolworth's claimed would change them into parquet. Rex was about to move into the hall when Enid dried her hands on her apron, dropped the scrubbing brush into the bucket and announced, 'We need to talk about how we're going to manage. We ought to discuss money.'

To Enid, a discussion was a process which began with her announcement of what was to be done and ended with the other participants agreeing that she was right.

'It's careful from now on.' She looked at the bar of carbolic soap, which she had been careful to take out of the bucket, as if it was the ultimate extravagance. 'We mustn't spend any more for a bit. Except for the curtains. We can't do without them. When Worksop have come round, I'll be able to make them on Aunt Anne's machine . . .'

'We've still got—' Rex had not quite mastered the art of recognizing the end of Enid's extended sentences.

'If Mam doesn't come for a day or two. And she can't come till we get the proper bed . . .'

'Everything put together, we've still got the best part of fifteen pounds. It's a fortune,' Rex told her reassuringly. 'You managed on that for nearly two months when you lived on miners' pay.'

'It won't last for ever.'

'It will last till I get a job. We can afford a carpet, a bed and a radio. We can afford to live in—'

'You can say that. But I'll have the managing to do.'

The world had burst in upon them. The idyll of the long weekend had ended in the quick calculation of hire-purchase payments and concern about grocery bills. Rex was not quite ready to surrender.

'I'm not saying spend it. I'm saying that we needn't worry.

Anyway sooner or later I'll get a job.' He noted Enid's intake of breath and added, 'Sooner, I reckon. Soon as I can. I'll go down to the Labour Exchange this afternoon, if you don't mind.'

'I've got all the windows to clean,' Enid told him as if he was preventing her from carrying out her proper duties.

Rex was genuinely apprehensive about leaving Enid in the virtually empty house – no carpets on the floors, no furniture in half of the rooms and an attic which they had not even dared to explore. He had hoped to use his apprehensions to justify postponing his visit to the Labour Exchange and the frank explanation which it required.

Rex put on his best black suit without a thought of Clare who had bought it for his ordination and, with some difficulty, knotted the knitted tie which Ernest Skinner had given him, together with the spare collar. As he travelled to town, he looked at himself in the mirror which was fixed at the back of the tram car to give the conductor a full view up the winding stairs. The tie did the trick. At the Labour Exchange he would look exactly what he was, an out of work clerk.

'What was your last job?' The man behind the desk was old enough to be Rex's father. He held the form still on the table with an artificial hand which he used like a paperweight. He had a regimental badge in his button hole.

'Clerk at I. and R. Morley's in Nottingham.'

'And before that?' The man did not look up.

'I did all sorts. I was abroad for a couple of years. I started at Morley's in their packing department.'

'What sort of work did you do?'

'Stamping the trade mark on stocking feet, mostly.'

Rex did his best to read what the old soldier was writing on the form. But the exaggerated long hand which would have been hard to decipher in any circumstance, was incomprehensible upside down.

'What sort of schooling have you had?'

The pause was fatal. The pen was lowered over the form. Rex felt under suspicion and, in consequence, he made the mistake of telling the truth.

'I was at Ratcliffe College in Leicestershire for a year or two.'

'Public school boy, eh? Have you been in some sort of trouble?'

'No. Certainly not.'

'It's no good getting on your high horse with me. It's the sort of thing an employer will ask.' The tone became more confidential. 'If you've done time, it's best to tell me. It'll come out sooner or later. Saying it now will save you a lot of grief.'

Without waiting for an answer. the clerk consulted a list.

'All I've got now is half a day. Five bob. Not bad for an hour or two. But it's just one afternoon.'

'I'll take it.'

A card containing the details of the half-day opportunity was held for a moment in mid air to heighten the drama.

' "Saturday afternoon. A half a dozen well spoken young men to meet at the pavilion entrance to Bramall Lane." Do you know where Bramall Lane is?'

Rex nodded.

' "Player's Weights. Special Promotion. Packet of two cigarettes to be given to spectators on way to football match. Ten till half past four." That all right?'

Rex nodded again.

'To be handed out in tobacconist shops round the ground.'

The card was put back in its drawer with a gesture of work well done.

He returned home in triumph, impatient for the congratulations which he knew that he would receive. As soon as he turned the corner into South View Road, he saw Enid standing outside the gate of number eleven. She was discussing her ancient sweeping brush with an Indian travelling salesman who had balanced his suitcase on the garden wall.

At the sight of her – in front of the house they shared and engaged in so obviously a domestic a task – his elation multiplied. What little gloom he felt at the thought of spending an afternoon giving away cigarette samples turned into pride. He was going to work for her. It was impossible not to give her the good news at once.

'I've got a job.'

Enid looked at him with real pride and the commercial traveller tipped his hat in acknowledgement of the achievement.

'Only a day. But it's a start.'

Enid took his hand. Her pride was clearly as great as his.

'I was just saying that you'd come back home after years
abroad.'

'I reckon,' the salesman said, 'that you can afford a new brush
head now. You certainly need one.'

'Of course,' said Rex. He had only been given enough to pay
his tram fare to and from the Labour Exchange, so he waited for
Enid to fetch her purse from the kitchen.

'And the polish?' With the dexterity that comes from years of
practice the salesman flicked at the locks of his suitcase and the lid
flew open. 'I've been having a most agreeable chat to your good
lady. She's been telling me about the antique furniture you
brought from Worksop.'

'The table,' said Enid as if Rex was not certain what the antique
furniture was. 'The table and the dining chairs.'

'This is the stuff.' A tin of polish was lifted reverently from a
corner of the suitcase and held within inches of Rex's *pince-nez*.
'She wants it, sir. I can tell you that. And your furniture needs it.'

'If she wants it, she must have it. How much?'

'One and sevenpence.'

'One and seven?' Enid asked incredulously. 'For a tin of polish!
No, thank you.'

'The brush head then?'

'This brush will do for weeks yet.' To prove her point, Enid
scraped the few remaining bristles along the footpath.

'So you want nothing. After all the time I've spent listening.'
The salesman turned to Rex. 'There's nothing about your family I
don't know. Or your bloody dog. I listened to all the rubbish
because she thought that she'd buy the polish if you got back.'

Shutting his case with a deft use of knee and arm, he swung it
off the wall with his right hand and marched down the road like a
man who was used to making a swift getaway. He called over his
shoulder as he went. 'Give my love to your little brother – the one
at the posh public school.'

Enid grabbed Rex round the waist and hung on as he tried to shake her free.

'No, Rex, you mustn't.'

'Oh yes, I must! Nobody is going to speak to you like that.'

He had got as far as the gate, with Enid slowing him down but not holding him back, before she said to him in an urgent whisper, 'Think of it. Think of what would come out if there was any trouble.'

He stopped and thought as she commanded – thought of the lies he had told to get the house, thought of the lies he had told in the Labour Exchange and thought, above all, of the disgrace of being unable to defend her for fear of lies being exposed. He walked back up the path. He was a prisoner, locked in the walls of their secret life.

They stood together in the kitchen, frightened by their isolation.

'I don't think I can keep it up,' said Rex. 'At the Labour Exchange the man knew that something funny was going on.'

'You've got to keep it up.'

'One lie leads to another. And you don't remember. In the end you contradict yourself. We've been living like this for less than a week and we can't keep it up. At least I can't.'

'You've got to. For my sake. It will get easier. I promise you it will. We'll have our own lives to talk about. Our own past to remember.'

'But do we have to? I'm not ashamed of what I did. I used to be a priest and I'm not one now. What's wrong with that? Why can't I tell anybody who asks? When I go to the Labour to sign on again next Monday, why can't I tell them?'

'That's telling them we're not married. And I am ashamed of that. I couldn't live with it. I told the woman next door that I was Mrs Hattersley. Do you want her to know that I'm not?'

'You've no idea how hard it is.'

'We can make it easier by putting the past out of our heads.'

'This,' said Rex 'ought to be one of the happiest days of our lives and it's like this.'

'It can be the happiest day of our lives – happiest up to now.'

Enid was washing her hands and face at the sink. 'We've just bought our first bed.'

Enid did not make supper until after it was dark and, because there were no curtains in the living room, they took two chairs into the kitchen and ate off their laps. Rex spilt mutton fat down the front of his new shirt, the shirt he had only bought two days before and put on for the first time that afternoon. Enid tutted and leaned forward to dab the spots with the moistened corner of a towel. He caught her head in his arms and was going to pull her towards him, but she struggled free.

'I want to tell you something.'

He waited anxiously.

'From today,' she said, 'I have no past except you. The world began last Saturday. I've never been married and you've never been a Catholic priest. Didn't you feel that upstairs? Could you believe that you'd once taken a vow against women? I couldn't believe that I'd ever been married, before I was married to you. That's all that matters. Anybody who doesn't understand that won't be welcome in South View Road. Anybody.'

GEORGE HATTERSLEY and his aunt Clare sat in the hall of Bishop's House waiting for the housekeeper to tell them that tea was served.

'This,' said Clare, 'is extremely impolite.' She looked at her watch for the tenth time in five minutes.

'You don't have to wait.' George believed that he was old enough to see Monsignor Payne alone. 'It's only the last rites.'

'Your mother would expect me to be here. I've got to meet her in heaven one day. I don't want her to ask why I didn't come with you for your confrontation with the old monster.'

'It isn't a confrontation. It's just proving that we're all being civilized about it. Anyway, in heaven, Mam would understand.'

'You may know about heaven.' Clare had grown tired of theology. 'But I know your mam. She never did like Francis Payne.'

'That's all in the past.'

'Everything's in the past. That's no reason for forgetting about it.'

Clare made another attempt at patience. It only lasted five minutes.

'Tell me again what you're going to say if he asks about your brother.'

'I don't know anything, so I can't say anything.'

They waited for another ten minutes and then the Vicar General himself appeared and boomed his greeting with the air of a man who was jovial without conviction. As soon as he had pronounced his blessing, he launched – without change of tone or volume – into an account of the golden opinions which George had won in Spain. Before his aunt could express her agreement, he added that many young men developed doubts before ordination and that the best of them always heard the call a second time.

'You behaved with great courage and with proper respect for your faith. Not everyone in your circumstances does so.'

Clare stared at George, willing him not to assume that the Vicar General was contrasting his admirable conduct with Rex's furtive fall from grace. He remained calm and Monsignor Payne went on to urge involvement in the work of the local parish. A cup of tea was offered and declined and the ordeal ended. Aunt and nephew hurried down the drive.

'Did you ask him?' Bill Ellis was not his usual suave self.

'No, Father. I did not.' The Vicar General seemed offended by the question. 'I had no need to. I found out yesterday.'

The bishop's secretary looked gratifyingly astonished.

'The rector telephoned from Valladolid. A telegram arrived for George Hattersley a couple of days after he left the college. After agonizing – typically, I might say – for rather too long, Father Henson opened it and rather belatedly told me of its contents. Father Hattersley is in Sheffield.'

'So you told George?'

'I told the rector to post the telegram to his father's shop where he's staying. That will be time enough.'

The Vicar General was anxious to emphasize that there was no more to be said on the subject, so he added, 'You'll be pleased to know that I've also spoken to Ushaw about Jack O'Hara.'

'But what are you going to do about Rex?'

'I shall write to him this afternoon. He owes the Bishop's Trust three pounds. So called "out of pocket expenses" for his visit to Valladolid.'

FATHER ELLIS had never seen a man pack with such meticulous attention to every necessary fold and potential crease. As the second best shoes and spare socks were carefully arranged in the suitcase, the priest did his duty and told Jack that the marriage vows required a serious attempt at reconciliation. And mercifully, as the two clean shirts went in on top, Jack had replied that he knew that all such attempts were sure to fail.

'But you are going to write and tell her where you are going to live? Just in case she comes to her senses.'

'Yes, Father.'

It was clear that only a direct question would produce the information that he sought and there was no risk of a direct question being resented.

'Do you mind telling me exactly what you're going to say?'

'No, Father.'

The silence which followed lasted throughout the time that it took Jack O'Hara to spread a Fair Isle pullover across the contents of his almost full suitcase, cover it with a sheet of tissue paper and then lay half a dozen ties, side by side, in his final act of packing.

'What will you say?'

'That I will keep my marriage vows and if she ever wants to come back she can. I know she won't. But that's what you told me to say and I will. I'll write as soon as I settle down . . . settle down in my own mind.'

'Anything else?'

'That I've left the key with Mrs Ferguson and she ought to take the stuff out before the colliery let the house again. That's if she wants it. I expect she will.'

'Very generous.'

'Well, I won't want it, will I? She'll be round here the day after she gets the letter. You take my word.'

They travelled together in silence to Nottingham and sat together in the station buffet without speaking. When, five minutes before the Newcastle train was due to arrive, they walked out on to the platform, they made an incongruous pair. Father Ellis – small, neat and bespectacled – was obviously in command. Jack O'Hara – tall, tawny and high cheekboned – walked deferentially a pace behind, concentrating on holding his suitcases out from his legs so that they would not rub against the expensive serge of his wedding trousers. The men looked at the little priest and the women at his handsome companion.

'I'm sure you're going to like it, Jack.'

The train was late and, after a desultory quarter of an hour, Bill Ellis made his apologies. Jack felt nervously in his pocket. To his surprise and relief, the ticket was still there. Bill Ellis held out his hand.

'Do you think that you'll see her, Father?'

'I'm sure I shall.' He felt certain that he would be expected to go to Sheffield within the week. 'Do you want me to give her a message?'

'No, I just wondered. She knows all I've got to say. In the old days she worked it out before I said it. She's a clever one, is Enid. She understands.'

'Does she?' Bill Ellis said under his breath. 'Does she know what sort of life she has to look forward to?'

IT WAS George's idea to go to Sheffield. His father took some convincing but after a couple of days gentle, though insistent persuasion, he agreed. Before Herbert had time to change his mind – or Betty had the chance to change it for him – George went to the station to find out the time of the trains. He returned with a plan which he had designed to suit his own convenience and which would prove irresistible to his father.

'No need to start too early. We get the two o'clock. It gets us into Sheffield just after three. You can show Betty round for a bit. Then come up to see Rex.'

'I wish you wouldn't call your brother Rex.' Herbert was exerting his authority over the details so that he would not feel quite so ashamed of leaving the big decisions to his son.

'It's what everybody else calls him. His wife calls him—'

'She's not his wife.'

Betty's correction was greeted with shocked silence

'You'll like her.' George ignored his stepmother's look of respectable offence. 'I saw a lot of her in Langwith last summer. She's great fun. Bossy, but great fun. We got on famously. Same with Syd.'

'Are you going to write to tell them?' asked Herbert.

'No,' George told him, not adding that he was afraid that they would run away. 'No need. I'll go straight up there and you come along after you've had a look around.'

'She's never been to Sheffield,' Herbert said, nodding in his wife's direction with a combination of pity and incredulity.

They both assumed that Betty's silence was proof of her enthusiasm.

Mr and Mrs Herbert Hattersley walked arm-in-arm up Exchange Street and along Fargate. They rested briefly on one of the seats in the Peace Gardens which, Herbert explained several times, had been a church when he was a boy. The pause was not wasted. He pointed out the extension to the Town Hall (which the Prince of Wales himself was due to open) and the strips of brass, set out into the wall, which marked off every minor distance of imperial measure – inch, foot, yard and perch. He emphasized the word imperial. The idea of Empire was very important to Herbert. Despite Betty's aching feet, she made a fair imitation of enthusiasm when he suggested a visit to the General Cemetery. They failed to find his father's grave but they were more successful in their search for both the house in which Herbert was born and the house in which he was brought up. To his wife's relief, he decided not to knock on the door of 16 Aline Road and ask permission to visit the room in which he had come into the world.

'Now Bramall Lane.' He said it as if he was offering her a prospect of pure bliss. 'It's United's first home match of the season. Never went much when I was a young man. Always playing myself.'

The Shoreham Street tram car took them to one end of the ground. Betty could hear the excited buzz from inside the ground and as they walked to what he called the pavilion entrance, a great roar, which Herbert identified as a near miss, exploded into the cool afternoon air. To her relief he stopped to look in the window of Jack Archer's sports shop.

'He sells the footballs to United. And the shorts. Look – *Official Suppliers!*'

Betty was more interested in the tobacconist and confectioner's next door, so Herbert tore himself away from the display of shin pads and goalkeepers' jerseys and offered his opinion on the neighbouring window. Since his wife had worked for John Player and Sons, he had nothing to say about the pipes, cigars and cigarettes in case she proved the greater expert. But the sweets and chocolates afforded a welcome and unexpected opportunity to brag about his native city.

'Thornton's toffee. Best in the world. That's made in Sheffield. So are Bassett's Liquorice All Sorts. Do you know how they came to be called "All Sorts"?'

'Yes,' said Betty. 'You told me.'

'And did I tell you that Bassetts made their sweets in the barracks in Hillsborough? I used to play football for the Barracks Inn. In those days of course, the barracks was a barracks.'

'Yes,' said Betty with sublime patience. 'You told me that as well.'

'Would you like some toffee? It gets stuck in your teeth, but it's—'

'Fry's, I'd like a bar of Fry's Chocolate Cream.'

Herbert was hurt by her disloyalty, but, being a man of generous disposition, he pushed at the shop door. Instead of swinging open, it rattled against two men who were arguing just over the threshold. One of them peered out of the darkness into the sunlit road. It was clear from his fawn linen jacket and his air of authority that he was the proprietor.

'Do come in. I have told this young man that he ought to stand outside on the pavement. But he claims that he was instructed to remain inside the shops. Says it's to associate me with the promotion. Would you like a couple of Player's Weights with my compliments?'

Herbert was about to say that his wife had once worked for Players', when he noticed the young man who would not stand on the public highway.

Rex was still wearing his heavy black jacket and the waistcoat which had once imprisoned his stock. His collar was limp with sweat and the heat of the September afternoon had dappled wet patches on the parts of his shirt which were visible below Uncle Ern's knitted tie. A tray was suspended round his neck – a tray of the sort from which cinema usherettes sold sweets during the intervals between pictures. Herbert looked into his son's face. The film of moisture on the lenses of his *pince-nez* made him look blind – blind and ridiculous.

'What the bloody hell are you doing?'

'Earning my living, Dad. Or trying to.'

'It's my lad,' Herbert told the shopkeeper. It was clear from his manner that he held the man personally responsible for his son's degradation. 'Do you know that he's—'

'It doesn't matter, Dad.'

'. . . didn't finish his education until he was twenty odd.'

'These are hard times, sir. We have to do what we can.'

'How much does the whole lot cost?' Herbert felt in his back pocket. 'The whole lot?'

'They're not for sale, Dad. I have to stay here till five when the match is over and the crowd comes past the shop again. They're samples.'

'Samples be buggered.'

'Dad, can you wait till I've finished?'

'We were just on our way to see you. George is up there already.'

Rex's only thought was of getting his father out of the shop.

'Have a walk for an hour and we'll go up there together.'

Betty, who until then had not dared to speak, tugged at Herbert's sleeve.

'He's right. We're only making things worse.' She sounded desperate. 'Let's wait for him outside.'

They were all afraid that another customer would come into the shop. The confectioner feared that he would acquire a reputation for attracting troublemakers. Rex feared he would be required to perform his patter in front of his father. 'Two Player's Weights with the company's compliments. John Player is confident that when you've tried them you'll never smoke another brand.' Herbert feared that he would have to witness his son humiliate himself by pressing samples on reluctant customers and his wife feared that her husband would hit anybody who treated Rex with anything short of total respect.

'Come on, love. Let's have another little walk.' Betty tugged harder.

'Have you got that docket?' The confectioner was sweating no less than Rex.

Rex took a crumpled piece of paper from his trouser pocket. The shopkeeper licked his pencil and signed it.

'There won't be many people come in when it's finished. Too busy getting home for their tea. Most of the trade's before the match starts.'

'I'm very grateful,' Rex told him, wriggling out of his harness. 'Very grateful indeed.' He unclipped his spectacles and mopped his face with a grey handkerchief.

'We came in,' said Herbert, dignity regained, 'to make a purchase. A bar of Fry's Chocolate Cream, if you please.'

'Have it with my good wishes.' The confectioner who – out of habit – had rung up tuppence on the cash register, pressed the 'No Sale' key. 'It's not often that you have the privilege of meeting a good father these days.'

★

BETTY SAT in the easy chair. At first she thought that Enid's insistence that she sank into the shabby cushions was a mark of respect. But when she looked across the room at the other four – her husband, his sons and that woman – sitting round the table, she only felt excluded from their family circle.

'How have you spent the time?' Rex asked Enid and George, loosening the laces in his shoes.

'We've been to the Ruskin Museum,' Enid told him.

'Hell of a walk,' George added. 'No pictures or anything. Just a collection of stones. "Onyx and other examples of quartz and chalcedony." '

He was reading from a catalogue which he had brought home from the museum. As he read, he squinted furtively over the top of the illustrated guide. George prided himself on understanding people and he was sure that he understood Enid in a way which Rex, because of his infatuation, could never match. He knew that Enid was no less nervous than his stepmother and he wanted to provide time for her to sink into the security of Rex's company, for he knew the destructive potential of Enid's raw nerves.

' "A form of quartz with crystals arranged in parallel fibres." We walked all that way to see—'

'Malachite,' said Enid. 'It was malachite not onyx.' She looked across at Betty. 'They're all semi-precious stones.'

'That's not what it says here.' George flapped the brochure across the table. "Ruskin's collection consisted mostly of—" '

'Ruskin,' Enid was speaking directly to Betty again, 'was a painter and an art critic and an essayist. I'm very fond of him. We all are.'

Betty was not sure how to respond. She had never heard of Ruskin but she did know what was what. This woman had left her husband and was living with another man. There were no carpets on her floors and no curtains at the windows. She possessed only four cups and saucers, a deprivation which her claim not to like tea had been unable to hide. Yet she behaved like Lady Muck. Betty did not understand that all Enid's talk was the product of fear and a determination that she expected rejection.

'What I miss most,' said Enid, 'is my books. We've hardly any books at all. Just a few that Rex could bring.' She looked across at Betty again. 'You'll not believe it, but I doubt if there's two dozen books in this house. I think that a day without reading a book is a day wasted, don't you?'

The emotional reunion, which Betty assumed was the purpose of the visit, had never taken place. Once in the house, Rex and Herbert had shown less affection than they had exhibited in the shop. Instead, Enid had told endless anecdotes about the time she and the three Hattersley brothers had spent together during the previous summer. She recounted each story as if Rex and George could not remember it for themselves and, more improbably, as if Betty and Herbert would be interested. Sometimes she reminisced to the dog which lay under the table, growling from time to time for no apparent reason.

'It's time the three men had a word,' said George.

'Why the three men?' Enid's manner had changed from maudlin to severe. 'What about?'

'If it's important,' said Rex, 'I'd like Enid to come too.'

That, thought Betty, means everybody except me.

'It's not important. It's only about me and my future,' George smiled his secret, superior smile. 'Just the three men for a minute or two in the kitchen.'

Betty felt less offended and more apprehensive. She was used to women being excluded from all the decisions which mattered and felt no offence at the men going off to hold secret male discussions, but the idea of being left alone with Enid horrified her. The opening salvo justified her worst fears.

'Do you still work in the cigarette factory?'

'I gave up when I was sixty. Too much like hard work.'

'I always wanted to work. I wanted to work in a library, but Mother being ill, I couldn't. That's why I couldn't go to university.'

Betty looked blank and Enid tried again.

'Do you like poetry?'

'I don't know.'

'I couldn't live without poetry. Browning in particular. "I'm

your friend. What a thing is friendship is, world without end?"
Fancy not liking poetry. I couldn't manage without.'

'I didn't say I didn't like it. I said I didn't know any.'

The intention was to be firm without being rude. Enid was
prompted by no such admirable instinct.

'If you wanted to, you would. The public libraries are free. No
matter how poor you are.'

Betty looked again at the badly painted floor boards and marvelled at Enid's effrontery.

'We're not poor. We never have been.'

'I didn't mean that. I was just making the point. It's like soap.
Nobody needs to be dirty. Soap and water are cheap enough.'

It was not possible, Betty decided after some thought, that this
woman was accusing her of being dirty. Against the background
of Enid's unremitting dialogue – Ramsay MacDonald, rheumatoid
arthritis, Bernard Shaw, Squire Hodding, home rendered lard, the
Lyceum Theatre, new-laid eggs, A. J. Cook, Ashleigh House
private school, *Angel Pavement*, Aunt Anne – she concluded that
Enid was a lunatic and must, therefore, be treated with patience
and caution. So she nodded from time to time, and made clucking
noises which she hoped signified agreement. After the first ten
minutes, not even that was necessary. She sat absolutely still and
let Langwith tennis club, Percy Ford, gastric ulcers and Walt Whitman all wash over her. Then Enid, as was her habit, suddenly
asked a direct question.

'Have you not noticed . . . ?' Enid used the negative to imply
negligence. 'Have you not noticed that the buttons on your husband's suit aren't in line? He must have let them out when he put
on a bit of weight. He must have done it himself, before you were
married. It's very difficult with a double-breasted suit. Men aren't
any good at that sort of thing.'

Betty, who had readjusted the buttons that morning, decided
that it was safest not to answer.

The long pause which followed was only broken by George's
return. He launched, without pausing or thinking, into an
announcement of the conclusions to their deliberations. Betty
swallowed hard.

'Tomorrow,' he said. 'I'm bringing my clothes tomorrow. I'll go with Rex to sign on next week.'

Revenge, thought Betty, is sweet. Lady Muck is to take in lodgers, without even being asked if she is willing to do the extra drudgery. Enid, she felt sure, wanted to burst into tears and ask how she could be expected to look after two men and the bedridden mother who had figured so prominently in the one-sided conversation. She almost felt sorry for her.

Enid ran, but she ran to George not to Rex.

'That's wonderful,' she said, putting her arm round his shoulders. 'I knew you'd come. Why you had to have all that daftness about asking Rex and telling your dad, I'll never know.'

She turned to Herbert, who had taken refuge on the arm of the easy chair next to his wife.

'I know you'll miss him but it's best for him to be here.'

Why, thought Betty, does son not defend father as father defended son in the confectioner's shop? How could these two young men – knowing that her Herbert had worked his fingers to the bone to give them a proper education – allow this woman to treat him so badly? But Enid had not yet done.

'But we're still part of the same family. I know you're old enough to be my mother so perhaps I better call you Mrs Hattersley. At least for a bit. But I hope you'll call me Enid.'

Betty's nerve snapped.

'Well, I'd better not call you Mrs McNamara, or whatever your real name is.'

CHAPTER SIXTEEN

FOR THE whole of Sunday evening, they talked about Betty. George said that her behaviour was barely credible, Rex judged it unforgivable and Enid said that she was more to be pitied than blamed.

'A normal woman wouldn't behave like that.' She grimaced to indicate that she suspected an ailment which it was best not to mention.

Despite her innate good nature Enid did not argue with Rex's pronouncement that Betty would never be allowed inside South View Road again.

'I shall go to see Dad, though.' George felt defiant without being clear what he had to be defiant about.

'I shan't,' his brother said. 'Not if she's there.'

Enid, who had been staring at George as if he had betrayed her in some way, smiled and gripped Rex's knee under the table, after negotiating her way past one of the balusters in the carved legs of the mock-Jacobean dining table.

As always, she passed an untroubled night. Rex dreamed that his mother had forbidden him ever to speak to his father again. The brothers were up early. They were in the living room – smoking, drinking tea and feeling slightly apprehensive about their future – when the letter arrived.

George picked it up from the empty door-mat well and carried it into the living room at arm's length, like a bomb which he feared would explode.

'I bet it's for Enid,' Rex said.

'Why do you say that?' George asked looking at the envelope as if he knew that he must give it to Rex but wanted to delay the moment.

'Process of elimination. Four people know where we live. You are here. Dad was here yesterday. Syd's too lazy to write. Enid expects her mother to make peace any day. That's the peace treaty.'

'It doesn't look like a peace treaty to me. It's addressed to Mrs Enid O'Hara. I thought you said her mother was with that funny lot in Worksop.'

'She is.'

'Not according to the postmark, she isn't. The letter comes from Newcastle. Are you going to open it or not?'

George's question was meant to suggest impatience rather than imply doubt.

'It's Enid's letter, not mine.'

'You are going soft in the head. Do you realize what this letter means?'

'Of course I do. It means that the postman – and because of him probably the neighbours – think that the O'Haras live here. When they find out that I'm called Hattersley there will, to say the least, be confusion.'

'That's only the beginning of it.'

'It also means that somebody else – somebody besides Dad, Syd and Enid's family at Worksop knows that she's here. Do I pass the test? Do I qualify as intelligent enough to be your brother?'

'I'm glad you're so calm.' It was an attitude which George much admired.

'I'm calm because I've thought about it. We were always going to have difficulties with the name. And I knew that, sooner or later, they'd find us. I'm calm because I'm not surprised.'

He shook Enid gently and she smiled at him before she was fully awake. He tried to smile back. It was not a convincing imitation of confidence and contentment.

'What's the matter?'

'Nothing we didn't expect. It's just come sooner than we thought.'

'Is there somebody downstairs? Have they come to take you back?'

Enid pulled the bedclothes back up under her chin to protect her against whichever priests were waiting in the hall to reclaim Rex for the Church.

'There's nobody there. It's just a letter.'

He handed her the envelope.

'How have they found out?' She was too surprised to be afraid.

'Open it and see. But don't worry.'

'I'm not worried about losing you, if thats what you mean.' She put her finger under the loose corner of the flap. 'But we could have done with a quiet week or two.'

Enid tore at the envelope, cut her finger on the sharp edge of the stiff manila paper and watched as a thin line of blood ran along the crease behind the knuckle. Then she pulled out the thin sheet of cheap writing paper. When Rex looked impatient, she told him, 'I know who it's from. It's from Jack. That's his handwriting.'

'From Newcastle? Jack?'

She started to examine her cut finger. Then she sucked the wound. It was several minutes before she felt ready to read the letter. Rex stood nervously over her, trying to read Jack's opening sentence.

'It's him all right. But they must have told him. They must have found out.' To Enid, the Catholic Church had become a menacing conspiracy. 'He hasn't found out for himself. How could he? They've told him. They know.'

'They know all right,' said Rex adopting her language. 'The question is, what will they do next?'

'Are you frightened?' Enid asked.

Rex wondered how she could imagine that it was possible not to be frightened. They stood, the two of them, against the might of Rome, possibly even against the will of God. All that he had been taught conspired to make him feel afraid. When the priests came, as come they must, it would not be one man who stood at his front door but the representative of a million martyrs, the College of Cardinals, the company of saints, two thousand years of belief, the worldwide Church and an infallible Pope. He would have to stand out against them and she asked him if he was afraid.

'Nothing to be frightened about,' he said. 'Read it.'

'There's nothing in the letter to bother about. I can tell you that without looking at it. Jack won't do anything to hurt me.'

'Read it.'

The thought of Jack – abandoned but still devoted – renewed her confidence. Curiosity and self-esteem drove from her mind all feeling of fear and shame. Speaking in the voice which she assumed when repeating important conversations or delivering messages of significance, she read the letter out loud, interrupting her flow from time to time with comments of her own.

'. . . "Father Ellis kindly found me a job as a gardener" . . . Gardener! He was never interested in gardening when I knew him . . . "at Ushaw College" . . . So now we see why he's not in Langwith.' She spoke as if she had found him out in something shameful. 'Ushaw's not like the English College in Rome, is it, Rex? I mean, you wouldn't have wanted to go there?'

'It's all very much the same. We *thought* we were special . . .'

Although she had seemed fascinated by the question, the answer did not interest her.

'He says we can have all the furniture in Langwith. I should hope so. Mam bought most of it. "I have left the key with Mrs Ferguson" . . . How stupid. Leaving it out there in Hucknall! Why didn't he leave it up the road with Brack?'

The question was meant to do no more than emphasize Jack's stupidity, but Rex chose to answer.

'Too painful to meet him.'

'Not too painful for me to trail out to Hucknall.' She put the letter on the floor next to the bed. 'Well, that's that then. It'll be nice to get the furniture. George will have something to sleep on.'

'There's more to it than that. I'm not sure I want that stuff.'

'Why on earth not?'

Rex could not explain why he did not want the chairs on which Enid and Jack had sat, the table at which they had eaten and, above all, the bed in which Enid and Jack had slept. He did not dare to admit his sudden feeling of sympathy for Jack.

For the first time, he felt a deep disapproval of Enid's behaviour – not irritation or annoyance but an irresistible feeling that she was wrong. The experience was so strange that he could not bear to look at her. He resented the barrier that her insensitivity had erected between them.

'It won't be long now before they come and say that I ought to

go back.' He wanted her to think about something more important than retrieving the furniture. 'I'm surprised they haven't been
already.' He looked at the postmark on Jack's letter. 'They must
have known for a week or more. They've been planning what to
do.'

The idea of a planned campaign was far more frightening than
the expectation of a sudden and spontaneous recrimination. Enid
gave a gratifying shudder.

She took his hand. 'A goose walked over my grave,' she told
him.

Rex, having achieved his objective, felt immediately guilty.

'It had to happen, sooner or later. I know how much it all
matters to you.'

'Last night was different.' She was out of bed and already half
dressed. 'What I was worried about then was *people* finding out.
People who don't know now. Neighbours in particular. Nobody
from the cathedral is going to make a fuss in public.'

Rex knew what she said was true, but she said it in the offhand
manner of a woman who was preoccupied with a greater endeav-
our. He followed her out of the bedroom.

'Where are you going?'

'Hucknall of course, silly. Then on to Langwith. I'm getting
that furniture before Mrs Ferguson writes to Newcastle and
changes Jack's mind. You know how soft he is and she always had
an eye on him for her daughter. I'll telephone Dad on my way and
get the lorry or the van . . . The van will probably be best.'

'You don't really mean that you're going out to Langwith?'

'Indeed I do. We can't afford pride. Not without a kitchen
table, we can't.'

'And you're going to Hucknall first?'

'I have to. It's the only way to get the key. I'll have to take her
by surprise or she'll think of ways to keep it from me.'

Enid arrived in Hucknall wearing what she described as her
best coat and what Mrs Ferguson called her film-star hat. The
hat was undoubtedly impressive – broad brimmed with artificial
flowers at the front and two strips of ribbon which hung half way
down her back. It was the last relic of the carefree days before her

marriage, bought in a fit of frivolity in Mansfield, and not even worn on her honeymoon journey to Worksop because her Aunt Anne had told her that it was flashy. She wore it to her meeting with Mrs Ferguson because she felt frightened and did not want to show it. Because she wore it, Mrs Ferguson was confirmed in the opinion that 'Enid O'Hara is as bold as brass'.

Mrs Ferguson refused to let her take the key away so they set out together, silent and resentful, to Langwith Junction. Mick, who was infected by their solemn mood, walked to the bus stop without once pulling on his lead or having to be dragged away from a lamp-post. All three sat motionless at the back of the bus.

Enid spent her first hour in Colliery Row folding tablecloths, rolling up rugs and piling crockery and saucepans into the wicker washing basket. Brack's van – promised for half past one – was late and she had nothing to do except feel out of place. Her plan had been to make the man who brought the van pull the linoleum from the floor – cheap lino which she feared would crack when it was lifted, as it had almost cracked when it was laid less than six months earlier. But lifting the lino was better than sitting with Mrs Ferguson, so she began to pick at the edges where it almost touched the wall.

'Are you leaving the glass in the windows?'

'What do you mean?'

'I mean that I've never moved into a house where lino hadn't been left on the floor.'

'This is nearly new linoleum. I bought it myself at Mansfield Co-op. It's very high quality. It cost—'

'It isn't linoleum at all. It's oil cloth.'

'No, it isn't.' Enid pulled hard and the lino tore from wall to hearth. 'There you are. Oil cloth doesn't tear like that. I hope that you are satisfied.'

'I'd only be satisfied if everything broke in your hands. This was all Jack's and you've no right to any of it. When I think about what you've done—'

'You don't know what I've done. You couldn't understand.'

She had intended to say what she honestly believed, that her love for Rex – a love which was too great to deny – was something which was beyond the comprehension of ordinary people. But Mrs Ferguson, sweating inside her heavy coat and easing her aching feet out of her shoes, did not look as if she would be responsive to any argument which was concerned with romance. So Enid changed tack.

'If you knew what I've been through—'

'Not with Jack. You couldn't have had a better man. You didn't deserve him. A real gentleman. You didn't appreciate it.'

'It was before that,' Enid said mysteriously. 'I was desperate to get away from home, when Jack asked me to marry him. Things that I can't tell you, or anybody. But if you knew, you wouldn't judge me so harshly.'

Mrs Ferguson had no idea what Enid was talking about and, being a pious Catholic, had no wish to find out. So she said no more. When the van came and the moving began, she lifted one end of the sofa whilst the driver carried the other. It was her way of ensuring against the sin of the Pharisee. As they were manoeuvring it through the door, she noticed that Enid was taking the kitchen light bulb out of its socket.

THE CLERK at the Labour Exchange told George that he had nothing to suit them.

'Nothing?' asked George. 'I know times are hard. But surely there's something. I can clerk,' he said, implying that anyone could do that.

'We've more clerks than jobs. And before you ask me, the answer is yes. I got the job because I'm an ex-service man. If you'd had your arm shot off . . .'

'I didn't mean that. I just thought that there must be something.'

'Only labouring.'

'Then I'll labour.'

'Oh yes.' The clerk was aggressive again. 'I can see you sweeping up in a steel works.'

'Done,' said George, clapping his hands together, as if he had just made a deal in the market in Valladolid. 'I'll start sweeping up tomorrow.'

'It's no use being smart with me. It doesn't work like that. Sweeping up is done—'

'By lads. It's done by lads. Old men. Wrecks, called lads.'

'How do you know that?'

'My father was a time-served cutler. Scissors-maker, as a matter of fact. So was my grandfather.'

'Get away. I thought you were a foreigner. You certainly look like that.

'With a name like Hattersley?'

'Plenty of Hattersleys went abroad with their trade. I met a Wolstenholme once, who was a Frenchman. And there's something funny about you.'

'I lived in Spain. But I'm as English as you.' George decided that it was not the time for biographical niceties. 'Any jobs for a Sheffielder?'

'Can you play an instrument? Brass?'

'"Fraid not.'

'Pity, 'cause you're big enough.'

George looked bewildered and the clerk explained.

'The police are looking for bandsmen. Any good at games?'

'Cricket. Football. Tennis.'

'Ever done any boxing?'

'I did at school. But it's a long time ago.'

'That sort of school. I thought as much. Well, it won't do any harm. Hillsborough Boys' Club. Assistant manager. Ask for Captain Royle. Get the hundred-and-one tram to the Hillsborough Barracks. It's where they make—'

'I know. Liquorice allsorts. My dad told me. Is there anything for another Sheffield lad, my brother?'

'Attendant at the new museum, would he do that?'

'Like a shot. Just his style.'

Captain Royle wore a scarlet polo-necked jumper and white flannels. His interviewing technique was brisk. 'School?' he enquired. When George answered 'Ratcliffe', he asked 'Catholic?' As soon as his worst fears were confirmed he opened his office door and said, 'Morning.'

Rex went first to the Graves Art Gallery and was redirected to the Western Park Museum where he was sat down opposite a case of stuffed birds. After waiting for almost half an hour, the head attendant told him that no interview would be possible that afternoon.

'They shouldn't have sent you today. It's the annual visit. The committee's all here. Councillor York's in with the director now. We told them not to send anybody today.'

'How many are you expecting?'

'We saw seven yesterday. I don't know how many more.'

It was not so much desperation as the wish to boast to Enid about his initiative that made Rex hang about in the park. At four o'clock the black limousines drew up outside the main gates and the committee – Labour and Conservatives indistinguishable in their municipal respectability – filed out.

'Councillor York,' Rex called in the general direction of the shuffling councillor.

A thin-faced man with fair wavy hair turned round.

'Can't it wait till Saturday? Labour Hall. Ten o'clock.'

'I'd welcome a word now.'

'Quickly then.'

It was, he decided, time for almost all the truth. Benefiting from George's experience, he spoke of his grandfather's business and his father's affection for the city, of his extensive education amongst the antiquities of Rome, his familiarity with Latin, his love of old churches and his enthusiasm for English history. It required a partial confession. Although he admitted to the English College in Rome, he did not confess to ordination.

Councillor York was growing impatient. 'And what can I do for you?'

'I'm after the attendant's job at the museum.'

'Pity,' said Councillor York. 'Pity. You seem just right for it. Pity that canvassing disqualifies. It's written into the standing orders.'

FATHER CREMONINI had tried to postpone the official visitation until Christmas in the hope that by then there would be a real bishop to entertain at Ratcliffe. But Monsignor Payne had been adamant. The visitation was always held in September and the rule could not be broken. The Vicar General was in no way influenced by the hope of enjoying an afternoon of *pro tempore* authority. His only concern was precedent. As things had been in the past, so should they be in the future, world without end.

The college had done its best, but its best had been disappointing. The cadet corps had been slovenly. When Monsignor Payne's car arrived, the guard of honour appeared to hold an inconclusive discussion on the merits of coming to attention. During the service the whole school had been restless and audible giggles had followed the announcement that the Vicar General would take as the text of his sermon St Matthew, Chapter Ten, Verse 6, 'He that endureth to the end shall be saved.'

The lunch was a fiasco – the food cold and half cooked, the senior refectory hot and airless, the head boy speechless with fright on the Vicar General's right hand and the Bishop's Prize-winner garrulous with nerves on his left. The presentation of prizes and certificates passed off without major disaster, only because the boys had been told to keep whatever they were given and exchange it for the right presentation later. The football match which followed was a farce. The school had only recently switched from Rugby to association football and lapses in memory combined with confusion of roles to result in continual fouls. When, in the middle of the second half, a wing forward caught the ball and ran towards goal, the referee abandoned the game.

Father Cremonini had dreaded the conversation with which the visitation always ended, but on that day he led Monsignor Payne to his study with something approaching relief. At least his humiliation would continue in privacy.

'Congratulations,' said the Vicar General. 'Congratulations on a very successful day.'

The President was not sure if his guest of honour was being sarcastic or if he had merely spoken the traditional, and therefore obligatory, opening words of the visitation's formal conclusion. Father Cremonini poured the Vicar General a glass of madeira with shaking hand. It overflowed on to the table and he waited in terror to watch it drip down Father Payne's cassock when he lifted it to his lips.

'Which, President, leaves us with only one matter outstanding. Sydney Hattersley. I take it you have told him as I requested.'

'I hoped we could think about it.'

'I have thought about it during the weeks since his brother's apostasy. I resent the implication that I have not.'

'And perhaps talk about it.'

'There is nothing to talk about. It is the new bishop's wish.'

'On your recommendation . . .' Father Cremonini was shaking. 'On your recommendation without consulting me.'

'I don't propose to argue with you, President.'

'But the young man has done nothing wrong.'

'You bewilder me. What this Sydney – this Charles Sydney – has or has not done is hardly the question. The question is the reputation of the Church and – if I may say so – the reputation of this college.'

'I cannot see how his presence has damaged that reputation. I feared that it might but . . .'

'Because he will become a cause of gossip. He will become notorious as the brother of the priest who lives with a married woman. The school will become notorious in consequence.'

Father Cremonini did not find it easy to argue with the Vicar General, but he forced himself into one last trembling disagreement.

'What I find difficult . . . I do not mean to question your decision, only to examine my own conscience . . . That is, I am sure you will agree, my moral duty . . . The problem, for me is the fear, which I hope you can dispel, that the boy is being sacrificed.'

'Of course he is being sacrificed. But the sacrifice is necessary. Do I need to remind you that our faith is built on sacrifice?'

Father Cremonini knew that he was about to capitulate and he knew, with equal certainty, that capitulation was contemptible. He was in his own study, with his own books on the shelves, his own missal open on the desk in front of him and his own crucifix – the symbol of Christian sacrifice – on the wall above his head. Yet, with all the reminders of comfort and confidence around him, he did not have the courage to take his own decisions for his own school.

'If you insist—'

'I do. There is no possible argument about it. To doubt that is mere self-indulgence, the pretence that personal feelings are more important than—'

'It is my duty to consider the personal feelings of the boys in my charge.'

'Your personal feelings, President. Yours. It is your personal feelings that you place above the clear interests of the Church. I trust that you will bring yourself to tell him. If you do not feel up to the task, I will see him on your behalf.'

'I shall do my duty, Vicar General. If your mind is made up, I shall tell him tonight.'

'Tonight. Good. It would be best if he were out tomorrow.'

The worm turned.

'He needs to make his plans. And I have an obligation to warn his father.' Father Cremonini called on all his reserves of courage. 'I will tell him tonight. But he cannot leave at once.'

'His father will not understand. He is not of our faith.'

'He will understand that his son needs a bed.'

To Father Cremonini's relief, he was accused of neither flippancy nor impertinence. The Vicar General's mind was concentrated on discretion.

'Can you be sure that he won't make a nuisance of himself? We've avoided fuss so far. Not a word in any of the papers? If he goes charging about the school . . .'

'He's a very level-headed young man.'

Father Cremonini might have added that Syd would be so concerned to protect his brother that he would probably lie about why he was leaving, but he was not sure whether the Vicar General would be relieved at the guarantee of continued secrecy or offended at the idea of calculated deception, so he merely repeated his reassurance.

His business done, Monsignor Payne left without finishing his madeira. The car had not been brought round to the front door.

The coffee table (made by the fourth form woodwork class and presented to him at the end of the prize giving) was missing. And the cadet corps, which should have formed up in a guard of honour, lay on the lawn which separated the college from the Fosse Way. One of them was smoking.

It was almost time for lights out when Syd got the message that the President wanted to see him. It was, he decided, the moment of decision which Rex had warned him would come before the end of the year. If he told the truth and admitted that he had no intention of becoming a priest, he would risk losing the bishop's scholarship. Without the bishop's scholarship he would be forced to leave Ratcliffe.

Until that moment, he had never understood Rex's feelings about the college. He had barely noticed Pugin's pointed latticed windows, the gothic letter M embossed upon the flagstones of the Lady Corridor and the statue of the Virgin at the corner where it ended. But as he walked past them on his way to the President's study he felt that all that mattered was to spend his eighteenth year at Ratcliffe. He decided to lie about his vocation.

Father Cremonini spoke without looking up from the missal on his desk.

'Sydney. I'm afraid you can't come back after the Christmas holidays. I'm sorry. It's out of my hands. I did what I could.'

'But I've decided, Father. I want to go to Rome. I want to become a priest.' Rex had told him that if he continued to proclaim his vocation, the bishop's scholarship would be saved. He could not believe that Rex was wrong and the scholarship lost. All he had to do was convince the President that he still heard the call. 'I prayed and asked for guidance—'

'It isn't that, Sydney. It's your brother. After what he's done—'

'That's not fair.'

It was the reaction of a boy of ten – spontaneous, naive and entirely justified. Father Cremonini had no adequate answer.

'Nobody's blaming you. I'm sorry. There's nothing that anyone can do. We don't want to cause you any embarrassment. Finish off this term.'

'Finish off this term?'

'I've put it all very badly. You're not being expelled.'

'If I have to go, I'll go tonight.'

'You can't do that.' Father Cremonini sounded nervous. 'The last bus goes in half an hour.'

'Tomorrow then.'

'That's foolish, Sydney. If you do that, everybody will know what has happened.'

'What do I tell them if I stay?' He sounded calmer. 'I can't talk about next term. I can't talk as if I'm coming back.'

'I hope that you don't feel bitter.'

Syd did not reply to what, even at the age of eighteen, he regarded as a contemptible observation. Of course he felt bitter – bitter about the President, the college, the Church and most bitter about the brother who had ruined his life.

That night, instead of kneeling on the hard floor, he said his prayers after he got into bed. The other boys noticed – as he intended – and assumed that he had not said his prayers at all. The next morning he told them.

'I'm off. Off today. I've got a job. I'm going to earn some money. No more being treated like a kid.'

His friends, who said they would miss him, particularly resented the contempt with which he spoke of the school which, until that minute, they had all assumed that he enjoyed.

'IT'S NOT half term.'

It was hardly a warm welcome, but it expressed Rex's surprise and relief, for he had begun to believe that every knock on the door was made by a representative of the unforgiving Church. Syd stepped inside without waiting to be asked.

'They've sacked me,' he said.

Enid arrived in the hall just in time to hear his explanation.

'What have you done?'

Until that minute, Syd had been calm – calm enough to decide, as he packed his bags, that he wanted to go neither to his father's house in Nottingham nor to his aunt Clare. Rex was the architect of his misfortune, but he would still rather live with Rex and

George than anywhere else. He had travelled to Sheffield full of forgiveness and understanding. Then Enid asked him what he had done.

'It's what you've done,' he said. 'You two. You've ruined everything.'

He was shaking with anger and Rex feared that he was about to cry.

'They can't have expelled you because of us!' Enid was more outraged than guilty.

'Of course they can. They have.' Syd turned on her. 'You don't want to believe it but it's true. You've done it. You've done it to me.'

Rex wanted to comfort Syd, but he wanted to defend Enid even more.

'You mustn't speak to her like that,' he said. 'If it's anybody's fault it's mine.'

He led his brother into the living room and Enid, after taking a couple of tentative steps after them, hung back in the hall. She had just closed the living room door as a sign of a selfless wish for the brothers to make private peace, when there was another knock on the door. She grasped the latch without pausing to think that the second caller of the morning might be the priest they so much dreaded. Mick, excited by the commotion, threw himself at the door. Afraid that he would run out into the road, she bent down and held his collar in one hand and opened the door with the other. It was a feat of considerable physical agility but one which made it difficult to preserve proper dignity. Crouching on the doorwell, she looked up into the startled face of Father William Ellis.

'Good afternoon. I hoped to see Father Hattersley.'

CHAPTER SEVENTEEN

ENID DECIDED to give as good as she got.

'He's not Father Hattersley now. And he's out. Mr Hattersley is out.'

It was, Bill Ellis knew, not the right moment for theological disputation. But he could not let the heresy pass unchallenged.

'He is still Father Hattersley, but no matter for the moment. I really do need to see him. Will he be out long?'

'I don't know. You'll have to forgive me.' She pushed the door half shut. 'This isn't a very convenient moment.'

'Does he still live here?'

It was a straightforward, if insensitive question, which implied no more than a determination to find Rex. But Enid was scandalized.

'Of course he does. He's just out at work, that's all. He won't be back until late.'

'Could I come in for a minute?'

Father Ellis tried his best to sound reassuring but he only managed to make Enid feel threatened. She stepped back into the hall and he feared that she was going to close the door.

'I must tell him something, or at least, if you won't let me see him, I must send him a message. It would be better inside, really.'

Enid shook her head.

'I really am a friend. William Ellis is my name. Perhaps Rex has spoken to you about me . . .'

Rex had spoken to her of the bishop's secretary, the priest who had come out to Langwith Junction to persuade him to give her up and return to the Church.

'I haven't come here to persuade him to change his mind.'

'You couldn't do that. He won't change his mind now.'

'I'm not going to suggest that he does. I'm here as a friend to tell him something that he needs to know. I'm afraid it's bad news and I wanted to tell him myself. I'll give you a message, if it's the only way. But it would be better to do it inside, rather than out here.'

'You better come in. Careful of the dog. It's a bit fierce.'

They stood together in the hall. Enid took up position in front of the kitchen door. In her mind, she was protecting Rex from a vengeful Church. Father Ellis moved from foot to foot, still hoping that he would be taken into the living room and asked to sit down.

'Go on then. You're inside now.'

'I'm afraid that his brother Syd has been asked to leave Ratcliffe. He took it rather badly. Walked out early this morning. No one's quite sure where he has gone.'

Before Enid had time to answer, the living room door opened.

'He's here, Bill. Beat you by about ten minutes . . .'

There was another long silence whilst Rex and Bill Ellis adjusted to the sight of each other and Enid wondered if Rex knew how badly he had let her down. She decided, from his confident manner, that he had not heard her tell the priest that she was alone in the house.

Bill Ellis had been sent to meet Rex at the Termini Station on the day that he had arrived in Rome, hot, tired and frightened to be away from home. He had watched him become a priest and, in Nottingham and Langwith Junction, he had witnessed his degeneration. But the man in the badly fitting tweed jacket was a stranger who lacked the hope and quiet confidence of his old friend. Rex, the man, seemed quite different from Rex, the priest – smaller, paler and infinitely less distinguished. He even spoke more quietly than before.

'It's a rotten business.'

'Anyway,' said Enid, unable to comprehend the feeling that the two men shared, 'he's all right now. He's with us.'

'Come into the living room, Bill. He's in here. Come in and sit down.'

Father Ellis began to apologize to Syd, but he directed his apology towards Rex and that made it sound like an accusation.

'The circumstances of your going made all the difference. I

wish they'd taken a different view. I was worried . . . I just wanted to make sure . . .'

'I'm very grateful, Bill,' Rex said.

'Grateful?' Enid asked. 'What have we got to be grateful about? God is love! Or he's supposed to be. It doesn't sound like it to me.'

Bill Ellis looked gratifyingly shocked, and Syd glowered, uncertain whose side to be on. Rex thought it best to postpone the justification of his gratitude until Bill Ellis had left. He would not risk giving the impression that he and Enid argued with each other. So he said, 'It was good of you to come.'

His casual manner was intended to convince Enid that he meant to do no more than meet the needs of formal courtesy.

'There's one more thing.' Father Ellis was already on his feet. 'It's a rather embarrassing subject, I'm afraid. Money. Now I'm here, it's best to tell you. Better than writing.'

'So that's it,' said Enid.

Bill Ellis ignored her and Rex prepared to decline with thanks a grant from the Impoverished Clergy's Fund.

'It's rather petty too. But it can't be avoided.'

Father Ellis took an official looking document from his inside pocket.

'First of all, will you sign this? It's the refund on the Valladolid ticket. You have to apply yourself.'

Father Ellis took out his fountain pen, but hesitated before he offered it to Rex.

'You'll see, if you read it, that they'll only repay two-thirds.'

'I'm sorry.'

'If he'd gone,' Enid said, 'you wouldn't have got any of it back.'

'If he'd gone . . .' Bill Ellis decided that it was best not to finish the sentence. 'I'm afraid that the Vicar General wishes you to repay the rest . . . And the three pounds that you kept for out of pocket expenses.'

Even Enid was speechless.

'You don't have to pay it all at once.'

'Just as well,' said Rex, 'since we can't. It comes to more than twelve pounds.'

'Of course we can pay it back.' Enid's anger was transferred from Bill Ellis to Rex and back again. 'He doesn't know how much we've saved. I do all the housekeeping. You can take half now.'

'I wouldn't dream of it.'

'And we'll get the rest from my aunt. And we'll send you every penny. Don't you worry about that.'

It was, Bill Ellis knew, no more than a figure of speech. But it annoyed him and revived his composure.

'I'm not worried. I trust Rex implicitly.'

He did not mean to be as rude as he sounded, but as he walked down South View Road, Bill Ellis did not regret what he had said. By standing up to Enid, he felt that somehow he had struck a blow for Rex.

It was Syd's arrival as much as the Vicar General's demand that made them talk about money when they got to bed that night.

'I'll have to write to Worksop,' said Enid. 'They'll help.'

'They can't help for ever,' Rex told her.

'Then you think of something.'

He had thought of something already. Despite the special indignity which they would have to endure, there was no alternative to applying for National Assistance. It had not been an easy decision to make, for they lived in the age of the 'means test', and protest marches through every town in Britain proclaimed the prospect of humiliation for those who applied for 'relief'.

George, the most assiduous student in the reference library, had looked up the actual paragraph in the Act and copied it out on the inside of an old cigarette packet.

> It shall be the duty of the father, grandfather, mother, grand-
> mother, husband or child of a poor, old, blind, lame or indigent
> person or other person not able to work, if possessed of suf-
> ficient means, to relieve and maintain that person.

Enid was the daughter of a coal merchant and wife of a working gardener. Rex, George and Syd were the sons of an ironmonger. Agnes was still married to Brack. But George had also found a note written on the cover of the Act by instruction of the Libraries Committee. The courts had ruled that relations were only required to support indigent relatives who lived in the same house.

'That's what all the fuss is about,' George had explained contemptuously. 'They say that it splits up families. It's just sentimentality. Typical of the Labour Party. We ought to sign on tomorrow. It'll take a day or two before we get anything.'

He had gone on to explain why they would have to wait and Rex, lying in the dark next to Enid, braced himself for the trauma of repeating the explanation.

'We qualify for assistance,' he said, fearful that she would interrupt him with the sort of emotional tirade which George so despised.

'The poor law?' Her antagonism was not as great as he had feared.

'It's not that any more. The town halls run it now.' A more political man would have told her that they would make their application to the socialist city council of Sheffield. 'Between us we could get six or seven pounds.'

'Then let's get it. What do we do?'

'We all have to sign on, down at the town hall. Except Mrs Brackenbury of course. You sign on for her.'

'Can't you sign on for me?'

'No.' Rex could not bring himself to give the true explanation. 'Then the Relieving Officer comes round and takes particulars—'

'Asks questions?'

'Of course, but all the answers would be kept private.' Even as he said it, he thought of the entry in the box marked 'Relationship'. It would be 'Common Law Wife' or 'Co-habitee'. 'George says that's the law. And there's no doubt that we're eligible. That's the word, eligible. I asked him to find out about it. He copied out part of the Act.'

'And I thought that you understood.'

'Understood what? I understood that we need the money.'

'I thought that you understood how I felt in there.' Although it was dark, she laid her hand with a theatrical gesture on where she believed her heart to be. 'And in there.' She tapped her forehead, hoping that he would sense the agitated motion. 'I thought that you understood that in there, *I am Mrs Hattersley*. And I'm not going to say anything different to the Relieving Officer. Not for six pounds a week or six hundred pounds a week. *I am Mrs Hattersley*. That's what the neighbours call me. That's what I call myself in the shops. When Worksop write, that's what they'll put on the letters. That's what it's going to say on my ticket at the library.'

It was, Rex knew, the final proof of their permanent union.

It was not the first of Enid's outbursts which he had enjoyed. Usually he had admired them as a sign of her strength and determination. The declaration of the name inside her heart and head was different. She was strident for him and frantic in the best possible cause.

'That's wonderful.'

'Yes – it – is.' She kissed him in between each word to confirm how wonderful it was. 'And this is wonderful too. I've got a nest egg.'

She reached down by the side of the bed and opened her handbag. After much fumbling and some incredulous muttering, she held up her hand in triumph.

'Look.'

It was too dark for Rex to see Jack's engagement ring, but Enid described it in detail.

'It's quite good. Nine carat gold and diamond chips. We'll get a pound or two for that.'

He had not the heart to tell her that it would not keep them for a fortnight.

IT WAS almost another month before Worksop began to relent. Weekly postcards confirmed that Enid was thinking of her mother and that Agnes was well. But although Agnes or Lottie bought the stamps and helped to decipher Enid's writing, they sent no message of their own.

Then, on General Election day – just as George was trying to cause trouble by saying that it did not matter that Rex and Enid could not return to Langwith to cast their votes because they would only have cancelled each other out – the envelope with the Worksop postmark came through the door. All it contained was a five-pound note, but Uncle Ern's message was as clear as and reliable as E. S. Peppiat's promise to pay on behalf of the Bank of England. The time had come for Enid to be welcomed back into the family.

She sat down and started her letter of thanks at once. It began with the reassuring news that with Uncle Ern's special bed retrieved and erected under the window and the rest of the Colliery Row furniture in place, South View Road was ready to receive her mother. All that remained was a discussion of dates. The letter ended with the announcement that details could be discussed on the following Sunday. She had returned to the old habit of inviting herself to Brook House. The final sentence was a risk that she knew must be taken. 'We hope to arrive at about three.' It was the first time that she had risked the use of the plural pronoun.

She posted the letter on Friday afternoon. The telegram, with which Aunt Anne replied, arrived at noon on Saturday. Instead of their going to Worksop, Worksop was coming to them and would arrive that evening.

Enid immediately assumed that her mother was mortally ill and was full of tragic remorse. Rex convinced her that, if Mrs Brackenbury was on the point of death, she could hardly be left alone whilst her sister visited Sheffield. He feared that they were coming to make on last desperate effort to take her away from him. Enid took his hand.

'They know it wouldn't work. Nothing is going to separate us. Ever. We haven't gone all this way to turn back now.'

She kissed him by way of reassurance, but there was no time to talk. Pots had to be washed. Windows cleaned, furniture polished and steps scrubbed. Rex was sent to the corner shop to buy a better brand of tea. Mick was bathed and brushed. At two o'clock, Enid withdrew to have her own bath. To general relief, George suggested that he and Syd could go out and find a football match to watch. Enid would have been reluctant to exclude the brothers from the talks on her mother's future, for she was determined that the close knit little family would not unravel. But she feared that her aunts and uncle would not wholly understand George's mocking manner or Syd's anxious exuberance. They had barely left the house when Rex, on look-out in the front window, sighted Uncle Ern. He opened the front door in courteous anticipation and held out his hand.

'How's Mrs Brackenbury?'

Ernest Skinner ignored him and spoke to Enid over his shoulder.

'Danged train half an hour late. We walked. Your aunt didn't like the idea of a tram car.'

Anne lowered her wicker basket on to the hall floor. A brown liquid spread out from one of its corners. She looked up in a way which the uninitiated might have imagined was lifting her eyes to heaven. Enid, with years of experience to rely on, understood the coded message.

'Top of the stairs, Aunty. Right opposite. The lock doesn't work, but nobody will come in.'

Uncle Ern stood guard in the hall whilst Enid unpacked the basket in the kitchen. She asked Rex to notice and remember the quality of each item. Worksop's generosity was taken as absolute proof of their wish for an immediate reconciliation.

Rex was surprised by his own reaction. Normally, poor as he was and always had been, he would have resented being given half pork pies, the remnants of joints and bottles of caramelized jam. But Worksop were different. The normal rules of human conduct did not apply to them. He had already been drawn into Enid's magic circle.

When he heard the lavatory flush, Rex turned back towards the hall, but Enid – who understood the routine – held him back. Five minutes later, the cistern began to fill again. They met Ernest as he descended the last step.

'You're going to have trouble with that tank. I took the liberty of having a look inside. The ballcock has rusted through. Overflow hasn't been going, has it?'

Rex, who did not know where the overflow was, felt so

flattered by Uncle Ern's attention that he nodded out of gratitude.

'If you get a new ballcock, do you reckon you'd be able to fix it? It's an easy enough job. Need to turn the water off, mind.'

'I'm sure I can do it.'

'Then I'll get you one from my place of business. I'll pay for it, of course. I'm not in the habit of helping myself out of the stores. And I'll pay the right price.'

'Of course, Mr Skinner. And I'll pay you.'

'Now, I didn't mean that. I didn't mean that at all. It will be my pleasure. A little help is worth a lot of sympathy.'

It seemed the right moment for Rex to make his declaration.

'We have a lot of things to talk about, Mr Skinner.'

'We do, at that.'

'I want you to know that Enid and I love each other. What we've done hasn't been easy and some people will say that it wasn't right. We've hurt some people and we're sorry for that.' It was, he thought, exactly the right mixture of defiance and apology. 'But we've no choice. We can't live apart from each other.'

'But can you live together?' Uncle Ern almost smiled underneath his neat, military moustache. 'That's the question. Can you live together? Not unless you got something to live on you can't.'

'Has he got a job yet?' Anne Skinner, who had a talent for asking difficult questions, seemed to find it difficult either to speak to Rex or look at him.

'I sign on. Sign on every Monday. I've done some casual work. I've told them that I'll do anything.'

'When you get something,' Ernest Skinner said, 'take a bit of advice from me. Look after the pennies and the pounds will look after themselves. Let her do the managing. She's a wonderful manager. Always has been.'

'I've had to be,' Enid reminded him.

'You're right, Ern. He should let her do it.' Anne Skinner spoke with real admiration of Enid and a clear suspicion that Rex might want to take charge of the housekeeping. 'Walk her feet off to save a halfpenny on the price of a lettuce. She should manage the money.'

'Are you going to the Public Assistance?'

It was the question that a practically minded relation should have asked, but when Ernest Skinner asked it the sudden challenge unnerved Rex. He was about to give a complicated description of the old poor law regulations – the doubts about Enid's status, the complication of Agnes's legal dependence on Brack and the risk that they would be asked to sell their furniture before they qualified – when Anne addressed him directly.

'We've stood for a lot. More that we should. But we're not having our sister put in a workhouse.'

'Workhouses don't come into it, Miss Skinner. Mrs Brackenbury is coming to live with us.'

'Don't you try to tell Miss Skinner about workhouses.' Ernest's habit of referring to close relations as if they were casual acquaintances always added to the surrealism of the conversation. 'Our father was master of the old Wisbech workhouse. There's nothing you can tell us about workhouses.'

'I can tell you,' said Rex in desperation, 'that there's no question of Mrs Brackenbury going into one.'

'We'll help. Agnes is our responsibility, not yours.'

'She's mine too, Miss Skinner.'

'She'll become yours,' said Ernest, 'on the day that you and Enid get married. Not until. And I can't see that happening for a bit. In the meantime Mrs Brackenbury can rely on us.'

There was a clear implication that she could rely on nobody else and that Rex, whatever his romantic intentions, was beyond the pale of reliability.

'It is particularly kind of you in the circumstances.' Rex, having acquired Enid's strange reverence for Worksop, felt genuine gratitude was necessary. 'Particularly since we know you disapprove.'

'So we do,' said Ernest. 'So we do. And always will till you marry her. Nothing's going to change that.'

'I'll marry her the moment I can—'

'In the meantime,' Anne Skinner looked straight ahead. 'We shall do our duty.'

Her tone made it clear that there was no joy in the fulfilment of their family obligation. Indeed she was obviously sickened by the idea of association with a pair of libertines, but she was determined to keep her niece and sister out of a pauper's grave.

'We do not,' she said to Enid, turning her back on Rex, 'believe that your mother should come here until there's a wage coming in.'

To Rex's horror, Enid meekly agreed. Although he had learned to treat Worksop with reverence, he was not yet in thrall. Enid was apparently under their spell. It frightened him.

'As soon as Rex gets a job,' Enid seemed almost grateful, 'we'll come and get her.'

'Better not,' said Anne, her steady gaze wavering for the first time. 'We'll bring her.'

'But we can save you the trouble.' Enid was eager to be instantly and totally involved in the process of reunion.

'It's better . . .' Uncle Ern spoke with a carefully measured cadence. 'It's better to be safe than sorry. There might be customers at Brook House. Your aunt and Miss Harthill have got their business to think of and their customers come at funny times. I've known 'em as late as ten o'clock. We can't expect your aunt and Miss Harthill to risk losing business as well as everything else. Some of them wouldn't think the business respectable if they knew that you two were in the back kitchen.'

Enid was only briefly disconcerted. Then she switched her enthusiasm from fetching Mrs Brackenbury from Worksop to welcoming her to Sheffield. After the Skinners left, Rex abandoned all attempt to disguise his depression.

'They're ashamed of us.'

'They'll come round,' Enid told him. 'They'll realize that they've nothing to worry about. Jack only went to Worksop once. Nobody knows him. In a week or two we'll be going to Brook House and the woman next door will be calling me Mrs Hattersley.'

'But they're ashamed of us and that's terrible.'

'No, they're not. They're just being sensible. They're on our side. You'll see.'

Every day, the drawbridge was pulled up a little higher. Syd and George were already inside the battlements and when the besieged family was completed by the arrival of Mrs Brackenbury, it would increasingly turn in on its own isolation. It was a strange life to which Rex had to look forward, but because it was a life with Enid it was enough for him.

'Are you very unhappy?' he asked after they had left.

'Why should I be?'

'Your mother's not here. Your uncle doesn't like me. I've got no job. You've got plenty to be unhappy about it.'

'I've got you,' she said. 'And that's all that matters. I've got what I want.'

When George and Syd got back they were nowhere to be found.

CHAPTER EIGHTEEN

THE WAITING – waiting to find a job, waiting for the money to run out, waiting for Mrs Brackenbury to move in and waiting for the priests to come for Rex – grew increasingly painful. Waiting for the priests was the most painful waiting of all. Indeed Rex began to suspect that the Church was delaying its attempts to win him back in order to undermine his confidence and sap his courage. Enid's nerve snapped first.

Sunday dinner at South View Road, like Sunday dinner at Worksop, was a ritual – but it was a ritual for which the participants had to wait rather longer than young men, like George and Syd, found tolerable. They went early to mass in good Catholic style, leaving a long morning of boredom and hunger before them even if an early Continental lunch had been in prospect. Enid, who preferred to talk about cooking the dinner to actually cooking it, put the leg of lamb into the oven at one o'clock. Syd, who had been sitting at the table since noon, knew that Rex was trying to calm everybody's nerves by carrying from the kitchen visible signs that the food would not be delayed much longer. Knives, forks, salt, pepper, eventually a plate of cut bread were bought out in turn. Syd watched the thick slices drying and curling at the corners for almost half an hour. Then he ate one.

He was unlucky with his timing. Enid – about to mix the batter for the Yorkshire pudding – stood in the doorway, holding a wooden spoon in one hand and a bowl in the other.

'I was hungry,' he said, looking absurdly guilty.

To Enid the admission was a criticism of her failure to feed him earlier. He was accusing her of negligence.

'I don't know how you dare!'

'Dare what? It's just a piece of bread.'

George retreated behind the *Sunday Express* whilst Rex tried to mediate from the kitchen.

'He didn't mean any harm.'

'Why did he say it then? Why did he say he was hungry?'

'Because I was.' Syd did not mean to be provocative. 'I just ate a bit of bread.'

'What time did you get up?' Enid asked him.

Syd shrugged his shoulders in admission that he did not know.

'Well, I was up at six. And I've been working ever since. I sometimes think you don't know what it's like looking after the four of you.'

'You work too hard,' said Rex, who was still standing behind her in the doorway. 'We all know that.'

It was an unacceptably calm reaction. Enid wanted Rex to turn on his ingrate brothers and remind them of the sacrifices she was making on their behalf or – better still – to defend them in a way which justified the accusation that all he had wanted was a housekeeper to skivvy for him and his relations. It was necessary to increase the emotional temperature.

'We're not even related. You're not even family. It's like slaving for three lodgers.'

Rex turned white, Syd red and even George was provoked into looking at Enid over the top of the *Sunday Express*. None of them spoke.

She was still waiting for the full effects of her bombardment to ricochet round the room when Rex stepped out into the hall. The front door opened and then slammed shut. Through the bay window she could see him, hunched and hands in his pockets, hurrying down the road.

'Where's he gone, George? Where's he going?' Anger had turned to anxiety.

'Who?' George asked, reaching towards the sideboard for his packet of cigarettes.

'Didn't you hear the door? It was Rex. He's gone out.'

'Breath of fresh air,' said George. He lit his cigarette. 'Working up an appetite for his lunch.'

'Run after him, Syd, and tell him to come back. Tell him not to be so silly.'

Syd, being only eighteen, did Enid's bidding whilst she began to imagine all the possibilities from desertion to suicide.

'Seriously, George. Where do you think he's gone?'

'Nowhere that you need worry about. You've upset him and he wants to walk it off. He'll come back in half an hour, right as rain.'

'I can't see why he's so upset. Can you?'

'Of course I can.'

George did not care whether or not she exploded into another fusillade of self-pity. And Enid, knowing it, remained composed.

'Tell me then.' She was worried, but not yet repentant. 'I'm getting the dinner as quick as I can.'

'It wasn't the dinner. It was what you said about family. You must know that. It's not his fault you're not related. He'd like to be. You shouldn't rub it in.'

Enid knew that she had gone too far. She had known it as she spoke the intentionally offensive words. At that moment, going too far had been her conscious objective. She needed to relieve her feelings with a thoroughly good row. But the row should have ended with Rex assuring her that she was loved, wanted and appreciated, not with him leaving the house.

'You can't understand how a woman feels about these things. Every time I walk outside this house I wonder who's looking at me and thinking that we're not married.'

'That's not Rex's fault, is it?'

'I suppose it's my fault for being so proud. So sensitive and so proud. But I can't help it.'

'That's not what I meant.' George did not enjoy rubbing salt into the self-inflicted wounds. He simply described the obvious truth. 'Rex could get married tomorrow.' He seemed only to want an acceptance of the facts. 'If you really do worry about living in sin, don't blame him.'

'He could have been more understanding about it all.'

George stubbed out his cigarette in the ashtray which was built into the arm of Rex's armchair.

'What could he have done?'

It took her several seconds to think of an answer.

'He could have arranged for me to change my name by deed poll. He knows I would have liked that.'

★

SHE RETURNED to the kitchen where, despite the running of taps and the crashing of saucepans, no progress was made in the preparation of Sunday dinner. Syd and George exchanged increasingly exasperated glances. Both of them knew that something must be done, but neither of them knew what it was. George was about to play the older brother's part and ask Enid if there was anything that he could do to help when Rex appeared at the back door.

'It's all right,' he said.

'What is it?' Enid asked near to tears.

'I understand. Don't talk about it now. After dinner.'

His hope was not to talk about it at all. Calm had been restored. That was all he asked.

Sunday dinner was served at half past three. The meat was hard, the vegetables were soft and, because of the strange way in which it had been cooked and cooked again, some of the food was too hot to eat and some of it was too cold to enjoy. But each of the plates – carried fully laden from the kitchen – was heaped so high that corners of Yorkshire pudding poked out over its edges and mashed potatoes bulged under the weight of beans and roast potatoes. They ate in silence.

Syd and George announced that they were going to Whitely Woods to see if there was a scratch football match in which they could play. Both Rex and Enid were too preoccupied to say goodbye.

'I'll wash the pots,' said Rex. 'Then I'll have a look at the paper before those two get back.'

'I thought you wanted to talk.'

'I did. But it doesn't matter now.'

'You sound as if we've got nothing to talk about.' She was tense but composed. 'We can't keep pushing it all behind us. We've done that for too long.'

It was a calmer Enid. Her need for emotional gratification had for the moment been satisfied.

'I'll talk about whatever you want.'

Rex lied. His instinct was to push unpleasant truths to the back of his mind. *Tu ne cede malis, sed contra audentior ito.* He had tried to believe Bishop Dunn's homily, but he wanted to be happy, which to him meant being at peace now, not in a month or a year's time. Enid could not see an obstacle without wanting to surmount it. Rex was willing to rest on the easy side of trouble. Twice he had faced up to his destiny with a courage which none of his family and friends thought that he possessed and – having been braver than ever he thought possible – he felt entitled to take life easy.

'There's a lot to go over,' Enid said, pulling her chair round the corner of the table and sitting so close to Rex that their shoulders touched. 'I hoped that money would be the first item on the agenda.' Rex could barely disguise his relief; although she would not be satisfied with his answers, he had something to say about money. To some of her other questions, there could be no reply.

Nothing he could say about the prospect of marriage would cause anything except pain. Even though Enid felt an occasional compulsion to draw up an inventory of despair and disappointment, Rex thought it was his duty to stand between her and reality.

'It can't be all that long before I get a job.'

'It's not about the money. I don't know why I pretend that it is. We'll manage . . . somehow. The truth is, I'm frightened, frightened that you'll leave.'

Rex turned and made a brave attempt to hold Enid in his arms, but their knees were under the dining table and their hard chairs were side by side. So he managed no more than to put one arm round her shoulders whilst the other hung loosely in her lap.

'I love you. How can you think that I'd ever leave you? You're all I want in the world.'

There's not much here for you. Nobody would blame you if you went.'

'There's nothing for me anywhere else. It's too late. Happy or not, I can't choose any more.'

'Don't say happy or not.'

He had been about to ask how she could think of him leaving her when he had stayed despite all they had suffered together. But it sounded too much like a complaint and an admission. He did not want her to think that he was staying because, having crippled himself in her cause, she had a duty to supervise his recovery and convalescence. He wanted her to know that he only felt complete when they were together. But he dared not tell her that he would die rather than lose her for fear of sounding as if he loved her despite their love bringing him nothing but pain.

So, knowing that he sounded pathetic, he told her, 'I don't know how you can think that I might leave you.'

'Because you never talk to me about them trying to take you back. They must have tried by now. But you haven't told me.'

'The only priest who has been here is Bill Ellis and you were here when he came.'

'I know that you think that you're protecting me. But you're not. I never walk down the road without expecting to meet them coming round the corner. It only makes it worse when I find out.'

'There's nothing to find out.' For once he said what he thought without bothering about the consequences. 'We've got enough troubles to face, without you inventing ones that don't exist.'

'You're telling me that nobody's tried to persuade you to go back. All these weeks? More. And they've just let you live here with me. I know about your Church. They've sent somebody. But you haven't told me about it, because you haven't decided what to do.'

'Enid, just stop and think for a moment. I haven't been to church for a month. I commit a mortal sin, day after day.'

'What do you mean by that? If you think it's a sin—'

'I don't care. I commit half a dozen sins a day and all of them different. And I don't even think about it. The idea of going back is ridiculous.'

Then a terrible thought came into his head.

'That is unless you want me to. You'd probably have an easier time without me. Is that what you are trying to say?'

'I'm not *trying* to say anything. I want you to tell me what you want.'

'I want a bit of peace—'

'So you do want to leave me. Just tell me.'

'I'll tell you.' He was very near to losing his temper. 'I want to live a normal life – as normal as possible. I don't want to row over nothing. Why do you have to have these arguments? I don't understand it. It's all invention and imagination. And I've had enough of it.'

Enid took the complaint as proof positive that Rex was considering returning to the Church. As always when she was afraid, she escalated the tension. Give the choice, she would always gamble on sudden death or total reprieve rather than wait in the hope of receiving a less severe sentence.

'Go. If that's what you want, go. You've ruined my life. But don't worry about me or Mam. We'll be all right. Worksop will look after us. So will Jack. He'd come back tomorrow if I asked him to. You haven't got the courage to be a real man and live in the real world . . .'

Rex could do nothing but watch, white-faced and trembling, as she punctuated each sentence with choking sobs.

THEY TRIED to make the evening normal. All four of them behaved with conspicuous consideration and a courtesy which was so artificial that it heightened the general feeling of embarrassment. George talked more than usual, Syd less. Enid was as loquacious as always but tried hard to pause at the end of each question until someone had answered. They drank tea, ate bread and mutton dripping, went to bed.

The attic was lit by gas. Both George and Syd always forgot to turn it out before they got into bed. That night they did not argue about which of them should get out again and wrestle with the rusty knob of the tarnished bracket.

'I'll do it,' said George.

Syd watched, half asleep, as his brother folded up a dog-eared copy of the *London Gazette* and carefully laid it on the floor for further examination next morning. George had no particular interest in Court Circulars, Army Lists and Orders in Council. He had found the week-old publication in the foyer of the Central Library the previous day and brought it home as another source of useless information. He felt his way carefully back to bed through the dark, lay on his back and spoke to the ceiling.

'All that rowing. Enid shouting and crying. I've had about enough.'

'I thought you liked her,' said Syd.

'I did last summer. She was fine when we were cycling about and playing tennis. Talked too much, but she was good fun. She isn't good fun now.'

'I don't know what to do when she's like that,' Syd told him. 'If you say anything she snaps your head off. If you just sit there, she says you're ignoring her.'

'I think we should go.'

'And leave Rex?' Syd was genuinely incredulous.

'He'll hardly notice we've gone. All he cares about is her.'

'What would we live on?' Syd, who had been regularly reminded of Worksop's generosity, was more reassured than humiliated by their benevolence.

'We'll get relief. If it wasn't for her we'd have done it already. We'll get a room somewhere and sign on at the Assistance until we get a job.'

'Not go home to Dad?'

'Not on your life. Not with that woman there.'

'Funny, isn't it. Dad ran away. Uncle Joe ran away . . .' Syd was well versed in family folklore.

'We're not running away. You can't run away when you get to our age. We're just leaving.'

'I'm not.' Syd's first loyalty was to Rex. 'I'm staying here.'

'Suit yourself,' said George and turned over ready for sleep. 'I'll tell him after we've been to the Labour Exchange tomorrow.'

THERE WAS no reason why George should have taken precedence over his brothers, but he stood up as soon as the clerk shouted 'Next' and walked up to the counter. Neither Rex nor Syd felt inclined to argue with the assumption that he had been called and might be chosen. He was away for barely five minutes and returned to the rows of battered wooden benches in quiet triumph.

'Wath-upon-Dearn,' he said. 'They're opening a temporary Labour Exchange for a couple of months. They're sacking miners and men from the railways. It's definite for a week or two and might become permanent. I'll start Monday.'

'That,' said Rex, half turning to congratulate his brother and half hurrying to his interview, 'is marvellous.'

Desperate as he was for good news of his own, Rex was delighted by his brother's success. He was not incapable of envy. During the months which he had spent alone in Langwith Junction, he had envied every married man he saw. But had he thought of competing with George, he would have regarded the idea as both wicked and absurd. He vaguely wondered what would have happened if he had answered the first call. But fate, and his brother's instinctive self-assurance, had placed him second in the queue. So George had got a job. It was an occasion for unequivocal rejoicing.

'Where's Wath-upon-what's-it?' Syd asked when Rex was out of earshot.

'Wath-upon-Dearn. It's near Rotherham. Ten miles away. At least I think so. That's what the man told me.'

'So where will you live?'

'I don't know. I've hardly had time to think about it.'

It was the first time that either of them had spoken of George's decision to leave South View Road. Until that moment, Syd had still hoped that by not mentioning the idea he could contribute to its destruction. Such superstitions should have been anathema to a good Catholic and Syd paid for his impiety by the disappointment which he felt when his brother did not announce a change of heart and mind.

Rex reappeared, so obviously downcast that there was no need to ask what had happened. He sank back on to the bench and struggled to smile.

'Thank heavens, at least you got something. I'll keep my fingers crossed for next week. When do you start?'

'Day after tomorrow.'

'How are you going to get there?'

'I've not worked it out.'

Syd reappeared through the cubicle door. His brothers stared at him, hoping to notice the beginning of a satisfied smile. He stood, uneasily, in front of the lines of benches, waiting for them to join him on the journey home.

'Did you get anything?' Rex asked.

'Course not. Did you expect me to?'

They went on top of the tram car so that they could smoke and in the hope that they could all sit together. But both bays were full, so George and Syd sat side by side, and Rex turned to talk to them from the seat in front.

'How much?' Rex mouthed the question silently.

'Three pounds.'

George spoke in the loud confidence of success. The other passengers looked at him furtively. Syd waited for the terrible announcement.

'Enid will be delighted. Not just . . .' He reverted to his barely audible whisper, 'Not just because of the money. She'll be delighted that you've got a start.'

'I'll be a civil servant.' George was only partly joking. 'Red tape, tea.'

'You'll have to buy a bowler hat.' Syd joined in the celebration.

'Given a chance, you'll get on,' said Rex. 'This might be the first rung of the ladder.'

As always they all got off the tram before the nearest stop to South View Road. By walking the last half a mile, they saved a penny on the fare. George went into a newsagent to buy a *News Chronicle* and Rex told Syd, 'We must do something to celebrate.'

Syd nodded, agreeing without thinking about his agreement.

'What are you going to do after dinner?'

'Don't know. Nothing much.'

Rex searched in his pocket and pulled out a shilling.

'Think of an excuse to slip away. Nip into town, to Woolworth's. Do you know where it is?' Syd looked blank so Rex told him, 'Just off Fitzallen Square. Get a pair of cuff links. In a box. Sixpence. They cost sixpence. You can choose . . .'

George was reading the *News Chronicle* as he walked out of the shop but, although his head was buried in the paper, he strode down the step with the certainty of a man who knew exactly where he was going.

At first, Rex and Syd walked together, talking about the usual things, whilst George followed a pace behind accumulating facts about the new government in Austria, the United States Senate's reaction to its first woman member and the likelihood of the Milky Way interfering with wireless reception on clear nights. As always, when they turned into South View Road, Rex accelerated away, spurred on by a determination not to delay his reunion with Enid by a single unnecessary second.

'You haven't told him.'

Syd pulled at George's arm and his brother's face appeared from behind a corner of the newspaper.

'Haven't told him what?'

'Told him that you are going.'

'I'm not, am I? I can't now, can I? You know that.'

'Why not?' Syd had no wish to argue, only to find out why the miracle had happened.

'Because I've got a job.' George spoke to his brother with an undisguised impatience. 'It's obvious, isn't it? I can't shove off now. I can't go off with my three pounds and leave you all to starve. If Rex had got a job, it would have been different. Or if I hadn't. But there we are.'

They stood at the front garden gate, Syd grinning with delight and George smiling with self-righteous resignation. Syd saw a stone on the footpath and, out of pure high spirits, kicked it down the road. Then he leaned over the gate and swung in with it as it opened. As he walked towards the door, he tore a handful of leaves from the weeds which grew alongside the path and threw them at his brother.

'We'd better get inside,' George said, 'before I knock your block off.'

CHAPTER NINETEEN

THE TELEGRAM to Worksop was not quite a lie. It simply said, 'Job at Wath-on-Dearn Labour Exchange. Starting next Monday.' And Enid had every intention of explaining in a subsequent letter that it was George who was, at last, in work. But when her aunt Anne replied that Agnes could wait no longer for the reunion with her daughter, there seemed no reason to waste another one and sixpence on clarification. After all, Rex, George and Syd were the Three Musketeers. It said so on the fly leaf of the *Golden Treasury* which they had given her. All for one. One for all. George's wages would be spent on the whole family.

Agnes arrived in Sheffield on bonfire night. Her journey from Worksop had been accompanied by the sound of thunder flashes and the sight of rockets exploding into cascades of coloured lights across the cloudless sky. The hills which surrounded the city sparkled with bonfires and outside the public houses in its centre little boys demanded 'a penny for the guy'. It was, Anne and Ernest knew, a bad night to travel with a nervous dog. But their sister's determination to be immediately reunited with her daughter was irresistible.

For almost all the journey, Chum lay trembling and silent apart from his heavy breathing. When the hire-car turned into a deserted South View Road it seemed that the journey had ended without incident. Enid rushed out to greet her mother with Mick yelping at her heels. Ern pulled the folded bath chair from the boot and began to shake it into shape. Then, two little boys with sparklers in their hands ran out of number thirteen.

Chum – a moment before supine by the open door – rose, leaped, pounded and closed his arthritic jaw around the calf of the nearest child. Both boys screamed, dropped their sparklers and ran for home. The silence, which had been so welcome when the visitors arrived, was terrible.

Agnes was bundled into the still-not-stable wheelchair. Anne picked up the suddenly jovial dog and made for the front door. Ernest pressed more money into the driver's hand and snatched the bag of comestibles from the back seat. Rex hurried out of the house to help the invalid up the steps. It was too late. The bitten boy, his brother and their parents were back at their garden gate.

'We,' said the father, 'are going to send for the police.'

The wound was displayed and Enid observed, with more accuracy than tact, that the skin was not even broken. The diagnosis enraged the mother who spoke of rabies and lockjaw.

Rex tried to be emollient.

'If it hasn't drawn blood, there's really no need to worry. But we are very sorry. Very sorry, indeed.'

The soft answer only increased the wrath.

'That dog ought to be shot,' the mother said.

'I'll see it doesn't happen again,' said Rex. He would have liked to offer the frightened boy a threepenny bit with which to buy a lollipop. But, as always, there was no change in his pocket.

'Don't think,' the father told him, 'that it can all be hushed up with an apology. If the copper comes round tonight, I'll report you. I hope you've got a licence, that's all.'

The copper came round just as Anne and Ern were leaving for the Worksop train. He was a young officer who had not yet lost all his enthusiasm for thorough investigation. He wrote down Rex's full name in his notebook before asking who was the dog's owner.

'I am,' said Enid.

'And you are Mrs Hattersley?'

Rex said 'No' and Enid said 'Yes' simultaneously. Enid recovered first and explained.

'That wasn't my name when I bought the licence.'

The dog licence was produced and the officer left mumbling about his duty to make a report when he got back to the station. Enid just managed to contain her anger until her aunt and uncle had left.

'How could you? How could you say we weren't married?'

Rex, genuinely sorry for her distress, held her in his arms.

'We couldn't do anything else. Not with a policeman. We couldn't tell him a lie. It's a criminal offence.'

It was Enid's turn to say that she could not stand the shame of deception. But she meant that she could not stand the shame of the deception being found out.

'I've been thinking,' she said. 'There's only one thing to do. I'll have to change my name by deed poll.'

'I've looked up how it's done,' said George. 'It's easy enough. Cost's five bob.'

Walter Clegg and Company were adjudged too grand for so simple a legal task, so on George's advice, Enid wrote to make an appointment with Messrs Slater, Son and Elliott, whose offices he had passed each morning on his way to the reference library. Syd was left to guard Mrs Brackenbury whilst George led Rex and Enid to Surrey Street in the manner of a man who feared that they would get lost on their own. It was a wet November morning and he sheltered in the side entrance to the town hall whilst they went in for what Rex regarded as an ordeal. He felt diffident at the thought of confronting a solicitor face to face, for he had forgotten that, only six months before, he had himself been a professional man of sorts.

Young Mr Elliott was pink and plump and brisk. A tasselled cap hung by the side of his fireplace and Rex, in awe, wondered if it had been awarded to him for some particular sporting merit. Enid explained.

'I want to change my name to his.'

There was no need for her to give the reason. That was obvious enough.

'It is,' said the solicitor, 'easily done. Deed poll's the usual way. You swear before me, or any other Commissioner of Oaths, that you mean to be known by a different name. Do it today, if you like.'

'Yes, please,' said Rex.

'How much will it cost?' asked Enid, opening her handbag. She was relieved that it had all been done so easily.

'Half a guinea. That's the standard registration fee.' Mr Elliot smiled. 'That pays off the Inland Revenue for its stamp and me for my signature. The advertisement will cost three and sixpence.'

'What advertisement?' Rex asked.

'You have to put a notice in the legal columns of the local paper. It's a standard form. You can fill it in here and now.' ' "I, Enid Brackenbury of 11 South View Road do hereby announce that I shall hereafter be called and known as—".'

'So everybody will know?'

'Exactly,' said the solicitor, hoping that he sounded reassuring.

'Is that the only way?' she asked.

'By no means. You can call yourself whatever you want to call yourself. That's been established in the courts. Du Boulay *versus* Du Bulay, 1869. Cawley *versus* Cawley, 1901. What did you say you wanted your name to be?'

'Hattersley.'

'Then Hattersley it is. You don't need a deed poll.'

Enid stood up.

'How much do we owe you for the advice?' Rex asked.

'Nothing. Not for five minutes.'

Young Mr Elliot, who was a kindly man, assumed that the cost of a deed poll had been beyond their means.

Unlike young Mr Elliot, George – who had put the idea of changing her name into Enid's head – was clearly resentful that his advice was not taken and he argued the merits of taking the formal legal path. Half way home, Rex told him to 'give it a rest', but he was still arguing when they got to the front gate and saw Syd looking anxiously out of the window. There was no way of interpreting his frantic signs but Enid, who felt sure that they signified her mother's sudden collapse, rushed up the path, with Rex a yard behind. George took his time and whilst the others dashed into the back room, sidled to join Syd. Sitting at one end of the front room sofa was the fat priest who, on the previous three Sundays, had given the two young men communion in the local church.

GEORGE, who prided himself on remaining composed in all circumstances, held out his hand.

'Hattersley,' he said in his unnerving Continental way. 'George Hattersley. You've met my brother Sydney.'

The fat priest stood up. His response was entirely English.

'How do you do?'

'What can we do for you, Father?'

It was not the sort of question that was normally asked of a priest. Priests do not have to explain themselves or justify their actions. Syd was properly embarrassed.

'My name is Father Emery. I'm the parish priest at Saint Marie's.'

'We know,' said Syd, anxious to ingratiate himself. 'We go there to mass.'

'It's not really your parish.'

'I can't believe that you've come to warn us off.' George laughed in a way which made clear that he was not feeling jovial. Father Emery became suitably nervous.

'This has all turned out very badly. The old lady in the back seems very upset. If I'd have known what trouble I'd cause, I would have thought of some other way.' The priest seemed determined not to state his business. 'I really am so sorry.'

'She isn't very well,' George told him. 'It often goes on for some time.'

'I seem to have upset everybody. Perhaps we ought to take a little walk.' It was clear that Father Emery would feel better out of the house. 'I really had no idea.'

George led the way in silent agreement. Enid heard their footsteps in the hall and shouted from behind the closed back-room door.

'Mr Hattersley does not wish to see you. He's sorry that he cannot show you out, but he is very busy at the moment.'

Syd imagined her standing like the centurion at Pompeii, faithful unto death, in the protection of all that she held dear.

'We're just going out for a bit,' George shouted.

Enid neither recognized his voice nor his message through the closed door. She shouted back. 'Please don't come again.'

Elated by his escape, the priest skipped down the garden path.

'I can tell you now that Rex won't go back.' George saw no reason to prevaricate. 'We couldn't persuade him and we wouldn't try.'

'That's not it. That's being dealt with by my superiors. I'm here to see if we can help you and your brother.'

'We don't need any help.' George wanted his reply to be a rebuff, so he paused before adding. 'Thank you very much.'

'I'm only the messenger.' Father Emery was sweating. 'But I know the message was true. I don't think you fully realize what you are dong.'

'What are we doing?' Syd asked imitating his brother's aggression.

'Just think about it. Last summer you were going into the Church. Now you're lodging with a priest who lives with a married woman—'

'We're not lodging with him,' Syd said. 'He's our brother.'

Father Emery was too exasperated to argue. They walked on in silence for a few minutes. Then he tried again.

'That's not the real message.'

They were passing the Wheatsheaf Hotel and, it being twelve o'clock, the landlord was pulling open the front door.

'Let's sit down for a moment,' the priest said. 'Let's sit down and think about what the Church suggests.'

Even George, at his most cynical, was impressed by the idea that the Church as a whole had a suggestion to make about his future. He followed Father Emery into the empty public house.

Father Emery ordered the drinks with the easy familiarity of a man who had done the same thing twice a day for the last ten years. George sat composed in a corner of the snug whilst Syd, feeling slightly out of place, pretended to study the ancient sepia photographs which hung on the walls. All of them were pictures of the devastation caused when the dam at Bradford burst and flooded northern Sheffield.

Father Emery, carrying the three half-pint glasses with practised grace, had barely reached half way across before he began his attempt at ingratiation.

'This is very pleasant,' he said. He stared into his glass. 'John Smith's here. Sam Smith's in Leeds. Sam Smith's Tadcaster Ales. This isn't bad.' He took another gulp. 'Not bad at all.'

George did not respond. He hoped that his silence would force the priest into coming to the point.

'We just wondered about how you were managing. Then by good fortune somebody in Leeds heard of two jobs that were going. We thought they might suit you . . .'

Syd was about to interrupt, but George put a restraining hand on his knee.

'They'd find you lodgings, of course. We hoped that you might at least try it out. And there's always Oscott.' He turned to George. 'If you changed your mind and wanted to go into the Church, after all.'

'And if Syd wanted to finish his education?' George asked.

Father Emery, believing that he felt a tug on his line, began to haul in what he hoped was a catch.

'I'm sure that something can be arranged.'

George's smile was genuine. Father Emery really believed that he had caught his fish.

'I think we ought to have the other half.' The priest drained his glass. 'Drink up.'

He was half way back to the bar when George told him. 'I got a job this morning. And I don't think we'd better have any more. We really ought to be on our way home.'

As they walked back up the hill Syd asked George what he was thinking.

'Would you have left? Would you have gone if you hadn't got a job this morning?'

'We're all in it together. I realized that morning, after I got a job and Rex didn't. I saw his face. The thing now is to warn him that they're cooking something up. Let me do it. And not a word to Enid.'

When they got back, the house was calm and quiet. Rex was trying, without much success, to fasten a coat rack on to the hall wall and Enid was watching in a way which further reduced his already inadequate confidence.

'Where have you two been?'

'Just for a walk,' Syd told her. He had begun to fall into the habits of the house, and tailor-make his answers to win Enid's approval. 'We thought that it was the best way to get rid of him.'

George was already half way up the stairs when she replied.

'There was no need to do that on my account. I could have dealt with him all right.'

Syd shrugged his shoulders to imply that they had acted for the best. Enid stared at him as if she had suddenly noticed a new defect in his appearance.

'Have you been drinking?'

She would have gone on, but the coat rack fell from the wall and broke in two on the hall floor.

ON THE morning that George started work he cycled off from South View Road with the announcement that on the following Sunday they would all have a day out. Rex doubted if an excursion was possible since the trip could not include Mrs Brackenbury and he was sure that Enid would not even consider leaving her mother alone. He also doubted if she would agree to the purchase of four bus tickets. But he did not express his doubts until he was alone with George. Syd, blinded by the extravagance of youth, sometimes forgot that Enid's preoccupation with thrift was necessary for the family's survival. Rex wanted Syd to admire Enid.

Despite Rex's warning, George quietly persisted with his plan and, at the end of his first working day, he handed Enid a copy of the *Sheffield Telegraph*. It had been neatly folded open at page five. The advertisement published by the Sheffield Corporation, LMS and LNE Railways Joint Omnibus Committee was headed 'Suggestions for winter walks in Derbyshire'.

'What about it? What about Sunday?' he asked and, before anyone had time to answer, added the magic words. 'It'll be like old times. Just like old times.'

'Sunday's too soon,' said Enid. 'Worksop need more notice.'

'For a celebration,' George insisted, 'it has to be the first weekend.'

'They might like to make sure that Mam's really settled in.'

The task of self-persuasion having begun, Enid completed it with the most compelling of all arguments for half a day in the country.

'Mick needs a really good walk. He'll get hard pad just walking about in the road. The dust gets between his toes.'

'Try for next Sunday.' George waved the paper at her as an encouragement and read the advertisement as if the endorsement was his own invention. ' "A visit to one of the following will be well repaid." '

'They're all a bit more expensive than I imagined.' Enid stared at the paper, willing the prices to be less.

George was ready.

'I thought Hathersage. Two shillings return.'

'Castleton would be nice.' Rex suggested, looking over Enid's shoulder. 'There's a Norman castle.'

'It's three and six return. Nearly twice as much,' George told him. 'Let's go to Hathersage. Let's go next Saturday. Write to Worksop tonight, Enid, and I'll walk down to the GPO.'

Enid wrote, Worksop agreed and the excitement mounted all week. There was a brief frisson when the partners arrived without Ernest Skinner, but Anne explained he was neither ill nor still alienated but tidying his parents' graves at Steetly. There was another moment of doubt when Mick, who had been much excited by the talk of 'walkies', rushed screaming out of the front door which Enid thoughtlessly left open. Fortunately the car which was passing at the time was able to swerve. It was with some relief that they all boarded the tram car to Moorhead bus station, where they arrived with five minutes to spare before the journey west began.

They started to marvel as they passed the great Victorian houses in Whirlow – Syd because they were so big, George because they must have cost so much, Enid because it was clear, even in winter, that the terraced gardens which ran down to the road were almost as carefully cultivated as her grandfather's masterpiece at Harness Grove, and Rex because they had been built for the great steel families of Sheffield. When they crossed Houndkirk Moor, they marvelled even more at the great blocks of stone which nature had piled along the skyline.

Enid held her breath and grasped Rex's hand every time a sheep lumbered towards the bus's front wheels, and Mick had to be held down whenever a pheasant or partridge fluttered up from the heather and bracken by the side of the road. They approached Millstone Edge, consciously preparing themselves for what the leaflet, thoughtfully provided by the bus company, promised them would be the greatest marvel of all.

The moors came to a sudden end which might have marked the edge of the world but, once the bus had negotiated a sharp bend and braked hard down a steep slope, they realized why the route was called 'The Surprise'.

Below them was what looked like all of Derbyshire displayed for their delight – field after field, moor upon moor and, behind the valley, a faint purple line of hills that turned, almost imperceptibly, into blue sky.

Syd, who had read the leaflet from start to finish, was the first to recover. He wanted to go at once to Little John's ten-foot grave in Hathersage churchyard. Rex, who had not forgotten boyhood summer afternoons spent with bread and butter and bottles of water at the side of the Trent, suggested that they find a place to eat at once. George said that they should walk to Padley.

They toured the village, found a tea room which did not forbid 'the consumption of own food on the premises', and, over their sandwich lunch, discussed an expedition to the stone circle and burial mounds.

George said, 'Let's go to Padley.'

'What's so special about Padley?' Enid asked.

'There's a chapel. Or used to be. It's in the manor house. Two Jesuit priests were captured there. Elizabeth, I think. It might have been Henry. The family's called Fitzherbert.'

'What fits me, fits Herbert,' Syd said.

They all ignored him.

'Are you sure we can see it?' All Rex's old interest in ruined churches was revived. 'If it's in a house, it may be private.'

'They're rebuilding it and making it public. It's being consecrated next year. It's worth a try.'

'How do you know all this?'

Enid asked the question out of genuine interest. There was no resentment that she had been left out of the conversation or that her wishes were not even being considered. She just wanted to be part of their expedition.

'I read about it in the paper, weeks ago when I went to the

reference library.' He looked at Enid as if he expected some sort of argument about visiting a Catholic church and then added, 'It said in the paper that it's not consecrated till next year. It's only a ruin.'

The walk took almost an hour. For most of the way they sang 'Tiptoe Through The Tulips, 'Three Little Words' and 'Time On My Hands'. Their breath condensed on the cold air as the afternoon wore on. Syd attempted the verse of 'Stardust' and failed miserably. When they got to Padley, the gate in the high wall round the ruin was locked.

'Let's go round the back,' Syd said.

'There may be a caretaker or something.' Enid, usually a keen trespasser, seemed reluctant to risk the anger of the Fitzherberts.

'It's fifteenth century.' George was trying to enthuse Rex for an expedition over the wall. 'And it's got a hammerbeam roof.'

'How can it have a hammerbeam roof,' Syd asked, 'if it's a ruin? How can it have a roof at all?'

'Steetly's got a roof,' Enid told him. 'And Steetly's a ruin.'

'Let's have a look round the back.' Rex's interest had, at last, been excited to the point where he was prepared to face an angry owner.

'You go and look,' Enid told him. 'I'm taking Mick for a run in the field across the road before it's dark. He's been on his lead too long, poor little thing. Will you come with me, Syd?'

Syd, being young and chivalrous, agreed.

George and Rex followed the wall for a quarter of a mile and then decided that it could not be breached. When they got back to the gate, they could just see Enid and Syd, three fields away, faint figures following a blur, which was Mick, along the horizon.

'She seems to be enjoying herself,' George said.

'She needed a day out, a day away from her mother and house-work. She deserves something better. It was a marvellous idea of yours.'

'I thought she was going to object to coming here. When she heard the word chapel—'

'It was Jesuits that made her prick up her ears, not chapel.' Rex challenged the slightest suggestion of criticism. 'Can you blame her?'

'I don't think that she's afraid any more. I think she knows by now that you'll never go back.' He paused. 'I hope the Church does too. I've done my bit to convince them.'

Rex was so happy at the thought of the confidence that he had given Enid that he did not even think of what George meant by his own contribution to the Church's understanding.

On the way home, Rex tried to sit next to Enid, but Syd had the dog and Enid wanted to comfort Mick during what she thought might be an unpleasant journey. So the two of them sat at the back of the bus, with the dog spread out and asleep along their knees. Occasionally it twitched in its sleep and Enid suggested to nearby passengers that it was dreaming about rabbits.

George and Rex sat at the front with their eyes in line with the notices which forbade smoking, prohibited spitting and warned that non-payment of the fare was a prosecutable offence.

'It's not the ideal place,' George sounded uncharacteristically apprehensive, 'but there's a couple of things that I'd better tell you whilst I have the chance.'

'I thought so.' The thought of having an intimate conversation in a bus was to Rex only slightly less terrible than the prospect of having to wait for a suitable moment before he could find out what George had to say. Reticence and anxiety combined to make him add, 'Quietly then.'

'Monsignor Payne went to South View Road this afternoon.'

'What?' Rex spoke so loudly that half of the bus turned and stared at him.

'Monsignor Payne and the new Bishop's Secretary went to South View Road today. At least, that's what was planned.'

'How do you know?'

'Father Emery told me after mass last Sunday. I was supposed to soften you up for the big assault.'

'What did you tell him?'

'I told him that, if you took my advice, you wouldn't be there. Of course he didn't believe me. He couldn't imagine us leaving the Vicar General standing on the step.'

'So that's why you wanted the day out?'

'I wanted a day out. Heaven knows, we all need it.' He grinned. 'But today seemed a good day. You've all enjoyed it, haven't you?'

'It's been marvellous. Will you tell Enid that you knew the Vicar General was coming?'

'Course not. And you're not to tell her either. Let you and me have a secret for once.'

'There are too many secrets, George. Half of what I say isn't the truth, half of what I do is pretending.'

'Then one more pretence won't matter. And it's in a good cause.'

'I hope you think so.'

'Listen,' George's voice had sunk to an earnest whisper. 'I told you that I was on your side. I do understand. You don't have any choice, either of you. If I still believed in heaven, I'd think that it had all been arranged up there. Perhaps it was in a rather nasty heaven which made you indispensable to each other but also made you cause each other so much pain. Anyway, I know that you're locked together. Mr and Mrs Spratt—'

'Who on earth . . . ?'

'Jack and his wife. Nothing in common. Quite the opposite. But they fitted together because they were so different.'

'That's nonsense. That's not like us at all.'

'She likes being run after. You like running after her. She likes taking all the decisions. You like leaving all the decisions to her.' George drew a deep breath. 'You love her. She loves you.' It was not the sort of language which he enjoyed using, but he wanted Rex to know that he understood. The old cynical mood returned. 'So you'd better make the best of it.'

They were almost at the Moorhead bus station before either of them spoke again. Then Rex made the promise which, whilst intended to be reassuring, convinced George that the secret would have been better kept.

'I'll try to look surprised . . . and I'm very grateful.'

'They'll be back, you know.'

'I know.'

'Time after time.'

'I know that too.'

'But I'm glad that, just for once, we showed 'em that we didn't care. I've only one regret. Didn't you see my face drop when they said Mr Skinner wasn't coming. I wanted Uncle Ern and Monsignor Payne to meet at the front door.' He sighed. 'I suppose you can't have everything.'

CHAPTER TWENTY

It was, Rex reluctantly agreed, typical of George to be late home even on the great day, but he mumbled something which approached contradiction when Enid suggested that his absence confirmed that he had no real affection for Syd and that she was the only one who cared for the youngest brother's happiness and welfare.

The great day was an event of Enid's creation – a Saturday set aside to prepare for Syd starting work on the following Monday. The three men had accepted – with varying degrees of reluctance – that there could be no visit to Bramall Lane that afternoon. George had complained that Enid had been looking for an excuse to stop them from hanging around the entrance to the football ground until they, and two or three hundred more poor and unemployed men, were allowed in for the enjoyment of the final twenty minutes of the football match. But the force of her will had, as always, swept all opposition aside. By Friday night George was pretending that he looked forward to helping give Syd a proper start. Then, instead of getting home at half past one as usual, he was still absent without Enid's leave at four o'clock.

Syd was to become what amounted to an errand boy at Wheeler and Company, a firm of cloth merchants which carried on its business from a warehouse in a dingy alleyway behind the cathedral. Only Agnes said that the job was unworthy of his talent and long education. Enid told the neighbours that he was to become a commercial traveller and came so near to convincing herself that her invention was true that she went to extraordinary lengths to make sure that he would leave for work looking the part of a prospective salesman. Making sure that he was properly kitted out was the designated task for Saturday afternoon. Enid was to do most of the work, whilst Syd and George were allocated the job of watching and admiring.

Rex had mended Syd's shoes early in the day, cutting out the leather to the shape of the soles with the carving knife, bruising his fingers as he drove the tacks home with a coal hammer which he had found in the yard and smoothing the edges with sandpaper. It was not the way in which he would have chosen to spend his Saturday morning, but Enid looked at the mended brogues with such admiration, that he would gladly have worked his way through all the shoes in the house.

Worksop had made their contribution earlier in the week. Syd's best Ratcliffe suit – worn so often that it was best no more – had been sent to Brook House, where the elbows had been patched almost invisibly and the frayed trouser bottoms so cunningly mended that the turn-ups were preserved almost intact. It was returned to South View Road, packed so carefully in tissue paper and cardboard box that it did not even need ironing. By Saturday afternoon all that Syd needed was a decent shirt. Enid even thought of visiting the Co-op and buying him one, but prudence prevailed. She spent the afternoon turning old into new.

Enid sat in the front-room window to make the most of the fading light, picking away at the double rows of stitching which fastened the frayed cuffs to the arms of what had been Rex's ordination shirt – best white poplin to go with the black suit which Aunt Clare had bought him. The tail had already been cut off just below the waist. It lay at her feet ready to be cut – as the shoe leather had been cut into shape – as soon as the template was ready. From time to time, she looked up in the hope of seeing George come up the road. When the light faded and she could see her sewing no longer, she let her mind wander over all the possible reasons for his being so late. Having reduced the alternatives to death and desertion, she called to Syd in the kitchen with an instruction to switch off the football commentary and run to the police station for news of dead cyclists on the Wath to Sheffield Road. Before Syd's protest was finished, a man was hurrying towards the front gate. It was not George but Bill Ellis.

She did not even bother calling Rex. She swept up the sewing and hid it under the cushion on the sofa as she would have hidden it if any other visitor whose high opinion she valued had come to call. As she hurried to the door, she picked up the stray threads of cotton which had fallen on to the carpet.

'Come inside,' she said. 'I'll get Rex.'

Rex told Bill Ellis that he was wasting his time – told him before the priest had time to explain why he had travelled all the way from Nottingham.

'I've not come to persuade you of anything . . . anything at all. I've come to say goodbye and, believe it or not, good luck.'

'And all the best to you,' said Rex, holding out his hand as if the meeting was over.

Bill Ellis had not quite done.

'I'm going as parish priest to Hatfield . . . I don't suppose that we'll meet again. But if you ever need any help—'

'It's no good.' Rex, remembering how Bishop Dunn had behaved when he first left Langwith, was suspicious of friendship. 'I'm never coming back.'

'Believe me, I'm only speaking as a friend . . . for once. I don't think we've managed all this very well . . . the cathedral, that is . . . I'm sorry.'

'There wasn't any better way it could be managed, Bill.' Rex softened at last. 'It couldn't be managed at all. It was always out of control.' He held out his hand again.

'Just to prove I'm your friend, a piece of good advice . . . .'

Rex put his head on one side in a gesture of resentful resignation.

'The Vicar General is coming to see you next Saturday afternoon. It's the big push. Don't run away again. Get it done with. He'll catch you sooner or later. It will only hang over you. Finish it. Once and for all.'

When George got home, ready to deliver his well-rehearsed speech about playing table tennis and forgetting the time, Enid seemed not even to have noticed that he was late.

THE PHRASE 'hang over you' haunted Rex all evening. As soon as they were alone, he asked, 'Does it hang over you? Hang over you all the time?'

It was not like Rex to ask questions which might have painful answers and Enid – astonished that he prejudiced the evening's happiness for no better reason than trying to make it last beyond tomorrow – was frightened by his new intensity.

'I still think about it. Not as much as I did. I can live with it now. At first I wasn't sure that I could.'

'Is it because you know that I'll never leave you? Do you believe that now?'

'Whatever I said in my temper, I've known that from the start . . . Anyway I've known it from our first night together. You need me. I know that I need you too. I was afraid that I couldn't stand living in sin. The neighbours whispering and laughing. After your father's wife had been here . . .'

She was crying too much to go on.

'I'll never forgive her for that. Never. I still can't understand.'

'Oh I can.' Enid, who could not find her handkerchief, sniffed inelegantly. 'She wanted to bring me down a peg or two. I make people feel like that. She didn't understand that I was more frightened of her than she was of me. They just think airs and graces. And ideas above her station. I suppose I have . . .'

Rex expected her thoughts to trail off into a miasma of whimsy – Ruskin College, poetry, politics, painting and the compliments which had been heaped upon her as a girl. But she wrenched her mind back to the subject.

'That made me all the more worried. The people back in Langwith Junction rejoicing at the fall of Miss High and Mighty. I wasn't sure that I could stand it.'

He was afraid to ask the question, but even more frightened of leaving it unanswered.

'You're sure that you don't feel like that now?'

'I never wanted to go. And I would have loved you for all of my life. I don't know what would have happened to me. Gone back to Worksop with Mam, I suppose. I would have always loved you—'

'But you don't feel like that now?' He could not stand another moment's doubt. 'You don't even think of leaving me now.'

'Can't you tell? Can't you tell the difference since that day in Derbyshire. That's what did it.'

Rex, breathless at the thought of what seemed to him to be the miracle at Padley chapel, could not think of anything to say. He remembered the sun on the dark hills and the grey ridges of timeless rock which marked the line where sky and land met. It was, he felt sure, as she walked along the horizon, that the truth was suddenly revealed.

'It all changed on the way home on the bus.'

'But that was . . . such an ordinary thing.'

To argue with her explanation was a denial of everything on which he hoped to build his life. For as long as he could remember it had been his ambition to become so ordinary that nothing ever happened to disturb his peace, and he had put that idea behind him because turmoil with Enid was better than tranquillity without her. Yet she had been convinced of his love by a two shilling char-à-banc ride.

'I knew that you'd understand,' Enid told him. 'That's why I didn't need to explain. When I sat there talking to Syd and with Mick on my knee, I felt like everybody else. We were all a family. I suppose that Syd and George being there helped. And Worksop waiting at home with our tea. But it was really the ride home. I felt as married to you as it was possible to be. Just an ordinary married couple. I wasn't going to worry about a bit of paper. Not any more.'

'That's wonderful.'

'There's just one more thing. When that awful old man comes on Saturday I ought to be wearing your ring.'

He believed that she was doing no more than saying that she longed to marry him. The pain of knowing that her wish could never be granted was greater than the joy of remembering that she wanted to be his wife.

'I only wish it could happen.'

'Of course it can.' She pulled off her wedding ring and put it on the table.

'People will notice.'

'You don't think that I'd go out without one, do you?' Before he had the chance to answer she began to search in the recesses of her handbag. When she had found the ten-shilling note that she always kept hidden in the lining, she handed it to Rex with a triumphant smile. 'Here you are. I want our ring to cost more than you get for the old one. I don't care if it's only a few pence. But it's got to cost more. That way it will be ours without Jack having anything to do with it.'

Enid gave her detailed instructions.

'Sell Jack's ring at one shop and get ours at another. That way the jeweller won't wonder what you're up to. Try not to spend any more than you have to. If it gets on your little finger, it will fit.'

'Would you like to come with me?' There was not a hint of sarcasm in his question. 'Wouldn't you like to choose your own?'

'How could I go into the shop without a ring on my hand?' She assumed the plummy accent which she imagined characterized jewellers. 'Congratulations, sir. And you, Miss . . . er . . . er when's the happy day? A white wedding is it?'

Rex laughed, but she was not joking.

'When will you get it into your head? We're married already. If you forget that next Saturday I shall never forgive you.'

THEY TIDIED the house with particular care and, after much discussion, agreed that it would be best if Syd and George went to the pictures. Then Enid and Rex sat and waited, looking at each other, from time to time holding hands and occasionally reiterating their determination to act with composed dignity. Several times, they imagined that they had heard the Vicar General's motor car pulling up outside the front gate, but when they squinted through a gap in the curtains the road was empty. For the first hour of the vigil they talked normally to each other and for the second Enid spoke an almost continuous monologue. The speed of delivery increased and the quality of the content deteriorated as she grew more and more nervous. By half past nine, when Monsignor Payne had still not arrived, the tension had forced her into a strained silence. At ten o'clock George and Syd burst in and waited impatiently to be told every detail of the confrontation.

When at last it was accepted that the Vicar General would not call that night, they felt only relief. The brothers drank tea, smoked so many Woodbines that the air was filled with fumes and they listened to Carol Gibbons and his Savoy Orpheans on the radio that Enid had retrieved from Colliery Row. When Enid went into the back room to prepare her mother for the night, they were all behaving as if Monsignor Payne, having not come that evening, would not come at all. Only Rex wondered if Bill Ellis had been mistaken or if, for some Byzantine reason, had intentionally deceived them.

It was the late night, more than any sudden dramatic conversion, that prevented George and Syd from going to mass next day. It was the first time that they had missed but, far from behaving as if a momentous decision had been made, nobody seemed to notice. There had been no anguished discussion or profound debate. They had simply turned over and gone back to sleep. Lying in bed on a Sunday morning seemed, to the whole family, a perfectly natural way to behave.

The brothers no longer remembered the details of the Church Calendar by which they had once lived, so nobody in South View Road realized that it was the first Sunday in Advent until the morning service on the radio – to which they only listened because every broadcast was a novelty – blared out the hymn of hope and expectation.

> Oh come, oh come Emmanuel,
> And ransom captive Israel.

Enid, who was sitting in the kitchen peeling Bramley apples for a pie, said that it was her very favourite hymn and Syd, who was eating the spirals of peel as they came off the knife, proved that it was a Catholic hymn as well by joining in.

> Rejoice! Rejoice!
> Emmanuel shall come to thee, oh Israel.

There was a shuffling of feet in the yard.

'He's here. He's come!' cried Enid. Syd, who was still proving that the Church owned him no longer, laughed more than the joke deserved. The peeling being done, Enid led Syd into the living room so that he could enjoy hearing the joke again when she repeated it to George and Rex.

'Enid! Enid!' It was Agnes from the back room. 'There's a man in our yard.'

'Jehovah's Witness,' George predicted. Nobody of any importance went down the passage to the back door.

'I told you.' Enid was still celebrating her witticism. 'Emmanuel shall come to thee.'

'Emmanuel or not,' said Rex, 'he might be stealing the bike.'

Reluctantly, George laid down his Sunday paper and left for an inspection of the wash house. An unknown Catholic priest was peering in the kitchen window.

Father Hugh Fisher, newly appointed secretary to Bishop McNulty, did not condescend to step back or look ashamed. He gave a half bow. George pulled open the kitchen door and asked him to wait in the yard. Father Fisher bowed again.

'It's a priest,' George announced when he was only half way into the living room. He sounded perfectly calm but he could not hide his fear that his news would cause panic. 'He's only a young chap.'

'Ask him in,' Enid told him, taking off her apron and rolling down her sleeves. 'Stay if you like.'

George returned to the kitchen perfectly composed, but he could not resist telling the visitor how much he resented his day of rest being disturbed.

'It's about time you packed all this nonsense in. It won't get you anywhere.'

Father Fisher looked hurt.

'I don't want to be here. You know that as well as I do. I was told to come and I came.'

'They've invited you in.' George tried to make it sound like a privilege.

'Just a moment.'

Father Fisher, to George's astonishment, disappeared into the wash house. He re-emerged with a distressed and obviously embarrassed Vicar General.

'Monsignor Payne,' he explained, 'is not well. I sat him down in there whilst I made sure that you were back from mass.'

George could not imagine the Vicar General propped up against the boiler or sitting on one of the orange boxes in which Enid's chattels had been brought from Langwith. Father Fisher did not recognize the cynical smile but Monsignor Payne himself – being at least sensitive about his own reputation – began to bluster. It was not, he said, his habit to hide in wash houses in order to mount surprise assaults on the families which he visited. George noticed that he was breathing heavily and would have accepted his assurance at face value, had he not undermined its credibility with a characteristic recrimination.

'I've tried very hard indeed to talk to your brother. I came a few weeks ago, but he was either not here or unwilling to talk to me.'

It was an unpleasant recollection. A strange middle-aged woman in a long black coat had ordered him from the door and threatened to call the police if he touched her. When he attempted to explain his good intentions, she threatened to set her dog on him.

'Is that why John the Baptist here came to the door first?' George asked.

It was the sort of question that enabled the Vicar General to regain his poise.

'I would be grateful if you kept your profanities for your secular friends.'

George indicated with a flourish that the Vicar General should go through into the living room. Syd passed him in the corridor. They did not speak.

Rex stuttered a barely comprehensible greeting. Monsignor Payne ignored Enid and gave a bad imitation of humility and gratitude.

'It is good of you to see me, Father.'

'Please don't call me Father. Mr Hattersley. Rex for preference. Roy or even Frederick. But not Father. I'm no longer a priest.'

'My dear young man, you can't stop being a priest just by saying so. The Church isn't a club that you join when it interests you and leave when you lose interest.'

It was a cold morning but the Vicar General was sweating. He mopped his face with a huge spotted handkerchief. A vein throbbed in his neck.

'I don't want to argue, Vicar General. We – my wife and I – just want you to understand . . . I'm sorry, I should have introduced you. Enid, this is—'

The Vicar General turned away.

'It's you I have come to see, Father. I have nothing to say to this young lady.'

'Then you have nothing to say to me.'

There was, Rex knew, no point in prolonging the agony and he hoped that the Vicar General understood how fruitless an argument would be.

'May I sit down?' Monsignor Payne asked.

'I'd rather you left,' Rex told him. 'For all our sakes.'

'The Vicar General is not a well man.' Father Fisher intended the reproach. 'He has taken a great risk by coming at all.'

'If I might have a glass of water, Father. Then I'll be on my way.'

Despite the Vicar General's obvious distress, Rex felt unable to ignore the challenge.

'Monsignor Payne. Not Father, please. I am not a priest. That's all behind us. I can barely believe that it ever happened.'

'Ever happened!'

The Vicar General gasped for air and clutched at his side. Then he ran his hands across his huge belly in a desperate search for his waistcoat pockets. Before he found one, his head slumped on his chest.

'Hold him up,' ordered Father Fisher.

Rex obeyed without argument. The bishop's secretary found what Monsignor Payne had been searching for, prised open the little silver box and took out a phial which he broke under Monsignor Payne's nose.

'Angina,' said Father Fisher knowingly. 'He's suffered from it for years. It will kill him one day.'

The Vicar General raised his head and pulled at his collar. It flapped free of the stud and the stock flapped loose on his chest.

'He needs to lie down.'

Rex looked at Enid, but even before she nodded her agreement, he began to help Father Fisher drag the Vicar General towards the sofa. There was almost a collision as Syd and George hurried back into the living room to find out the cause of the commotion. Enid ushered them back into the kitchen. Then she went to reassure her mother. Her voice was just audible as she explained that there was nothing to worry about.

Even at that moment of tension, Rex rejoiced at her choice of words. As she said, everything was all right.

Monsignor Payne drew a deep breath and opened his eyes.

'I am so sorry. Believe me, Father Hattersley . . .'

Father Fisher laid a restraining hand on Rex's arm. Rex seemed not to notice.

'Please don't upset yourself, Vicar General. Just lie still. You'll be right as rain in a minute. Just lie still.'

Monsignor Payne, even in distress, was not willing to take instructions from subordinates. He pushed himself up on his elbow.

'I assure you that I shall intrude no longer than is absolutely necessary.' He noticed that his stock had escaped and he tried, unsuccessfully, to stuff it back under his waistcoat. 'You must excuse me.'

Having rearranged himself and his clothing, the Vicar General returned to the charge.

'Frederick,' Monsignor Payne was not a man for sobriquets, 'you really must consider the consequences of the course you are following.'

'This is not the right moment.' Rex did not want a dead Vicar General in his living room.

'It is exactly the right moment. When I first felt the spasm, I prayed for forgiveness that I had delayed this meeting for so long. I feared for my soul. I might have met my Maker before I had done His will and warned you — '

'You're wasting your time, Vicar General.'

'How can I waste my time on God's work?'

'No disputations this afternoon,' Rex told him. 'I don't want to make you ill again.'

'Sick or well, Father, I must do God's will. And it is God's will that I tell you to end this wickedness.'

'Vicar General, you're taking advantage of my good nature. So I must make one thing clear. There is no question of me leaving my wife.'

He was going to go on to say that he resented the talk of wickedness, but Monsignor Payne pounced before he could register his complaint.

'Your wife, Father Hattersley? Did I hear you aright?'

'Yes, my wife. That is how I think of her and that is what she is. I told you. I can hardly remember being a priest. And sometimes I cannot believe that I ever was one. Life for me began when Enid and I came together. She taught me that. Nothing before that matters. Nothing before that happened.'

'But, Father, you cannot live by such fantasies. You can't push the truth aside.'

'I was taught to do exactly that for seven years in Rome.'

'Father Hattersley, you may be as offensive as you wish.' The Vicar General sank back exhausted on the sofa and then spoke in a voice which was made almost inaudible by fatigue. 'But you will not stop me from telling the truth.'

A year before, Rex would have listened patiently and allowed the Vicar General to hope that there was still a chance of redemption. But that afternoon he had no time for anyone's feelings but his own.

'The truth, Monsignor Payne, is that we have built a new life—'

'A new life without religion. A new life built on a lie.'

'Built on a greater truth.'

'All this is meaningless mumbo-jumbo.'

'Perhaps. I don't know and I don't care. Life is more than lectures in doctrine at the Gregorian University. I believe in something different now. I have my own creed and my own catechism. All I want is here.'

The Vicar General decided to change his line of attack. The demon which possessed Father Frederick Hattersley prevented him from understanding that, as always, vice would be vanquished by virtue and that he could only look forward to a life of pain and sorrow.

'And you have dragged your brothers down with you. They are very young. They look to you for guidance and you have persuaded them to jeopardize their immortal souls.'

'Ask them if they want to leave.'

'You have locked them in a prison of loyalty.'

'This is not a prison, Monsignor Payne. It is a fortress. Syd and George chose to come inside before we pulled up the drawbridge.'

The metaphor had stretched beyond the Vicar General's powers of further invention. Enid's return enabled him to attack on a second front.

'What about this young lady's father? A most respectable man, I understand. A councillor. What does he think of all this?'

'My father is dead.'

It was the turn of Father Fisher, who had sat in a trance throughout the argument, to confuse image with reality.

'I really had no idea . . . When I left Langwith Junction . . . He seemed such a healthy man.'

'I am so sorry,' said the Vicar General. 'God rest his soul.' There was not much time to be wasted on sympathy. 'And what about your aunt and your sisters? They are profoundly distressed by all this.'

'They're as good as dead,' said Rex. 'When they had to take sides, for one reason or another they didn't choose us. Remember, Vicar General, those who are not for us are against us. People have to decide, inside our little world or outside it.'

The Vicar General pushed himself up off the sofa. He had not been taught how to deal with invincible complacency. The man had sold his soul for less than nothing – for the right to live with a young woman who stood by the door, unashamedly anxious to see her aged visitor off the premises whatever his state of health. It seemed a strange compensation for the pains and punishments of eternal damnation.

'Help me up,' Monsignor Payne said to Father Fisher. 'You'll have to drive back to Nottingham.'

IT WOULD, Rex decided, be the best Christmas ever. Worksop, who had encouraged his optimism by announcing that they would have to spend the holiday at Brook House, brought their contribution to the festivities a full week before the great day: a hen which was alternately referred to as a chicken and a capon, a jar of sugary slime which was described as Anne's 'special' mincemeat, a plum pudding which had been boiled in the summer and left to mature throughout the autumn and a fruit cake which was too obviously magnificent to need the constant commendation that it was made according to the Harness Grove recipe.

In common with every Christmas, Lottie had made Enid a new dress and the last fitting was still going on in the back room, under the critical eye of Mrs Brackenbury, when George burst in. The three women were too astonished to be shocked. Before they had time to remonstrate he asked, 'Where's Rex?'

When none of the women answered on the instant, he disappeared, exuding the same air of mysterious excitement as when he came in. Rex was in the front room examining the original Grove Cottage Christmas decorations, which Aunt Anne had carried by train from Newcastle Avenue. In Anne Skinner's awesome presence even George had to wait for the right moment to speak.

She was looking lovingly at a *papier-mâché* replica of a parish church. The coloured paper in its windows was broken. But, with a candle behind them, they would still have shone like stained glass.

'When Ern was a boy, he always wanted to light it up. But we never let him. Too dangerous.'

'Rex,' George seized his moment. 'Do you want this job or not?'

'What?'

'I've got you a job.'

'I don't believe you. Where?'

'The Assistance Board. Next room to me in the Miners' Welfare. They need a new clerk, starting Monday.'

'Are you sure I can get it?'

'You've got it. I play ping pong with the manager. He knows that you're looking for something. Turn up half past eight on Monday and it's yours.'

'Definite?'

'Definite.'

'I must tell Enid.'

Anne would have followed him into the back room, for she never felt at ease with George, but she rightly anticipated that (even with Lottie to suppress their ardour) there would be much rejoicing around Agnes's bed, and Anne felt even less at home with rejoicing than she did with George.

Ten noisy minutes passed before Rex returned.

'I can hardly believe it!' He felt no need to express his gratitude. What George had achieved was his gift to the whole family.

'You'll have to buy a bike.'

Anne, who had not quite slipped away, began the complicated business of unbuckling the large leather purse that she always carried with her. She took out a pound note and handed it to Rex.

'Our contribution.'

'Bikes – second-hand bikes – cost ten shillings,' said George unhelpfully.

'Use the rest as you wish.'

'We ought to celebrate,' George suggested.

Rex having again rushed out to tell Enid the good news, Anne was once more left with the difficult choice between George in the front room and rejoicing in the back. She chose George for a second time.

'He's a good man,' she said. 'He deserves a bit of luck.'

GEORGE WAS insistent on a celebration. Enid made her normal protest about the very idea of leaving her mother but, when Syd told her that *Lilac Time* was on at the Heeley Electric Picture Palace, agreed 'just this once'. There was an awful period of anticipated disappointment when Lottie wondered out loud if she could stay in Sheffield so late. Anne gave her permission.

They walked home singing 'Marche Militaire', with Rex, his hair ruffled and his spectacles pulled down his nose, giving a bad imitation of Richard Tauber playing Franz Schubert. From time to time, he put down his imaginary violin and turned round to encourage the children who were following him through the

Vienna woods. Enid said that she could not remember when she was last so happy and Rex told her that, for ever more he would think of the tune as the Public Assistance March.

The night passed in joy and excitement and a bleary-eyed Rex was outside the second-hand bicycle shop half an hour before it opened, just in case it had only one on sale. There were several dozen models from which to choose. He picked a Raleigh for no better reason than that it had been made in Nottingham.

Rex, who had cycled since he was a boy, practised his cycling for much of Saturday afternoon. On Sunday morning, George rode with him in search of the old Heather Works in which their grandfather had hoped to make his fortune. They did not find it. On Sunday afternoon, Syd borrowed George's bike and went with Rex in search of the Empress Works into which old Frederick had rashly, and disastrously, expanded. Their search was unsuccessful. In the early evening dusk, when there was nobody about to see, Enid, who had cycled across Nottingham with Rex during the summer when they fell in love, climbed indecorously over the crossbar of George's Rudge and attempted to relive the past by peddling in what she believed to be the general direction of the Derbyshire countryside. After half a mile, she swerved danger-ously close to the tramlines that ran along the centre of the road. Rex, paralysed by the fear that she would lose her balance, lost his. He lay in the road with his cycle wheel spinning on top of him.

'It's a good thing that you've got your old trousers on,' she told him. 'Have you seen what you've done to the knee?'

The cloth was torn and the skin below it was grazed. But that, and a little grit in the palm of one hand, was the full extent of Rex's injuries. The bicycle fared worse. The front wheel was buckled.

They walked home, terrified that Rex would not get to Wath-upon-Dearn next day. Enid's solution was for George to feign illness whilst Rex used his bicycle.

'I couldn't ask him.'

'I could.'

Rex trembled in the knowledge that it was true.

George avoided a direct answer to the request by suggesting that Rex's bicycle could be made rideable. They took it in turns to hit the wheel with the coal hammer which, long ago, Rex had found in the yard. At the end of an hour's hard pounding, the wheel was flat but not round. After another forty minutes, it was still oval, and the tyre was punctured. They pulled out the inner tube, sank it in a bucket of freezing water and located the hole by marking the place where the bubbles rose. The third patch stuck. George peeled the rubber solution off his fingers and pronounced the bicycle roadworthy.

Syd made a test ride. The oval front wheel rose and fell, but there was no doubt that anyone who was prepared to look like a circus clown could pedal to Wath and back.

'I'm still worried,' Rex said.

'Of course you are,' George told him. 'But take it from me, tomorrow morning won't be any different from the rest of your life. There'll be ups and downs but you'll get there in the end.'

'You're right,' said Rex. 'It is not by avoiding bumps in the road that you get to Wath, but by riding straight over them.'